PRAISE FOR

RADIO GIRLS

"Sarah-Jane Stratford's *Radio Girls* is an achievement of historical fiction so believable that you'll wonder if the author has access to a time machine. Maisie's trajectory—from mousy, fearful underling into assertive, independent powerhouse—mirrors that of the nascent BBC for which she works. The promise of postwar prosperity and the looming threat of fascism make for an engrossing background against which Maisie finds herself involved in international intrigue and national rights movements that will make the reader turn the pages frantically, utterly enthralled until the very end. By turns funny and fascinating, *Radio Girls* is a triumph."

—Allison Amend, Author of *Enchanted Islands*

"*Radio Girls* carries readers on a memorable, eye-opening journey to London in the 1920s and '30s, a pivotal time in the history of women's rights, politics, and the arts. Sarah-Jane Stratford's storytelling skills are on vivid display throughout, and the strong, believable, and immensely human Maisie Musgrave is the best imaginable guide to that vanished time and place." —Joseph Wallace, Author of *Slavemakers*

RADIO GIRLS

SARAH-JANE STRATFORD

 NEW AMERICAN LIBRARY

NEW AMERICAN LIBRARY
Published by New American Library,
an imprint of Penguin Random House LLC
375 Hudson Street, New York, New York 10014

This book is an original publication of New American Library.

First Printing, June 2016

LIBRARY OF CONGRESS CATALOGING-IN-PUBLICATION DATA:
Names: Stratford, Sarah-Jane, author.
Title: Radio girls/Sarah-Jane Stratford.
Description: New York City: New American Library, [2016] |
Identifiers: LCCN 2016000672 (print) | LCCN 2015047085 (ebook) |
ISBN 9780451475565 (softcover) | ISBN 9780698195295 (ebook)
Subjects: LCSH: British Broadcasting Corporation—History—20th
century—Fiction. | Radio broadcasting—Great Britain—History—20th
century—Fiction. | BISAC: FICTION/Historical. | FICTION/Literary. |
FICTION / Biographical. | GSAFD: Historical fiction.
Classification: LCC PS3619.T7425 (print) | LCC PS3619.T7425 R33 2016 (ebook)
| DDC 813/.6—dc23
LC record available at http://lccn.loc.gov/2016000672

Printed in the United States of America
10 9 8

Designed by Kelly Lipovich

Penguin |
Random |
House |

"*If we have the sense to give [broadcasting] freedom and intelligent direction, if we save it from exploitation by vested interests of money or power, its influence may even redress the balance in favour of the individual.*"

—HILDA MATHESON, Broadcasting (1933)

RADIO
GIRLS

London 1930

She ran, weaving in and out of the startled pedestrians, but her pursuer was still close on her heels.

All their meticulous planning, all that work in spinning the web and catching all these flies, but they hadn't factored in this possibility: the chance that the papers in her bag were worth so much that someone would chase after her to get them back.

Chase after her with a gun.

She heard it, heard the click, even above the sounds of shoppers, of traffic, of her own pounding feet and pounding heart and the steady gallop of the man behind her.

He didn't know, though, that she wasn't alone. A small comfort, as she leaped over a pair of Yorkshire terriers and ducked around their sable-clad owner to sprint down the alley, but she would take what comforts she could.

And he had no idea what she was about to do. No idea of the power she really wielded. He was like all the bullies who had chased her as a child, hoping to frighten her. They had succeeded. He would not.

She ran harder, knees high, sure-footed as a gazelle, and gazelles didn't wear well-polished heels with fashionable double straps.

2 · SARAH-JANE STRATFORD

Thank goodness for short skirts. Ten years ago I'd have been dead by now.

She just needed to get to the car. He was getting closer, though. She put on a burst of speed.

Would it help to scream? No, it never helped to scream. Besides, she wouldn't give him the satisfaction of knowing she was afraid, just as she wouldn't give him the satisfaction of getting the papers he wanted so badly.

She tightened her grip on her handbag, slick with sweat, and ran harder.

ONE

November 1926

Although everyone in the boardinghouse had seen the letter and assured Maisie that it was genuine, she couldn't help continually unfolding and rereading it, until the typed words along the creases were nearly illegible, only five days after she had received it.

"You ought to be careful," advised Lola from her perch on the straight-backed bedroom chair, where she was buffing her nails. "You'll soon have that in pieces, and aren't you meant to present it at your interview?"

The interview. After months of unemployment, with only the occasional two or three days of work that everyone was sure would turn into something more substantial and never did, Maisie was at last invited to interview for a full-time position. A junior secretary was needed at the BBC.

"I do hope it's for whoever it is who puts on the plays and things," Lola said at least once a day, with some variation. Maisie promised faithfully that, if this was the job on offer and she secured it, she would make every effort to have Lola brought in to broadcast. Privately, however, she hoped the job was as far away from the "plays and things" as the BBC's offices in Savoy Hill allowed.

She read the letter again. The letterhead was a plain, modern type, giving the address and exchanges for phoning (Temple Bar 8400) or sending telegrams (Ethanuze, London). The text was in the succinct, formal style she associated so fondly with Britain, directing her to arrive at the BBC at three o'clock Thursday, November twenty-fifth, and ask for Miss Shields. She was to bring "appropriate references."

"I wish I knew what they meant by 'appropriate,'" Maisie said, running her finger up and down her pointy chin. She had a note from Sister Bennister, head matron of the Brighton Soldiers' Hospital, pronouncing Maisie an effective and considerate nurse—generous, considering Maisie had scarcely been more than a nurses' aide. The certificate of completion from Miss Jenkins's Secretarial College was more relevant but less impressive, as it was dated 1924, from New York, and there was no great way to explain her failure to provide anything else.

"Ah, don't fret so much," Lola advised. "They have to say that sort of thing, don't they? But I don't reckon those references matter so much. It's really all about the impression you make when they meet you."

The longer Maisie studied herself in the black-stained mirror at her dressing table, the less encouraging that prospect became.

Both Lola and their landlady, Mrs. Crewe, had been nonstop fonts of advice since the ceremonial slitting of the envelope. Even the other boarders, women who rarely seemed cognizant of Maisie's existence, shared the thrill. Listening to the wireless was a sore subject in Mrs. Crewe's house, as that intractable lady pronounced the whole concept a "nonsensical passing fancy" and refused to spend her hard-earned money on such a thoroughly unnecessary and, she emphasized, *unnatural* contraption as a radio.

"Why on earth would anyone want to hear bodiless voices? Sounds irreligious to me, not to say dangerous. Who knows what they can do, if they can speak to you through some machine or other? First cinema, now this. It's not right."

Not right it may be, but Mrs. Crewe was a stout champion of

"her girls," as she described her boarders, and was willing to put aside some of her hard feeling in the cause of Maisie being properly employed.

"And once you're working there and not growing two heads or whatnot, she'll have to agree it's all right and buy us a wireless!" Lola crowed. "Of course," she went on more musingly, penciled brows furrowing, "like as not we'll have moved somewhere a bit more smart by then, I'd think. Don't you?"

Maisie did, though only because Mrs. Crewe wasn't likely to buy a radio anytime before doomsday.

Lola and the other boarders all had friends willing to host "listening in" parties, where everyone gathered to enjoy something or other from the BBC, usually the plays or music, but of late the Talks. Maisie was not so lucky, which was part of why she was so interested to know more. She secretly agreed with Mrs. Crewe that there was something terrifying about a disembodied voice, and it was bizarre that it could originate from another part of London and yet sound as clear as someone sitting across the table. A lot of people were afraid of the wireless, certain that all this new technology was a harbinger of evil spirits, or a means of bridging the gap to the spirit world. Maisie wasn't sure what she believed.

What she knew for an incontrovertible fact, however, was that her funds had dwindled to one pound, thirteen shillings, and ninepence. Despite her nonpareil expertise with frugality, this little pile of coins represented a week of food and shelter. Her family, such as it was, lived in New York and Toronto, and none of them would respond favorably— or politely—to a request for assistance. There was nothing else for it. She had to get this job.

"Let me put some makeup on you. All those BBC girls wear makeup, I'm sure," Lola insisted. Maisie demurred. She couldn't risk the unknown Miss Shields thinking she was fast.

Or stupid enough to think makeup would improve me. Maisie sighed, focusing on the nose people called "Roman" when they were being kind and wishing her gaunt face boasted at least one other notable feature. *I suppose I should be grateful I haven't got a boil.*

She saved her gratitude for the popularity of the bob. It was a great gift to women like herself, cursed with fine, lank hair, and she wholeheartedly embraced it. Her hair might be dull and dirty-dishwater brown, but was less offensive for being short and unmoving on her head, with a severe fringe laboring hard to give her face something approximating a shape. She wished she had a decent cloche, something with a rhinestone flourish near the ear, or perhaps a little feather. Her tired black wool hat was so plain and obviously cheap. But it was clean, and careful brushing masked the worst of the patchiness.

The forcible English tones of her Toronto-born and -raised grand-mother echoed as Maisie rolled her stockings up her thighs and clamped them in place: "Well? Aren't you going to thank me?" And Maisie *was* grateful that the woman's passion for thrift and sharp things had given her the skill to mend her black wool stockings so well. Modern women wore beige or pastel stockings—some of them silk!—but black was still acceptable and these weren't too awful, so long as no one looked closely.

Lots of luck there. She frowned at her skinny, shapeless legs, wishing she'd appreciated longer skirts more when they were still in style.

As for her shoes, she would just have to keep her feet flat on the floor to hide the holes. The cheap Oxfords had tarried valiantly for five years, but even if they could be repaired again, she couldn't bear it. Every time she put them on, she wanted to cry.

As she tied the laces, she remembered one of the few pieces of advice her mother, Georgina, occasionally offered: "It is always best to have less if one must, so long as everything you wear is of good quality."

Fine words from a woman who, as a struggling young actress, wore skirts to the ground and was now successful enough to always have what she called a "sponsor" to keep her in all the silk stockings she wished.

Maisie stood and put on her coat.

"Gosh, Maisie, I wish you'd borrow something of mine," was Lola's response as Maisie presented herself for inspection.

"Your clothes would never fit me," Maisie said, with perfect truth. Lola was shorter than Maisie, and though she made assiduous use of straps to render her luscious figure more fashionably boyish, she wore her dresses as low-cut as daylight hours allowed. If Maisie tried to wear one, she would look like a chorus girl in a sideshow.

"Well, I suppose no one cares what anyone looks like for radio anyhow," Lola said in her most comforting tone. "At least take a taxi there. No, you must. You'll feel awfully grand. Here, I'll lend you the fare."

The coins glinted in Lola's palm, shiny temptation. Maisie had never set foot in a cab and couldn't imagine such extravagance, but the sudden vision of a cloth rose to pin to her hat arrested her. She might find a milliner's on the Strand. Her hand hovered, but refused to land. She could not be pretty or smart, but as she was, she looked steady and practical. Someone must appreciate those qualities in a secretary. Besides, she hated being in debt if she didn't have to be. She had no idea what next week was going to bring.

"Thanks awfully, but that's all right. It's only two o'clock. The tram will get me there in plenty of time," Maisie assured Lola.

"Well, good luck." Lola grinned. "They'll want you. I'm sure of it."

Parting with one of her precious pennies for the fare, Maisie hoped Lola was right. No one had wanted her in a very long time, and those that had taken her hadn't kept her any longer than Richard the Third kept Anne Neville in Shakespeare's invention.

Georgina always said Maisie didn't belong in London.

I can't have her be right.

Outside the handsome stone building with the brass sign reading: BRITISH BROADCASTING COMPANY beside the door, Maisie had a sinking feeling that Georgina knew whereof she spoke, though she had only ever visited a London suggested by stage sets. Maisie laid her fingers on the dark wooden door, feeling the pull of a place bursting with life. She forced her hand to stop shaking and to remember how to work a doorknob.

The door opened onto a vast reception room, vehemently modern, with a marble floor polished to the gleam and hazard of a skating rink and wallpaper featuring incongruous tropical trees. Two women in a corner, swathed in fox furs, twittered and chirped to each other, rhythmically tapping ash from their cigarettes into a burnished brass tray.

A clatter heralding imminent devastation—the earthquake of San Francisco, come to London—sent Maisie's arms around herself in feeble protection as two men pelted down the stairs, cramming on hats and straightening ties, faces glowing with purpose. They zipped past on either side of Maisie, close enough to knock her both east and west, a billiard ball on a table, and sprang out the door, never seeing her.

Maisie straightened her coat, congratulating herself on staying upright. She edged up to the cherrywood table, where the much-Marcelled receptionist turned away from the telephone to appraise her.

"Have you an appointment?" the receptionist asked in a deep voice, pleasant enough to be welcoming and authoritative enough to be respected.

"Please, I'm . . . I'm to see Miss Shields at three o'clock," Maisie whispered, unfolding the precious letter to prove her credibility.

"Hum," came the answer. A bell must have been rung, because a moment later a plump young boy with a shock of red hair appeared. He could not have been more than twelve, and bore himself with the imperiousness of a courtier.

"Ah, Rusty," the receptionist greeted him. "This is"—a glance at the letter again—"Miss Musgrave, for Miss Shields, right away, please."

"Yes, miss! This way, please, miss." An exuberant wave of the arm, inviting Maisie into the bowels of the BBC.

"Did you want to take the lift, miss, or the stairs? It's up at the top, you see."

She knew she should save her strength where she could, as it was hours before supper, but there was a buzz emanating from all those floors above and she wanted to walk through as much of it as she could.

"I don't mind the stairs," Maisie assured Rusty, and was rewarded by an approving grin.

The BBC had existed only four years, so Maisie didn't expect the sort of ponderous grandeur that characterized a steady establishment, places that filled her with awe, wonder, and desire. The sort of places she dreamed of spending her days in, and her nights, too. Savoy Hill was a different narcotic. The bright, pulsing energy of the new, of a staff enveloped in a technological marvel, in a venture that might turn in upon itself and disappear tomorrow—though they would all battle like they were at the walls of Agincourt to prevent such defeat. Behind some of these doors, people were certainly shut in soundproof rooms, speaking out to the nation. But in the corridors, it was a rush of thundering feet and rustling paper and rapid conversation.

"Did you hear? Old Matheson landed us Anthony Asquith."

"Pah. I'm holding out for Tallulah Bankhead coming to broadcast."

"You'd likely pass out stone cold!"

"Worth it, depending where I land."

The colloquy buzzed and whirled around Maisie's head, cloudier than perfume, and just as dizzying.

"I say, anyone fancy the American tonight?"

Maisie stumbled.

The bar, you idiot. He means the bar at the Savoy. Was that the sort of place these people went after work? Her presence on its pavement would provide the doorman with a good laugh before he directed her back to the main road.

The voice continued. "They've got a new bartender, straight from the 300 Club in New York!"

"Any man can mix a drink, he puts his mind to it. Tell me when they've got that Texas Guinan and her girls!"

He pronounced it "Gwynen."

Quite unintentionally, Maisie stopped and spoke into the din.

"Guy-nan. Her name, it's pronounced Guy-nan. And she's not one of the . . . er, dancers. She owns the club."

And was, allegedly, a friend of Georgina, though a life's experience had taught Maisie to query any information that sprang from the maternal font. Georgina described Texas Guinan as "no actress, nor beauty, but she has a force of personality, child (which Maisie still had to be, as Georgina never aged). Well worth cultivating" (because what else were people but hothouse lettuces?).

Through the vapor of her rising mortification, Maisie felt several people staring at her in amused interest, spurring a sudden fondness for her own well-cultivated disguise of Invisible Girl, the foe she had made friend, usually so useful in cloaking her. Even Rusty had abandoned his sacred duty to gaze upon his charge in wonder.

A young man loped up to her, all sunshine grin and summer freckles. His hair flopped over one side of his head in untidy brown curls, and he wore fashionable baggy trousers and what Maisie guessed was a school tie.

"You're American?" he asked in a well-bred accent. "Are you from New York? You are, aren't you?"

Maisie struggled to remember how to breathe. That grin. Those freckles.

"Well, I . . . sort of . . . I mean, I lived . . . grew up . . . in New York, but . . ."

Rusty, remembering himself, intervened. "Ever so sorry, Mr. Underwood, sir, but I must deliver the miss to Miss Shields for an interview."

"Oh!" The young man looked stunned. "I rather thought you must be a Matheson acquisition."

"Not likely," someone said, and sniggered. A chorus of whispers ensued.

"Well, enjoy Miss Shields, then," Mr. Underwood encouraged. Sapphire eyes smiled, charmer to her snake, but his tone suggested enjoyment was futile.

Maisie wished the blush burning her face and neck was hot enough to turn the floor liquid and let her sink into nothingness. She trotted robotically behind Rusty, taking no notice of the number of stairs, only waking up when they reached a hushed corridor, more polished and solemn than the lower floors, with every door closed.

Rusty strode up to one of the doors, gave it a respectful knock, then edged it open.

"Miss Shields, Miss Musgrave for you, miss," Rusty announced in his best impression of refinement.

"Thank you, Rusty," came a ringing voice. Maisie forced herself into the office, hoping her blush had dissipated. Miss Shields looked down her nose at Maisie, her handsome features unblemished by such frivolities as a smile. She wore a brown tweed suit whose simple lines spoke the epitome of quiet good taste. A gold watch was pinned to the lapel, reminding Maisie of the Sisters in the hospital, except their watches didn't feature a spray of tiny rubies and a diamond.

"Do sit down, Miss Musgrave," came the invitation, polite enough. "Would you care for a cup of tea?"

Maisie hesitated. She never turned down refreshment on principle, and all the chill November had to offer had seeped through her worn shoes. On the other hand, she was shaking enough to possibly upset that tea all over her thighs. But this was not the sort of woman who brooked refusals, so Maisie nodded and smiled.

"Yes, please, thank you. Very much."

Miss Shields gave Rusty the order. Maisie waited awkwardly, feeling rather than seeing the room, hot little pinpricks of excitement dancing up her limbs, forming pools of sweat under her arms. Quite a thing, sitting in an office all your own. Miss Shields's chair had curved arms and swiveled. Maisie longed for every bit of it, and wondered how fast the chair spun around.

"Would you like milk? Sugar?" Miss Shields asked.

"Yes, please, both, thank you," said Maisie, wishing the bounty extended to a tea cake or even just a cookie (or "biscuit," as she'd taught herself to say). She didn't remember what it was like not to be hungry in the long hours before supper.

"Yes, you Americans do like your tea sweet," Miss Shields observed, pleased with her knowledge as she handed Maisie a cup and saucer with bluebirds flying around the rim.

"Oh, I'm Canadian," Maisie stammered, and went into her usual apologetic patter. "Half-British, as my father was British. My mother is Canadian and I was born there. Then my mother and I went to New York, where she was an ac—where she had work. I mostly lived there but spent summers in Toronto until I joined the VAD in 1916 and was assigned to the hospital in Brighton."

She trailed off. Her biography was such a terribly unimpressive hodgepodge. She handed Miss Shields her two letters of reference and managed only one sip of tea before they were read through and set aside.

"Where was your father born?"

"Oh. I . . . I don't . . ." She couldn't see how the question was relevant, but glanced down at her shoes and settled on "Oxford," as that sounded gorgeously respectable. Very not Georgina.

"I suppose his name was Musgrave."

"Edwin Musgrave," Maisie specified, which was true as far as she knew. The familiar pang tapped her behind the breastbone, and she suppressed a sigh. The father she apparently—and unluckily—resembled almost exactly. Whom she still hoped to find someday. Had he taken one look at his infant daughter and walked away, or did she have memories of him locked away somewhere, if only she knew where to search?

"And do you know where he was educated?"

"Where he . . . ? No, I . . . I'm sorry . . . I—I don't." She forced herself to keep looking into this woman's cold eyes.

"I see. Well, we've grown quite busy of late, and I need someone who will provide a bit of extra assistance when the typing pool is at full pressure. I am the personal secretary to Mr. Reith."

She pronounced his name with the sort of fervor Lola reserved for Rudolph Valentino.

"The director-general, yes," Maisie put in, attempting to demonstrate that she had made an attempt to learn something of this place.

"Mr. Reith expects everything done well and on time. He expects a serious and dedicated staff. We are growing, gaining in importance. Everything we do must reflect and enhance that. I require an assistant who can manage a number of tasks at once and yet be ready to add something more when called upon. You having been a nurse, that is—"

She narrowed her eyes at Maisie.

"You must have been *quite* young when you joined."

Maisie never knew how to respond to that observation. Surely someone must appreciate her patriotism and initiative—or at least her need to escape—in having procured a fake birth certificate so as to be eighteen when she first came to England, instead of several months shy of her fourteenth birthday. But she had never yet found anyone to whom she dared mention it.

"Most of my nursing was after the war," Maisie explained, truthfully enough. "I left because we had discharged enough men that I wasn't needed anymore."

"And you didn't seek a job with another hospital?"

"I . . ." *Wanted to stop washing blood off my hands. Wanted to be part of the living world.* "I wanted to do something a bit different." And she hadn't been much of a nurse anyway.

"So you went to secretarial school." Miss Shields nodded briefly at the certificate. "And in New York, it seems."

"Yes. I, er, I . . . returned there for a short while."

I was penniless, my grandparents wanted nothing to do with me, and Georgina wanted to show off her generosity to her newest sponsor. She is always so happy when I fail. Though in fact Georgina had called Maisie her niece, not her daughter, and it was the sponsor's money that paid the way.

"I see," said Miss Shields. "And where did you work after completing your course?"

"A number of offices, but they were only short-term assignments, I'm afraid."

Everyone wanted secretaries to be glamorous and bubbly and modern.

"I see. When did you return to Britain?"

"Last year. My mother, er, knew I was happier here." And she and Georgina were both happier with an ocean between them. "I am indeed very happy in London and hope to stay, provided I can secure a good job." Maisie kept her tone prim.

"Mm," was the sole reward. "Now, aside from your nursing and secretarial training, where did you go to school?"

And we're at that question.

It was a question asked in American interviews, too, for formality's sake. Maisie's single criticism of the British was that they were inordinately obsessed with education, even for girls. Or at least, girls who interviewed for the sort of jobs she wanted.

Oh, just lie! she scolded herself. *One more can't hurt. Make up a name. They're not going to write somewhere overseas just to confirm it. It's so easy. Miss Morland's Free School for Girls. St. Agatha's Girls High. Gramercy Girls Academy. She won't know they're not real. Just say something!*

"Er, I . . ."

"Yes?" Miss Shields's eyebrows danced the dance Maisie knew too well.

"The fact is, we moved a great deal, so I couldn't go to the same school for very long."

"But you did go to school?" Despite the inflection, it was much more of a statement than a question, one that expected nothing but affirmation.

The School for Scandal. The School for Wives. The School of Hard Knocks. Miss Witless's School for the Criminally Uneducatable.

"I was predominantly educated at home," Maisie answered, hoping she sounded starchy and governess-trained.

"Was this a general all-round education, or did you have a specialty?"

Maisie wasn't sure what the woman meant. All she could think of was Georgina instructing her never to wear two shades of red together.

"Just general. I, er, I liked history. I've always liked reading. Reading everything, really."

"Hmm. Well, I didn't exactly expect the equivalent of Cheltenham," Miss Shields remarked, making a note.

Cheltenham! That was one of the poshest girls' schools in Britain. Was Savoy Hill filled with women who had gone there? Had Miss Shields?

"We need people who are sharp and well organized, Miss Musgrave. For this job, your educational background is less critical than your ability. Now, the post also demands some assistance given to the new director of Talks"—Maisie was quite sure Miss Shields swallowed a sneer—"but your main attention is to me, which is to say, Mr. Reith. I expect that's quite clear?"

"Yes, Miss Shields." Maisie nodded.

"Because we can't have someone who's got one eye somewhere else."

"No, Miss Shields."

"It is useful, of course, especially in Talks, if you know a great deal about the important people of the day and things taking place. Do you read the daily papers?"

Maisie used to, but the long period of irregular employment made it impossible to focus on anything other than the "Situations Available" pages. She had, however, become adept at picking up abandoned papers from collection piles and cutting out shoe linings from them. They kept her feet warm. She wondered what stories she had walked on to get here.

"I certainly do look at them, Miss Shields."

"I see."

Miss Shields didn't seem likely to say more, and Maisie finished her tea, thinking *she* ought to ask a question.

"Would I, that is, would the person you engage be working in this room with you?" It seemed unlikely, given the room's size, but she wanted to steel herself if she were going to be subjected to that stern gaze half the day.

"In my room? I should say not. We are pushing through a cupboard to create space."

Maisie glanced at the door to her left.

"No," Miss Shields corrected her. "That is Mr. Reith's room."

Maisie's heart jumped. Was he in there? Had he been listening? What if he opened the door?

"This is the space we are designating," Miss Shields said, pointing to the door on the right. "There will be space enough for a type-writer, and it will do. Much time will be spent in managing files and papers. Energy, Miss Musgrave, I need someone with energy."

"I have energy," Maisie assured her, wishing there were some way to prove it. *Shame I can't turn a cartwheel.*

Miss Shields set down her cup and saucer, then looked at Maisie's references again.

"What I cannot understand, Miss Musgrave, is why, if you've had such trouble securing regular employment, you haven't returned once more to your people in Toronto or New York."

Beneath the impertinence, Maisie sensed the woman was exhort-ing her to leave and save jobs for those who deserved them, especially as so many men were unemployed. It was a fair point, although no man would be hired as this sort of secretary. And in fact, despite the enticement of the office, Maisie planned to quit the moment she was sure her hoped-for husband was a certainty, bringing her closer to the loving family she had wanted since she knew such things existed.

She forced her shoulders back and her breath steady.

"Miss Shields, I may have been born and raised in what's some-times still called the New World, but my heart lies in the Old World. There's nothing that makes me happier than walking around London. History's lived here. So much began here, so many stories. This is still the center of the universe, and there are still . . . conventions here. I came here hoping to do my bit for Britain, and leaving was so stupid, so cowardly. I made it back and I've got to stay. I've just got to. This is home. I hope," she tapered off—her blush was making her face hurt.

But it was true. She needed this job, needed this room with the desk, the swivel chair, the bird-festooned teacup and saucer. She even needed the terrifying Miss Shields. And the hidden Mr. Reith. If the

BBC's brazen raw newness chafed against her passion for the starch and certainty of tradition and opulence, it also enchanted her with its brightness and bustle. She couldn't be turned away. She just couldn't.

"Very nice, I'm sure, Miss Musgrave," Miss Shields said dryly. "Thank you so much for coming in." Miss Shields pressed a button by the door and held out her hand. "You will receive a letter in due course telling you of our decision. Rusty shall show you out."

Rusty popped up like a groundhog and hovered as Maisie shook Miss Shields's hand and thanked her with what she hoped wasn't an excess of sincerity. She tagged after Rusty, feeling her heart oozing through the holes in her shoes. The most important thing was to get outside before the tears came.

"Hey, New York!"

Just as she reached reception, Maisie was stunned to be accosted by Mr. Underwood of the school tie and baggy trousers, pattering down the stairs after her. Still grinning. Still freckled. Eyes still blue—inviting enough that she wanted to learn to swim. Had she ever been smiled at by a man this handsome?

"Have you been to a speakeasy, then? What's it like? Is Broadway really so bright at night it's like day? Gosh, I'd rather like to spend just a week there. Must be jolly great fun—not that our London isn't the best place on earth, of course, and we can get drinks legally, but maybe it's more fun when you can't? I'd give a lot to see the Cotton Club. Or do they let white people in?"

It was like being blown through with machine-gun artillery. The fellow's interview skills were more daunting than Miss Shields's, and the questions more impossible to answer. But he was looking at her with interest, which was more than Miss Shields had done and remarkable from a man. Grateful to him for distracting her from her misery, Maisie gave him the one answer she could manage.

"Well, 'Broadway' itself is a street, but you mean the theater district. It's . . . rather . . . well, glorious, really. All those theaters, one after the other, marquees all lit up. I daresay you could read there, though I suppose you wouldn't want to."

To her dismay, he looked disappointed.

"You don't talk like an American, not like some of the others who've been here, or in the stories."

"Oh. Well, I . . ." She was eager to explain herself using as many choice bits of American slang as she could muster, but those eyes and freckles made syllables hard to come by.

"Oi, Underwood!" someone shouted from the top of the steps. "What the devil are you doing, having another tea break? Get yourself back here before the man takes your head off and uses it for a football."

"Suppose I ought to dash, then," her interrogator remarked, unruffled. "You'll be back, will you? I do want to hear more!"

"Er . . . I—I don't think so," she mumbled, but he was scaling the stairs two at a time. "Thanks anyway," she said to his back as it disappeared.

She glanced at the receptionist, wondering if she should be marked as leaving. The receptionist was simultaneously directing a man with a parcel, asking someone on the phone to please hold the line, and scribbling at a pad with a pencil.

Maisie closed the door on the painted trees and the gleam and the polish. She swiped impatiently at her eyes, rounded her shoulders against the chill, and trudged up the appropriately dark street.

"Miss! Miss!"

Rusty was sprinting toward her, a fiery little Olympic torch.

"Lucky you're here, miss. Didn't think I'd find you, but I took the chance. Miss Shields, miss, she asked if I did find you, would you return a moment, please?"

He ran back to the BBC, gone so fast Maisie was sure she was hallucinating.

But Rusty was decidedly solid, standing in the light spilling from the open door, beckoning to her with the impatient exasperation of boys universal, and was only mollified when Maisie finally walked back toward him. Her heart was behaving in a most peculiar fashion, as though it were holding its breath, wondering if it should crumple completely or take a leap of hope.

Miss Shields was descending the steps into reception. Her expression was resigned, with a soupçon of fury, and her words sounded rehearsed.

"Ah, Miss Musgrave, that is convenient. It has been decided to offer you the position. You may begin on Monday. Be here promptly at nine."

Maisie knew she should close her mouth or say something, but she was thoroughly incapable of doing either.

"Are you interested in the position?" Miss Shields snapped.

"I . . . yes, that is, yes, abso . . . Thank you!"

"I will allow for your surprised enthusiasm, but do know that Mr. Reith expects clear-spoken decorum in his presence at all times. As to—" She pursed her lips and appeared to change her mind. "The position pays three pounds, five shillings a week, and we are not accustomed to negotiating. Is that understood?"

It would never have occurred to Maisie to negotiate. This woman had just offered her life. She only hoped she wasn't hallucinating after all.

"Thank you. Thank you so much. I can start tomorrow, if you like?"

"Monday, Miss Musgrave. You'll report directly to me and we can begin. I expect you to be fully prepared."

"Yes, Miss Shields." Maisie nodded fervently. She had a bad feeling "fully prepared" meant better clothes. It was tempting to hop a tram to Oxford Street right that minute. But she wasn't the sort of person to whom the shops gave credit. Shoes and clothes would have to wait. She would just be prepared to do a good job.

A squeal escaped her as she bounced back to the street, which seemed much brighter. What had turned the cards in her favor? Miss Shields hadn't seemed to like her much. Maybe she was one of those people who were hard to read. Lots of people were like that. Maisie hoped to be one of them someday.

Her Charleston-dancing heart reminded her that she would get to see Mr. Underwood again, too. Those eyes, that smile . . . *I'll go to the library first thing tomorrow and catch up on all the papers. New York ones, too, if they have any. I most definitely want to have something new to say about New York.*

TWO

Monday morning Maisie tumbled out of frantic dreams and into the uneasy darkness of the predawn hours. Trepidation marched down her arms and shoulder blades, pinning her to the iron bedstead. The short gasps of breath allotted her lungs pounded in her ears and felt loud enough to endanger the sleep of the other boarders. Except Lola, who wouldn't wake up if a biplane crashed into the house.

Maisie crawled out of bed, wishing she had slippers and a dressing gown. Instead, she wrapped the thin, fraying blankets around her like a Roman senator and tiptoed across the equally thin rag rug to the window. Everything in Mrs. Crewe's house was worn and thin, though impeccably clean. Including Maisie.

The view was moderately improved by being in shadow. This sliver of London insisted it was for the respectable working poor, not a slum, but the rows of identical dingy Victorian terrace houses to which people clung by their fingernails were hardly the stuff that was featured on a picture postcard.

More like the cover of a penny dreadful.

Maisie hugged her knees to her chest and watched the sky slowly grow lighter, waiting, wondering what the day was going to bring her.

In the hospital, Maisie had changed bandages on men whose eyes had been destroyed by poison gas. She dressed wounds on nubs of wrists, no longer extending into hands. She was doused in blood, in vomit, in tears. And not a bit of it prepared her for the rigors of the BBC.

Miss Shields spared her one critical glance, clearly displeased that she still looked like a companion to Oliver Twist, but waved her into her work space, a cramped closet with a typewriter and a hook for her coat and hat. There was no swivel chair, just a straight-backed spindly terror, but nor was there any sitting. Rusty was deputized to give her a "general tour" of the premises. He did so at a near run, Maisie tracking his bright red head while trying to absorb something of her surroundings.

"That's the Schools Department, miss. They broadcast to classrooms specially. And down here is the Music and Drama Departments, thems that do plays. Some of them quite funny they are, too, miss, sometimes. There's a control room in the basement. Ripping machines they've got in there, too, but the engineers, and Mr. Eckersley who heads them, they don't like anyone messing about near them, nor asking questions."

On and on his buoyant speech ran them around the L-shaped corridors, so fast that a place was no sooner mentioned than lost in a tangle of syllables. The artistes' waiting room, the sound room, the offices of this man and that one, Department of Whatsit, Office of Whosit, the typing pool, the room where broadcasters stored the evening dress suits worn when they were on the air—the tumult slowed just enough to allow Maisie to be beguiled—then on and on. The rabbit-warren building seemed much larger on the inside than it looked from the street. The only room whose location she was able to commit to instant memory was the tearoom, from which emanated the most enticing scent of buttered toast.

Throughout Savoy Hill was that glorious—terrifying—noise and rush and whirl and people who must be delighted in their importance and glamour. It was a heady cloud around her. The accents, the chat, the speed. Despite their varied ages, they possessed a glow of youth that eluded Maisie, even at twenty-three.

Rusty deposited her back with Miss Shields, who stacked an Everest-sized pile of papers on Maisie's desk—"typing and filing and familiarizing yourself"—and ordered her, in a tone that suggested a lengthy quiz would follow, to read and memorize the week's programming schedule and Mr. Reith's packed diary.

Maisie started reading, her lips curling into a grin. Nearly her whole childhood had been spent in windowless corners, reading. Now she was getting paid for it.

"Miss Musgrave!"

The grin vanished and Maisie scurried to her mistress. Miss Shields pointed a pencil at a chair and began dictating a memo. It was understood that Maisie had, of course, snatched up her own steno pad and pencil.

Miss Shields didn't pause in her remorseless dictation, not even when a slim, spotty young man with a crooked grin wheeled in a basket threatening to shatter under the weight of envelopes. He deposited a leaning tower of correspondence in a wire in-tray on Miss Shields's desk, nodded to her politely, and turned, untroubled by a lack of acknowledgment. He started on seeing Maisie and glanced back at Miss Shields, who roused herself enough to ask, "Was there something else, Alfred?"

"No, miss, that's all for now," he said. "Good luck," he whispered to Maisie as he maneuvered the basket out.

"And that's to go to all the men of the Engineering Department," Miss Shields finished with a snap. "Read back the last line."

Maisie skirted from the glinting eyes to her shorthand.

"'I expect this investment means we will not see so many technical errors in the future and that I may assure the governors thereof.'"

"Yes." Miss Shields nodded, a vaguely disappointed frown creasing her forehead. Maisie wondered what technical errors there were—with radio so new, how could there be mistakes? Or perhaps the opposite, and it was rife with error?

Miss Shields beckoned Maisie to the in-tray.

"We are most exact in our handling of correspondence. Everything is stamped and dated properly." She pressed a large rubber stamp into Maisie's palm. The word "RECEIVED" was cut into it in neat capital letters, and underneath were tiny wheels for setting the date. "This is yours to keep at your table." As if it were a prize. "Set the correct date every morning upon arrival." Her tone insinuated that failure to do so would result in an apocalypse to make the destruction of Pompeii look inconsequential.

Maisie turned the wheels carefully, Miss Shields's eyes circling along, to "29 Nov. 1926."

Miss Shields continued her lecture.

"When you have ascertained a letter has been read, you are to draw a pencil line down the page. You will be *very* neat." A cocked brow queried Maisie's capacity for neatness. "Well, get started, then, and mind you type the memo promptly."

Maisie gathered the correspondence and bore it back to her little desk. She wasn't sure which she was supposed to do first, though the typewriter, a gleaming black Underwood with sleek rounded keys, was a seductive siren. *It's like Miss Jenkins said at the secretarial school. Don't ask anyone's opinion or assistance. Just find a way to do everything at once.*

By midmorning, when she was dismissed to a cup of tea, Maisie was exhausted. Perhaps those afraid the radio would turn everyone into robots had a point—the staff of the BBC seemed tapped into the very transmission wires, able to buzz along without even pausing for breath.

"Well, hello, New York!"

Maisie's spine seized up and that pestilent hot flush danced over her neck and cheeks. She supposed controlling one's color was part of the privilege of gentility. Certainly, they never seemed to get embarrassed.

Mr. Underwood (eyes, grin, freckles) swung a leg over a chair and sat down opposite her.

"The old battle-ax brought you on, eh? Well-done. You must be a good one. Or perhaps they're trying to diversify?"

He seemed to be joking, and Maisie risked a smile.

"Cyril Underwood," he announced, extending a hand in the manner of one taught how to do so shortly after mastering a rattle. "Yes, like the typewriter, but not our branch of the clan."

Cyril. It could not have been more perfect.

"Maisie Musgrave," she said, wishing her voice sounded less wobbly.

"How d'ye do? So! Are you from New York, then?"

"No, not . . . I suppose I grew up there, mostly."

"How do you mean, 'mostly'?"

"Er, well, I was born in Toronto . . . That's Canada, I mean."

"I'm familiar with its work," he assured her.

If I blush any harder my hair might catch fire.

Cyril supplied his own laugh and persisted. "But New York, that's something, if the stories are to be believed. If you don't mind me saying so, you don't seem to be quite the sort of New Yorker they describe."

Maisie yearned to point out that this might be why she was in London instead. Those sorts of thoughts always charged into her brain unbidden and had to be subdued. Men didn't like sarcastic girls. The glossies all said so.

"Well, that might be the effect of Toronto? But I . . . I prefer it here."

"Clever girl, then. The grapevine was a bit unclear. You're with the Great Shields and the typing pool—is that it?"

"No, I'm assisting Mr. Reith. I mean, Miss Shields, but helping her with Mr. Reith. And I'm a part-time assistant to the director of Talks, but I haven't met him yet."

Cyril's eyes twinkled. He opened his mouth, then swallowed his thought in a schoolboy's unmistakably mischievous grin. He stood and gave her a rather elaborate salute that she hoped was friendly, even though it looked ironic.

"Good luck, Miss Musgrave, and welcome to the madhouse. I hope you enjoy it!"

"Very much, if it has such people in it," she answered, but only in a whisper, and only to the safety of his back again.

Five minutes later, she forgot she'd ever sat down. No Olympian could have trained harder than under Miss Shields's direction. Nor was there anyone in Savoy Hill who seemed to move at any pace slower than a canter, as though they were eager to reach the future that much more quickly and make sure it wasn't gone by the time they got there.

Maisie saw the usual glances slanting toward her, the familiar half smiles. And, of course, the muffled chuckles. Her clothes, her nose, her nothingness, it was the same record, turning around and around. But it didn't matter. Invisible Girl would rise again. She concentrated on keeping her head down, hugging the walls as she scurried along the corridor, ignoring the ancient echo of the Toronto gang children as they chased her: *Mousy Maisie! Mousy Maisie! You can run, but you can't hide!*

Oh, but I can.

She shut the door to her tiny haven and grinned as she settled herself to another mountain of typing.

Too soon, she was shunted back to the corridors. It wasn't even lunchtime and she was contemplating writing the hospital to ask if they'd post her some Ephedrine.

"Here." Miss Shields thrust several heavy folders into her arms, papers peeking out from the string binding, yearning to breathe free.

"These belong to the Talks Department. I can't think how they came to be here. Oh, and this." She added a large brown envelope with the imposing words: "Interoffice Memo: Dir. Talks H. Matheson" emblazoned across it. She also added a disparaging sniff. "I suppose you'll need a steno pad. You remember where the Talks Department is."

Since it was a statement, not a question, Maisie pressed her tongue to the roof of her mouth and nodded.

Let's see. It was on the fourth floor, I think, and at the far end of the corridor. Or, no, wait. Maybe it was down this way . . .

Everything Rusty had rattled off that morning sat piled in her brain like unsorted items for a jumble sale. No one took the lift—that much she remembered—unless they were transporting something awkward. It was faster to run up and down the stairs; the more impressive noise was a bonus.

She walked with purpose, drawn to the clatter of loud typing and louder chat. Too late, she realized it was only women's voices she heard and thus the typing pool. She was accosted by a statuesque blonde, a sketch artist's dream of curves and curls and country-pink cheeks, depositing work in a tray marked "Output."

"Hullo! Is that all for us?"

"Er, no," Maisie muttered. She couldn't discern any of the women individually, but collectively they oozed glamour and modernity, a sea of red lipstick and snapping eyes. "It's for the Talks Department."

The curvy blonde's interest was further piqued.

"No! You must be the Shields hire! Well, I . . . What are you doing along here?"

Maisie was not about to let the entire typing pool, who, if past was prologue, were the beating heart of gossip and judgment in Savoy Hill, know she was less than thoroughly competent and capable.

"Nothing," she answered. "Do excuse me." She strode away fast to avoid hearing giggles.

Down another flight and scooting around an awkward bend in the corridor, Maisie, eyes firm on the polished floor, collided hard with a man carrying a tuba. One of her overworked shoes slid forward, then the next, and then she landed with a hard "phlumph" on the floor. The files gave one great leap—dozens of papers flew free and fluttered down on her, burying her like a pile of autumn leaves.

A musical giggle landed on top of the papers, and Maisie looked up at a girl every studio in Hollywood would have offered a mansion and the moon. Her dark red hair curled in the natural waves only a Mayfair hairdresser could concoct. Enormous green eyes, lashes that could have doubled as hedgerows. She tilted her head; long jet earrings rested against her jaw. Even from the distance of the floor and her infinite humiliation, Maisie could tell the girl's jersey and skirt were Chanel. And her stockings were most definitely silk.

"Need a hand?" another man volunteered, though not going so far as to set down his own box full of unidentified objects, or even come to a complete stop.

Maisie scrambled to her knees, wondering if there was any chance no one had spotted the holes in her shoes.

"No, I'm all right, thank you," she told the papers on the floor, sweeping them into piles.

"You've got to move quickly around here," the Chanel beauty told Maisie in the most aristocratic accent she had ever heard. "Can't blink even for a moment, you know."

"Yes, I . . . I'm learning that."

"Miss Warwick!" one of the men called in a deferential but hurrying tone.

"Oh, this is a super place for an education!" she trilled, ignoring him. "Better fun than Cheltenham, and I've told my teachers there so. Mind you, I think they were pleased to see the back of me." Another melodious giggle.

Maisie's knees stayed glued to the floor.

"Miss Warwick!" the man called again.

"You don't look the BBC sort," she went on. "Unless perhaps you work in the tearoom? Oh, no, you've got papers. Oh, are you giving a Talk? You rather look like a bluestocking. It must be awfully relaxing, not being bothered with your clothes. I suppose that's how you find time to write, or whatever it is you do."

Maisie had never heard an insult delivered with such sunny politeness.

"I . . . No," Maisie said. "I've just been brought on by Miss Shields."

"You're American!" the Chanel cried, with all the pleasure of having discovered Tutankhamen's tomb.

"Canadian," Maisie grunted obstinately, attempting to get up while gripping the gathered papers. "I mean, that's where I was born."

"I say, *Beanie*, look sharp!" the man bellowed. "Can't have dead air, you know."

"Hopping, skipping, and jumping over!" she chirped.

"Wait!" Maisie cried in desperation. "Sorry. Can you, I, er, I actually am looking for the Talks Department, please." She wrestled any hint of interrogation from her tone.

"Second floor, just down the end. Can't miss it—always a hotbed of activity. Shame the Talks are so soporific, but I'm for the jazz and drama. Not everyone can like action, I do understand. No need to be ashamed. Cheerio!"

She pranced away after the two men. Maisie, despite her anxiety about the time lost, couldn't help but stare after her. She ran on her toes in an elegant little trot that would be the envy of every dancer in the Ballets Russes. Her skirts bounced around her hips and knees, demonstrating to any naysayers that the modern fashions could indeed show a woman's figure to its finest turn under the right circumstances.

Dazed, Maisie wended her way to the Talks Department, clinging to the mad hope that she could sort out the papers without anyone knowing she'd dropped them. Miss Shields undoubtedly considered such an offense to merit the cutting off of hands before being bowled into the street.

For all the Chanel-clad "Beanie" had described Talks as a hotbed of activity, the department was church-like quiet, and Maisie slowed to a tiptoe.

Her reward at last, a crisp, polished sign on a door, glistening with newness: DIRECTOR OF TALKS—H. MATHESON. She took a deep breath, rehearsing an apology as she crept to the office.

The door was ajar. Maisie peered in and saw a severely tidy desk. There seemed to be a building block in the in-tray, but as Maisie drew closer, she realized it was only correspondence stacked so meticulously as to appear smooth. A half-written letter in a rather scrawly hand lay on the blotter. A pile of books. A green leather diary. Maisie chewed her lip as she studied the desk, wondering where to lay her burden.

"Hallo. Is it anything urgent?"

Maisie shrieked, and the papers went flying again. She whirled to see a woman sitting on the floor by the fireplace, smiling up at her.

"Are you off your nuts?" Maisie cried, surprising herself both by the decidedly American expression she hadn't realized she'd ever known and the volume of her speech, which showed that she'd learned one thing from Georgina: how to project to the upper balcony.

"Steady now," the woman advised, her smile broadening. "Carry on like that and you'll be part of the transmission. Indeed, they'd hardly need the tower."

The head of a grim-faced young man in tortoiseshell glasses slithered around the door and glared at Maisie.

"What was all that ruckus? It's not a mouse, is it?"

"Hardly," the woman on the floor responded, her gaze boring into Maisie.

"So what's the matter with you?" the man scolded Maisie. "Pick those up. Don't you know how to deliver things? I've always said girls have no place working in—"

"Now, Mr. Fielden, do calm down. You're in danger of being

ridiculous," the woman chided. "The young lady was simply startled by my presence, and you must agree, I am astonishing."

Fielden's thin lip, unimproved by his haphazard mustache, curled. Maisie could feel how much he longed to keep scolding her.

"I shall handle this," the woman concluded. Her voice was pleasant, cheerful, but rang with an absolute command that would not be countered.

Fielden nodded obediently, and his head slid back around the door.

The woman chuckled. Maisie couldn't understand her ease. If *she* had been caught lounging on an office floor—not that she would ever contemplate such an action—she'd be lucky to retrieve her hat and coat before being shown the door. But this woman took a luxurious sip of tea, set her cup on a lacquered tray, and swung to her feet with an almost acrobatic leap.

"Now, then, what were you delivering?"

"Er . . ." Maisie bent to gather the papers, now far beyond hopeless and well into disaster.

Why didn't I just look for work picking potatoes?

The woman helped her up, and Maisie balanced the papers on the desk.

"Are you . . . ? I, er, I thought the director of Talks didn't have a secretary," Maisie said, her hands still shifting through the papers to hide their trembling.

"Not as such, no, and that's something that badly needs rectifying," came the jaunty reply. Maisie had the uneasy sense of being read from the inside out, despite the placid sweetness of the huge blue eyes. The woman was rather lovely, with soft blond hair cut into a wavy bob and an elegant figure shown to advantage in a practical, and obviously bespoke, tweed suit. Her skin was the pink and white of first bloom, but Maisie felt sure she was in her thirties. It was just something about her bearing. This was a woman who had seen and done things.

And now she had seen the interoffice envelope, addressed to the director of Talks.

"Ah!" she cried, catching it up and opening it.

Maisie was galvanized. "No! That's for Mr. Matheson, Miss Shields said."

"I know of two Mr. Mathesons, and neither are here." The woman grinned. She had the air of an infinitely patient teacher.

Maisie had the horrible sense she was being set up for a joke. That any second, Cyril, Beanie, Rusty, and the boys were going to swarm around the door and laugh at her. That the story would fly through the whole of Savoy Hill and follow her wherever she ran, even if she fled to deepest Saskatchewan.

"You . . . Are you . . . the director of Talks?" Maisie whispered, hoping everyone waiting to laugh wouldn't hear.

"I am," the woman announced with a pleased nod. "Hilda Matheson. Miss. And you are?"

"Maisie Musgrave."

"Aha!" Hilda pumped Maisie's hand, her eyes snapping with delight. "My new secretary! Or as much as Mr. Reith and Miss Shields are willing to spare you. Thus far. Marvelous! Now, don't you mind me sitting on the floor by the fire. It's a grand way to think and just one of my quirks."

"I didn't mean to—"

"You most certainly did, and don't you apologize for it. It was glorious." Hilda laughed. Her musical laugh was very unlike Beanie's. It was boisterous, rolling, and deep—Maisie found it a touch alarming.

"I expect you thought I was a secretary," she went on, not waiting for Maisie's embarrassed nod. "Wouldn't I get into the hottest water for such impropriety? Well," she added, eyes twinkling with an unsettling roguishness, "I might anyway at that. But it is chilly and one must stay warm. I appreciate your looking after me, Miss Musgrave, though I might suggest in future moderating your tone just a nip."

Maisie could hear an echo of that laugh.

"Of course, Miss Matheson," she whispered.

"That's going to the other extreme. But quite all right. It's always useful to try a few possibilities. Else how can you be sure what's right?"

"I . . . I don't know, Miss Matheson."

"Well, we try, try again. Now, are all these for Talks as well?" she asked, indicating the folders.

"Er, yes, but I'm afraid . . ." Maisie squeezed her eyes shut, both to avoid seeing this exacting woman too closely and to stop the tears from spilling more freely than the papers. "Oh, Miss Matheson, I'm so sorry, but I'd already dropped them, even before now. They've got to be put all back together and I don't know—"

"Folders dropped twice, and on your first morning, no less! That is a feat. You don't make a habit of tossing paper thither and yon, do you?"

"Oh, no! No, I was . . . Well, I ran into a tuba."

"Occupational hazard in Savoy Hill. But you're all right? Good. Now, let's have at these papers and see how quickly they submit to order."

Could she possibly be facetious? Maisie thought with yearning of Miss Shields's disapproving candor, which was at least comprehensible. She gazed, fascinated, as Hilda organized the papers, small neat hands flying through them, nails manicured, left finger brazenly unencumbered by a wedding ring, a silver-and-enamel Mido watch clamped around her wrist.

"There!" She patted the neat folders with satisfaction. "I shall let you in on a little secret I've unearthed, having been here only since September myself. Few of these papers are of the earth-shattering consequence they're considered by some. It's all about what's *going* to happen, Miss Musgrave, not what's already been and done. Which isn't to say I don't like to keep very complete and tidy records. That is something I do expect, along with a strict attentiveness to all that goes forward. But I daresay Miss Shields and Mr. Reith wouldn't have approved you if you weren't sharp."

At the moment Maisie had no idea why she'd been approved. Miss Jenkins at the secretarial school always withheld from giving her full marks. "You're the most technically proficient and capable,

Miss Musgrave, but the best secretaries have *brio*, dear." *Does anyone ever use the word "dear" when they aren't insulting you?*

Maisie was grateful to Miss Matheson, who in any case was a good deal more pleasant than Miss Shields, but now, the emergency over, she felt deflated. She'd been expecting a man. A clever, charming, well-spoken man who would intimidate and dazzle her. Under his influence, she would learn how to behave in such a way that would allow a man's genius to flourish. Such skills would hopefully attract another clever and exciting man (dark blue eyes and freckles came to mind) who might be enticed to become her husband.

But a woman. As director of Talks. That seemed to be taking the BBC's audacious modernity a bit too far.

"We have some time before the meeting," Hilda announced. "Let's discuss the department. I'll detail what we've been doing here and some thoughts I have towards the future and how to implement some plans. We're very small as yet. You'll meet us all by tomorrow. You've already had the pleasure of meeting my junior, Lionel Fielden, very good at his job but rather willfully bad-mannered—you'll get used to him. He's handy, but it's not the same thing as having an energetic, clever young woman to really organize things and keep us all well oiled." She studied Maisie, assessing those oil reserves. "We're a bit short on time. What say we be wild and I send out for some sandwiches? Anything in particular you'd like?"

"Er . . ."

For heaven's sake, at least use a different syllable!

Hilda grinned.

"Can a person ever go wrong with egg and cress in one hand and ham and cheese in the other? Do sit down." She waved at the room as she pressed a button to summon a page, another brisk and eager adolescent boy.

Hilda's office was larger than Miss Shields's, more militantly well ordered, but also more inviting. Slivers of gold-and-blue walls peeked around bookshelves, which were stuffed with the sort of books Maisie had always wanted to own. It was a struggle not to reach out and run her finger across them, feeling each embossed leather binding sing under her skin. What wall space remained was decorated with pictures; an Italian landscape, the Scottish Highlands, Paris on a lavender spring evening. A water jug and two glasses sat on one trestle table, the tea tray on another, next to a tempting plate of biscuits. Maisie wanted to hug the room, kiss it, swallow it whole.

"Why are you standing on ceremony?" Hilda asked. "I wasn't intending for *you* to sit on the floor, you know, though of course you're very free to do so."

Maisie sank into a chair. A fat round cushion with a red-and-blue Italian print cover nestled into her back. Its fellow was on the floor, having performed its good service for Hilda. Just as Maisie was reaching for it, Hilda caught it up, set it on her own chair, and turned to Maisie.

"I don't want a fetch-and-carry sort of secretary. We're far too busy. Now then, I've been organizing Talks into series. I think regular programming is useful and builds an audience, but of course we don't want anything so routine that it becomes dull. I like to keep things in categories. So, literary Talks, political, scientific, educational, artistic, household, general, those are what I've put into motion thus far, and I think will form a useful frame within which to operate, but of course it's really only just the springboard for launching any manner of interesting broadcasting. From one person speaking, to interviews, to a series of debates, wouldn't that be splendid?"

Maisie nodded, concentrating on her shorthand as Hilda rattled off names of people she was hoping to persuade to broadcast. Maisie recognized some of them—T. S. Eliot, Virginia Woolf, George Bernard Shaw. But she was soon drowning under the scientists, mathematicians, writers, artists, politicians, butchers, bakers, candlestick makers. Hilda talked as if she knew every one of them, her giddiness catapulting her from her chair so she paced the room, both it and Maisie shrinking to accommodate her expansive vision.

The sandwiches arrived, along with two bottles of ginger beer.

"Ah, excellent," Hilda crowed, pressing a large coin into the happy page's hand. "Bit outlandish, sending for victuals from the pub when it's just our little meeting, but first days must be marked." She busied herself finding napkins.

Maisie's gratitude mingled with mortification. Hilda shouldn't be spending her own money like this. It made Maisie feel indebted to her before she'd earned a penny.

"I mean to make 'efficiency' our byword here in Talks."

Hilda was so efficient as to be able to eat while talking and somehow remain elegant. Maisie's attempt at combining efficiency with elegance was far less successful. She wrote with her pad balanced on her knee, leaving her other hand free to shovel in food, and hoped Hilda was too absorbed in her soliloquy to notice.

Women notice everything, though. I bet she's seen every mend in my stockings. I bet she knows I have to cut my hair myself. I bet she thinks she's drawn a straw so short, even Thumbelina couldn't drink out of it.

Hilda dabbed her lips.

"Terrific challenge, talking about new art on the radio. Let's schedule a meeting with Sir Frederic at the British Museum and Charles Aitken at the Tate—very able man, Aitken. We'll explore some possibilities . . . I think it might be really compelling to have a curator or art historian speak with an artist about a current piece. Wouldn't that be thrilling? Paint a picture, if you see." She smirked.

The glossies also said that men didn't like women making jokes, but perhaps it was different when there were no men present. Maisie didn't want to laugh. That would imply she was relaxing.

"You've done fine justice to those sandwiches, Miss Musgrave." (Was that a compliment?) "Before we segue to biscuits, do tell me something of yourself."

"Er, well, there's nothing much to tell," Maisie demurred.

"Nonsense. And if you don't mind me saying so, that's a very bad habit, playing yourself down. We all have a life story, age notwithstanding."

Maisie didn't want to talk about herself. She did, however, badly want biscuits.

"What made you apply to work here?" Hilda asked.

"There was an advertisement," Maisie answered, surprised.

"There are always advertisements. Why the BBC?"

"I . . . er, well, I . . . It was a job I thought I could do. And it, er . . ."

Blissful distraction wheeled in with the basket post. Hilda glowed with Christmas joy.

"Ah! The second round!"

"Here you are, Miss Matheson. Enjoy it." Alfred balanced another foot-tall pile of papers in Hilda's in-tray. He started even more violently than before on seeing Maisie again, and she was too busy inhaling a biscuit to greet him.

"Have you met Miss Musgrave, my new secretary?"

"Hallo." He nodded, and shook his head all the way back out the door.

Hilda moved to tidy the letters. Maisie hoped that wasn't going to be one of her assignments. It looked as though it would be lethal simply to breathe too close to the pile.

"You look alarmed, Miss Musgrave. Correspondence comes in by the veritable hogshead all day long. Didn't Miss Shields tell you?"

It seemed rude to say no.

Hilda gave the now-symmetrical mound an approving pat. "I call it my Tower of Babble. Though in fact nearly all of it is interesting. Or useful. And some of the criticism is downright entertaining."

The white-and-pink guilloche enamel carriage clock perched in pride of place on top of the desk sang out the hour. Hilda glanced at it and tossed back the last of her ginger beer.

"Time to face the DG! Director-general," she clarified, seeing Maisie's blank face. "Our master, Mr. John Reith, director-general of the British Broadcasting Company. But nearly everyone here calls him 'the DG.' Are you finished?"

Maisie nodded, her longing to see Mr. Reith eclipsing her desire for another biscuit.

Hilda plucked the green leather diary from her desk and glanced at a bookmarked page. Maisie shifted her gaze downward, noticing Hilda's smart mahogany shoes, low-heeled, with three straps and a double-stitched edge. They gleamed like new, though they might have been several years old. This was what Georgina meant about buying good quality. Hilda, though she obviously had money, didn't seem the extravagant type, or one to buy every latest thing, leaving still-good items to languish in a cupboard or be dispatched to a church's charity box. Perhaps she rubbed saddle cream into the leather every night to keep her shoes so fresh.

I'll do that with my new shoes, from the first night.

For a fairly petite woman, Hilda walked fast. Maisie gave full leash to her own speedy walk (not very feminine), and noticed, even above the din of people thundering all around them, that Hilda's footfall was almost silent.

"Apologies for the lack of girlish heel clicks," Hilda said, seeing Maisie's puzzled face staring at her feet. "Just trying to set a good example. However good the soundproofing is, that's no excuse for carelessness."

Maisie thought Hilda was fighting a losing battle there. Carelessness seemed to run amok in the corridors.

"Mind you," Hilda continued. "I learned to walk quietly some time ago. It's quite useful, not being heard when you approach. Or leave. In my experience, it suits rather a few situations."

They reached Miss Shields's office, and Hilda sailed in.

"Good afternoon, Miss Shields. Here we are. Is he ready?"

"Mr. Reith is always very punctual, Miss Matheson, as you well know," Miss Shields informed her. Now Maisie understood the sneer when Miss Shields mentioned the director of Talks. She glanced at Hilda, who, if she even registered Miss Shields's electric dislike, was wholly untroubled by it.

The inner door opened, and Maisie involuntarily stepped back. The imposing figure of Mr. Reith towered in the frame, heavy eyebrows drawn together, dark eyes boring into the women assembled before him.

Resplendent in Harris Tweed, a gold watch chain glittering across the dark fabric, shoes so polished he could inspect himself in them, Mr. Reith could not have been more what Maisie had hoped for than if she had crafted him herself out of the same fine cloth that made his suit.

The fierce eyes settled on her, the one unknown amid the familiar.

"Ah, you are the new girl," he told her, scowling, though his voice, upstanding King's English laced with a Scottish burr, wasn't without warmth. "The one who is fond of the Old World."

Maisie reeled. Miss Shields hardly seemed the sort of person to repeat such information.

"I'm—I'm so pleased to make your acquaintance, Mr. Reith," Maisie stammered, hoping all the words came out in the right order.

"We're pleased to have you here, Miss . . . ?"

"Musgrave," Hilda put in.

"Ah, yes." Reith nodded, brows drawing together again. "Well, do come in, ladies."

It was the grandest room Maisie had ever entered. The heavy pile of the carpet tickled her feet through the newspapers in her shoes. Velvet drapes, heavy enough to suffocate her, were looped back to allow for a view of the Thames. The ceiling seemed to stretch up for miles, appropriate to accommodate both the immense rosewood bookshelves and a man of Reith's stature, as well as helping Maisie feel minuscule.

Reith settled himself into a chair behind an oak desk that nearly spanned the width of the room. Once he ascertained that they were all waiting on his preamble, he drew some papers toward him and began.

"Your programming schedule for next week is most satisfactory," he told Hilda. "The series on winter gardening sounds very pleasant. I will be sure to alert Mrs. Reith to it."

"Oh, excellent. Do tell me how she likes it. I'm quite pleased with our speakers, though I haven't managed to get anyone from the Botanical Society to agree to broadcast. I think they find us a bit shocking."

"Hm. You wrote to Charlie Simms? Old Gresham's chum of mine; should be game."

"Yes. Here was the reply, from his secretary." She handed him a small square of paper. "She sounds the dragonish sort, guarding the gate against all comers."

A sharp intake of breath from Miss Shields, even as she dutifully continued to take the minutes.

"Hm," Reith said again, passing the square back. "Bit of rum nonsense. I'll phone him; due for a coffee anyway. Miss Shields, you'll make the arrangements?"

"Of course, Mr. Reith," she replied, her voice so warm and deferential, Maisie looked up to be sure it was the same woman.

"That's very good of you, Mr. Reith," Hilda said.

"All in it together, eh, Miss Matheson? And if the Talks keep going as they've been just in the last few weeks, or so I gather from these correspondence reports, you should have less and less trouble beating down dragons."

"Onwards and upwards, yes, indeed! But in the meantime, I shall continue to be my best St. George," she assured him.

"Good, good." He nodded seriously. "Now, about Christmas. You've put in far too many suggestions—it's not as though we broadcast twenty-four hours a day, and even then we wouldn't have time."

Hilda's laugh bounced off the leather folios.

"I suppose I got a bit carried away, though you did ask that I give you a lot to choose from, this being my first time arranging our holiday broadcasts."

"Yes, yes," Mr. Reith agreed, tapping his pen along the typed list. "Important we do well, nothing inappropriate. Though Miss

Warwick tells me it was your suggestion the Drama Department do a specially designed performance of *A Christmas Carol*. A jolly good thought; should be most entertaining."

"Ah, thank you. Yes, I am afire with anticipation," Hilda said. "They've secured a marvelous cast. Mr. Hicks, you know." Another minute sniff from Miss Shields, though whether for Dickens or actors, it was impossible to guess.

"Hicks, yes," Reith murmured, eyes on Hilda's list. "Rather hard to choose."

"I ought to have tried to edit more," Hilda said, cheerfully unapologetic, "but we can always make use of extraneous ideas for another time. And you know, the holidays might be a time to press for more broadcast hours, what with—"

Reith made a noise like a bull sneezing.

"More hours, indeed. You've never been to a meeting of the governors. What a rum lot."

"I would be happy to join you at one, if you would like?"

His scowl crinkled upward.

"Perhaps one day, if it can be managed." He sounded so fatherly. Maisie's throat constricted.

"Well, if we've only got the hours we've got, let's give this a bit of a thrashing, hm?" Hilda consulted her copy of the Christmas list. "So let's see, something to accompany the Dickens broadcast, obviously, a Talk about the traditions, the tree. I'll ask Peppard at Cambridge, and do let's have a Talk about gift giving. Gilbert at the V&A should do, and Nellie will be game for a decorating Talk. She's at *Home* magazine now—"

"Wonderful, wonderful," Mr. Reith broke in, nodding vigorously and marking the list. "And then this and this, yes, yes, and what do you reckon to the Archbishop of Canterbury?"

"He does fine work, I hear."

"Pardon?"

"Just a jest, hopeless habit. He should be grand for a reading if he isn't fully booked. Would you like to send the letter, having met him, or shall I?"

Reith had met the Archbishop of Canterbury. And here was Maisie, serving him.

"I'm happy to make the request, yes." Reith made a final tick on the list and slid it back to Hilda. "Very, very good, Miss Matheson. You're doing splendidly. Exactly why I was pleased to hire you."

"Begged me to come aboard, as I recall it." Hilda pealed with laughter again. Miss Shields did not sniff, but the scratch of her pencil spoke volumes. "Lady Astor had quite a job convincing me. Still, she succeeded, as of course she always does, and I am very pleased indeed."

"Yes, well." Reith turned over another set of papers. "It was a good show of you, not to want to leave your employer."

Maisie looked up from that shorthand mark. Even with her scant interest in British government, she knew the name "Lady Astor." Everyone did. But to Maisie, she was an object of glorious inspiration that had nothing to do with being the first woman elected to Parliament. Nancy Astor had been born and raised in Virginia, and managed to marry a British nobleman. She was one of Maisie's personal goddesses.

"I think the chaps at the *Radio Times* could be making a better show of writing up the Talks programs," Reith went on. "Perhaps you can give them more specific notes?"

"Certainly," Hilda said. "Though we are always very clear. The fellows seem to have this idea that they add pizzazz, I think."

"But if you can write things up for them more exactly, that will be of use."

"Having Miss Musgrave will be a great help in that regard," Hilda told him.

"Hmm? Oh, yes." He gave Maisie a pleasant nod, and she blushed.

"I beg your pardon, Mr. Reith," Miss Shields broke in, "but it is nearly half past two."

"Is it?" He consulted his watch to confirm. "Ah. Well, we can discuss plans for next year later in the week. Thank you, Miss Matheson, and do keep on with the fine work."

"I absolutely shall," Hilda almost sang as they trooped out.

Back in Miss Shields's office, Maisie hovered, waiting to be dismissed so she could type the minutes. She was eager to relive every second of that meeting.

Hilda turned to Miss Shields. "Have I got Miss Musgrave again now?"

"Not just yet," Miss Shields said, snap and chill fully restored. "I have quite a bit of typing for her to complete. Weight must be mindfully distributed."

"Well, indeed, but—"

A brilliantined man burst in, straightening his tie.

"He ready for me?"

"Do go in, Mr. Eckersley." Miss Shields indicated Reith's office. "Was there anything else, Miss Matheson?"

"No, thank you," Hilda said. She turned to Maisie. "Welcome aboard, Miss Musgrave. I hope you can be spared a few more hours this afternoon."

"Yes, Miss Matheson," Maisie murmured politely. Having basked in the glory that was Mr. Reith, she wanted to stay as close in his circle as possible. But she wasn't forgetting the sandwiches.

Hilda nodded briskly and was gone, her footfall so silent, she might as well have evaporated.

Miss Shields took Maisie's pad and examined her shorthand. Despite her scrutiny, she didn't find any errors. Again, she looked disappointed.

"You could be tidier. You will type the minutes for our office from my notes, and I daresay Miss Matheson will request a copy."

"Yes, Miss Shields."

Half an hour later, Miss Shields's voice rang out over the typewriter.

"Miss Musgrave!"

The secretary was still seated, her chair fully turned to face Maisie's cupboard.

"I have nearly had to shout," she scolded Maisie.

"Oh, I'm sorry," and she was, but it was only seven steps across the room to the threshold. Which Maisie herself now crossed to hear instructions.

"Mr. Reith needs his tea. He's asked that you fetch it, rather than a boy." Her voice was crisp, her face irritated. "I am assuming you can manage that."

"Yes, I can," Maisie answered proudly, and set off at a sprint. If Reith needed tea, he must have it, and she was going to run faster than Mercury to bring it to him.

The tearoom proprietress, neat and busy with graying hair coiled in an austere knot at her neck, nodded at the request and wheeled out a tea tray.

"Mr. Reith's only," she warned.

Maisie was prepared to guard it against all comers during the return trek to the executive offices, but she was unaccosted. Miss Shields sighed and waved her through, and she entered the throne room again, alone.

"Ah, Miss Musgrave," Reith greeted her. "Very nice, thank you."

It would have been easier to lay out his tea things if her hands weren't shaking, but he continued to nod approvingly as she set the pot, cup, milk, sugar, and—a pang of longing—two iced buns before him.

"I can manage from here," he assured her, though she would have been so much happier to keep waiting on him.

"Yes, sir," she said, trying not to sigh. She edged toward the door.

"Sit down a moment, Miss Musgrave."

She'd never known an invitation could be barked. She perched on the club chair he indicated. The leather was probably repelled by her cheap wool dress.

Reith devoted himself to the pouring of tea and adding milk in a manner only slightly less ritualized than the preparing of Communion, and Maisie's respect for him grew. He was unhurried, comfortable in his silence, allowing Maisie to drink him in at leisure. He was balding and had a cleft in his chin thick enough to hold a cigarette. Something that would be an amusing parlor trick for his children, but the heft of his eyebrows, drawn together into one, indicated that Reith was not a man given to whimsy.

He raised the lid of a teak box with an ivory inlay design and drew out a cigarette.

"Do you smoke?"

"No, sir."

Couldn't possibly afford it.

"Glad to hear it!" he barked. "I don't like seeing a female smoke. It's unseemly. Modern girls," he said, sighing as he lit the cigarette, "so uninterested in decorum."

He scowled at her again, and she wondered if it would be inappropriate to say that she was a devotee of decorum.

At least my skirt covers my knees when I'm sitting.

"You're a nice girl," he announced. "I heard what you said to Miss Shields in your interview. I don't have anything to do with the hiring of the girls, generally, but in this instance I thought it best to have a small hand in."

He was still scowling, and now she discerned that the creases around his eyes turned up slightly, creating his version of a smile.

This man was responsible for hiring me.

Her fingers were gouging into her knees, preventing her from sliding to the floor in obeisance.

If Reith noticed her naked gratitude, he hid it under his scowl as he stirred sugar into his tea.

"There are two questions I like to ask of potential BBC staff," he said, taking a sip of tea and sniffing in approval. He leaned closer to her, eyebrows tight, chin jutted. "Are you a Christian, and have you any character defects?"

Maisie's jaw unhinged. Since the true answers were "no" and "countless," there was nothing to do but stare at him hopelessly.

Reith took a big puff on his cigarette and laughed. Or anyway, it sounded like a laugh; she didn't want to swear to it.

"Not to worry. Not to worry. I only ask in earnest when interviewing men for top positions. I was merely curious to see how you would respond, though of course I don't doubt you are a well brought-up girl."

Maisie was beyond relieved he had answered for her. During Toronto exiles, her grandmother (the incongruous Lorelei, who had spent an admirable life's work exorcising the name's implied sensuality) marched Maisie to the First Anglican Church every Sunday, carrying a birch switch to remind her of consequences. "Your mother is the first and last whore in this bloodline. I shall beat every last sin out of you if I must, so help me." Certainly, all the local hoodlums were happy to assist—the unwanted daughter of an actress must deserve beating. Georgina's neglect was a welcome relief on a Sunday, as she slept all day.

As to character defects, between Maisie's assessment and Georgina's, there couldn't be enough letterhead in the BBC to complete the list.

Did Reith expect everyone to say "Yes" and "No"? Would he believe the latter? There wasn't such a man, was there? Would he be absurdly dull or irritatingly perfect?

"I hope you are a hard worker," Reith barked, his scowl twisting into expectation.

"Yes, sir," she squeaked. "I mean, I am."

"Excellent." He nodded, taking another sip of tea.

"Your next appointment, Mr. Reith," Miss Shields announced from the door.

"Thank you," he said, which sufficed for both women.

"Back to Talks with you, then," Miss Shields ordered Maisie. "You have those minutes?"

The typed pages, neat and exact, were received with a resigned grunt. Maisie wondered how Miss Jenkins would react to a supervisor who seemed to resent a lack of error. "You have to be prepared for anything," she'd lectured her students. *I think I'll write and suggest a new course for the curriculum.*

Hilda's lamps were turned up full, making the room cozy in the chilly November afternoon. She handed Maisie a typed script covered in illegible red writing.

"A Talk runs fifteen minutes; we're rather firm about that. Except when we're not. Some Talks warrant more time. Unfortunately, every speaker thus far seems to think their subject is one of the latter." Hilda grinned. "Can't blame them, can you? I'm developing a set of guidelines that should help them. You can type my initial notes tomorrow. No time to lose."

Imagine knowing so much about a topic, you can talk and be interesting for fifteen minutes. Be considered an expert, invited to broadcast. Be listened to and paid.

Maisie looked at the script. It was for a broadcast by Joseph Conrad. Perhaps that meant Maisie was going to meet him, going to meet all such men when they came in to broadcast. This job might be something close to heaven.

"You'll have to type the script again, implementing my changes," Hilda directed, waving a hand at the illegible red scrawl. Maisie felt a slight descent from heaven.

"You're making changes to Mr. Conrad's work?" she asked.

She hadn't meant to speak out loud, but however much power Hilda might wield, she couldn't think it extended to altering a syllable of a man's words, not a man like this.

"Many can write; few can broadcast. Thus far," Hilda added with a cackle. "There's a trick to it, I've found. I mean to devote myself to developing, refining, and teaching it. You'll see. You shall come to rehearsals with me soon, and you'll see."

All Maisie could see were typed words slathered in red graffiti.

"Yes, I am sorry about that." Hilda laughed, not sounding sorry at all. "Never had much of a neat hand. But I'm sure you'll soon decipher it and be raring away. You'll get used to me in time."

Maisie settled herself before the typewriter.

I'm not so sure about that.

THREE

"Tremendous congratters. Knew you'd land it, but I miss us gadding about during the days," Lola mourned, as though there'd ever been any gadding. Maisie knew she was only missed as an audience to the drama that was Lola's ramshackle—and indeed, often entertaining—life, and that as soon as Lola was cast in a show again, she would disappear, and Maisie would be forgotten.

Maisie embraced her new routine with all the ardor of a new bride. Up at seven, washed and dressed, all in the space of fifteen minutes. *The length of a Talk.* This efficiency, she decided, marked some small advantage to being poor. With so few clothes to choose from, getting dressed was no quarrelsome effort. It was almost an argument for *not* acquiring more blouses and skirts, jumpers and jackets, else how much time would be lost in dividing and conquering them? But she still sighed as she buttoned herself into her blue serge dress, the dullest of her three outfits. She lined her shoes with fresh paper and went down for breakfast.

Though inflexible on points like acquiring a wireless, Mrs. Crewe was admirable about breakfasts. There was porridge and toast, corn-flakes and coffee, with the boarders free to use as much treacle, butter, and cream as they wished. Maisie craved eggs and bacon, but it was a lovely porridge. And the other girls' desire to be fashionably slim meant she could be even more extravagant with the cream and butter.

After breakfast, she put on her coat, hat, gloves, and scarf. Her handbag, empty save for a handkerchief, two pennies for lunch, and emergency sixpence, went over her wrist, and she hoped her rickety umbrella could stay folded.

She was one of the lucky ones, as it took her only one tram to reach the Strand, the street above Savoy Hill. The ride was long and she had to stand, but she didn't mind. The car had a rhythmic sway, the bell tinkled happily, and one never knew when a sudden screech or thrust would disrupt the song, jolting them all out of their morning meditation. It was a kind of jazz, the only kind she could afford, and so she exulted in the fizz of cigarette smoke, the lingering smell of coffee, and the crinkle of newspapers that added to the hum and percussion. It wasn't stealing to read the paper over a man's shoulder, gleaning nuggets of the world and enjoying the smell of Palmolive shaving cream. And she watched London unfold before her.

The dark rows of unloved terrace houses gave way to streets wide enough to encompass history, close enough to wrap that history around you and make you feel how fleeting and finite you were within it. Maisie exulted in the oldness of the buildings, their grandeur and glisten, stoically gazing down on the throng of people and trams and buses and cabs and horse-drawn carriages, with a snake of private cars looping in, men encasing their wealth in sleek metal and leather and wire wheels. Women, too, occasionally, nearly always driving open-top cars, bursts of impertinent sunshine in beaded cloches, cherry-red lips widespread in ecstatic smiles, eyes fireworking from behind their motoring goggles. Racing their way somewhere they no doubt called important.

Maisie turned from them and held her breath, waiting for the entrance onto the Strand, this last mile of the marathon. So many magnificent buildings to pass on the way, the Royal Courts of Justice, the charming and appropriately antique Twinings tea shop, and then at last, the Savoy Hotel, an almost-palace on a street that once boasted palaces. She alighted at the corner of Savoy Street and revolved once on the spot, drinking in the day before measuring each step down the hill to Savoy Hill House, home of the BBC. The pub on the left, the Savoy Tup, was still shuttered at this hour. It and the Lyceum, just up on the Strand, were popular lunch spots for the denizens of Savoy Hill. Until she was paid, Maisie confined her lunches to an apple and a bun, but the Tup had been the purveyor of the sandwiches Hilda ordered that first day, and so Maisie hailed it with respect.

She hadn't yet visited the decrepit Savoy Chapel, just outside the BBC, but knew it was the subject of many jokes, its location considered ideal for the days when one's entire department was imploding (at least once a week) or as a hiding place from Mr. Reith when he was on the warpath (at least once a day).

No less worthy of worship was the Thames, at the foot of the hill. Maisie stopped outside the BBC's door and looked down at it. Some bright day, it would be the height of bliss to eat a sandwich and cake on the Victoria Embankment.

The BBC shared its home with the Institute of Electrical Engineers, who, being more than fifty years the senior, showed its scorn for this damp-eared upstart by designing the carved-out space so that the two entities never met. The IEE commandeered Savoy Hill's majestic entranceway on the Embankment, and it was said they had a good laugh whenever some grand person came to broadcast and had to use the BBC's unprepossessing entrance at the side of the building. Maisie thought that since the BBC was the natural and rather exciting outgrowth of the IEE's work, they should be hovering like proud mothers. Instead, each organization went about its business as though the other didn't exist.

And indeed, once through that wooden door, nothing else did exist.

It was easy to maintain her status as Invisible Girl as she whizzed back and forth between the executive offices and the Talks Department. Maisie had a long experience of listening to many conversations at once and gleaning anything that might be useful, and information flew through the narrow corridors of Savoy Hill at a speed Lindbergh would envy. Thus, as the week progressed, she learned that Cyril Underwood-not-typewriter worked in the Schools Department, where they produced broadcasts heard in schoolrooms throughout Britain, considered a daunting task. Scores of complimentary letters from teachers and heads did nothing to allay the staff's horror of a scalding letter, or even worse, negative commentary in a newspaper. They soldiered on, both pets and prodigals under Mr. Reith's watchful eye. There was a woman producer there, too, a Mary Somerville, apparently hired through "an old girls' network, who knew?" and quite brilliant. The curvy, curly blonde in the typing pool was Phyllida Fenwick, the de facto head of the consortium by dint of being the tallest and loudest. The proprietress of the tearoom, her temperament both leonine and motherly, was Mrs. Hudson. Then there were those who simply announced themselves, like Beanie.

"It's Sabine, of course, Sabine Warwick, not of the Greville side—wouldn't want to look after that pile anyway—but baronets just the same. And new creations, but 1780, so well entrenched in Debrett's. Bit scandalizing, me working, but Mama thinks I've not got the stamina, so must prove the old dear wrong. Pater's pleased for once. Thinks it shows moral fiber, good example to the ordinary folk, and very modern. Keen on being modern, he is. Bought some of the West End theaters in his wilding days, and proud to be a patron, don't you know. So here I am in our mouse hole of a Drama Department! The DG thinks I bring refinement, and Pater is bursting his buttons, contemplating all the edifying drama I'm bringing to the poor wretches who never saw a play. Great good fun, really."

Maisie was the one left breathless after this one-sided exchange.

She was quick to drop Invisible Girl whenever she saw Cyril, and was pleased to be rewarded by his grin.

"Well, New York! I'd heard you were a Talks fixture now, and here it is true."

"Oh, no, the Talks only have me part-time," she reminded him.

"Until Matheson comes to like you, I'll warrant. Massive apologies for not setting you straight on her your first day. Rotten of me. What say I apologize properly someday and you tell me all about speakeasies, hm?" He seemed to take her blush as agreement. "I'll hold you to that," he said, and loped away, which spared Maisie's having to either admit ignorance of speakeasies or ask how particular he was about the truth.

Phyllida and a minor contingent of the typists chose that moment to walk by, smoking and chatting. They went silent on seeing Maisie, glanced at her sideways, then dissolved into whispers and giggles once she was behind them. Maisie was suddenly contemptuous. Had any of *them* lied about their age to join the war effort? They had probably grown up in loving families, who didn't begrudge them food or education or upkeep. Or existence.

It doesn't matter. I've spent my whole life not having friends. I've gotten good at it. And that's not why I'm here.

She was still uneasy around Hilda. It was one thing to have had Sister Bennister as a superior. That was comprehensible. The world of nursing was emphatically female. This world wasn't, and Hilda's comfort with it unnerved Maisie that much more. Hilda was friendly to her, but she was friendly to everybody. Georgina always said, never trust a friendly woman. She herself was always friendly, to anyone who wasn't Maisie, and Maisie certainly never trusted her.

According to the Savoy Hill buzz, Hilda had not exaggerated— Reith had indeed begged her to leave her post as Lady Astor's political secretary (how did she *get* these jobs?) and come to the BBC to head this, the most important department in the company, and it was Lady Astor, not Reith, who had convinced Hilda.

"That Matheson knows everyone," Billy, one of the engineers, pronounced to a shiny new boy as they wheeled equipment along the third floor. "Brings loads of ladies in to broadcast. Between her and that Miss Warwick in Drama bringing in the actresses, you get to see some of the finest in the land. And if you need to adjust the sub-mixer during broadcast, you can get an up-close of their legs."

So much for the glory of the new technology.

"Managing all right?" Hilda asked, seeing Maisie waver over some filing.

"Oh, I, yes, thank you," Maisie muttered.

"Excellent. I hope you're feeling robust. I've got a few revisions for you to type." She handed Maisie another script sagging under the weight of red writing. "Tell me, Miss Musgrave. I'm bursting to know. What sort of Talks do you like best?"

Maisie tried to remember the last time anyone had asked her personal opinion. Hilda liked answers, so Maisie pondered. She felt the most affinity for the morning Talks, considered the purview of women and primarily focused on household issues. The afternoon and evening Talks were more taxing in comparison, though she liked the book reviews and discussions. But a bluestocking expected a more intellectual response.

"Er, well, I . . . They're all different, aren't they?" she asked, opting instead for diplomacy.

"I certainly hope so. But you needn't fear being marked up or down. I'm merely interested in your opinion."

Maisie also liked Talks where great men spoke of great things in a great way. *And you* really *can't say that to a bluestocking.*

"I really can't say."

Disappointment tinged the edge of Hilda's eyes. "I hope you've seen that I encourage free speaking around here, Miss Musgrave. It would hardly be the Talks Department otherwise."

"I don't understand," Maisie said, although she had a feeling she did.

"I prefer when everyone is open and honest. Makes for far pleasanter conversation, and more efficient, too," Hilda explained. "Mind you"—a grin teased around her lips—"an enigmatic conversation is not without its enchantments. One does enjoy a challenge."

There was a ream of things Maisie hated. Umbrellas that turned inside out. Newspaper ink on her fingers. Plays featuring Georgina. Hunger. And being made the subject of a joke. That was Georgina's favorite trick. The nurses had picked it up as surely as if they had been sent instructions. And now Hilda was teasing her.

"Speaking of challenges," Hilda went on, as though Maisie wasn't inching toward the door, longing to escape to the typewriter, "we must arrange for you to be here more frequently. You'll be worn to ribbons in a month, otherwise."

"Please don't fuss on my account," Maisie said, horrified at the thought of spending more time in this quarter of the BBC. "I can manage just fine."

The grim head of Lionel Fielden swooped around the door.

"Mr. Bartlett for his rehearsal, Miss Matheson."

"Ah, yes. Thank you." She turned to Maisie. "I assume you can take notes whilst being discreet?" She didn't wait for Maisie's answer. "Of course you can. Come along! It's high time you saw our studios properly."

"I hope your shoes and hands are clean," Fielden muttered into Maisie's ear.

"Was there something else, Mr. Fielden?" called Hilda, already at the stairs. Maisie, pad and pencil pressed to her chest, scuttled after her, eyes fixed on her shoes.

A sign on Studio Five's door warned against bringing in any outside dirt. Vernon Bartlett, MP to the League of Nations, was obediently attempting to brush what looked like half of London off his hat.

"It's very nasty out," he apologized. "It would take an industrial Hoover to make me suitable."

"Quite all right, Mr. Bartlett. The sign is ultimately a suggestion. Only don't tell the engineers I said so," Hilda confided, sweeping them all inside.

"Oh!" cried Maisie, an outburst that would result in a string of demerits from Miss Jenkins. Billy, busy with something or other at the big black boxes with all the intriguing buttons and dials, squinted at her and turned away, smirking.

She hadn't expected such a friendly space. Presenters sat in a pale green upholstered chair, comfortable enough to feel relaxed, firm enough to remind one of the gravitas of the event and thus remain regally upright. Beside the chair was a stuffed bookcase. Notes and elbows rested on a writing desk. And at the top of the desk was the microphone.

The microphone was oblong, tapered inward at the top, not unlike a tiny coffin, which seemed inauspicious. It bore the legend BBC, a presumably unnecessary but highly photogenic label. Maisie longed to touch its mesh exterior, run her fingers over the wires. Take it apart to see what was inside. She had to force herself to turn to Bartlett and take his hat and coat.

He gave Maisie a polite nod. Like Reith, he had a fatherly quality. Unlike Reith, Bartlett's rumpled suit and impish grin gave him a cheerful, rather than imposing, mien. He was the type to give hair an affectionate tug and feign surprise at the discovery of a peppermint in his coat pocket. He eyed the microphone with nervous amusement. "I really can't fathom how I've let you talk me into this," he said to Hilda.

"Because you'll be marvelous and you know it," Hilda answered. She had a way of saying something that made it sound patently obvious, with further argument impossible. "People want the horse's-mouth view from the League, if you'll excuse the rather rank-sounding metaphor."

"I think the six people interested in the League are the sort to prefer a newspaper," he pointed out.

"Scores of people are interested and don't know it. That's where we come in. And anyway, not all the papers would print your columns. This is going to be far more riveting, trust me. After a good rehearsal, of course."

Rehearsals for Talks were one of Hilda's new policies. Maisie had heard Miss Shields sniffing about the "waste of time." But as Mr. Bartlett ran through his first attempt, in a tone both prattling and ponderous, leaning so close to the microphone he was in danger of swallowing it, she could see where a rehearsal might be useful.

"A very fine first attempt," Hilda said, sounding sincere.

"That's what you said about this script you rewrote three times," he said, laughing as though they were old friends. Which Maisie realized they might be.

"I meant it, too!" Hilda grinned. "Now, the easy part is to mind the mike—get too close or make any sort of noise like coughing or even rustling paper and you deafen all our listeners. And then those afraid of technology are allowed to be smug, and we can't have that."

"Oh, come." He laughed again. "Since when do you indulge in hyperbole?"

"Begging your pardon, sir," Billy broke in. "But Miss Matheson's quite truthful, sir. It creates a dreadful bit of interference that's a nasty thing to hear."

"Almost as much as 'there's a bit of trouble with your taxes,'" Hilda added.

"It's why we keep the room so clean, sir," Billy went on. "Got to control dust."

"Sensitive little device, isn't it?" Bartlett observed.

"But powerful," Hilda said, smiling fondly at the mike.

"All right, so not too close and no paper rustling. What's the tricky bit?"

"The actual reading. Because you don't want to sound like you're reading, you see?" (He didn't, as far as Maisie could tell, and neither did she.) "No one likes a declamation. Turns them right off. I'll bet the best speechmakers in the League sound as though they're extemporizing—am I right? Think of yourself as speaking to a friend. They're genuinely curious and want to know all about the work of the League and its goings-on. Try addressing yourself to Miss Musgrave here, if it helps."

Maisie almost fell off her chair. She just caught sight of Billy shaking his head, sneering at the idea that looking at her could ever help anyone.

"That won't make you uncomfortable, Miss Musgrave?" Bartlett asked.

Desperately! Horribly! Completely! I'd rather eat this pencil, type a thousand pages of Miss Matheson's writing, ask Miss Shields for a pay raise!

"No, not at all, Mr. Bartlett," she murmured.

So he began again, looking right at Maisie. "'We know it's shocking to consider an ongoing slave trade in 1926,'" he told her, "'but the traffic in human lives is a tragedy still occurring in some areas of the globe. The League's successful treaty to end this shame once and for all begins implementation in March. This is how . . .'"

Maisie realized she hadn't registered anything he'd said during his first reading. Now that he was talking to her, she was fascinated and full of questions, many of which he answered as he went along. But more kept cropping up, questions that had nothing to do with his script. *You couldn't have something like the League before, could you? Gather people from around the world in one place and talk about things? If we'd had it before, would it have prevented the war? What . . . ?*

"Very well-done, Bartlett," Hilda crowed, treating him to a small applause. Even Billy nodded in approval. "Do you want to try once more for luck?"

He did, and was so engaging this time, Maisie had to bite her tongue to stop herself from entering into dialogue. *I'd look an imbecile besides getting sacked. What's wrong with me?*

After Bartlett left, Hilda commanded Maisie's attention.

"I think that went rather decently. Didn't have to bully old Bartlett too badly, did I?"

"Er, I don't think so?"

"You should have seen his original script, dear, oh dear." Hilda shook her head. "As if some people couldn't happily ignore the League enough. Very sporting of you to act as audience. I appreciate it."

"Oh, certainly," Maisie said.

"Some of them will insist on declaiming. You'd think they were doing Euripides in the Parthenon," Hilda mused. "Mind you, the worst ones are usually the actors." She drew several neat lines down interoffice memos to indicate they were read and handed them to Maisie. "DG-bound, these. What say we go through some fresh scripts this afternoon, shall we? You can get your first glimpse of the sausage ingredients at their most raw!"

"Er, well, I don't think I'm really, that is—"

"Not so much fun typing up revisions if you don't see from whence they began. And that's the best way to learn how to help make them better. Oh I know, that's not in your job manifest, but I like all my staff to have opinions and feel free to air them."

"But I don't know how—"

"Not yet, certainly, but you'll learn. Onwards and upwards! And on up to the DG for now."

"At one of those rehearsals, were you?" Miss Shields sniffed when Maisie entered the office a few minutes later. More points for the Savoy Hill buzz. "Rehearsals!" Miss Shields went on. "Give that woman an inch and she takes the entire British Isles. Honestly, just because reviews of Talks have been so good, she thinks she can dictate terms. What, pray tell, was the subject?"

"Mr. Bartlett was talking about the work of the League of Nations."

"I see. Well, I suppose someone must like that sort of thing."

Maisie was hard-pressed to imagine what sort of thing Miss Shields would like.

"Dull, was it?" Miss Shields asked hopefully.

"Well, I, er, I don't think so, actually. I mean, I sort of thought—"

Miss Shields sniffed again and pointedly turned back to her desk. Maisie scuttled to her own little table. She rolled fresh paper and a carbon sheet into the typewriter and got to work. She didn't miss a key, even as her mind was roving through other Talks scripts, wondering what was in them. It seemed so odd, Hilda suggesting she should do anything more than type and file and take dictation.

Maybe I really did *look interested? Good grief. I think I am.*

Saturday morning. A half day. The end of her first week.

Maisie stirred sugar into the cup of tea she was clutching tightly enough to absorb via osmosis. Sometime today, she was going to be paid. The bottom was not going to be hit. The floor would not be fallen through. The abyss was not going to have her to swallow. Not today.

Three pounds. Five shillings. These would be counted among her possessions this evening. Her room, her board, her lunches, pennies toward shoes, some small savings. All hers.

Lola swanned into the kitchen, carrying two dresses.

"Another audition today! I can't decide between the green and the yellow. I don't know if I should look refined or sultry, you see."

"The green," Maisie advised, not sure which category it fell into.

Lola gave the green an approving pat and helped herself to tea.

"Ooh, end of your first week. You're getting paid today!"

"I suppose I am," Maisie acknowledged. "I've been too busy to think of it."

"We'll get a celebratory drink if the audition doesn't run too late," Lola promised.

"That sounds super," Maisie agreed, cringing at the thought of what sort of Armageddon must be befalling them if an audition of Lola's didn't run late.

An hour later, as she was hanging her hat on the rack, she realized she had no idea when, or where, she was to collect her pay. Rusty must have told her on their breakneck tour, but no friendly syllable of "salary" came to mind.

"Miss Musgrave, I do hope you're planning to start soon. I know that many Americans don't work on a Saturday, but here we are keen on being industrious."

She hadn't planned on asking Miss Shields anyway.

It will be in the buzz. It must be.

Saturdays had a lighter broadcasting schedule. Apparently, it was bad form to think that people might use their increased leisure time to listen to the wireless. Or maybe the idea was not to encourage them. Maisie wasn't sure.

The buzz certainly didn't care about the listeners. Today it was full of the ineffable sense of the self. Any evening held the potential for adventure, but a Saturday evening was portentous. It was stuffed with hours in which things could happen and could keep rolling on and on and on. Unblocked time—provided you weren't obliged to attend church in the morning—in which a whole life could unfold. Worlds could turn. The weight of everyone's anticipation was making Maisie a little nauseous.

The tearoom's happy chatter felt like an insult, especially when snippets of plans to spend money arrowed into her ears.

"Can you believe it? I'll finally pay off that dear silk frock! I can't wait to see Maurice's face when he sees me in it."

"I'm taking Doris dancing at that new spot everyone's been rabbiting on about." (*Billy? A date? Poor Doris.*)

"We're getting our fittings for that masquerade ball. What an absolute hoot!"

Maisie reminded herself she didn't care. She would keep herself fed and sheltered and could start improving herself and become someone that a man (*not* Billy) would want to take dancing at the new spot. *Provided I learn how to dance.*

Any moment now, someone would say something. She was so sure she was about to hear Cyril's voice saying, "Hallo, New York. Payday, what? Come along and pick up your pennies," that she stopped hearing the rest of the din and was only roused when she took a sip and saw her cup was empty. The room was empty, too. She ran back to the executive offices.

"Now, see here, Miss Musgrave. I can excuse your foreignness only so long. You ought to have been back three minutes ago, and please tell me you are not panting." Miss Shields sniffed.

"No . . . I . . . Sorry," Maisie muttered, backing to her table.

She typed, hardly knowing what keys she was hitting. Would Alfred or another mail boy come in with an envelope? It was ridiculous not to ask, but questions were verboten for Maisie long before she met Miss Jenkins. Lorelei had no interest in any granddaughter, much less an inquisitive one. Georgina felt the same about a daughter. Librarians welcomed questions, but Maisie had already learned to be cautious with her curiosity, hugging information as it was provided, but letting her wondering mind explore the stacks alone, satisfied to stumble upon scraps of knowledge in her quest for whatever she originally sought.

Sister Bennister hadn't been one for encouraging questions, and all Maisie really wanted to ask in the hospital was why this war had had to happen, and the opinions on that front flew at the same rate as the bullets on the Western front.

But no one was as violently opposed to questions as Miss Jenkins. "You must appear from day one to know your work intimately. Never give anyone reason to query your capacity. If there is something you don't know, up to and including where the ladies' room is, simply keep your eyes and ears open and figure it out."

Maisie plucked the correspondence from Hilda's in-tray. Her eyes and ears were open, but all she could see or hear was Hilda, on the phone.

"Oh, certainly," Hilda was saying. "I haven't got any quarrel with his politics. We're all allowed to hold whatever opinion we wish. That's the beauty of a free country . . . Precisely, even if it's irretriev-ably silly . . . No, no, my hesitation with inviting him to broadcast is that his work is painfully dull . . . Yes, the BBC is committed to air-ing all points of view, but we're also very keen on keeping listeners awake. No, I assure you . . . If it were bad work, that would at least be a conversation point. Dull is simply pointless."

Hilda hung up a few minutes later, and Maisie handed her a sheaf of letters.

"Thank you, Miss Musgrave. Been a good first week, wouldn't you say?"

"I suppose so, Miss Matheson."

"Many more to come, I hope," Hilda said. Maisie nodded absently, trying to control her nerves. She was dizzy, and couldn't feel her fingers anymore.

Hilda looked over the next week's schedule, her pencil running a steady gauntlet through all the broadcasts, each name provisionally knighted as she went along.

"It's horribly impertinent of me, I'm sure," she said suddenly, eyes still on the schedule, "but I'm given to understand that this is about the usual time for a weekly employee to collect pay at the cashier window."

"The cashier window?" What—and where—on earth was the cashier window?

Hilda's smile was infuriatingly kind.

"I'm sure you've passed it a dozen times without noticing. On the fourth floor, the little cage at the south end of the corridor." She paused, grinning. "Looks not unlike the sort of jail cells you see in Western films."

"Do I go now?" Maisie asked, half standing. "I'm not done with this."

"We will never be done with the post. Go and get your money. You don't want the cashier to run out before your first pay."

She laughed at Maisie's traumatized face.

"I'm pulling your leg, Miss Musgrave. Run along and collect your wages."

Maisie was a fast runner. She could have leapfrogged anyone who had a five-minute start on her. But she walked, forcing sedateness into her stride. She wasn't going to let anyone laugh at her eagerness.

There was a queue for the cashier's window, a retired corner that Maisie had indeed never noticed.

A clutch of typists was queued ahead of Maisie, headed by Phyllida. She smiled on seeing Maisie, took a luxuriant puff of a cigarette in a pink Bakelite holder, and nudged the others.

"Pah, I told you it was just a gentlemen's bet." She turned back to Maisie. "We didn't think you knew how to collect your wages."

I'm so sorry to have disappointed you.

"Oh," Maisie said, hoping it was enough to end the conversation.

"I suppose someone told you."

Maisie couldn't see how that required a response.

"Would you have asked if they hadn't?" Phyllida asked, her expression uncomfortably shrewd.

"I'm sorry?"

"I'm not trying to be impertinent." (Though she was succeeding admirably). "You just don't seem the asking sort."

A point to Miss Jenkins! But the crease between Phyllida's brows made Maisie feel guilty.

"I guess I don't know what sort I am," she told Phyllida.

That made Phyllida laugh, a deep, boisterous laugh that echoed centuries of raising tankards in the remote countryside on a rare night off. She muttered something, and Maisie realized Phyllida's usual voice struggled to tamp down a strong Yorkshire dialect, the sort that was generally sneered at in London.

Maisie was still thinking about Phyllida's accent when, at last, it was her turn at the barred window.

"Oh, yes. Miss Musgrave," the cashier, Miss Mallinson, responded when Maisie gave her name. She wore round spectacles and a masculine tie and worked with brisk purpose, but gave Maisie a wide smile as she slid the brown pay packet under the bars. "Welcome to the BBC."

Maisie half nodded and tiptoed away, not hearing the whispers and ill-suppressed giggles her trance accorded.

It was real.

Pound notes. Her previous pay packets had been so small, she had never received paper, only coins. Which she liked. Coins had heft, and history. Their value was irrefutable. She liked the way they jingled in her purse. That was the song of solvency. The cheerful assurance that there would be food and comfort through the day. It was better than any hymn.

Paper had no such assurance, and far less romance. But Maisie knew it imparted its own power. There were many working people, far more deserving than herself, who never saw paper wages. She was still poor, but in the last twenty seconds, she had entered a new class.

She hadn't thought it was possible to walk sedately when really she was running, skipping, bounding. But she managed it just fine.

FOUR

February 1927

"New sign, new letterhead, new memos, new everything; who's paying for this, I ask you?" Fielden grumbled at no one in particular.

Maisie rolled a piece of the offending letterhead and carbon into her typewriter. She didn't pretend to understand the significance, but as of January 1, the BBC was now the British Broadcasting Corporation, not "Company" any longer, and vast quantities of paper were sent to be pulped into something else. Hilda would explain it to her if she asked, but Maisie didn't ask. She did, however, think that the new name looked even more impressive on paper, and this pleased her.

By now she knew that grumbling was the standard form of communication for Fielden, and though he was senior to the two producers and Talks assistants wedged into two rooms across from Hilda's office, they mostly ignored him.

"Spend a king's ransom on stationery and can't spare a penny for the gas fire," Fielden went on, and here Maisie agreed with him. A rainy January had turned into a rainy February, and the fires were not holding up their end.

Hilda was blithely untroubled by the weather. She strolled in at seven minutes to nine every morning with a punctuality that would have intimidated a naval officer. Just as the carriage clock sang the hour, her coat and hat were hanging on the rack, galoshes discreetly behind the stand, drying on an oilcloth, and she was at her desk looking over the day's schedule, sipping coffee. She had already read the papers but brought them in to annotate.

"Why bother?" Fielden asked. "The Reuters fellows give us our news report."

"For now," Hilda corrected him. "Besides, I'm marking items that could be fodder for Talks. Or potentially useful broadcasters. Contrary to popular opinion, I don't in fact know *every*one." She gave them a broad music-hall wink.

"Don't you believe it," Fielden warned Maisie later as she was headed to Sound Effects. "Our Lady would be a brilliant gossip if she weren't so above that sort of thing."

When Maisie first heard Fielden refer to Hilda as "Our Lady," she assumed he was being sarcastic and mocking, as he was about everyone. Now she knew that Hilda was, in fact, the only person in the BBC whom he respected. Even worshipped. She wondered if Hilda knew his term for her. Probably. Hilda knew everything.

It was universally agreed that Sound Effects was more in need of soundproofing than the recording studios. Maisie tapped politely on the door, next to the sign that read: EVERYONE MUST KNOCK BEFORE ENTERING. NO EXCEPTIONS, NOT EVEN YOU! There was no answer, which didn't wholly surprise her, as it sounded like dinosaurs were having a boxing match inside. She knocked harder.

"That's not likely to work, miss," Rusty advised as he ran past, bearing a lumpy package. "Most just go on in."

"The sign says not to," Maisie argued, though he was halfway up the stairs. She pounded on the door, ignoring giggles from passersby, till Phyllida, on her way to the favored ladies' lavatory, reached under Maisie's arm and flung the door open.

"Spares you bruising your hand," Phyllida called behind her.

Maisie stepped to the edge of a blazing battle. Billy and another engineer were apparently unimpressed with the planned effects for some upcoming program.

"It has far too much range; it's going to burst eardrums," Billy yelled.

"Aren't your machines fine enough to accommodate whatever we create?" The lead effects man, Jones, was fiercely protective of his creation.

"Aren't *you* able to work within parameters?"

"See here, you're not creative people—"

"And you have no brains for technology!"

The other three sound effects men were busy with designs and tests, unruffled by the conflagration. Maisie recognized the wild-eyed glee of theater people, even in men who were respectably married and not so very young—although young in the way everyone in Savoy Hill was young, except Reith.

"Did you knock?" one of them challenged her. She was fairly sure he was called Fowler; they all looked alike. "Oh, you're Matheson's girl, aren't you?" he went on, gaining animation. "Anything good?"

"We've got three pilots coming in, talking about planes and the future of flight, but they'd like to give a sense of what flying sounds like—"

"I say, that sounds difficult!" Fowler purred happily.

"They all flew in the war, and wouldn't mind re-creating the sound of a dogfight for a portion of the Talk, if that's possible?"

"Gunfire!" Fowler clapped his hands. "That's one of the hardest effects to get right! And for a Talk, too, not just a play. By Jove, that'll be rough!"

"They'd like to come and hear it first. They're scheduled to rehearse on Wednesday."

While Fowler pondered the calendar, Maisie glanced around the room. The shelves were sagging with all manner of objects. It looked as though the men had looted every shop imaginable—and a few that weren't.

"Wednesday at two would be splendid," Fowler said.

Maisie nodded and hurried out of the room to the sound of something smashing against a wall and the cry, "Oi, that's my abacus!"

"Go all right?" Hilda asked when Maisie returned to the office.

"Mr. Fowler said Wednesday at two. He's very keen."

"Well, the lads like a challenge."

Half the BBC liked a challenge, Hilda especially. What Maisie liked were all the small details that composed her work. She liked the way the words DO NOT WRITE ON THIS SIDE were printed on the backs of BBC internal memo forms three times, cascading down the paper-like steps. She liked the bright harvest-moon orange of the Talks Department memos. She liked her typewriter. Each click of the keys sang with the crispness of Beanie's heels tapping down the corridor. The clatter, the ping, the neat rolls as the carriage was reset—she understood the passion of the sound effects men. Sound was visceral; she'd never realized it before.

No wonder the wireless is becoming so popular. It's capturing imaginations and holding them ransom.

It wasn't just the sounds, or the music, or the drama. She was growing more enchanted by the Talks every day. It was like coming out from under ether when she started to really hear them. From the morning Talks, like *England as Viewed by a Frenchwoman* and *Old Arts in Modern Villages,* taking a pickax to ignorance she didn't know she had, to *Mechanics in Daily Life, A Week's Work in the Garden, A Brief History of Highway Robbery,* it was better than her so-called education, gained wholly in libraries. A series called *Straight and Crooked Thinking* made her brain hurt, but Dr. Thouless, the presenter, was an exuberant speaker with a booming voice Hilda struggled to keep from blowing the transmitter, and Maisie soaked up every bizarre word.

And the counterpoints! Hilda was keen on political Talks, such as the effect of trade unions. In fifteen minutes, Maisie was convinced that unions were the best thing to have happened to the working classes since the Peasants' Revolt of 1381 and a great boon to modern life. But then another speaker neatly laid out all the ways in which unions were a danger to society. Maisie was surprised to feel her own opinion hold firm, but she could see how these discussions could force a person to consider things from a variety of views and *that*, she was starting to understand, was something new.

"This is how it ought to be," Hilda said, signing letters. "Even the illiterate can receive a range of information and form opinions. Of course, there's affording a wireless and license fee, but access is increasing daily."

"How do you know for sure you're providing that range of information, though?" Maisie asked. Miss Jenkins would be appalled at Maisie's open inquisitiveness.

"Oh, we can never be absolutely sure!" Hilda was gleeful. "That's part of the challenge! But we do our due diligence and research and work our damnedest, and you can hear it yourself when it sounds right, can't you?"

Increasingly, she could. And she wanted to hear more.

Though the Talks provided more excitement, Maisie remained devoted to Reith. And in fact, there were things to hear in the executive offices as well. Things she only heard as Invisible Girl, which made them more enticing.

Today, unfortunately, it was only the irksome Mr. Hoppel, an executive at Siemens-Schuckert, the company who made wireless sets, among other things. He was haranguing Reith on one of his favorite topics.

"I tell you, Reith, that's what it's going to be, you want our partnership. Proper advertising on the radio. Make us all a fortune."

"I don't disagree with you, but you must know the BBC is overseen by a board of governors. Accountable to Parliament and meant to represent the public. Very keen on the BBC being a public entity, quite different from the American model. Independent and what." Reith shrugged in a "What can you do?" sort of gesture.

"Oh, public, public, public." Hoppel grinned, leaning over Miss

Shields to tap the contents of his ivory pipe into the ashtray on her desk. "I'll say this for the interminable public. Not only are they dreary, but they fail to know their own interest. Besides which, who appoints those governors? I warrant it's the government, yes? So all the more argument for a government more sympathetic to business interests."

"Ah, it's a bit trickier than that," Reith said, chuckling and shaking his head. It was impossible to tell if he agreed or was simply trying to end the discussion. Maisie suspected this was the technique he employed when meeting with the governors themselves, and wished she could see such a meeting in person. She couldn't resist tagging after them into the corridor, seizing a folder to lend credence to her activity.

"See here, Reith," Hoppel went on, undeterred. "You've got to come to one of our political meetings. You keep saying you're keen, but you don't follow through." He sucked on his pipe and blew a smoke ring.

"Yes, I do apologize," Reith said. "My schedule is a barely tamed beast, for one, but I do need to be a little mindful, too. I can't be seen supporting a nontraditional political party. Must maintain the proper image." For punctuation, he pulled out his pocket watch, shook his head at the time, then tucked it back in his waistcoat.

"Exactly," said Hoppel. "The image of a right-minded man, the sort to make sure this country runs as it ought to. Ah, Reith, I know you're not your own master entirely—I suppose few of us are—but it comforts me, having a man like you in a place like this. Bodes well for the future."

Reith laughed agreeably and shook Hoppel's hand as he called for the lift. Maisie hurried downstairs to avoid being seen when Reith turned, and then struck a circuitous route back. She passed Sound Effects just as Fowler was leaving. He brightened on seeing her. "Hullo. Have you got something for us?"

"Oh, I . . . No, actually. Sorry."

He frowned. "You in Talks need to put on a better show. Drama and Schools are constantly giving us marvelous challenges. Yours are the best when they happen, but they are far too rare."

"I'll let Miss Matheson know."

Not that Talks was short on challenges. The following week, Maisie was leaving the tearoom, brushing crumbs from her skirt, when Hilda came at her at a dead run, looped her arm through Maisie's, and barreled her down to Talks.

"Bit of a crisis, I'm afraid," Hilda explained, though she didn't look afraid at all. She was glowing hot with excitement.

"Oh, excellent. Reinforcements," Fielden said with heavy sarcasm on seeing Maisie. "Are you sure you don't want to ask any of the cleaning crew to help?"

"Mr. Fielden," Hilda said, and it was enough to silence him. She parked Maisie in front of a telephone and handed her a list of names, phone exchange codes, and a steno pad. "Somehow a program on Turkey has been thrust upon us, and it's all hands on deck for research."

Turkey?

Fielden sniggered at Maisie's expression.

"The nation, Miss Musgrave, not the Christmas dinner."

What a shame. It'd be so nice to shove a whole turkey in his mouth.

Hilda ignored him. "We must find someone, preferably Turkish, who can speak at length, be comprehensible, and be interesting. Oh, and some music. One of those silly exotic restaurants will have a player or a group. Just be sure they are genuine. And some poetry or a reading from a novel, that will be nice."

"There doesn't seem to be anything original," Fielden informed her in his most dour tones. "I'm just off to King's College and the library to be sure."

"Good." Hilda nodded, frowning at her watch. "I'll have to cancel my lunch, poor Fred." She turned back to Maisie. "Ready to begin?"

The only thing Maisie felt ready to do was hyperventilate.

Answering a phone was one thing—which Miss Shields didn't allow anyway ("you're not as twangy as most Americans, but your accent will still put people off"). Reaching out to a stranger on behalf of the BBC was not in her bailiwick.

"I'd really rather type and things," Maisie begged. "My voice just isn't—"

"Of course it is," Hilda interrupted. "And we need more notes before there can be any typing." The clear eyes lasered in on Maisie. "You have a very pleasant manner, you know."

She always sounds so sincere. Why isn't she a politician?

"We just need to find something that won't shame the BBC."

Was that meant to be encouraging? Hilda was halfway into her own office but stuck her head around the door again.

"And warn everyone that if I hear the phrase 'Turkish Delight' they'll get a hose turned on them."

Maisie picked up the phone, though she could barely keep it steady, and asked the operator to connect her.

Maybe no one will answer anywhere.

But someone did, and she had to speak.

"Er, hullo. Um, this is Miss Musgrave calling from the BBC Talks Department, and, er . . . I . . . That is, we were hoping you might be able to assist . . ."

The voice squeaked and crackled—it would have rained fuzz through the airwaves. But the words got out. And Maisie hadn't reckoned the effect of "BBC." The man on the other end didn't know she was Mousy Maisie, Invisible Girl, dogsbody extraordinaire.

"Yes, Miss Musgrave, what can I do for you?"

She'd never heard anyone address her so deferentially.

"We're preparing a Talk on Turkey, and we're a bit pressed for time—" Was that really her voice, gaining confidence and competence by the syllable? This man deeply regretted not being able to help, and meant it. Maisie thanked him politely and soldiered on.

"This is Miss Musgrave of the BBC Talks Department." The voice was getting crisper and more commanding, with a mixture of warmth and politeness. "We are looking for a knowledgeable person to speak about Turkey for a program that's come up rather suddenly and were hoping you might be able to assist us."

Maisie reported it all: the restaurant managers who thought maybe, perhaps, could they ring back? The expert in Byzantine history who insisted the capital be referred to as Constantinople, even though it had been renamed Istanbul in 1923. ("I'm all for adding controversy," Hilda said, "but he doesn't sound like someone who can be bullied into decorum in a timely fashion.") The diplomat who wanted to pontificate on the successful eradication of the Ottoman Empire and the proven brilliance of the Sykes–Picot Agreement. ("Practically begs the imperialists in the Turkish embassy to march on the BBC with torches and pitchforks. Certainly good for publicity, but a nuisance for the fire brigade and awkward if we want lunch.")

The phones rang in—Hilda had sent telegrams to "a few Foreign Office chaps I know." The representative of the Turkish consulate was glad to speak to Miss Matheson if she was a friend of Mr. Winters, but was concerned the BBC was making light of his nation.

"Nothing of the sort," Hilda insisted. "We want listeners to gain a real understanding of the Turkish nation, not just its history, but what its people are really like. If you can send over a few notes this afternoon, we can turn it into a script and send it back for your approval."

"That seems satisfactory," came the grudging, but also eager, response.

"Thank you so much!"

"I'll carry on looking for musicians," Maisie offered.

"No need," Fielden announced with grim smugness. "I've found us a trio, Miss Matheson, who play instruments called a 'saz,' a 'sipsi,' and a 'darbuka.' I suppose we can't expect Bach."

"I should jolly well hope not!" Hilda crowed gleefully.

"They probably won't fit in the lift." Fielden sighed, stumping out of the room.

"I expect they'll have a remarkable sound," Hilda told Maisie. "The engineers will be run to exhaustion, which should render them ecstatic. You did very well, Miss Musgrave. Thank you. I'll give you a note for Miss Shields to explain why you're a bit late getting back there."

Cripes, I forgot all about the executive offices. She came in expecting the worst, but Reith was locked in a meeting and Miss Shields only gave her a withering glance as she scurried to her typewriter. The in-tray was invisible under the weight of correspondence.

Maisie concentrated hard, fingers barnstorming over the keys, steadily reducing the mountain of replies requested, but couldn't help looking up when Reith's door opened. She got a little thrill on seeing him, breathing in the power he emanated. He walked out with yet another man in a black bowler hat saying that Reith must dine with him at his club the next week.

"I should be delighted. Miss Shields will be in contact with my free days. Cheerio, then!"

Clubs were where important men gathered to talk about important business. Maisie couldn't imagine what it must entail, but she thought how wonderful it would be to find out, just once. To be part of the life of a man who lived this way.

She brought the correspondence to Miss Shields.

"You look a bit melancholy, Miss Musgrave," Reith observed, sending her spirits soaring. She loved when he singled her out. "I hope there isn't anything troubling in that." He indicated the letters.

"Oh, no. Not at all, sir. I think we get busier every week."

"That is the idea," he answered, pleased. "Bringing culture and education to all Britain, isn't that right?"

"I should think so, sir," she answered reverently.

Miss Shields handed him a report. He glanced at it, lit a cigarette, and scowled back at Maisie.

"I do worry about you young girls, left all on your own after that nasty war. Rum business, having to work during prime marriage years."

Maisie didn't dare look at the ageless, but perhaps not prime, Miss Shields.

"I hope you don't devote yourself too much to work that you don't try to seize a good chance," he advised. "There are still some sound chaps out there for a working-class girl, even if you're not British, so long as you aren't too particular."

"Thank you, sir," Maisie whispered, still blushing when Eckersley, the chief engineer, strode in.

"Ah, Eckersley!" Reith barked. "Good, good, do come in. Spot of something?"

"No, thanks, sir. I'm all right."

They disappeared behind the door of the inner sanctum. Maisie lingered, twisting her hands together, and inadvertently glanced at Miss Shields, who was frowning at her left ring finger. She felt Maisie's gaze and looked up, angry triumph lighting up her face.

"Loafing, are you? I'll report that to Mr. Reith. People get sacked for less."

Maisie slunk away. For the rest of the day, their typewriters battled to see which was loudest.

Miss Shields's report went unmentioned and the secretary's snubs continued. Maisie thought more about Reith's warning (or was it encouragement?) regarding marriage. *But who am I kidding? Look at me. Not pretty, no money, an actress mother and an unknown father.* Her attempts to make her father less unknown continued to fail. She had written to the General Register Office, hoping Edwin Musgrave's birth was in their records, but there was no reply.

Family. A home. Love. All the things she'd dreamed of as a child. It was hard not to still want them. Desperately.

At least her work here kept her so busy, and interested, she had less time to want things she wasn't likely to get.

"Hallo, New York!" Cyril's usual greeting sounded over her thoughts—and set them into a tumult—as she navigated the corridor.

The ever-shifting schedules and constant crises made it impossible to count on seeing anyone at any given time, even tea breaks.

Several days could pass without seeing Cyril. Even when she did, each of them was always rushing somewhere else.

But he does see me. That's more than anyone's ever done. And a man like that, intelligent, interesting, charming, handsome . . .

She shook it all out of her head, reminding herself that he just liked the idea of New York, and called her that because he couldn't remember her name.

Still. She wished she could ask someone's opinion, get advice. If nothing else, she might stop jumping and twitching like a rabbit when she saw him. She envied the easy camaraderie among the typists and other secretaries. How did a person make friends with someone?

"Ah!" Hilda cried as Maisie entered her office. "More typed scripts, wonderful."

Maisie half wished she could ask Hilda's advice on how to speak more with Cyril. Or at least find out if he already had a girl. But she never would. Hilda, able to speak to anyone, about anything, was on a different plane. Maisie was, however, watching the way Hilda gleaned information. The woman had a remarkable way of framing a question that didn't seem to be probing at all. She knew the birthdays of everyone in the Talks Department, and it was understood she had not presumed upon the office manager, Miss Banks, for the personnel files. She also knew everyone's favorite cake. It was considered unfortunate if one's birthday fell on a Sunday, though Hilda was admirable about day-after cakes.

"It'll be a ghastly day if she ever gets married and leaves us," Collins, one of the Talks assistants, said through a mouthful of his vanilla sponge birthday cake, courtesy of Hilda. Fielden stared the stare of a man who had never beheld such inanity, which Maisie thought a bit harsh, even for Fielden. Probably it was because Hilda was senior, and the BBC one of the few places in Britain that allowed senior women to work after marriage. Or maybe because the man to woo and win her was hard to fathom? Or maybe, simply, there was no one who could run Talks like Hilda.

By the calendar's estimation, it was summer, but the weather had its own opinion on the subject. Despite the damp and chill, the young men of Savoy Hill regressed to school holiday deportment, heralding the change in season with a raucousness that threatened to shatter the windows.

Maisie, tucked in a corner, heard nothing. She was comparing Georges Lemaître's original script against Hilda's revisions. The priest's upcoming broadcast rendered Hilda giddy, though Reith insisted she have another priest denounce his big bang theory. "A name as repugnant as the concept!" the DG fumed. Hilda argued it was important that science have its say, and much of Oxford and Cambridge agreed, which silenced Reith.

Lemaître himself insisted the real revelation was Hilda's revised script, and Maisie agreed. There was never enough time to study the scripts she typed—the Talks assistants were the ones who enjoyed that privilege—but even when she was able to read them thought-fully, she had yet to understand how Hilda was able to take a treatise and turn it into a conversation, every time. This man had seen some-thing transformative in the stars and Hilda had figured out how to tether his words back to earth for all the ordinary Britons having their tea.

Maisie sighed and shifted her mind to Cyril, across the room.

Maybe he'll shout, "Hallo, New York. Come tell us what you have for tea over there. And it's not tea, is it? It's coffee." And I'll go over, and say how the puddings aren't as good as they are here, and he'll say something, and I'll say something . . .

He wasn't looking at her. She ran the last bite of buttered scone around her plate to pick up stray crumbs and had just popped it into her mouth as Beanie sat down next to her.

"You're still hungry, aren't you? I don't think I can manage the rest of this."

Beanie, resplendent in green-and-gold silk, looking more glamorous than the actresses she booked for broadcasting, slid half a buttered scone to Maisie.

"It's lucky you're not too particular about food, having the appetite you do," Beanie went on conversationally. "Personally, I make sure to eat a gargantuan breakfast before I come in. Having a cook helps. Mind you, she's nothing to the cook at the family manse, but what can you do? Still, it's great fun, isn't it, lunching in pubs and things? So different from hotels and restaurants, well, my usual sort of restaurant. You ought to see the shock when I tell a school chum I can't lunch with her because I have to work! And they always say, 'Now, Beanie, of course you don't *have* to,' and that's perfectly true, *merci la famille*, but I've really grown very fond of it. Certainly isn't a bore, anyway."

Maisie finished the scone, and Beanie accompanied her as she took her tray to the shelves for washing and then out into the corridor.

"Mind you, the chums can't imagine anything more fun than shopping and parties. I rather think it depends on the party, don't you? Or I suppose you wouldn't know."

It was often annoying when Beanie was right.

"Hallo, Beanie. Hallo, New York. How's tricks?"

Maisie's heart jumped.

"She's not 'New York.' She's Canadian. I rather thought that was known," Beanie scolded. "But I must say, Maisie, I think you'd do better for yourself saying you're from New York. *Très* glamorous, and you should really play up any glamour anyone associates you with. Besides, most people don't think of New York as America, exactly, or not in the same way."

"What does that matter?" Maisie asked. Beanie's commentary might be rude, but it was fascinating, and Cyril was enthralled right alongside her.

"It matters enormously. There are those who are still cross with Americans, what with being rather late to join the war, and they do tend to run on and on when they talk, and at a volume that presumes we're all deaf," Beanie boomed. "Not you, of course. The average titmouse is louder than you, and you never have a great deal to say for yourself. Probably anyone would guess you're Canadian anyway, if they remember Canada exists."

"I rather thought we were guessing she was a spy," Cyril interjected.

"Oh, Mr. Underwood, are you still here? You've got the most unique sense of humor. A spy, now really! Spies are meant to be dreadfully clever and good with language, you know."

"And beautifully mannered, I imagine." Cyril grinned.

Beanie considered.

"No, I've never heard of that mattering. But perhaps, why not? Well, must be getting on, cheerio!"

Maisie watched her skip away. It must be so liberating, being so totally at ease with yourself and never caring what anyone thought of you. Then she realized she and Cyril were alone. Or as alone as it was possible to be in a Savoy Hill corridor.

"I . . . I . . . ." The pages in her hand were dampening in her sweating palms. "I think I need to be getting back."

"I as well," he agreed, frowning. "Another wild and woolly afternoon looms. We're the storm before the calm, is what I say."

She smiled. He was so handsome, so charming, so . . .

"Do you know, you've got an awfully pretty smile, New York. I do hope you don't mind me calling you that."

"Oh, no, not at all," Maisie assured him, wishing her voice weren't springing about like a pogo stick.

"You don't sound very certain."

"I'm sorry. I do. I mean, I am. Certain, that is."

"How is it possible that you've been working here three months—"

"Seven," she interjected. Then hated herself for interrupting him.

"Good Lord! That makes it yet more scandalous that we've not had the opportunity for you to tell me all about New York. Let's rectify that, shall we? I don't suppose you have dinner plans Saturday night?"

The pogo stick scooped up her heart and sent it bouncing down the corridor.

Her tongue remembered to move.

"I . . . er, yes . . . I mean no. I mean I don't have plans, so I'd love that." She hoped she didn't sound as squeaky to him as she did in her head.

"Wonderful," he said. "You'd best be off now—we don't want you having to slink back to the States because you've been sacked!"

"Oh. Yes, no, right, thank you!"

She couldn't decide if it was encouraging or disconcerting that she could hear him chuckling as she jogged away, her run so very different from Beanie's.

FIVE

"You really haven't any choice." Lola was adamant, brandishing the dress she called her "pink silk"—though the fabric had no more met a worm than Maisie had the king.

"I don't know," Maisie demurred, valiantly trying to neither insult Lola nor cry. A date should mean a new frock, jewelry, perfume. Hair in soft waves. A smaller nose. The smile he called pretty radiating as though powered by the BBC's new transmitter at Selfridges department store.

"At least your shoes are smart," Lola encouraged. "They're not evening shoes, but they'll do."

The longed-for new shoes had at last been purchased without an ounce of the expected ceremony. Increasingly, and to her astonishment, the BBC dominated Maisie's mind even when she wasn't there, so her life outside it, tonight excepted, was rendered mundane. She needed shoes; she saved the money; she bought them. Chocolate-brown, double-strap, low-heeled beauties that would last. Comfortable, practical, and smart. They would do.

"I bet we can do something with that dress." Lola waved a hand at the stalwart brown wool that comprised nearly the whole of Maisie's wardrobe.

A strip of mulberry-colored velvet ribbon from Lola's bottomless stash was tacked to the top of the drop-waist skirt. A matching ribbon wrapped around Maisie's head, set off with a pink flower. A pink-beaded necklace.

"You've got to have some makeup, you know," Lola insisted.

The mascara, shadow, blush, and lipstick didn't transform her, but even Maisie could admit the effect was rather nice. As she finished touching up her lips, she wondered what would happen if Cyril tried to kiss her.

The lipstick dropped, and she concertinaed to the floor after it. She had no experience, none. Miss Havisham was the local good-time girl compared to Maisie. By her age, most girls had kissed at least one boy. Nurses used to giggle about it in the hospital.

"I kissed him in the altar boys' changing room at our church!"

"I think he thought he'd won the prize—didn't have the heart to tell him anything worthwhile was too far under the corset to be felt."

"He really knew his stuff. I barely held on to the goods—sometimes wish I hadn't. But who wants the first time to be in his father's motorcar?"

The stories were endless—kisses, pinches, squeezes, giggles. Filling the hospital ward with men who were hale and hearty and ribald and laughing, hiding the shadows of the men lying bandaged and broken. Some days it had felt as though there would never be any kisses again. The memories had to be made bigger, filling the space despair created.

"Much better," Lola said, appraising Maisie. "But do try not to look so terrified."

Maisie nodded, too scared to talk.

"Best get downstairs," Lola advised. "You don't want Mrs. Crewe to open the door to him."

Maisie catapulted down the stairs. The bell rang as she reached the hall, and she skittered around Mrs. Crewe, yelping, "Sorry, sorry,

so sorry," and flung open the door to receive Cyril, smoking a cigarette, handsome and at ease.

"Well, New York, don't you look smart?"

"Good evening, Cyril. Thank you," she said, attempting poise
between pants.

"It's almost properly warm tonight, but you might as well bring
that wrap anyway."

Wrap? She looked down to see Lola draping a pink shawl—more
fringe than fabric—over her arm. She took the bag Lola held out,
smiling at Lola's enormous gestures of approval.

"Well, then." Cyril grinned. "Let's see where the night takes us."

At Cyril's direction, it took them to the outskirts of Soho, to a street
whose scruffiness unsettled Maisie. But she felt safe with Cyril.

"I think you'll like this." He waved her into a steamy fish-and-chip
shop, so packed, every other chip shop in London must be empty.

"The place is always stuffed to the gills," Cyril confided, his eyes
twinkling.

"Stuffed? Looks fried to me," Maisie rejoined, pointing to
"Plaice" on the menu, quite forgetting her role was to giggle prettily.

Cyril gaped like she was an exotic zoo creature. And didn't laugh.

Stop it, Maisie. Stopitstopitstopit.

Disappointment had loosened her tongue. In the fantasy, she was
accepting a glass of something sweet right now, her senses entranced
by the heft and curve of the glass, the one-note song it made as it
touched Cyril's, the bubbles tickling her nose, the smell of grapes and
the essence of a French countryside turning her tipsy even before she
took a sip, or maybe that was his eyes, smile, freckles.

*Oh, what did you expect, really? Drinks at the Dorchester, dinner at the
Criterion, dancing till two? You don't know what he earns, and at least he
wants to feed you. And you can't dance. Just trust him. He knows what he's
doing. Trust him.*

Cyril seized Maisie's elbow and pulled her through the throng, murmuring his most refined "Please excuse me" and "I do beg your pardon" as he nudged past this one and that until they slipped into the seats of a couple just leaving.

"The cod's the best, all right?" Cyril asked her, and shouted an order that was somehow heard above the din before Maisie could answer. She would have preferred rock salmon. *Trust him. Trust him. Trust him.*

He was right. A steaming plate of fried glory was soon laid before her. The mingled smells of fish in batter and plump chips with crisp skins infused with oil worked on her like barbiturates. It may not have been the elegant meal of her dreams, but she nonetheless ate with gusto.

"So, you're enjoying it?" Cyril's voice wafted across to her.

"Everything is perfect," Maisie said, grinning. "Thank you. Thank you so much."

He couldn't have been blushing. It was just the heat.

"That's all right. You looked like you could use a decent feed."

Now *she* blushed. She hated looking undernourished. *Keep the conversation on him. New York or no, men want to talk about themselves.*

"How did you find this restaurant?"

"Chap's got to know a good chipper. I've always fancied things that maybe don't look the best, but get to know them and you find they're better than anything posh could ever be."

"So you don't like posh things?" She fought down the idea he was talking about her.

"If I did, I wouldn't be working at the BBC." He laughed. "Though I think my job's a doddle compared to yours, working for the biggest taskmasters in the building: Matheson, the Shield, our Lord and Master. Tell me, which is the most maddening?"

Even though he'd asked, Maisie knew the contempt men had for women's gossip. She considered how to change the subject, but he wasn't waiting for her answer.

"Funny thing with Matheson," he said, "having what you'd think would be a man's job, hm?"

"I suppose that's part of us being modern? She seems to do well, anyway."

"Oh, yes, audiences are very keen on the Talks," he said. "That's one advantage you have over us Schools lot. You know your audiences choose to listen."

"But you get plenty of letters from students saying how much they like the broadcasts."

"If they're anything like I was at school, they're being forced to write them."

"Oh, I don't think so. You know you're doing very good work. Mr. Reith wouldn't be so pleased otherwise."

"Ha! The DG governs Schools with a tyranny I think Vlad the Impaler might have thought a tad overbearing. It's why I'm such a heavy smoker." He lit a second cigarette for emphasis and shrugged. "But it's a good laugh. And what about you—do you like your job?"

She did. More than she'd ever imagined. But she didn't want him to think she wanted to be a woman like Hilda. He had to know she was eager to move on to the real work of life, as soon as she was invited.

Probably shouldn't say that on a first date, though.

"It's stimulating," she answered.

"It is that," he agreed. "Fascinating stuff, radio. Glorious being in on the ground floor, as it were, isn't it? Maybe we'll get to see how far it can go. Mind you, my father still hopes I'll give up this nonsense and go in for law."

"I'm sure he only wants the best for you."

"Oh, yes, nothing to be said against dear old Dad. Wants the best for all the brood. The best school, the best job, the best wife. Well, not for Kitty, I suppose. My sister," he clarified, with a laugh.

Maisie was still trembling from the word "wife."

In a dim and poky coffeehouse just up the road, he ordered for them again. Rhubarb cake with extra cream, drinking chocolate. And she trusted him, and it was good.

"You're all right, Maisie," Cyril said suddenly.

Her heart went pogoing again, around and around the shop.

Except he sounded surprised. Did he? Was he? She shoved the thought down, and while it was struggling to assert itself, Cyril reached over and patted her hand. The voltage sent all her thoughts scattering far beyond Galileo's reach.

Possibly, just possibly, she was going to be kissed tonight.

Cyril was talking. She watched his moving mouth; she was dissolving.

"I'd like to do some proper producing, as a lead. Bit off that Miss Somerville does and I don't, though she's quite good—not saying she isn't. Can't tell the chaps from school I'm junior to a woman, though. They'd rag me to death."

"You'd be brilliant at producing, I'm sure," Maisie told his lips.

"I wouldn't mind a stint in New York radio either, someday. Meant to be quite different, but maybe you know about that?"

She remembered that the supposed point of this outing was for her to describe New York. *Maybe he means for us to have another date? He must, surely. I hope. Please.*

"Tell me," he asked. "Why do they call it the Big Apple?"

Sooner or later he's got to ask a question whose answer I know.

"Oh, er, well, a lot of apples grow there," she ventured, half remembering reading something about the nickname, and that it had nothing to do with fruit.

"I thought it might be named after you," he said, waggling his eyebrows.

Maisie tried to remember to breathe.

"What?"

"Well, its skin turns red."

A treacherous joke about green apples entered her mind, but she couldn't speak.

Skin. Those freckles. She pictured him on the sand in Brighton, legs, arms, that wide-open grin lighting his face as he ran by the water. The smell of the sea on his skin, the tiny grains of sand caught on his flesh as he pulled her close . . .

"Maisie!"

"Sorry?"

"I asked if you were ready to go," he said, looking impatient. The plates and cups were empty.

"Yes," she answered, hoping she wasn't expected to use any more syllables.

"Let's get a cab," he suggested, and she was soon sitting on a plush upholstered seat, surrounded by dark wood and small windows. She'd never been in a London cab before. She longed to stroke the cushions and polished wood.

Cyril settled next to her, his lazy smile glowing in the semidarkness.

"New York girl, eh?" and he pulled her to him.

All she knew of kisses was what she had seen onstage. This was different. Better. Magic. His lips guided hers, encouraging her to melt into him. She trembled so hard, she was afraid she was going to bite his lip, but his hands were steady on her shoulders and he didn't pull away, so she must be doing something right.

Please don't let this stop.

The cab stopped and the yawning driver asked for the fare.

They were on a quiet street, moderately well-kept houses full of sleeping clerks and hardworking hopeful juniors. If it were New York, one house would hide a speakeasy. Maisie grinned. It would be just like Cyril to know of an underground place in London.

He kissed her again, his body pressed against hers. There was nothing except this man, this mouth, this moment.

"Quick, let's get upstairs," he breathed.

"What?" She was gasping, embarrassingly loud.

"Shush, come on, this way."

"Where are we? Is it a nightclub?"

"Ha. Perhaps tonight it will be. It's my flat. Well, a bedsit, but there's privacy enough. We'll take the back stairs. No one will see you."

"What?" She was still having trouble breathing.

"We ought to hurry," he urged.

"No, I . . ."

He wasn't really suggesting what he sounded like he was suggesting, was he? He couldn't be. This wasn't . . . His eyes were so bright and liquid. She wanted to kiss him more, kiss him forever. It would be so easy. *Say yes. Trust him.*

But it was too much at once.

"I don't think I should. I mean, not the first . . . I'm sorry."

His eyes chilled, raking her face. "Are you making a joke?"

"I . . . What?"

"You're not actually . . . ? Look, haven't I done rather nicely by you this evening?"

It was like walking downstairs and missing the last step.

"What?"

Because there weren't any other words.

"You can't . . . Haven't you done this before?"

She couldn't look like a girl who had, could she? Plenty of girls did, she knew, but were they ones who still got married?

"It'll be fun, won't it?" He took her hand. "You're not teasing me, are you?"

"What? I, no, I wouldn't. I'm not that sort, truly."

"Good. Let's go."

"Cyril, I'm . . . not that sort either."

"You are serious, aren't you?" His hand pulled away, and she was sinking. "Well, I never. Bit of a turn-up, that."

"What?"

Which asked so many questions.

"Ah, Maisie, go on. You're not . . . That is . . . A girl like you, I mean . . . Ah, what's a bit of practice between chums, eh? Just some fun, a laugh."

She was never going to laugh again.

"I have to go home."

Now. Before he saw her cry. He wasn't going to see her cry.

"I say, look, I'm sorry, all right? Maybe you being American, you can't understand. Never mind. We don't need to let them in the salt mine know about it, do we? I mean, you won't look any better than I will, and no harm done anyway."

If I had the money, I'd buy him a dictionary and show him the definition of the word.

"I'll get you a cab, shall I? Maisie! Wait, Maisie!"

She was running. He didn't have a hope of keeping up, especially now that she had her new shoes. She could hear them, the gang children of the Toronto streets, chasing her still. Mousy Maisie. Mousy Maisie. Mousy Maisie. They were never going to stop chasing her.

On the tram, she fought her stomach's urge to vomit. She was determined to digest that food. It was the only good thing to come of the evening.

After she'd yanked the velvet ribbons off her dress and thrown them under the bed, she remembered she might see Cyril Monday. It was the sort of thing that could happen.

I'll just be too busy to bother with him. Miss Matheson can probably guarantee that. And if not, I'll find a way to help her. Onwards and upwards.

She still wasn't going to cry.

Despite Cyril's assurance it wouldn't be mentioned, Maisie braced herself for an avalanche of humiliation at the BBC. Where the fellows talked, the women listened, and she would be marked: A for Ass.

Well, they can all go to hell. I'm not running away in retreat this time. I'm not the Germans. I'm the conquering army.

Which didn't stop her dreading their first meeting.

"You don't look very well," Hilda said, frowning at her as she typed.

"No, I'm all right," Maisie lied. She was coiled tight, bracing for a rude comment from Fielden, a knowing glance from Alfred, a smirk from Billy. A giggle from Phyllida. And Beanie would have a four-part soliloquy.

"Well, come along. We've got a meeting with the DG," Hilda

ordered. Maisie padded after her, pleased to discover she'd learned to walk almost as quietly as Hilda. Invisible Girl, upgraded.

They passed Rusty, Phyllida, Alfred and his basket, and dozens of others, including Samson the cat, but either Maisie was indeed not floating on the Savoy Hill buzz, or no one would dare even glance at her when she was with Hilda.

"Ah, Miss Matheson," Reith greeted them, scowling warmly. "Mrs. Reith wanted to pass on her congratulations about . . . well, some ladies' program. I can't recall which. Last week, I believe."

Maisie wondered if it was on home renovation or dressmaking or keeping fit. Possibly Mrs. Reith never listened to any of the broadcasts at all.

"That's very kind of her. Please thank her for me," Hilda said.

"Yes, yes. Now, I'm afraid there is a bit of unpleasant business."

"Oh dear."

"It seems you have a woman presenting *Odd Jobs Around the House*? Didn't you say that referred to mending small electrics and other such tasks?"

"Absolutely. It's very—"

"Isn't it awfully dangerous to suggest women take up tools? If they were to injure themselves, they could register a very strong complaint against us."

"Mrs. Fisher is making it clear that these tasks are quite simple. Anyone with a bit of common sense can do them. After all, sir, many women do live alone—"

"Poor creatures," he grumbled, shaking his head. He looked miserable, and Maisie wished she could get him a cup of tea. "It's a bad pass we've come to, Miss Matheson, very bad."

"Of course, it's very hard on those who wish to marry but can't," Hilda agreed, "but it's also rather exciting for women to have the chance at some independence."

"Too much independence is not healthy," he boomed. Maisie tapped her pencil in quiet agreement. She was convinced she'd be healthier in a state of warm dependence.

"I suppose it's different for everyone," Hilda said. "But what do you say I bring Mrs. Fisher to come and meet you before her rehearsal? I think you'll find her a very respectable, decent woman simply trying to help save women a little money by doing these things themselves."

"Taking work from handymen, too," he said with a heavy sigh. "Well, all right. I'm sure she is a very fine speaker. You've done well with them. We just do need to be mindful, is all I meant. Tread with care. You understand me."

"Perfectly so, Mr. Reith."

"Marvelous." He looked relieved, or as much as Maisie could tell, but she was learning to read his scowls. "Now, looking towards autumn, I very much like—"

The phone rang, and they all glared at its presumption. Maisie wished Miss Shields wouldn't answer so they could instead hear what Reith liked.

Miss Shields looked as though she wished she hadn't answered either.

"The Selfridges transmitter is having trouble again. We're switching to 2LO for the rest of the day," she reported in the tone of a nurse telling a man his leg would have to be amputated.

"Well, that's a rum bit of business!" Reith exploded, seizing a cigarette. Hilda edged away from the flame. "Where the devil's Eckersley?"

Miss Shields was already ringing the Engineering Department—people rang the fire brigade with less urgency. Hilda nodded to Maisie, and they sidled out of the room.

As soon as they were out of earshot of Reith's bellowing, Hilda sped up.

"Look sharp, Miss Musgrave. This is a great chance!"

"Pardon?"

"The 2LO, it's just up the Strand, at Marconi House. Will take us four minutes at a good clip. Don't you want to see our transmissions in action?"

"I . . ." Maisie had never really thought about the connection between the microphone and the machine that sent broadcasts into wirelesses around the nation.

"Everyone who works here ought to see a transmitter at least once," Hilda said, in that way she had that made you feel stupid for arguing.

So they hurried up the road to the Marconi House. Everyone there recognized Hilda—Maisie was pretty sure Hilda would be recognized if she walked into a meeting of the Ancient Order of Hibernians—and they were promptly ushered into an airy room where the 2LO transmitter was still housed.

Despite having made possible the first-ever words broadcast in Britain: "This is 2LO calling," the 2LO transmitter was an unholy relic, kept only for these occasional days when the newer, smaller, more powerful transmitter in Selfridges went down.

"Always good to have a contingency plan," Hilda murmured.

"Oh, hullo." Eckersley greeted them with a hunted expression. He was circling the transmitter, making minor adjustments, readying it to spring to life again. "I suppose the DG is baying for blood? It's nothing to do with us engineers, I've told him, but he can't seem to understand that."

"Of course it's not your fault," Hilda agreed soothingly. "Never mind, Mr. Eckersley. Have you met my secretary, Miss Musgrave? I thought she'd like to see a transmitter at work, and I'm afraid your misfortune is her great gain."

"I'll say one thing for the dear old dinosaur, Miss Musgrave. You can see the workings far more clearly than on the new beast," Eckersley told her, giving the transmitter a fond pat. "Come on, then, and touch the heart of the matter. But don't you dare actually touch it," he warned.

The heart of the matter. A battered anatomy book once taught Maisie that a human heart was the size of a fist. She liked that. Her own heart, always fragile, was bruised and shrunken after Cyril—a dandelion gone to seed; another blow and it would simply scatter. A fist, though, pounding away inside her chest, was much less likely to be crushed. It meant that somewhere inside her she was strong.

The 2LO looked more like a skeleton than an organ. Six meters of machine, comprising a line of valves backed by polished wood. Delicate and solid. Within this elegant contraption lay the power of communication.

Hilda was pointing, naming every segment, her knowledge as intimate as if she had built it herself, while Eckersley buzzed away at whatever he did, making the magic happen. But it wasn't magic. It was better. This was the result of endless questions, of the search for answers, of not resting until those answers were found. And then beginning all over again, with more questions.

The rectifier, the oscillator, the modulated amplifier, the modulator, the sub modulator. Valves and valves and valves. Making sound fly on airwaves.

How did anyone ask the questions that answered in this configuration of wood and glass and wire that was changing the whole world? Thousands of years ago, someone had gazed into the night sky and seen that some stars were planets. And then they mapped the universe. They unlocked mathematics. They saw the way the sun moved across the earth and how to harness its power, warming homes and baths, growing plants. And they developed tools. The capacity to sail around the globe, to build cathedrals, to run a factory, to capture images on paper and then on screen. And now, to send a story throughout the country, from a machine.

"In its infancy." That was the phrase. Radio was a form in its infancy. *This is the cradle of civilization.*

She stared harder, wanting to read the five pips that began each broadcast, before that call crackled through wirelesses up and down the country.

From Penzance to John o' Groats, anyone who had a wireless and the license fee could tune in and hear a symphony, poetry, gardening advice, a thriller, a debate, scenes from new plays, sporting events, stories about places scattered throughout the globe, because why shouldn't a farmwife in South Yorkshire know something of Shanghai, or San Francisco, or São Paulo?

"It's just so wonderful," Maisie breathed, wishing she could fold herself inside it and be part of those flickers, entering wirelesses in every home and pub and shop, seeing the faces as they listened to the stories.

"It is," Hilda agreed. "Quite an instrument for communication," she continued, her eyes traversing the length of the transmitter. "A magnificent tool. Of course, one quirk about tools is that many of them can also be wielded as weapons."

Maisie looked up at her, but Hilda was lost in the machine.

No wonder Reith was so particular about the BBC's content. With millions of listeners already, it would be catastrophic to broadcast something, call it fact, and then discover it was wrong. Broadcasting was only five years old, but it was becoming an institution. And institutions had power.

And I'm a part of this.

Her heart was pounding, the fist beating her ribs.

"Time we were getting back to the office," Hilda announced. "I imagine there are at least twenty new crises to corral. Such is life at our BBC."

No doubt. And Maisie couldn't wait to get back to it.

Her new vigor was a talisman, a shield against any arrow that might be slung her way, attempting to pierce Invisible Girl. She shoved Cyril to the back of her mind, where she was hoping he would fall out. There was too much else to think of, and it was all more important.

"Miss Musgrave, are you capable of bringing a broadcaster up for rehearsal?" Fielden asked. "Our Lady is still meeting with that ball of scruff from the Urban Allotment Society."

The broadcaster was a City man, Mr. Emmet, talking about the importance of investments and stocks, peevish because Hilda had revised his script four times.

Maisie guided him into the studio, where Billy and the new engineer were running tests and making adjustments to the mike.

"We're about to do a rehearsal," she informed them. They looked up at her, then turned back to their work, muttering something about being nearly done.

"I suppose there's no hope of a drink," Mr. Emmet asked, holding out his hat for Maisie to hang.

"Not in the studio, I'm afraid, sir."

He snorted and settled himself in the chair.

"I'll just run and tell Miss Matheson you're here," Maisie said.

"You should take him to the Tup," Billy said in an undertone. Maisie was astonished—Billy never spoke to her. "City chaps are awful lightweights. After a few, maybe he'll think you're one worth marrying."

The talisman pushed back her tears but did nothing to allay her mounting rage. It could just have been a matter of Billy being himself, but it was possible, just possible, that Cyril had told them.

Her talisman got its real test a few days later, when she was hurrying to the Talks Department. She saw Cyril before he saw her, and that fist in her chest flung itself in five directions at once. She concentrated on breathing and putting one foot in front of the other, thinking about the script she was about to type.

Cyril saw her and stopped. "Maisie, hallo. How are you keeping?"

She had to dig her nails into her palms to prevent herself from stopping or shaking.

"Copacetic," she answered, trying to sound like a brusque New Yorker, far too busy and important to even break pace. He jogged backward to keep eye contact.

"Good, good. I say, will you stop a moment?"

He put out a hand and she stopped, mostly to avoid his skin making contact.

"I, ah, just wanted to be sure . . . no hard feelings, hey? We can be chums?"

A fleeting image of fish bait swam through Maisie's brain.

"I'm sure you can be anything you'd like to be," she told him.

"Really must dash, cheerio," and she sailed around him and down the corridor, wondering if he was watching and refusing to care.

She was still roiling two hours later on her tea break.

"Goodness, what did that poor toast ever do to you?" Phyllida was moved to ask, hypnotized by Maisie's atavistic gnashing.

Everyone else in the tearoom, however, was focused on Billy and another engineer, Paul, who had built some ridiculous motorized contraption on which the handler could guide metal football players over a pitch. The clutch of BBC boys was enthralled.

"Seems to get a bit hot," Cyril observed, playing his round.

"Funny since you're such a rotten player," Billy said.

"Funny yourself!"

"Here, I'll show you." Billy nudged Cyril away and took over to a chorus of jeers.

Maisie lunged into another slice of toast, wishing they would shut up. As if solely to aggravate her further, the shouts grew louder. Then there was a sudden boom, puffs of black smoke, and the whole room chorused with shouts.

"What have those lunatics done?" shrieked Mrs. Hudson, ever protective of her abused tearoom.

The room was unscathed, the only casualties of the explosion being Billy, squalling and clutching his hand, and the toy, oozing unidentifiable liquid and an acrid smell. Paul keened over this destruction.

"We ought to get him to the hospital!" shouted Cyril.

Blood spilled onto the table, and several girls shrieked. Maisie, still chewing, hurtled over a table to get to Billy.

The cut wasn't deep, but it was just above the thumb, and spurting blood.

"My hand, my hand! I'll lose my job!" Billy's shrieks flowed as freely as the blood.

"I know it hurts," Maisie said, "but it's nothing much. No need to worry." She expertly wove a napkin around his hand to stanch the flow. "If someone runs to Miss Banks's room, she'll have a medical kit. This won't take but two stitches at most."

"Can you actually do it?" Phyllida asked, her face percolating with interest.

"I can," Maisie answered curtly.

Someone else must have thought of the medical kit, because Rusty came sprinting in with it. Maisie calmly selected a needle, wiped it with alcohol, and threaded it. Billy continued to yowl, convinced his career was finished.

"Oh, for Pete's sake," Maisie snapped, starting to stitch. "Quit casting a kitten, will you? See a doctor if you want, but you'll be perfectly fine, probably by tomorrow." And she finished stitching and cut the thread.

Cyril was the first to speak.

"Well, that's a turnup," he said, echoing the unspoken sentiment. "I'd have pegged you for the type who faints at the sight of blood."

"Yes," Maisie agreed. "And I'd have pegged you for a gentleman. Some surprises are nicer than others."

The others, even if they hadn't previously been given reason to speculate upon Cyril's gentlemanliness, were still delighted to see his deep blush, and congratulated themselves on a brilliant afternoon's entertainment.

SIX

"How is it possible?" Beanie wailed, channeling Sarah Bernhardt. "How could I have missed the greatest drama in the BBC? It is too tragic!"

Maisie wondered what version of the story Beanie had heard. Probably the one in which she sewed Billy's whole hand back on, although it might have been the one of her bringing him back from the dead.

Growing up with Georgina had taught Maisie not to enjoy a pleasant moment, because it was likely to be snatched away. So Maisie worried the story would be heard by Miss Shields and worse, Mr. Reith, and her reputation smeared due to what must have been some sort of improper something or other with Cyril. Reith was particular about morals, and any good credit she might have built up with him would be revoked in an instant, even if she explained. *I shouldn't have gotten in a cab with him. That was asking for trouble.*

"The local broadcast says there was quite a tempest in the tearoom the other day," Hilda announced from the floor, where she was marking up a script as Maisie came in with filing.

Well, of course Hilda knew.

"It was nothing, truly," Maisie insisted. "The chaps were being a bit . . . stupid, that's all."

"Yes, that would make it a day ending in 'y,'" Hilda agreed. "Although my secretary swanning in to mop up a bad injury rather ups the interest factor."

"I'm glad I was able to help," Maisie muttered. (Mostly. It *was* Billy, after all.)

"I suppose you think someone's going to ask an awkward question?"

That drew Maisie's eye.

"Miss Musgrave, if you wanted people not to guess that you lied about your age to nurse during the war, the expedient move would have been to use a different name or simply leave it off your list of experience."

"I didn't have any other references," Maisie protested, both stunned and not surprised by Hilda's guess. Though it didn't sound like a guess.

"You had the secretarial school," Hilda reminded her.

"Yes, but I had to offer some sort of work experience, too," Maisie said. "Please, Miss Matheson, I don't mind being reprimanded, but you won't tell Mr. Reith, will you?"

"Why on earth would I? Anyway, it's hardly news. I've known since your first week. Don't look so mutinous. You can't be surprised. As soon as I looked at you I knew you were never old enough to have done all you'd done in the proper way."

So I'm improper. No wonder Cyril asked me out.

"I did tell that lie," Maisie admitted, her old crime far easier to dwell on, "but I'm an honest person. I really am."

"Of course you are," Hilda said, astonished there would be any argument. "I wasn't reprimanding you, and it's no one else's concern. I was awfully pleased to discover it, though. It told me you were someone who was devoted to a cause. Or would do anything to be part of something bigger than yourself. Or wanted a great escape."

Am I supposed to say which it was?

"All worthy," Hilda went on. "It also told me you were someone who, when it came to it, was prepared to break rules."

Her eyes were sparkling. Maisie railed inwardly, determined to no longer be any sort of rule breaker. Mr. Reith wouldn't like it.

"Rules are useful, of course," Hilda noted, as though she were discussing galoshes. "But I find it's best to be flexible. You'd be amazed at who might turn out to be wrong." Hilda's grin turned conspiratorial. "The lads are keeping it quiet, but Billy was taken to the woodshed by Mr. Eckersley. He's also been given a few days off—without pay—to 'recuperate,' as it's being put. What with the shame, and a 'mere secretary' having done him such a good turn before all his friends, he'll never dare look you in the eye again, I should think."

Maisie couldn't help it. She laughed. Hilda laughed, too. She opened a biscuit tin and tossed one to Maisie.

"Butter. Your favorite, I believe." It was. "Let's forge on. We've a great deal to do. The lads can mess 'round if they like. We need to get things done."

"Perhaps . . . perhaps we can have a nurse do a series of Talks on treating injuries at home," Maisie suggested. "Not me! I mean, obviously, a proper nurse, a Sister from a hospital. Someone who really—"

"A very, very fine idea," Hilda agreed. Her smile was something different this time. Maisie had nothing to compare it with, but if she had to guess, it was respect.

"I'd have thought you'd be too brokenhearted to carry on there, after that rotten fellow," Lola said, watching Maisie put on her hat. "But you seem almost . . . jolly."

Imagine me, jolly.

"I suppose I'm still a bit cut up about it, to be honest," Maisie admitted. "But they keep me too busy to think about it much."

"'Too busy' is the problem. You'll never get a chance to meet anyone else."

"Ah well." Maisie shrugged, pleased with her fresh lack of concern.

"Perhaps I'll have more luck when I get some new clothes. What do you think?"

Lola, always a keen advocate of new clothes, waxed eloquent all the way to the tram stop, where she saw Maisie off.

True to Hilda's prediction, Billy melted into the wall whenever he saw Maisie approaching. When she couldn't be avoided, his addresses were to her shoes, or occasionally an elbow. Maisie marveled at the improvements humiliation could make in a man's character.

Phyllida, on the other hand, was so impressed with Maisie, she drew her into a circle of two. They quickly became friends.

"You're very lucky, working for Miss Matheson," Phyllida told her. "She's an absolute genius. She was political secretary to Lady Astor, you know."

"I know. I can't imagine. Or I can, but I can't."

Phyllida flicked some ashes off her cigarette and sipped her coffee.

"I trow . . . er, bet she was a suffragette." Phyllida's native Yorkshire dialect ceaselessly battled to break free of its London cage, scoring the most victories when she was animated. "I wanted to be a suffragette. I even came down to London for the last big fight!" She grinned and took a long drag of her cigarette. "I was ten years old. But tall, so no one noticed me till we were arrested. And just months before it was legal, what rot. The police didn't mither— bother—me, but I still have the scars from Father's whipping. Right nonsense women can't vote till we're thirty! I'm going to stand for office one day, you know, and get to changing things."

From a Yorkshire dairy farm to a typist at the BBC to an MP. That would be quite a story. Someone should be keeping notes.

"Did you vote, in America?" Phyllida asked longingly.

"I couldn't. I'm not a citizen there," Maisie reminded her. She'd still been in Brighton in 1920, and read about the American election with the same cursory interest she'd give a story about farming in India.

"The Talks are getting awfully fascinating. I wish I could have been Talks secretary." Phyllida looked mournful, not jealous.

"Did you put yourself forward?" Maisie felt guilty.

"Couldn't." Phyllida snorted. "If a lass is to shift from typing, she's got to be asked, not ask herself. That's just not the done thing. Besides, I'm a Northerner, officially uneducated, and nobody. So goes the assessment."

"But I'm not educated, and I'm nobody," Maisie said. "Why would—"

"Ah, but you're foreign," Phyllida pointed out, as though that answered everything. "Never mind. We're all here; that's what matters."

Back in the office, Hilda was radiating so much glee, the chilly summer felt almost warm.

"No, I shan't tell you until the meeting," Hilda teased. Her excitement was contagious, and Maisie tore through correspondence with hungry impatience.

The Talks staff usually held their meetings around a large table in the room that housed their files. It was the only room where the staff was guaranteed to sit still for an hour at a time, and so had the perversity to be the draftiest in the department.

Hilda sailed in, took a brief gauge of the temperature, and threw up her hands.

"Oh, this is just too absurd. Into my office, everyone, and settle by the fire. Room enough for all. Budge up, budge up," Hilda fussed, chivvying the staff into place. "Come along, we're all friends."

"Not all," Fielden muttered. He was sitting next to Maisie, but his disparagement was generously general.

Hilda's cheerfulness, as well as the novelty of holding a meeting on the floor, sparked a campfire mentality. Maisie thought they might open the meeting with a song.

"We've got weeks of business to discuss in one hour," Hilda warned them, the usual start of a Talks meeting. "But I have some rather ripping news to share. 'News' news, if you like." Enjoying the sight of their bemused faces, she plunged on. "We're finally starting a News section in Talks!"

"Won't we be prosecuted?" Fielden asked, looking almost perky.

"This comes down from the governors," Hilda assured him, eyes twinkling. "We can do things like in-depth analyses of events, and other such, and thus show off our capacity. It's a beginning!"

The BBC's governors, simultaneously dictatorial and distant, were Reith's benefactors and the thorns penetrating his tweed waistcoat. He bowed before their every whim, even as he cursed them fluently from a safe distance. But it was less the governors than the actual government that tied the BBC's hand when it came to news reporting.

At the BBC's birth, Fleet Street newspapers had banded together in an unheard-of camaraderie to insist that radio not be allowed to do original news. As certain as they were that radio was a silly fad that wouldn't last and no one except a few eccentrics was going to buy a license and who could afford a wireless anyway, if the BBC reported news, it would put the papers out of business. And Parliament, always keen on good press, agreed, so the BBC could only read news after seven p.m. and that was only the prepared Reuters bulletin.

"If we can prove anyone listens to those bulletins, I'll eat my hat," Fielden said. Maisie had never hoped so much that the bulletins garnered interest and decided they'd have to rent a cine-camera to record the meal.

"The ban is not lifted," Hilda told them, and they all wilted, even Maisie, who had never given news a thought. "But Talks such as Mr. Bartlett's broadcasts can be expanded and increased. So! Let's have some ideas!"

It was understood that Hilda had enough ideas to fill the Talks slots for the next seven years, but she expected her department to be a place where everyone had a dozen thoughts at any one time and should express them.

Fielden began, as usual. As second-in-command, he felt his position keenly. He rattled off eight ideas at a speed that made Maisie suspect he was testing her shorthand.

"Of course, that's just off the top of my head," he finished, giving Hilda a reverent nod.

"Very good indeed," she congratulated him. Always the same

script, but always sounding so sincere. "Anyone else? Let's really thrash this all out."

"What about a series of Talks on Russia?" suggested Collins. "So many people are so aerated about Bolshevism and spies and what, but maybe if we—"

"Get accused of supporting Bolshevism?" Fielden interjected. "Won't that do wonders for our reputation?"

"I agree that the more people know about Russia and the Russian people, the less afraid they might be," said Hilda, ever the diplomat. "Though a series would require a bit of finessing before the DG would accept it."

Less afraid. There were moments when Maisie felt the chill of walking shadows, all those vanished people under poppies. Sometimes, she was sure others felt them too, even the brightest and most beautiful, glancing nervously over their shoulders. *Maybe we're all trying to outrun something, like me outrunning the kids in Toronto.* They'd wanted to beat her till she broke, and not just her bones. The suffragettes had put themselves forward for breakage, hadn't they? That would be something, being the person who could put herself in harm's way, for a cause.

"There's meant to be an election, isn't there, in twenty-nine?" Maisie heard herself ask.

"Unless it gets called sooner," Fielden said.

"Maybe there can be Talks about aspects of the election, the candidates' platforms, what people hope—"

"Spoken like the American." Fielden sniffed.

"Canadian!" the entire Talks Department chorused.

"Go on, Miss Musgrave," Hilda encouraged. It was still alien, seeing someone look interested in her thoughts.

"I suppose, now that women vote, things must be different."

"Three general elections in almost as many years," Fielden said. "Hardly auspicious."

"I think it's something to think about," Hilda said, following the script, but Maisie believed her. "We'll give it a bit of a thrash."

After the meeting, Maisie heard Collins express his surprise that "the little occasional girl has a thought in her head. Who would have thought, a thought?" The others hadn't.

I can't blame them. I wouldn't have imagined it myself.

"If you could type up the minutes now, Miss Musgrave, that would be very useful," Hilda said. "Or do you need to get back to the DG?"

"Oh. I can do them now, yes," Maisie said, confirming from the carriage clock that she had ten minutes to spare. She lingered, turning the pad over and over.

"Was there something else?" Hilda looked up, surprised at the sudden lack of industry.

"Oh. No. Yes. Er, I was wondering . . ." The question was there, bouncing on her tongue, but it fell right back down her throat. Instead she asked, "Could I take your newspapers home to read, when you're done with them? The ones in English," she added, unnecessarily. Hilda came to work with an upholstered holdall in addition to her handbag, in which she carried newspapers, magazines, and at least three books in rotation. She also had the principal newspapers from Germany, France, Italy, and America sent to the office every week, and read them through. In the evenings, she went to the theater, concerts, salons, lectures, and, more nebulously, "events." When did she sleep? She always had more energy than all the rest of them.

"Of course," Hilda said. "Though I rather thought you read the papers on your tram ride."

Over men's shoulders, yes, but Hilda thought she bought at least one paper in the morning. Maisie was surprised to realize she knew something Hilda didn't: what it was to be poor. Hilda didn't know what it meant to have to mind each literal penny. Pennies were important, one after another meant a bun, soap, toothpaste. A penny spent on a newspaper might be the difference between being able to buy thread to mend stockings, and allowing a hole to show meant your status plummeted, even among the poor. Maisie was slowly rising out of penury, but all her savings now were for a dress. One good dress fixed your status. But she wanted to read more of the papers. That would change her status, too, if only at the BBC.

Reith was also a devotee of the papers, and assigned a phalanx of staff to mark every one of the articles on the BBC for his delectation.

"Ah, Miss Musgrave!" he greeted Maisie one afternoon as she brought in his tea. "Here's a fine thing. The *Times* writes that the BBC is 'doing good work in bringing more education to the British public.' And they don't just mean the Schools broadcasts. They mean music and the Talks. Very good, very good."

He continued to read aloud as he stirred in sugar.

"'Whilst many still think the wireless a fad of this peculiar modern age in which we live'—peculiar, indeed. I saw a couple dancing the other night and was of half a mind to call for an exorcist—'it cannot be denied that the BBC is presenting programming of an overall informative, enlightened, and elevating matter that is a credit to its purported mission.'" He raised his tea in a salute to the paper, though more likely to himself, then favored Maisie with his warmest scowl.

"It's a very satisfying thing, seeing this validation in the newspapers." Reith sighed happily, reading through the piece again. "Though they do say 'enlightened.' I often worry about that word. It sounds like a euphemism for 'too modern.'"

Maisie had been at the BBC long enough to learn that when the newspapers wanted to be critical of radio, euphemism was the last thing they employed.

"I'm sure they only mean in relation to the Enlightenment, sir."

"Hum." (Possibly he wasn't too keen on the Enlightenment either?)

"It's a fine testament to Miss Matheson," she said, hoping to restore his cheer. She thought she saw a shadow cross his face, but whether it was an ongoing meditation on the intricacies of Enlightenment or something else, she couldn't be sure. It might just have been the light.

"Yes, this piece singles her out for mention. Apparently she is 'the linchpin that makes the BBC more than just frivolous,'" he said, putting down the paper to stir more sugar in his tea. "And it congratulates me for being so visionary as to entrust a woman in such a critical post. Though not me by name, but the BBC. We're quite the avatars of daring, apparently."

"Yes, sir! Onwards and upwards," Maisie crowed. His scowl chilled. Maybe because it was Hilda's expression? "Oh, I only mean . . . everyone says the BBC is one of the few places where women can have more than clerical jobs."

"Yes. I daresay it is," he said. "Do go and file this newspaper, Miss Musgrave, and ask Miss Shields to come in."

Maisie obeyed, berating herself in a manner to do Georgina proud. Why didn't she say the article was a testament to him? That was what he wanted to hear, and it would have been so easy to say. Men loved compliments. Lola always quoted the glossies on this point. Maisie glanced through the open door, but could only see the back of Miss Shields's head, radiating triumphant disapproval at her.

They were indebted to him, all of them. Hilda, too. And no one more than Maisie. She hoped she hadn't given him any reason to regret it.

Hilda never seemed to mind what the papers wrote about the BBC, or her. If it was a compliment, she declared it "jolly decent," and if it was excoriation, she laughed and said, "Well, we can't please everyone and would probably be a horrid bore if we even tried." Articles were duly filed, fulfilling Hilda's particularity about order, but her real interest was in letters sent by the general public, and especially librarians. Literature and poetry were becoming mainstays of Talks, with a combination of reviews and readings, and librarians wrote with the enthusiasm of matinee-idol devotees to gloat about their increased circulation and even the formation of book and poetry circles. "Good Lord, there's one in Bradford, and I believe nearly the entire town left school at age twelve."

Maisie viewed poetry as one of those things you were supposed to like. A jumble of words, jazz without music, with a rhythm she couldn't follow. The poetry readings on the BBC didn't do much to enhance her understanding, but she enjoyed them more. Hilda engaged terrific readers and bullied them to her will. Maisie still preferred her words linear and clear, sword-sharp and a direct hit to her brain. But the general thrill that ran through Talks when a poem transfixed the listening audience was contagious. And these literary societies mattered. She wasn't sure what they meant, only that she was as ebullient as Hilda at their creation.

"Even though I've got nothing to do with it," she confessed to Phyllida on their tea break.

"You're there, aren't you?" Phyllida pointed out. "Keeping the wheels turning. That's plenty to do with it." She had Hilda's knack for pronouncing something as though it simply was, and there was no argument.

Maisie—the whole department—still gave all the credit to Hilda. She was so persuasive and adamant in securing broadcasters. It was getting harder and harder for anyone to say no to her.

"Excellent!" Hilda erupted, slamming down the phone and jumping for her hat. "I'm having a drink with T. S. Eliot." She wolfed down a scone and tossed a cup of lukewarm tea down her throat. "I think he's a bit of a champion with the drink. Best I don't go in with an empty stomach."

It was disturbing to see Hilda throw her things in her bag—Hilda being disorderly could only signal the apocalypse. Maisie glanced outside. *Oh good. It's only raining water. Not blood.*

"Wish me luck!" Hilda called, racing out the door. A pamphlet dropped. "Doesn't matter!" She was already halfway down the stairs.

Maisie picked up the pamphlet and hunted for a resting spot. The desk was, as ever, covered in neat stacks of papers, with several pages of a script filling the rest of the surface. Maisie set the pen back in its holder and straightened the correspondence so nothing peeked out from under the top pages. She could just fit the pamphlet in the bottom corner of the desk, but it didn't look right.

Have I always been this compulsive about order myself, or is it contagious?

The bookshelves were full. It would be scandalous to lay something on any other surface.

I'll just take it home. A little more reading for the tram.

Her initial disappointment on finding the pamphlet was in German was mitigated when she saw Hilda had made ample notes in English. Hilda's handwriting was still aneurysm-provoking, but Maisie was getting better at deciphering it.

Not that it made any of this any clearer.

One of the notes was torn from a German newspaper. Hilda had written in red: "equity drop!!! (disaster)." They'd had speakers on finance and economy, but Maisie didn't know what an equity drop meant, or why it was a disaster. If it hurt the Germans, she was satisfied—all those broken bodies, all those poppies, all the "Surplus Women," as the papers had it.

But why would Hilda be reading one of their pamphlets?

It was called *The Road to Resurgence*. Maisie could just make out the author's name, Adolf Hitler. Hilda's annotation said this wasn't meant for proper publication but was only to be distributed on the sly to leading German industrialists. So how had Hilda gotten it? Apparently, the contents were meant to assuage said industrialists about their fear that the Nazi party was anti-capitalist. Underneath that note were two tiny questions in writing even more illegible than usual: "Siemens?" "Nestlé?"

Maisie rubbed her forehead. Siemens. That man Hoppel was an executive at Siemens's British branch and Reith's good friend. And he had exhorted Reith to do . . . something; she couldn't remember what. As to the "Nazi party," she remembered reading that name over some man's shoulder. An article dismissive of Germans, but what article wasn't? Hilda's robot brain would remember all this information and put it all together, but that was the brain that was reading German publications.

Another question: "Socialists?" Socialists didn't like industrialists. You only needed to spend one evening listening to men in a pub to learn that.

Germany was a mess, the papers and pub patrons cheerfully agreed. Its economy tattered, government ineffective. Mussolini was said to laugh at Germany, he having taken a mess and turned it into a model.

"Miss? Miss!"

"What? I'm reading!" Maisie snapped. The tram conductor was glaring down at her.

"End of the line, miss. I called three times."

She had missed her stop.

"Oh. Er. Sorry," she murmured, closing the pamphlet. She slunk off, trying to ignore an exchange between the conductor and the driver about the flightiness of women.

SEVEN

Naturally, Hilda had secured T. S. Eliot for a broadcast and was celebrating with a pile of cakes for the whole department. Fielden glanced at it, then back at Maisie.

"I suppose you're wondering what the rest of us are having?"

I must remember to trip and spill tea on him sometime.

At last she found a quiet moment to return the pamphlet, feeling like she was passing over contraband.

"Ah, is that what I dropped?" Hilda said, taking it. "I'd ask you to type the notes, but it's not for the BBC. Or, I should say, not yet. What was your opinion of it?"

"I didn't read it," Maisie lied, outraged at the assumption.

"Really? That's disappointing." Hilda didn't frown, exactly, but her mouth was neutral, an expression so much more chilling than anything Miss Shields could accomplish. Then her eyes twinkled. "If you're going to attempt subterfuge, Miss Musgrave, which has its attractions, you must exert care and caution. You didn't put all the pages back in their original order, and this one is bent." She held out the page with the note "disaster" for Maisie's delectation. "You read my translations? Of course you did. What is your opinion?"

She looked both expectant and challenging.

"I . . . don't really know what to think," Maisie said.

"What rot!" Hilda snorted. "You need to mimeograph our guidelines for Talks, yes? Good. I'll join you."

"You don't have time." Maisie knew Hilda's schedule perfectly. "You've got to do the voice test of that fellow from Afghanistan, and—"

Hilda was not to be dissuaded. The mimeograph machine, crammed in its own room, was loud and slow and allowed for a private conversation. While Maisie set up the stencils, Hilda swung herself onto the table bearing the machine and crossed her ankles.

"Now, come, Miss Musgrave. Let's hear it. You read my notes on that wretched thing. What did you make of it?"

Maisie didn't have an opinion yet, just a thousand questions.

"How did you get a German pamphlet that's not meant for distribution?"

"Excellent question," Hilda congratulated her. "I can't answer it just now."

"Why not?" Maisie asked, frowning. "What's so important about it?"

"Is this distrust or bad temper?"

"Maybe it's distemper," Maisie said, unable to help herself.

Hilda's laugh almost drowned out the noise of the machine.

"Tell me, Miss Musgrave, if, just for fun, you thought I was a German spy, how would you go about ascertaining it?"

The question was posed like it was a party game.

"But I don't think you're a spy."

"Why not?"

"You can't be. You're too busy."

While she waited for Hilda to stop laughing, Maisie thought about espionage. Sensationalist literature was more abundant than sandwich shops, bursting with tales of Russian spies. *I don't know what Bolshevism's done for politics, but it's certainly feeding the creative mind.* Maisie envisioned cloaks and daggers, even though, of course, it was overcoats and pistols. Or perhaps poisoned darts? Why would

Russians spy in Britain anyway? What on earth did they hope to learn?

They wanted to conquer; that was the prevailing wisdom. Even most of the better newspapers thought the Bolshevist threat was real.

Hilda wiped her eyes. "God, I love your logic. Now go on, really. You must have made something of that bit of propagandistic dross."

"Not really," Maisie admitted. "I don't know what an equity drop is, or why it matters. I definitely don't see why socialists want to please industrialists, or what Siemens has to do with anything. Unless it's that they make wirelesses?"

"Very astute." Hilda nodded. "So! How would you answer any or all of these?"

"I'm asking you," Maisie said, liking the snap in her voice. Clearly, so did Hilda.

"And if you didn't have me to ask?"

"I don't know," Maisie cried. "I . . . Well, I suppose I would try to find a clever reporter on one of the better newspapers and ask him to help."

"You could do that, yes." Hilda nodded. "I think you'll find, though, that even clever reporters don't know things right away." She gathered the mimeographs and smoothed them into a neat stack.

"Miss Matheson . . . what *is* an equity drop?"

Hilda looked down at the pages in her lap and ran a finger under the words: Suggestions for Writing an Excellent Talk. When she glanced back at Maisie, her expression was almost rueful. "Probably nothing I ought to fuss about. I've sometimes been told I read too much. Think too much. Perhaps there's something to that." She chuckled, and slid off the table. "But one thing I do know for a fact is propaganda costs money, if it's going to work. A lot of money."

She took the mimeographs and headed back to the department, leaving Maisie to think dark thoughts about enigmatic statements.

And wish *she* were the clever reporter she needed to find.

How would they start, anyway? The library, I guess. And then a banker, maybe, or someone in finance? Someone like that Mr. Emmet we had in.

He'd be easy enough to get on the phone or meet with. And then maybe talking to someone in the Labour Party, asking about—

Oh.

One universal instruction Maisie had always been given was not to break rules. Her one great moment of disobedience was her lie—the false age that had brought her here, to her father's homeland, far away from Georgina and to work that seemed worthwhile. Despite the success of the venture, Maisie, unwilling to tempt fate, remained reluctant to try rule-breaking again. Certainly, no one else ever encouraged her to do so.

Neither had Hilda, or not openly. But the unanswered question pushed her past all the mountains of work she was meant to do and reaching into the wastebasket for discarded paper, which she sneaked into the lavatory with her to make a few notes in privacy.

Siemens. What was Hilda wondering about Siemens? *They're German, they're big, and they've got a huge operation here. All perfectly right as rain.* Maisie chewed on her pencil. That man Hoppel had said something to Reith, something Maisie wanted to hear, because she liked when people thought highly of Reith. Something about being right-thinking. An alliance, with the BBC. And some sort of meeting.

Two secretaries came in, chatting. The pencil fell out of Maisie's mouth. How long had she been in there? She flushed the toilet and ran back to the office, shoving the papers into her sleeve. *Please let Miss Shields be away from her desk. Please let Miss Shields be away from her desk.*

Miss Shields was at her desk. She looked up as Maisie entered, glanced at the clock, and made a notation in her pad.

Maisie rolled paper and carbons into the typewriter. She typed, she filed, she took dictation, she typed some more. But her mind wanted to think, to ask and answer questions. That fist in her chest swelled through her skin, pushing a grin onto her face.

She was typing: "I do not think Schools is managing to achieve its full potential as of yet. There is far more we can do to inform the youth of Britain," when something Hoppel had said sprang into her head. She yanked the papers from her sleeve and scribbled: "Right-minded man, making sure the country runs as it ought." *Funny thing for a businessman. Or is it? I suppose the right-minded should manage things, anyway. But who says what's right-minded? I suppose someone thought Nero . . .*

"What exactly are you doing?" Miss Shields asked. She stood over Maisie, arms folded, nose in full declension.

Maisie yelped, and the pencil cartwheeled out of her hand.

"Nothing. I—"

"Yes, I can see that. You certainly aren't finishing that memo. What is this you're writing?"

One arm unfurled and extended to its full length, palm full of expectation.

"It's just personal—" Maisie began in a squeak.

"Personal?" Miss Shields repeated, making the word seven syllables long.

"No! Not . . . That is, I mean, it's for Miss Matheson, but . . ." She trailed off, remembering too late that "being for Miss Matheson" was a graver offense.

"I see. Something for Miss Matheson. Even though you are on executive duty at this time. To which you have been late returning from Talks eight times this month. I have kept track." The arm was still extended. The fingers gave one insistent twitch and Maisie, defeated, surrendered the paper. Miss Shields glanced at the shorthand notes and sucked in her breath. "Who are you to be giving opinions about Mr. Hoppel?"

"I wasn't. It's not—"

Miss Shields raised an eyebrow, then turned and marched into Reith's office.

That fist inside punched all the way up Maisie's throat and nearly leaped out of her mouth. *Damn her, damn her, damn her.* A curse that worked for both Miss Shields and Hilda, with whom Maisie was equally furious. How dared she get Maisie interested in anything beyond the strict parameters of her work? How dared she . . . ?

"Miss Musgrave? Come!" Miss Shields barked.

Maisie walked slowly, feeling like Anne Boleyn on the way to her execution. She finally stepped inside Reith's office, and he nodded to Miss Shields.

"Thank you, Miss Shields. If you would close the door, please? Leaving Miss Musgrave and myself alone, I meant," he clarified, when Miss Shields tried to stay inside. Maisie refused to turn and see her expression, merely waited for the footsteps to fade and the door to click shut.

Her first instinct was to plunge to her knees—Anne Boleyn's last pose—and beg for clemency. But she stayed upright. "Sir, I can explain—"

"Sit down, Miss Musgrave." Reith waved her to the club chair with a flourish of his cigarette. "Miss Shields informs me you have committed a series of minor infractions, and all against your duties to this office, which is to say, to Miss Shields and myself. Infractions are not acceptable for someone so low on the ladder as yourself. I am most strict about duty and tasks, as you know, and I am quick to remove anyone unable to conform to these standards."

"I'm very sorry, sir. I really am. But they said, in one of the Talks meetings, it might be interesting to have someone who manufactures radios give a Talk. And I remembered Mr. Hoppel. It just came to me so suddenly. I had to make the note. I couldn't wait. I knew Talks wanted a right-thinking, right-minded sort of person to speak, someone who understands about managing things, and who would be better than someone intimate with yourself?"

Reith took a long drag of his cigarette, and as he exhaled, she was overjoyed to see his warmer scowl behind the smoke.

"I had a feeling it was something like that," he assured her. "And I daresay Hoppel will be glad to broadcast should his schedule allow. You may tell Miss Matheson so. But remember, each of your duties belongs in its own place. And . . ." He paused, pondering his cigarette before looking deep into Maisie's eyes. "I might warn you—not that you need it, I should think—but working for a girl like Miss Matheson,

Bloomsbury type and all that, you might start thinking you'd like to do something more than just secretarial work."

Maisie hoped he didn't see her gulp.

"I don't object to girls writing nice little stories, of course, although you're hardly . . . Well, you will always remember what your real duty is, yes?"

There was only one answer, and she gave it.

"Good!" He nodded. "Now, then, I think docking your pay this week will be sufficient punishment. Don't you, my dear?"

"What?" she shrieked. Too late, she clamped her hand over her mouth. Miss Shields had gotten her reward.

"Just a shilling," Reith clarified. "That compensates for your lateness. Even minor infractions cannot be allowed to go without punishment, or where would we be? Besides, you're a young girl, and unprotected. You need to be guarded against your weaknesses. Ambition is a dangerous thing in a girl like yourself. And it has a dreadful tendency to lead to rule-breaking. I should be very sorry to see that."

The words "just a shilling" zinged through Maisie's head. A shilling was nothing to Reith, casually lost in his trouser pocket. To Maisie, it was twelve pennies, precious armaments toward the new dress that would demonstrate her heightened respectability. She looked down at her knees, the overly mended stockings covered by the blue serge dress that bore a patch under the arm and was growing shiny in the elbows. Just a shilling. And she was lucky. There were families in her road for whom the loss of a shilling would mean the choice between having supper that week or losing their home.

"I'm only looking after your interests," Reith said. "Now, off you go, then, back to work."

Maisie nodded. She knew she should thank him for his benevolence, but couldn't get the words out. She breathed carefully as she measured the steps to the door. By the time it opened, her face must be neutral.

Miss Shields was at her desk, upright and efficient as ever, but her eyes sparkled with cold triumph. Maisie stood before her, ramrod straight and yet apologetic.

"I'm sorry if I've offended you in any way, Miss Shields."

The secretary simply looked at her, an unhurried, untroubled stare mindfully designed to make Maisie feel more uncomfortable.

"Don't flatter yourself, Miss Musgrave. Mr. Reith sees you as a pet, which is lucky for you. You should maintain that so long as you can. He has nothing to do with the hiring of the girls, and so he can't see that you don't belong here. You're a good enough worker and sharper than you look, but you lack—"

"Brio?"

"The right sort of manner," Miss Shields countered.

"I'm sorry. I do try, you know."

"Yes. But the BBC requires someone who doesn't need to try."

"I understand you," Maisie said, meaning it. "And I am sorry. But I'm not sorry I'm here. I know I'm not the sort of girl you want as your deputy, but I'm working on being the best sort for the BBC I can be."

"Much luck to you," Miss Shields said, with more amusement than acidity. "If I were you, I'd start with catching up on your typing."

Maisie returned to her typewriter. She hadn't needed this incident to tell her Miss Shields didn't want her here. But there were any number of people in Savoy Hill whom she wanted to see the back of, and when Maisie considered who was first on that list, she decided it wasn't a bad list to be on at all.

Despite the honor of the list, Maisie resolved to put aside equity drops, German propaganda, and anything else that wasn't strictly within her job specifications.

At the next meeting between Hilda and Reith, there was no mention of wireless sets or Hoppel. Reith didn't seem to notice, being too overwhelmed by Hilda's laundry list of plans and thoughts, several of which required vast technical improvements, until he interrupted her with a dry chuckle and said, "Miss Matheson, do try to restrain some of this unbridled ambition. It's not an attractive thing in a girl, you know, even at your age. You have to be patient, my dear."

"Certainly, Mr. Reith," Hilda conceded, a flap of her hand smacking patience aside. "But at least in so far as our content and its nature, there's a great deal we can—"

"Our content's exactly what it should be. You see how the papers compliment us. It's edifying and entertaining. What more could we possibly achieve?"

"We're doing well, certainly, but think of the opportunity for deep connection—"

"For what?" He turned pink around the edges, and Maisie thought he must have misheard something very rude.

"Connection," Hilda repeated, with a transcendent smile. "That's what people really want, you know. They want the feeling of immediacy, someone actually there and sharing an experience. A voice in the wilderness of the mind."

Maisie knew what Hilda meant. It was in the quieter letters they received, the sort Reith would never read, but she did. Radio helped people feel less lonely.

"It's not unlike a favorite book," Hilda went on, "the way it can be a friend. What's your favorite book?"

"The Bible," he answered promptly.

"And yours, Miss Shields?" Hilda said, turning around to draw the secretaries into the conversation.

Miss Shields's eyes rolled upward just enough to meet Hilda's.

"Just for a bit of fun," Hilda clarified.

Miss Shields looked as if she'd rank this "fun" slightly below getting branded.

"I can't but be curious, even if this is a colossal waste of time," Reith put in.

"Well," said Miss Shields. "I suppose it's the . . . *Jane Eyre*." She spoke with an almost defiance that seemed to surprise her. Reith's brows shot into orbit, and Hilda smiled, a minuscule glint of triumph in her eyes.

Maisie had never owned a book and couldn't imagine rereading anything when time was so short and the libraries so full. So as to a favorite, "Whichever one I have in my hand," was the only answer. She was just happy to know how to read and that libraries were free. Hilda looked pleased.

"I suppose mine is *Pride and Prejudice*, although I do so love poetry," Hilda mused. "But you see my point, that we turn to these books as old friends. They're always there and they speak to us. Radio has the same capacity, and we should make more of it, in all our broadcasts. That's how we'll build something that will find a home in any number of hearts."

Reith exhaled cigarette smoke through his nose. "Miss Matheson, you either read too much poetry or are simply a true Utopian. It's a charming picture you paint, I'm sure, but I don't think anyone thinks of radio quite so seriously. We simply will do our best with it for as long as it lasts. All right? Now, was there anything else on the agenda?"

Hilda was applying lipstick when Maisie brought the last of the day's letters for her to sign. She was lovely already, with that milky skin and those penetrating eyes, and the makeup she didn't need made her exquisite. Striking. Maisie sighed and turned her gaze out the window.

"Good, good, good," Hilda told each letter as she signed it. "Very good. Are you busy this evening, Miss Musgrave?"

"Me?" How did Hilda always catch her by surprise? It made her feel like part of her was sleeping, when in fact she was sure she was buoyantly awake.

"I'm attending Lady Astor's salon, and if you're free, I was hoping you might join me. It's not just for fun," Hilda clarified. "Scads of important people will be there. Actors, too, I believe, and so Miss Warwick will likely attend. It's a good opportunity to woo potential broadcasters."

"Why would they need wooing? Broadcasting pays." Maisie was dumbfounded. She'd never heard of an actor to turn down work, money, or food.

"You'd be surprised how often that isn't enough," Hilda told her.

"Remember, radio's still not wholly reckoned as a force for good. It might 'taint a career.'" She couldn't say that without laughing. "In any case, I'd be glad for your help. As it's work, I'll of course give you extra pay. And she serves a lovely buffet supper."

Extra pay? Had Hilda heard of the docked shilling? It almost didn't matter, as the enticement of Lady Astor needed little sweetening. Only . . . Maisie looked down at herself. Same old brown frock, same mended stockings. Same face, same hair, same her. She glanced at the carriage clock. Phyllida had left, so there was no borrowing lipstick.

Oh well. No one will look at me, even if I'm not wearing Invisible Girl. She plucked a fresh steno pad from the stash and they were off.

Lady Astor's house in St. James's Square was a jungle of tassels and ornaments and Baroque art. All this, for a house she lived in only when Parliament was in session. *Or for "the season,"* Maisie reminded herself, hearing Phyllida's snort.

The place teemed with sequins and feathers and glitter and gloss. True to form, it was the actors who were the most showily dressed. Those born wealthy had a studied ease to their glamour. The intellectuals had given themselves a dusting and the artists competed to see who could be the most avant-garde.

"Ah, Miss Matheson, marvelous!" rang a commanding voice. Lady Astor: a masterful confection of cut cheekbones and arched brows, hair twisted elegantly at her neck, pearls and eyes equally black and sparkling.

"Lady Astor! Wonderful to see you. May I present my secretary, Miss Musgrave?"

Lady Astor extended a gloved hand. Maisie felt all the breath leave her body as she took it. Lady Astor had the sort of grip that could pick you up and pitch you like a horseshoe.

"How d'ye do, Miss Musgrave?" Her voice was patrician English, but with the slightest twang reminiscent of her Virginia upbringing.

"I . . . I . . . It's such an honor. I'm so pleased to meet you.

Milady!" she amended, relieved the room was dim enough to hide her blush.

Lady Astor's smile was warm, but Maisie could see how just a twitch in her lips could turn it into a hatchet. She should have been an aristocrat back when they had had the power to order death sentences. No one would have ever crossed her.

"No need for any 'milady' nonsense. We're both born-and-bred Americans."

"Beg pardon, Lady Astor, but Miss Musgrave was born in Canada," Hilda interjected.

"Ah, yes. A Canadian and a New Yorker, too—isn't that right? Confusin' bit of backstory, Miss Musgrave, and good for you, I say. Always keep 'em guessin'. Don't you agree, Miss Matheson?" She turned to Hilda, with the expectant air of one who is rarely contradicted.

"Most certainly," Hilda obliged. Maisie would have agreed as well, but she wasn't asked.

"Now, then," Lady Astor commanded. "Come along and let me present you to some interestin' people. Might be good for your BBC, I think."

Maisie tagged along at a safe distance, discreetly taking notes as Lady Astor introduced Hilda to some of the throng with the air of a matron chaperoning a debutante—a titan in publishing, a magazine editor who eyed Hilda with suspicion, and the artist Laura Knight, whom even Maisie knew was famous for her *Self-Portrait with Nude*. "I knew I'd done well when the *Telegraph* called me vulgar," she said.

Eventually Hilda whispered to Maisie to get some food, and she didn't need urging. She gathered a treasure trove of salmon mousse and stuffed mushrooms and retreated to a corner, perfect for watching Hilda chat with each person in turn, that curious manner just enough on the edge of self-deprecation to make them feel how much of a favor they would be granting were they to come broadcast.

"Oughtn't you to be at her side?" A voice sounded suddenly, making Maisie jump. Her accoster looked a lot like Josephine Baker, only with darker skin and a more cynical eye.

"I'm observing," Maisie explained. "And she said I should eat something."

"You're American," the woman said, her enormous brown eyes glistening with interest. "I am, too. New Orleans," she clarified proudly. "Wisteria Mitterand." She held out her hand.

"Jeepers, that's a gorgeous name!"

"I'm glad you like it. I tweaked it for effect," Miss Mitterand said, with a wink.

"I'm Maisie Musgrave." (A name like a bland pudding.) "Are you an actress?"

"I am, and doing far better here than on Broadway." Miss Mitterand laughed.

"Broadway can be a little shortsighted, I know. My mother acts there."

"Oh. Will I have seen her in anything?"

"I'm afraid you probably have."

"Ah. Yes. I've acted in some of those shows myself. London theater's far more exhilarating." She lit a cigarette, not bothering to point out that she had a chance here to play something more than a maid. No wonder she looked so gleeful.

"Would you want to come and broadcast, do you think?" Maisie asked. Now that Maisie was in a position to advocate for friends, Lola was too busy onstage—or offstage—to come broadcast. But this woman, with her voice and story, might be a real coup.

Miss Mitterand raised a slim eyebrow. "It's not for you to invite me, is it?"

"Well, no, but I could—"

"You're very kind. But I suspect I might be a bit . . . racy . . . for BBC Drama." She chuckled. "But thank you. Truly. I'd love to chat more, but I must put myself back in circulation. I've got to secure a dinner date for the next few months or so."

"Sorry?"

"Steady work or no, I need to pad my income. And maintain appearances. I am the exotic creature here. Don't look embarrassed; it's just true. A few months of dinners are good for business. And maybe diamonds. They always love how diamonds look against my skin. Silly, hmm? Well, cheerio, as they say." She waved an elegant finger to Maisie and sashayed into the middle of the room. And was indeed soon surrounded by men.

"How have you got on?" Hilda asked, materializing like a genie and enhancing the legerdemain with a plate of tiny cakes.

"I think Miss Mitterand could give a very interesting Talk."

"Excellent. Write up your thoughts for my review Monday."

"Me? Isn't that a bit out of my—"

In the limelight of Hilda's merry, challenging eyes, Maisie's mouth snapped shut.

Hilda insisted on sending her home in a cab. Neither the luxury nor the pilfered cakes she'd wrapped in a cloth (also, she realized, pilfered—oops) distracted her from her thoughts. Miss Mitterand could tell stories of her working life, and why she was in London, and those stories might make people uncomfortable. Which would be most interesting, as Hilda would say.

She ate a cake. The jolt of joy that burst through her had nothing— she was pretty sure—to do with the excess of butter.

Maisie was still in the sitting room past midnight, her fingers black with pencil smudges, when Mrs. Crewe insisted she turn off the lights or else pay the entire gas bill. What did she need to write so much for, anyway?

"I don't know. I just do." There was some question as to who was more surprised—Mrs. Crewe, at receiving an answer, or Maisie, at the answer she gave.

"Early, are you?" Miss Shields sniffed, seeing Maisie stamping the correspondence. "It hardly compensates for all the times you're late getting back from Talks."

"No, Miss Shields," Maisie murmured.

"Mr. Reith isn't here yet, you know."

"Yes, I know." She knew his schedule better than he did.

Later that morning, he was interviewing a candidate for a Schools producer. Charles Siepmann was not exactly handsome, but he had a dashing quality that drew both Maisie's and Miss Shields's eyes. He had a slight acquaintance with Reith already and could afford a measure of familiarity.

"Nice to be waited on by two girls, I should say," he said when he arrived, laughing as he and Reith shook hands.

"I did warn you, we're very modern here." Reith laughed, too. "You'll find a girl producer in Schools, Miss Somerville. Capable little thing, quite clever."

"And of course that girl you have running Talks. Most bold of you indeed, sir."

"Very modern girl, Miss Matheson. Clever, certainly, though does tend to be a bit radical. Some of that poetry—if one can even use the word—she selects for broadcast is frankly shocking, but we try to understand current tastes."

"I deeply admire your broad-mindedness."

Reith gave his impression of self-deprecation and indicated for Maisie to take the minutes of the interview. Whether Miss Shields was aggravated or relieved, Maisie couldn't tell. Probably both.

Siepmann rabbited on about his education (Oxford, after having served in the army), which Reith already knew, his facility for the Schools broadcasts, and his general interests. He took out a cigarette case.

"The girl doesn't mind?" He jerked a thumb in the vague direction of Maisie.

"Hm? Oh, please go ahead." Reith gave a magnanimous wave of his hand.

"Ah, yes, modern girls." Siepmann chuckled, pleased with his own urbanity.

Maisie was surprised he remembered she was in the room.

"There are two questions I always ask of potential senior men," Reith said. "Are you a Christian, and do you have any character defects?"

Maisie expected Siepmann to laugh, but he didn't. He leaned forward, his look so serious that even his hair seemed less wavy.

"I am a proud member of the Church of England. And my greatest character defect is no doubt ambition, though perfectionism might also be rated a deficiency, as it can give me a warm temper, especially when others don't share the quality to at least some extent."

"Well?" Miss Shields asked Maisie, after the men left the office. "Will he get the position?"

"Most certainly," Maisie answered.

Ambition and perfectionism, my eye. As though half the BBC doesn't have one or the other. One person did possess both, though the ambition wasn't personal, and she'd never be so gauche as to parade either of them to score points.

I wonder if this Siepmann fellow even knows what perfectionism is?

She'd already made up her mind what she wanted to do in her own journey onwards and upwards. Now she just needed to go through with it.

"Ah, Miss Musgrave, wonderful," Hilda greeted her. "Five new scripts and we're rehearsing those fascinating people from the Chinese dance society—I don't know what I was thinking, but in for a penny now. People should adore the music, anyway, and the one fellow describes the dances awfully well. Incredible-sounding place, China. Wouldn't you just love to travel there?"

She wouldn't know the language, food, customs, clothes, or climate.

"I might, I think."

Though maybe not. Did they really bind women's feet there?

"I wrote up the notes on a Talk by Miss Mitterand," Maisie said. Her mind was still on Chinese women's feet. How did they walk? Or maybe that was the point. That they couldn't.

"Excellent!" Hilda said, skimming Maisie's notes. "Possibly too controversial, and of course we'd have to gauge Miss Mitterand's interest in sharing any of her biography. I propose we ask Drama to bring her in to perform, and if she does nicely, we'll be well positioned to invite her to give a Talk."

Maisie nodded, steeling herself, though she didn't know why.

"Miss Matheson?"

"Yes?"

"I, er . . ." Her eyes slithered to the carriage clock, ticking over a new minute.

"You know, Miss Musgrave, dead silence kills us."

"I . . . wanted to ask . . ."

Hilda set down her pencil to give Maisie her full attention. Which managed to be more disconcerting.

"One straight thrust, Miss Musgrave, a killing stroke," Hilda advised.

"I want more responsibility here. In the Talks Department. Please."

Looking at Hilda's face, Maisie realized she had never given anyone so much cause for pleasure. Georgina had been pleased to wave her off at the dock, but that hardly compared.

"Well killed," Hilda congratulated her. "Now we'll just have to see about arranging it."

Maisie, not being privy to the machinations involved in such arrangements, spent the next few days as jumpy as the typewriter keys she was currently abusing.

"He wants to see you at once, and he's very cross," Miss Shields said, eyes bright with triumph. Maisie leaped up, leaving "pursuant" only a mere "pursu." She paced her steps to be firm but obeisant as she entered Reith's office and sat down.

Reith not only sported a single eyebrow; it was so compressed the edges barely extended past the bridge of his nose.

"Well, Miss Musgrave, it appears Miss Matheson wants you all to herself."

"Yes, sir." Maisie exhaled. She didn't dare say anything else.

"I don't object to her having a full-time secretary. It's become necessary and speaks well for the Talks Department."

Was he pleased? Perhaps she should smile.

"But I'm afraid I'm not convinced that *you* should be that secretary, and I told her so."

She had never been more relieved not to smile.

"I know the department quite well, sir. Surely it would be inexpedient to engage a new girl at this time?"

A few threads of eyebrow arched upward.

"Well, you've learned something of good business. I appreciate that. But really, Miss Musgrave, do think this through. I know Talks brings in all sorts of literary men and the like. Very exciting for an impressionable young girl, I'm sure. But in my offices, you have the opportunity to meet the best sort of people."

Not "meet," she could point out. See them. Perhaps take their hat or bring them tea. Be rewarded with a nod or a word. Which was as much as an old-fashioned girl of no prospects should hope for and enjoy. Reith couldn't imagine her wanting more. Surely she should honor her love of the Old World by adhering to its strictest strictures, living and loving according to rules that even Maisie knew were growing mushy around the middle, a collapsing soufflé.

The new rules were being remade by the hour. One had to wonder what purpose there was in playing by them.

"Miss Musgrave, be straight now. Do you wish to work solely for Talks?"

She swallowed hard, lest her thoughts—ideas for Talks, for stories, for something—tumble out of her and spill all over the desk.

"Sir, I am more indebted to you than I can possibly say. But if this is what's best for the BBC, then yes, it's what I want."

His face remained impassive, but she knew better than to trust it. Reith tapped his pen against his lip.

"Miss Matheson is a girl of peculiar taste. I cannot say as I agree with her often. But she does seem to be doing well. So if she believes you are suited to be her permanent secretary, then I suppose I must acquiesce. And it is expedient. But if I see any faltering coming from Talks, I will insist she replace you at once."

"Yes, sir. Thank you, sir. I'm very indebted to you, sir. Again. Still." Maisie breathed, sucking in her cheeks to keep the smile from breaking free.

"Yes. I'm glad you realize that. I'd thank you not to forget it."

The smile sank into her throat.

"Yes, sir."

He replaced his pen. The eyebrows edged out a few millimeters.

"You're a sweet girl, but whatever Miss Matheson says, I don't think you're suited to her at all. And remember I warned you to guard against ambition."

"Yes, sir. Thank you, sir." She didn't dare tell him that ambition had triumphed.

He sniffed, popping a cigarette in his mouth.

"Modern girls," he muttered. Maisie knew he didn't mean her.

He didn't know she was one of them now. And if she wasn't yet suited to the job Hilda was putting her to, she was damned well going to be.

There was no fanfare when she settled permanently into a jerry-rigged corner of the Talks Department, within eyesight of Hilda's door. She could see Hilda if she was at her desk, though being Hilda, she was mostly sprawled on the floor, reading, writing, brain buzzing loud enough to disrupt the transmission waves.

The others were relieved to finally have a secretary at hand full-time and not have to run to the typing pool and be pecked incessantly about how some people were already working under full pressure. Fielden grunted: "I suppose it was inevitable, but Our Lady wants you, so I hope you don't let the side down."

"I'll need you to draft an announcement of the News division for the *Radio Times*," Hilda said. An inauspicious greeting, as the BBC's weekly magazine thrived on but despised content given to it by the departments. "And we're going to have to shift some files into storage—if they expand any further, they'll need their own postcode."

"Yes, Miss Matheson." Maisie nodded, biting down disappointment. She wanted a more exciting start to this new adventure.

"And, lest you think I forgot (When did Hilda ever forget

anything?), here." She pressed a florin into Maisie's hand. "For your good work at the salon. Lady Astor's going to come and broadcast. I've wanted her to do so since I started."

"But I had nothing to do with that!" Maisie hated false credit.

"Not directly. But I think she wanted to come when she saw me as well established, rather than as a favor. And one is never more well established then when one has one's own secretary."

Maisie rolled the coin in her hand. A florin. Two shillings. Her docked pay wouldn't touch her, and she still had a whole twelve pennies extra. She could get stockings with this.

"Not as much fun, perhaps, but have a go with this, if you like," Hilda continued, handing Maisie a large notebook overflowing in her exasperating handwriting. "Another after-hours job, so only if you don't mind staying a bit past the time, now and then. I could do it myself, but you're a much better typist than I, and I daresay some extra funds wouldn't go amiss."

They wouldn't.

"You're still a weekly girl for now, I'm afraid. I hope you don't mind."

"I don't. Thank you, Miss Matheson."

"Feel free to make any comment you like," Hilda said, tapping the notebook.

"What do you mean?"

"Just that." Hilda grinned. "I say, were you ever able to answer your question? About an equity drop?"

"I . . ." Maisie looked into Hilda's dancing eyes. "I'm working on it."

"Good. I thought you might be."

"I'll get an answer soon, I'm sure."

"I haven't any doubt of it."

"It's about flipping time," was Phyllida's assessment of recent events as they strode down the Embankment. "Can't think why the DG was being so tight about a Talks secretary, unless he trowed—thought—a woman wouldn't need one?"

"Why would he think that? Miss Matheson was a secretary to a woman."

"Aye, but a political secretary, and that's different. Ah, well, who knows with the DG. You were well in there and you can't guess, can you?"

Maisie couldn't. She still respected and even admired Reith. But she wouldn't dare question how his mind worked. He kept them all in Savoy Hill, and that had to be enough.

That Friday, Hilda left early on some sort of weekend adventure. The two producers and Talks assistants assumed "Field Marshal Fielden" would flex his muscle, but even Fielden claimed to have a weekend scheme ahead and so ducked out. Maisie paid no attention to the suppositions or the thoughts of a quiet Saturday morning. She had assignments to begin. She helped herself to some biscuits and opened Hilda's notebook.

It was such an effort, turning Hilda's scratch into words, that she had already typed two pages before the meaning began to sink in. She stopped typing and started to read, realizing her brain was still struggling to catch up.

Or catch on.

"Broadcast speech can be overheard by everybody; the printed word is often overlooked. This universality has its most obvious use in relation to what we call news—the announcement of events. But when we have said 'news,' we have at once roused the fundamental controversy. What news is broadcast?"

On and on and on—Hilda's thoughts on broadcasting. And news. And what made a valuable story. What radio was, what it ought to be, how to achieve that and then improve on it further.

An education.

EIGHT

"Will a shilling do?"

"Go ahead, pet. I expect you know how to use it."
Miss Cryer waved her to the phone at the back of the little post office.

Maisie pulled out her pad. There were several phone boxes within a hundred yards of Savoy Hill, but there was nearly always a queue, and anyway, she wanted to take notes as she talked. She expected the call to cost sixpence. The extra money was for Miss Cryer's confidence. The post office on Savoy Street that she managed with such tender respect, from morning till eight at night, was also a purveyor of rather good sweets and thus another pillar propping up the BBC.

A receptionist answered and hearing "Miss Musgrave of BBC Talks" put Maisie through with no waiting.

"Good morning, Mr. Emmet. Thank you so much. I won't take but a moment of your time."

"Not at all, not at all. Just having elevenses," he assured her. She could tell he was deepening and smoothing his voice, attempting to sound radio-perfect. *It wasn't his voice so much as his attitude—he's lucky Miss Matheson didn't beat him to death with a pencil.*

"I was wondering, Mr. Emmet, if you could explain to me a bit what happens if a nation experiences an equity drop. Is it a political concern at all?"

"Is this for an upcoming Talk?" he asked brightly. "Do you want to have me back again?"

Not on our lives.

"We are exploring a number of avenues, and hearing your thoughts on this would be useful," she said, opting for partial truth.

"Ah, I see. Well, in the simplest terms, it means negative equity. That is, a nation's holdings and general wealth are worth less. Its currency is less competitive. That can affect costs and national income— exports and the like. Mind you, it happens all the time. A strong economy overall can weather it. Look at your America, all those mad ups and downs over the last hundred years at least, yes? But the economy's soaring. Aren't people living better than ever before?"

Spoken like someone who's never walked through the Lower East Side in Manhattan. Or the East End of London, for that matter.

"Can you tell me what happens if there is an equity drop in a weak economy?" she asked.

"That's when you might have a problem," he said with an alarming chuckle.

"It's funny?"

"Oh, not for them, of course, but it's usually due to mismanagement somewhere, so it's deserved. And then they are ripe for someone to come in and sort things out at a good rate."

The man was making an argument for the benevolence of vultures.

"Someone? How do you mean?"

"An outside nation, perhaps, or someone with strong views and personality. Italy's still got any number of problems, but you see how Mussolini's created order. Order means a strong economy."

"I see. Thank you, Mr. Emmet. That's enormously helpful."

Back in the office, correspondence typed, calls put through, scripts marked, and rehearsal schedules fixed, Maisie found herself with a moment to think. Her eyes wandered over her notes and she remembered Hilda's word "connection." She had meant it differently, but . . .

"Miss Matheson?"

Hilda was reading through the listings for the *Radio Times*.

"Mm?"

"If we were to do a Talk on Germany's economy, could we perhaps draw a parallel to the American South after the Civil War?"

Hilda looked up at her, pencil between her teeth.

"It's not perfect," Maisie said quickly, "but the South's economy was a mess after the war and the North didn't do a whole lot to help, and then the South made some . . . well, not political changes, exactly, I guess, but policies that weren't very good. I'm not wording this well . . ."

The pencil dropped into Hilda's lap as she smiled broadly.

"You're very clear. It's a good thought. Everyone thinks the marginal parties in Germany, and here, for that matter, are just that, marginal. Worse, actually, a joke. But that's the sort of thinking that a party can use to advantage as it gains adherents." She picked up the pencil and brushed her skirt. "Probably want to be mindful of politics, keep it more historical, a Talk on the South and the years since the war ended. That would sound innocuously educational, but of course there's a bit more to it than that, for those really listening. I suppose there would be no way to mention that America does a fair bit to prop up the German economy—"

"Does it?" Maisie was surprised. "I haven't read that."

"Hmm. Really must get Mr. Keynes in here. A series would be ideal."

Maisie saw Hilda start spinning into the future and attempted to keep her in the present.

"Also, Miss Matheson, I know what an equity drop is."

"Yes, I thought you might," said Hilda. "Anything else?"

"Well, not really. Have you gotten any further—any more propaganda or anything?"

"Done!" Hilda ticked the top of the listings page and handed it to Maisie. "Off to the *Radio Times* they go."

It wasn't the answer to Maisie's question, and they both knew it.

Hilda was not only good at ferreting secrets from others, but she was a wizard at keeping her own.

"It's quite simple, Bert, really. You just need to make a bit more space in the layout for the article," Maisie explained, imitating Hilda's patient tone.

She didn't like Bert, but she liked the office of the *Radio Times*. As with most rooms in Savoy Hill, it was an awkward sliver of a space, cut at an angle like a layer cake. The higgledy-piggledy tables sported revolving exhibits of layouts in various stages and the tangy-sweet smell of the glue that pasted each article and photo into place hung in the air—a permanent, intoxicating perfume.

The magazine prompted a host of Savoy Hill snickers, not least because of its subhead: "The Official Organ of the BBC," which the boys all found hilarious. Maisie thought it was carrying a joke too far till Phyllida told her: "Well, you know it was founded by the DG and it's all his idea, so they call it 'Reith's organ.' Horrifying thought, hey?" Maisie was duly horrified.

It was an organ born of defiance. At the BBC's birth, the newspapers showed their pique by refusing to print program listings. So Reith had tapped his hat and ordered a magazine out of thin air. The first issue, brave and brazen in its scrolling font, appeared in 1923. It sold for tuppence and could take advertising, thus earning both keep and profit, so the magazine was one of Reith's darlings. But despite the prepared text from each department, the editorial staff, secure in their darlingness, continued to put what they dubbed "little flourishes" in entries, explaining with an amused patience to complainants that they were being paid to tend to the needs of the readers, not listeners, and were deaf to arguments that these were, in fact, one and the same.

An occasional cough from Reith restored order for a few weeks, until the determination of the "real" writers took sway again. The magazine was expanding, adding longer articles as accompaniment to the listening fare, and profiles of broadcasters. These were supposedly democratic, but the stage and film performers always held prominence, especially the prettiest women with the sultriest photos. Broadcasters like Vernon Bartlett shrugged this off—"I'd rather ogle Betty Balfour than my poor mug any day"—but Hilda was outraged. Maisie, convinced this was a lost cause, threw her passion into a defense of the prepared listings.

"It's dashed ugly for a girl to lecture a fellow, you know," Bert lectured her. "In medieval times, you'd be put in the stocks," he added, delighted with his wisdom.

"I don't mean to be impolite. It's only that we need you to print the listings as we write them," Maisie told him. "We shouldn't have to keep asking."

Or indeed, ask at all, but Bert required temperance. He was a young man trying to be old, thinking his journalist's requisition bow tie, tortoiseshell glasses, and pencil in permanent residence behind his right ear gave him gravitas.

"I keep telling you, we know what we're about; the magazine sells well and it's helping pull in more listeners. And we print those letters, too," he added with a gusty sigh. He'd have preferred real writing there, but letters from listeners were more of Reith's darlings, this effusion from the masses proof of his greatness. At Hilda's insistence, the *Radio Times* also printed some criticism. ("So long as they aren't the ones that sound like they came from Broadmoor, and via Mars at that," Hilda directed. "But thoughtful criticism is good for balance and makes everything more interesting.")

"Who's making the work that pays you, anyway?" Maisie argued.

"Awfully shrewish, aren't you? They always said you were a silent one."

I bet he wears glasses to keep people from seizing that pencil and cramming it into his eye.

"I'm sorry," she said, "but we do need these listings to be accurate, you see?"

He took the pages in false surrender and stalked away, a string of grumbles in his wake. Maisie lingered, eyes wandering over the layouts and the pile of magazines, fresh from the printers. A photograph of a large wireless was on front.

"Could I have the loan of some back issues?" she asked.

"What?" He hadn't realized she was still there. "What do you want them for?"

"Just to read. May I? Three months' worth? Oh, and the new one, please?"

He scrunched up his mouth. Eventually, the desire to thwart her was overcome by the reasonableness of her request.

"Well, all right, but don't get the idea I'm a lending library," he warned. He made a great show of finding a box and going to the storage shelves to fetch the magazines. "You'll be sure to keep them clean, of course?"

"I shall handle them with gloves," Maisie promised, lying with solemn ease.

"Now, if there's one thing Lady Astor cannot abide, it's being treated as though with kid gloves," Hilda warned the Talks Department. "The attention she demands for her status is as an MP, not as a viscountess. So long as anyone who encounters her employs the same general respect, politeness, gratitude, but firmness we have with all the broadcasters, you can't go wrong."

Meaning, "Don't bow thricely and no pulling of forelocks." Or, in the case of staunch republican Fielden, don't call her "Mrs. Astor." Maisie was excited. She wanted to bask in the great lady's presence again. Lady Astor was the sort of woman people stepped aside for, and Maisie wanted to study her mien. It couldn't all be position, could it? There must be something to learn.

Lady Astor swept in and greeted Maisie as a friend, or at least a favored courtier. She insisted on Maisie's remaining for the broadcast, which meant getting to see the engineers regard her with respect, but also appreciation. At nearly fifty, Lady Astor still radiated the mesmerizing beauty that had captured fascination, as well as a viscount, in her youth. Maisie could see the shadows of the piled-up curls, Gibson Girl silhouette, sweep and flow of long silk skirts. But what she couldn't have had then was the laserlike glitter in her eyes that could likely cut through someone more readily than any sword. That came with age.

On seeing Maisie, Billy attempted to melt into the machinery. Maisie, both because she was interested and it was fun to unnerve him, watched his work. *Wouldn't that be something, knowing how to make our broadcasts go?* Women weren't engineers, certainly not under Eckersley's fiefdom, but still . . . it would be something.

Lady Astor's broadcast was about Florence Nightingale, by way of introducing their new series on nursing. Maisie's idea, changed considerably, but from her kernel. As she listened to Lady Astor's lilting patrician voice—"Women have always nursed, but when Florence Nightingale set down the lamp and opened a school, she turned an expected avocation into a proper profession that has arguably done as much to save lives as vaccinations"—Maisie crammed her fist in her mouth to avoid squealing. Did Hilda feel like this every day, or did the thrill wear off?

Can't imagine which scenario is more painful.

"That was rather fun," Lady Astor proclaimed when the broadcast was finished. "Good lark, broadcastin'. I hope it lasts. Do give me a tour of the place, will you? I want to see more of our government's investment."

"Most certainly," said Hilda, "but—" She had twenty phone calls to make, plus the usual crisis management.

"Miss Musgrave can do very well," Lady Astor said. "You're far too busy; you always were. I'd say you'll work yourself sick, but you're healthier than all the colts at Goodwood."

Hilda's chuckle echoed as Maisie commenced the tour. Lady Astor might have been Queen Mary (or indeed, the *Queen Mary*) as she sailed through Savoy Hill. In the Engineering Department, Eckersley was reclined in his chair, reading *Electronics Today*. In Schools, Siepmann had his back to them, gazing out the window, hands folded behind him. Cyril and one of the assistants were playing darts and joking about their school days. Mary Somerville and the secretary were deeply immersed in revisions on a broadcast.

"I hear typin'; must be the girls," Lady Astor observed, and indeed the typing pool was, as usual, competing with a herd of stampeding rhinos for terror-inducing volume. But nothing was as deafening as Sound Effects. Lady Astor swung open the door to nod at the sight of the men engaged in a blazing row over a pile of coiled springs.

"Well, what do you think of our operation?" Hilda asked when Maisie delivered Lady Astor back to her.

"Very impressive. I congratulate myself on talkin' you into joinin'. And you must feel right at home—it's exactly like the House of Commons! All the men are loafin' about, and the women are the ones doing all the actual work."

Hilda's lips twitched.

"The House managed to get plenty done well before women were allowed in," she felt obliged to point out.

"Oh, certainly, certainly. But they're the ones with their feet up, loungin'. It's the women with their feet on the ground; that's all I've noticed."

Once Lady Astor was gone, Maisie observed to Hilda, "She's not entirely wrong about us, is she?"

"Thank heavens for that," said Hilda. "I certainly wouldn't want to be the one to tell her if she were. Would you?"

"Reading again? You girls work too hard," Mr. Holmby, proprietor of the Savoy Tup, chided Maisie as he set down her stew. She was very fond of the Tup, whose hot lunches had earned her loyalty from her third week at the BBC, and enjoyed Mr. Holmby's appreciation of her rounding face, to which he attributed his wife's cooking and his own liberal hand with the accompanying bread and butter.

Maisie preferred to lunch with Phyllida, but the vagaries of a day in Talks meant she often had to lunch alone. She didn't mind. The

Tup's patrons offered excellent eavesdropping opportunities, and she'd always enjoyed listening to people—it was almost like being in a conversation herself.

"I hear they caught some Bolshie spy in Walthamstow."

"Ah, go on. If any spy thinks that's a worthwhile place to do his work, he's not any good, is he?"

"Point is, bastards are everywhere, aren't they? And what are we doing about it?"

"A few rotten Russians can't overthrow Britain, though wouldn't I pay money to see them try? Those layabouts couldn't even make it to the Channel."

"Chuh, don't you read? It's about ideas now, not armies. Get inside the minds, is what it is. And they're working on it. That's what those trade unions are all about, softening people to Bolshevism."

Another group was fretting over the softening of the British mind and body, the "advanced and irregular" ideas of "all these artists and writers and unionists" who apparently lived in some namby-pamby world (Maisie didn't see how that was possible for someone in a trade) and didn't know what proper values were.

Then the inevitable: "I told her that if she dared cut her hair and wear a skirt too short, she'd get a good whipping, so that should hold her."

Most likely talking about a daughter. Though possibly a wife.

Maisie turned over the page in her pad and wrote: "Advanced Ideas"—perhaps a week of Talks about how new ideas were shaping society? Then she opened the latest *Radio Times* and turned to a story about performing for radio: "Miss Adelaide Whithouse is a comely performer of the stage, but her terror of the alien microphone in the BBC's Studio Two was evident as she prepared to broadcast an original comedy. Miss Whithouse had to be asked more than once not to twitch her papers, lest she disrupt the broadcast, and this only served to make her more . . ."

Oh, for goodness' sake, that's not how Beanie tells it. What rot. Honestly, I could write better stories than these.

Her spoon hovered inches from her open mouth.
Maybe I should try.

"Really, Maisie, do be careful," Lola scolded. "If you keep writing this much, your fingers will end up with permanent graphite stains."

Lola's penchant for hyperbole didn't seem misplaced. Maisie had worn down a whole pencil in a week. There was a Talk coming up on the rise of women as hairdressers, and she wanted to write a companion piece on the glory of short hair. Not the most exciting subject, but it seemed like an easy start. Or so she'd thought.

"At least it's just pencil," she said. Pens were an extravagance, and anyway, she was doing far too much erasing. Also doodling. She was good at drawing mice.

She was also very good at ideas, at notes, at beginnings. At writing sentences and rubbing them right out again, creating palimpsests before wearing holes straight through the paper. Her fingers hurt, her hand hurt, her arm hurt. And she loved every bit of the pain, with the love of a mother for her teething infant, screaming all through the night. Because increasingly, more and more sentences were being written, and staying put. She just wished her brain would remain focused on one thought at a time. She wrote, "The notion that women are given to excessive adornments and frivolity is generally just that, a notion. Most women prefer to be simple and practical, which doesn't have to mean Spartan," and start thinking about Sparta. From Sparta to war, from war to Hilda's notes on broadcasting, saying things like: "The general level of knowledge of the ordinary man concerning other countries, their politics, their people, their way of life, their interests, sports, recreations, would be enough to make them seem not vastly different in certain respects from his own. It would probably be less possible today to find a soldier's wife who thought the Germans were black than it was in 1914."

And then Germany and that propaganda Hilda pored over so carefully.

When Vernon Bartlett came in to broadcast—he had a regular series now, *The Way of the World*, widely touted as a "must-listen," a sobriquet he found both delightful and perplexing—Maisie asked him about Nestlé. He was in the League of Nations, after all, and they were based in Switzerland.

"Nestlé?" Mr. Bartlett echoed. "Big, obviously. I've never been. They're on the other side of Lake Geneva, you know. I will say I stock up on Cadbury chocolate when I'm here. But don't you let on, now." He wagged a finger and winked. It was hard not to feel like a ten-year-old with him, especially when asking questions.

"Would Nestlé have anything to do with Germany, do you think?"

"I'm sure they sell their foods wherever anyone's willing to pay for them," he said in surprise, not expecting basic capitalism to be beyond her grasp.

"No, that's not what I meant. You see, Miss Matheson had a pamphlet, from a German political party—"

"Oh, that. Yes, she wanted me to sound out the German League ambassador about those Nazi chaps ages ago. Mussolini-style Fascists, I told her, the usual lunatic fringe. We can't get hetted up about every crank with access to a typewriter and a mimeograph machine. We'd never get anything done."

"But some of those men, a lot of them, they were the ones who tried to commit that coup, in 1923," Maisie persisted. *Thank you, British Library.*

"There are always going to be crackpot parties, even here," Bartlett snorted. "Especially here, to be frank. But that's what democracy's all about, and rule of law sorts them out as well. The little Hitler fellow and his friends went to prison, and Germany's in the League, so no need to start picking away at them."

He absently reached for his cigarettes and Maisie snatched them from his hand, just saving him from Billy's flying tackle. Smoking was death to a clean studio.

On the tram ride home, Maisie wrote Bartlett's comments on

one page of her notebook. Then she doodled a chocolate bar. On the facing page she wrote: "There's no point in getting aerated over short hair anymore. Women love its style and practicality and the look is here to stay." She stared at the words for several moments. Then she looked back at all the paragraphs that preceded them. Then she shrieked, "That's it!" creating airspace between several passengers and their upholstered seats.

"So long as you're sure, dear," her solicitous neighbor murmured, patting her hand.

Now I just have to submit it.

NINE

Bert rolled his eyes up to her from the carefully typed pages. "Bit of a screed, isn't it?"

"I hope not," Maisie demurred, trying to keep the exasperation out of her voice. "It's just a supplement for our Talk this week. I thought, perhaps, at least for the women's stories, something written by a woman would be . . . useful."

"No, we can't have girls writing articles. That would be—"

"There aren't any bylines!" Maisie burst out.

"What does that have to do with it?" Bert asked, blinking in surprise.

"Well, only that, if it's good enough, no one should care who wrote it."

Bert gaped at her, whether overcome by her logic or struck dumb by her ignorance, she didn't dare guess.

"I only thought you might consider it," she amended, softening her tone. "Of course I didn't expect you'd necessarily take my first submission."

"I am awash in relief," Bert drawled. "Now, then, I suppose if you were capable of writing to our standards, a small interview, something nice and light, with one of the lady broadcasters, might be something I could consider. One of the prettier actresses, so we can do more photos. Oh, and mind the suffragette-y tone. Readers don't like it."

"But there are some women voting now. Why—"

"This is why I don't allow girl writers. Never take direction, always these questions, awfully tiresome. Are these the listings?" he asked, pointing to the sheets in her hand, his finger under the heading "LISTINGS."

"They are indeed, Bert," she told him. "And thank you," she added, because it was expected. In fact, she wanted to cry, but though they were tears of anger, not misery, he wouldn't know the difference and he was another man who wasn't getting her tears.

I'll just have to try again.

Her words, that was what she wanted. An interview didn't seem the same at all. *But why should I get* anything*, even in the* Radio Times? *I'm not a writer. Except maybe . . .*

She put aside the vacillations and took out her pencil for Hilda and Reith's weekly meeting. Writing shorthand wasn't what she meant at all, but at least she was stellar at it.

"I suppose you'll be pleased to know the governors have reviewed your proposal and decided to lift the ban on controversial broadcasting," Reith informed her, with a sigh sharp enough to peel paint from the ceiling.

"Glorious news!" Hilda bellowed, thumping Reith's desk so hard, his decorative mallard swam the length of the ink blotter.

"Yes, well, let's remember our decorum," Reith advised, sliding the duck back into position.

"It's a great triumph, Mr. Reith," she crowed. "Onwards and upwards."

"Some might say you have been thwarting the ban all along," he pointed out.

"Oh, not thwarting," Hilda assured him. "More like nudging the bounds."

Reith's scowl smiled, but Maisie could see it was perfunctory. In fact, it sometimes seemed to her that he was starting to dislike Hilda. But Maisie was sure she was wrong. More than two million households had found ten shillings for the BBC license fee to bring radio into their homes, with any number of listener letters expressing their pleasure in the Talks, and the newspapers regularly extolled Hilda's taste and original thinking.

Hilda, along with Arthur Burrows, the premier presenter, was becoming synonymous with the BBC. It was possible, Maisie conceded, that Reith's absence from the parade of praise was the problem, but he could hardly fault Hilda for that. Besides, he wasn't without recognition—he had been awarded the Knight Bachelor and was now "Sir John Reith." With the grace he decided came of being ennobled, he insisted the staff continue to address him as "Mr. Reith."

"Yes, well, you no longer have to nudge," Reith acceded. "But not *every* broadcast has to be challenging."

Maisie wasn't sure what Reith meant by "challenging," but her own opinion, born of Hilda's, was that a Talk should always have something new to say, in some new way.

Onwards and upwards, and all that.

It was a miserable cold spring in 1928, and the Talks Department was huddled on the floor again, everyone vying for a place nearest the fire. In the six months Maisie had been the proper Talks secretary, she felt her greatest skill was securing a prime spot with the most frequency.

"At this rate, we'll all have chilblains in June," Fielden muttered. He never cared that no one responded.

"We're going to expand the poetry and book discussions," Hilda announced, reading from her green diary. "Virginia Woolf is coming in for a few readings, and Rebecca West, but it looks as though Vita Sackville-West will be our permanent fiction reviewer."

"With so many bluestockings, we could compete with Selfridges' hosiery department," Collins hissed. Only Fielden heard him, and gave him a withering glare. He allowed no one to impugn Our Lady.

"We're fixed very nicely with political and household Talks, and Talks on the arts and sciences. But I think we could do with more in the way of general interest. And perhaps the occasional foray into light absurdity. Any thoughts?"

It started to rain, fat drops tapping at the windows. Maisie snapped a biscuit in half, liking the swishy crunch sound. She thought of something Hilda had written in her notes on broadcasting, that it was "a capturing of sounds and voices all over the world to which hitherto we have been deaf. It is a means of enlarging the frontiers of human interest and consciousness, of widening personal experience, of shrinking the earth's surface." Such a lovely way to describe this curious creature they were continually inventing. The stranger inviting itself into a silent home, asking to become a friend.

"Miss Matheson, what about a Talk on memorable sounds?" Maisie burst out, watching the drops splatter against the glass. "Sounds that mean something to people, something about their personal experience? A scythe in the harvest, or typewriter keys?"

"She would say typing," Collins again, more sotto, still voce.

"Marvelous," Hilda congratulated her. "We could thrill the Sound men for days. Of course, what would be really delightful would be to take a microphone up and down the country, asking people about sounds and perhaps recording those sounds in real time. Wouldn't that be evocative?"

Hilda sighed, momentarily despondent at radio's limits. There were valiant attempts at broadcasting outside the studio—the sports announcers were very keen on it—but it was a deeply cumbersome affair that thrilled and vexed the engineers equally and whose results were not quite on the cusp of satisfactory.

How do you choose just one gorgeous sound? Children laughing. Bees in a summer garden. The rattle of beads on a dancer's dress. A kiss.

"Why are you blushing?" Fielden asked her, not even trying to be sotto.

"I have tuberculosis," Maisie confided. Everyone laughed. Another nail in Invisible Girl's coffin. And she'd had another Talk idea accepted. She hummed as she headed to the mimeograph room, her cheerfulness compensating for lack of tune, when Cyril loped into place beside her.

"Hallo, New York. How are you?"

Cyril. She felt a rush of nostalgia for all the days he hadn't entered her thoughts. He had the nerve to still be deliriously good-looking, hair flopping over his temples, freckles, dark blue eyes. That high-voltage smile, so contagious as to almost make her smile back. She clenched her jaw.

"I'm doing very well, Mr. Underwood. How are you?" she asked, affecting what she hoped was a professional tone awash in detachment, sparing him only one curt nod as she continued to stride down the corridor.

He kept pace with her. "Never a dull moment—more's the pity. A chap could sit down then. The DG expects a great deal from Schools, you know. Minds of the youth, and all that." He gave a vague gesture to indicate all those minds.

"Yes, indeed. And how are you liking Mr. Siepmann as a superior? Awfully clever, isn't he?" she asked, hoping the question would annoy him. She was rewarded with a frown.

"Well . . . yes, actually. Likes details. We call him the devil in the details," he confided, eyes twinkling, inviting a laugh.

"Do you?" She nodded gravely. "I'm sure he'd appreciate that." Another prize: the flash of alarm turning him pale, his freckles poppy seeds in a milk pudding.

"You, er, you wouldn't mention that, would you? I was only joking."

"Of course you were," she agreed in a chirp. "I know better than to assume you're in earnest. Ah, here's my stop. Cheerio!" She bid him goodbye with a flick of her pinkie, swung into the mimeograph room, and set up stencils at record speed. Her ears were getting very good at picking up sounds, and she sensed him hesitate, swaying at the door, before he went on to wherever he was going.

"Honestly, I was happy never to talk to him again. What the heck was that for? 'Hallo, New York,' indeed, that beastly, blasted blackguard—"

"And we're still just in the 'Bs,'" Phyllida said. "You've certainly learned to talk like a Briton." She smiled and sipped tea from a flask. It wasn't really warm enough to eat outside, but it was the first bright day they'd had in weeks and they wanted the feel of sun and air, the tease of summer and country, even though the wind down the Embankment still had a pinprick chill that coaxed tears from their eyes and the mixed odors off the Thames were decidedly urban. They felt hardy and outlandish, the best of what flappers should be, though neither of them could afford to properly look the part.

"I told him I forgave him, or just as well," Maisie said, the injustice still stinging as much as the air. "It was more than a year ago, and *he's* the one who said it was trivial!"

"Maybe that wasn't so true?"

Maisie hooted with laughter and only stopped when she had to clamp her mouth over the bottom of her chicken pie to stop it oozing gravy.

"I know what the lads think of me," she said, grinning at the silliness of it.

"Thoughts can change." Phyllida shrugged, refusing for once to grin back. "You haven't run and hid, you're doing good work in Talks, and you're looking well."

Maisie hooted again, but Phyllida was not to be deterred.

"It's true! You're less scrawny now, and you've got nice color in your cheeks." She leaned closer to examine Maisie. "You've even got cheeks! And you don't look so frightened anymore. You look more . . . Well, you're still hungry," she said, breaking out the grin. "Have a banana."

Maisie finished her pie and took the banana. She knew she'd filled out and she liked it. A boyish look was fashionable, perhaps, but no one wanted to look unhealthy. Her new dress—still plain wool, but better quality—didn't hang like a rag on the line. Instead, it skimmed what was belatedly but unquestionably turning into a figure. The dress was a nice pale green. "Garland Green," the shopgirl had informed her in a proud, breathy swoon, as though she'd invented it. "And the trim is Briar Rose." Maisie still just called it pink.

"Hallo. Would you like company?" The women looked up, Maisie's cheeks bulging with banana, to see two young men walking their bicycles, grinning at them. Or anyway, at Phyllida.

"D'ye nae see we have each other's company?" Phyllida asked.

"Ah, go on," the bolder one persisted. "How's about we give you a lift on the bikes, hm? You'd make a fine figurehead," he complimented Phyllida.

"When I feel like having my bones broken, you'll be the first one I call," she promised.

"And we have to get back to work," Maisie added. "Some of us work, you know."

"Oh Lord," the other man groaned. "Northerners, Americans, working girls. A trifecta of misery. Come on," he urged, pedaling off. The bold one gave Phyllida another longing glance, but followed his friend.

"Which trait do you think was our gravest offense?" Maisie asked, though she assumed the men had only included her by way of convenience.

"Working, no contest," Phyllida said.

"I suppose it's not such an awful thing, fellows liking you," Maisie ventured, handing Phyllida a cake.

"Pah. They like that I've got blond curls, long legs, and an enormous chest," Phyllida scoffed.

She was very lovely. Tall and plumper than was fashionable, her dairy-farm roots evident even in her urbanity. The long legs were wonderfully sculpted, so it looked like she still hiked the hills after the cows every day, though she hadn't since she was seven. And despite her strident efforts, the loose fashions and flattening corsets failed to conceal her ample bosom.

"I thought I'd find a man to marry me in Savoy Hill," Maisie said. She concentrated on picking a currant out of her cake, glad her cheeks were already pink from the cold.

"Lots of lasses come in thinking that," Phyllida consoled her. "And I daresay it happens."

"What sort of man would you like to marry?"

"O-ho, no, thank you. No, I had quite enough being under the thumb of my father. I won't be subjected to any other man and that's that. One way or another I'm going to end up in Parliament. Is that the church bell?"

They braced themselves against the wind for the short walk up Savoy Place.

"Do you think there are Bolshevist spies in Britain?" Maisie shouted, her words buffeted on the wind. It was the perfect weather for asking such questions—you were lucky if the person right next to you could hear.

"If there are, they must feel right at home. Siberia's got to be warmer than this."

"But really, do you think so?" Maisie persisted.

"Communists believe in equality for women, so they aren't all bad, I'd say."

"If they believe in a single-party state, though, then no one would be allowed to vote."

"Mad way to cut down on paperwork, isn't it? And that's exactly why it's silly to be afraid of communism gaining a hold here. Even the illiterate know we British love paperwork."

They'd been gone less than an hour, and each returned to in-trays mountainous with paper, rather proving Phyllida's point.

Having new energy as well as new cheeks, Maisie felt she was becoming the avatar of the efficiency Hilda demanded for Talks. She read and sorted correspondence as though she'd taken a speed-reading course and could not remember the last time she missed a key when typing. She liked it all, but the constant bustle meant there was scant time for trying new things beyond the typewriter. There was her vague interest in Hilda's German propaganda, but Maisie wanted to do more within the world of Talks.

Hilda liked initiative in her staff, so Maisie felt bold enough a few days later, when Hilda was signing letters, to ask, "Could I be the one to start putting together notes and things for the Talk on memorable sounds, please, Miss Matheson? Or might I help Mr. Collins?"

"Hmm? Sorry?" Hilda looked up at her from a letter to Alexander Fleming.

"The idea, from the meeting, on sounds?"

Hilda's expression remained blank. Maisie blushed. "My idea. You said it was good, something we could . . ." She trailed off, feeling silly. Feeling worse than that, because Hilda was frowning.

"There are any number of good ideas, but as you very well know, only a few of them ever become Talks."

"But you said—"

"That it was a nice idea. It was. It is. And I always hope to encourage all of you, and see you all continuously exerting yourselves. But I am the only one who decides what will be broadcast, and once that decision is made, I delegate to the appropriate staff, as I hope you've noticed."

"Yes, Miss Matheson." Maisie wished Hilda would snap, like Miss Shields. Her calm, casual manner made Maisie feel ten times smaller.

"Ambition is a commendable thing," Hilda said, her eyes at last regaining some of their usual warmth. "And I've known from the start that you have a terrific capacity. It's good to want things, to work for them, and ask for them. Just don't expect to always get them."

"I didn't—"

But Hilda finished signing the letters and gave them back to Maisie for sealing. Maisie returned to her desk. Nice as it was to have terrific capacity, she could not stop blushing at the embarrassing realization that she had, indeed, expected to get what she asked for, just because she had the courage to ask.

The reprimand and its reason were forgotten the following day, when at midmorning Hilda asked Maisie to go down to reception and wait for Lady Nicholson.

Lady Nicholson. That was Vita Sackville-West.

Maisie glanced at the carriage clock. Lady Nicholson wasn't due for nearly half an hour.

"I know. I'm sorry," Hilda said. "But I've got to meet with the fellow from the Foreign Office, and I may not extricate myself in time. I trust you to keep her in good hands, should it be necessary. And you can read till she arrives."

Maisie grabbed a pad and pencil instead. Vernon Bartlett had just broadcast about Canada's work in the League, and she couldn't help thinking about America and its refusal to join. Which embarrassed her, despite telling herself she had no part of it. *But I lived in New York most of my childhood. It's part of me, isn't it?*

She smoothed the page. "Maybe the Congress should poll the theater community about American interest in Europe," she wrote. All the actors she'd known were eager to ply their trade in London, Paris, Berlin. And every third girl in New York sighed over foreign accents, imagining the romance of the French, the thrill of the Italians, the marvelous marriageability of the British. In the elite classes, many daughters were sent to Swiss finishing schools, many sons to Oxford or Cambridge. Americans, so fierce in their republicanism, their non-monarchy, yearned to meet aristocrats and monarchs, touch a fairy-tale past while scoffing at it. Wouldn't membership in the League of Nations allow a bit of that, while also getting to exert influence and show off a more perfect union to the world? And yet they stayed resolutely at home.

She crossed it all out. *I don't know what I'm doing. Why should I?* She doodled boxes and coils and radio waves. Then she scribbled:

"Ask the American embassy for someone to do a Talk about their not being in the League."

Would that be controversial? Miss Matheson would like that. Let's see. They'd have to address the war, de Tocqueville's idea of exceptionalism, or whatever it was, and maybe . . . She'd covered three pages when Rusty tugged on her elbow—she yelped and the pencil tip snapped off.

"Sorry, miss. I spoke to you lots, but you didn't hear me. It's the lady, miss. Her car's just coming. A jolly nice Daimler it is, too."

"Thanks, Rusty. Would you mind running these back to my desk?" She handed him the pad and pencil. *Awk! My fingers! I'm bleeding graphite!* She checked to make sure no one was looking, spat on her fingers, yanked her handkerchief from her sleeve, and attempted to wipe off the stains. Then she smoothed her skirt and pushed back her shoulders. Vita Sackville-West, a born aristocrat, might know Maisie was a commoner, but she was not going to be seen as common.

Maisie opened the door to prevent the lady's having to do so and immediately thought she was hallucinating, envisioning the great as truly overpowering. Then she realized Vita was over six feet tall and ramrod straight, making her even more imposing. She wasn't, perhaps, very beautiful, but she exuded something Maisie couldn't identify that gave her a peculiar attraction. It was hard not to stare at her. She glanced down her long nose and smiled at Maisie.

"Well, good afternoon. Are you my guide?"

"I am, yes, Lady Nicholson," Maisie answered, fighting the urge to curtsy. Vita's silky warmth was even more intimidating than Lady Astor's cheerful condescension.

"Please, no titles here. I'm in my capacity as a working writer. 'Miss Sackville-West' will do, thank you."

"Oh. I . . . Yes, of course. Well, please follow me, Miss Sackville-West," Maisie beckoned. She would never dream of subjecting Vita to the stairs, so the lift was summoned, and Bill cheerfully took them up. The noise of the lift tended to dissuade conversation, allowing Maisie to study Vita, who gazed straight ahead, utterly at ease. Her simple elegance was arresting. She was fashionable, of course—not like Beanie, who as a young unmarried socialite was expected to be ahead of the trends—but rather as a respectable, admired woman whom every tailor wanted to dress. Hilda's jackets and skirts were tailored, too, but there were tailors and tailors, and Maisie could see that Vita's was the kind that helped set the aristocracy apart.

Hilda met them at the lift.

"Miss Matheson!" Vita boomed before Hilda could speak, pumping Hilda's hand as though she expected to yield water. "Such a pleasure to see you again. I can't begin to express my excitement for this venture. I am deeply gratified to be asked to participate."

"We're very honored to have you broadcast, Lady Nicholson," Hilda said.

"'Vita,' please. Let us begin by being informal. Your reputation well precedes you, and I know I am going to be run absolutely ragged with rehearsal, so we may as well be the friends we're so evidently meant to be."

"Then you must call me Hilda."

"Good! Now, I'm absolutely longing to see the studio and get to work."

Maisie tagged behind, watching them. Hilda was always delighted to greet a speaker, but there was something different in her reception of Vita. She was radiating warmth and excitement, more than usual, but that wasn't quite it.

She almost seems nervous.

Hilda was never nervous. So it had to be something else.

The rehearsal was hardly needed. Vita was a born speaker. She had of course been given elocution lessons, but plenty of actresses weren't as readily engaging as she was. She simply understood at once what it was to give a compelling broadcast and employed her warm, elegant tones to perfection. She was someone who had expected to be listened to her whole life, and so spoke with total ease, knowing attention would be paid. And of course it would. No one who heard her would turn away from the broadcast. Hilda was tap-dancing on the ceiling again.

Rather than the usual bullying—or teaching, as Maisie preferred to call it—Hilda focused on making Vita as comfortable as possible. Which seemed unnecessary. The woman could be comfortable on an ice floe. But Hilda fussed to be sure her script was laid out so the pages would move with even more seamlessness than usual—she seemed to feel Vita should not have to handle her script herself. The great lady felt otherwise, and laid a steadying hand over Hilda's, holding it there while she assured her that such ministrations weren't needed.

"You are very kind, Hilda, but truly, these reviews are my honor."

"I think, Vita, we shall have quite a set-to deciding who is doing whom the greater honor."

"I suspect you might be the loser there. I'm quite a bit bigger than you."

"Ah, but I'm small and scrappy."

Vita's throaty laugh would have made the sound effects men swoon.

"I knew we should be great friends." Vita grinned at Hilda. "Miss Woolf said you were quite the tyrant, perhaps not realizing I appreciate a bit of tyranny. Well, I'm glad you think my efforts are up to scratch. I do hope you're not withholding any criticism due to some ceremony or other."

"Not a bit of it. Miss Musgrave can tell you there's little I despise more than a terrible broadcast. I won't have it, not on my watch. And I certainly won't have it from my friends, for my sake or theirs."

"Exactly as I would have thought of you. If I don't disgrace the BBC after my broadcast, you must come to dine. Will you?"

"You shan't disgrace us, so we may consider it a date."

"Jolly good!"

When Maisie stood to show Vita out, Hilda waved her aside.

"I'll escort our reviewer, Miss Musgrave, thank you."

Hilda often walked the more important broadcasters, or the ones she really liked, back to the main door. Which meant nearly all of them.

But she's never done so blushing.

"How did the great and powerful Vita Sackville-West get on?"

Fielden asked gloomily when Maisie returned to the Talks Department.

"She was superb," she raved. "People will just *have* to read whatever she recommends."

"Aristocrats. They still want to be dictators." Fielden sighed, shaking his head.

"I didn't mean it like that," Maisie snapped.

"I did," he said, with a shrug. "Did Our Lady bully her a good deal?" he asked in a more hopeful tone.

"Not a bit," Maisie said, rolling in a sheet of fresh letterhead and typing with extra force to drown him out. It was always nice to disappoint Fielden, and if he thought she was the type to tell that sort of story, he didn't know her at all.

Which was also nice.

"I don't suppose the *Radio Times* would like a little story on Vita Sackville-West's upcoming broadcast?" Maisie asked Bert when she dropped off listings.

"I don't suppose we would, no," Bert said, not bothering to stifle a yawn.

So she took her overflowing energy to the library, the place it had always found relief.

Neither the stack of books on Germany nor the backlog of newspapers distracted her from chewing on her pencil and staring at the ceiling. A passing librarian glanced at her.

"You've been in the exact same position over an hour," she whispered. "Are you all right?"

"How might someone in England get a piece of German propaganda not meant even for the general public in Germany to see?" Maisie asked, though she hadn't realized that was the question that had been plaguing her.

The librarian's black eyes sparkled with pleasure.

"Ooh, that's a tricky one! I would think he must be German himself, with close ties to whoever generated the work," she began. "He might be serving in an advisory capacity. Or he got it via an underground network, if he is engaged in some form of espionage activity."

"You mean a German spy? Here?" Maisie's stomach turned over. The unthinkable thought, the fly that had buzzed in her brain and eluded smacking. Hilda, so dedicated to informing the British, the world, about everything—it couldn't be a lie, could it?

"Not necessarily," the librarian saved her. "I daresay German spies exist, silly idiots, and Russians, too, but your man might well be in MI5 or MI6."

The intelligence agencies. Maisie had read about them. Spies, yes. But for Britain.

"How would someone know if a person was in one of those, though?"

"I should hope they wouldn't!" The librarian laughed at the idea—a totally silent laugh, mostly in the eyes. "A secret agent is hardly secret if people know who he is."

"Could she . . . he . . . He would have to have another job, wouldn't he? So no one would guess?"

"A man employed by MI5 might, perhaps, as that's the domestic agency. Must keep up appearances at home," the librarian agreed. "We have some books if you'd like—"

"What sort of person works for MI5?" Maisie interrupted eagerly. "She, er, he couldn't be too ordinary, could he?"

"I really couldn't say. All sorts, most likely. But a good agent would have to be enormously clever, know a great deal about the world, probably speak a few languages—"

"And care about the truth," Maisie murmured.

"As much of it as he's allowed to disseminate," the librarian warned. "Which I imagine is not a great deal."

But Maisie wasn't listening. She knew what she had meant. She knew, too, that if Hilda got that propaganda via MI5, it must have even greater implications than Maisie had thought.

And she's trusting me *to be a small part of this.*

The ambition of writing for the *Radio Times* was, Maisie now decided, silly and embarrassing. She had wanted to prove to herself that there was something she could do without Hilda's hand at her back, but why not quietly help answer the question of what giant companies like Siemens and Nestlé were up to? Why should they be invested in Germany's "road to resurgence" as led by a fringe would-be political party?

Ridiculous thing, the Radio Times. *Who cares if all the writing in it is virtually illiterate? Who cares if—*

"Heigh-ho, no trampling of the broadcasters!" Beanie's cry brought Maisie back to the corridor, and the mortifying discovery that she'd nearly trod on an actress. A sleek, beautiful actress with chocolate-brown eyes and skin. Wisteria Mitterand, from Lady Astor's salon.

Hilda had brought the idea of a Talk by Miss Mitterand to Reith, who had duly—and very fluently—shot it straight down. But given the hint that Miss Mitterand would be a fine performer, Beanie had sought her out. And lo, here she was.

"Miss Mitterand!" Maisie grinned, shaking her hand. "How lovely to see you again."

"Goodness, Miss Musgrave," she said, smiling. "I hardly recognize you. In the best way. You're absolutely blooming."

"Do you know," Beanie broke in, studying Maisie, "it's true. You're no Gainsborough, but you're not as Picasso as you were. All those harsh lines," she added helpfully. "Isn't that extraordinary?"

"It is," Maisie answered, which pleased Beanie. Maisie turned back to Miss Mitterand. "I wish I could come see you broadcast, but—"

"Maisie is quite the slave to the Talks Department," Beanie blithely informed her, with no thought for what that word might mean beyond her own idiom. Miss Mitterand's expression didn't vary by so much as a twitch, and Maisie thought again how excellent it would be to have her give a Talk. "But we must dash. Come along, come along."

"Glad to see you, Miss Musgrave," Miss Mitterand said, meaning it.

Maisie watched her go, wondering if her elegance was natural, like Beanie's, or if she had learned it from observation, like Georgina.

"What did her hand feel like?" Billy moved from his customary stance of hugging the wall when he spotted Maisie and into her circle of vision, curiosity overcoming his discomfiture.

"I beg your pardon?" Maisie wondered if Billy had developed a fixation about hands, after having injured his own.

"It's just, I've heard that Negresses' skin feels different, as well as being black, and I was wondering. Oh, but she was wearing gloves." He answered his question in crushing disappointment.

Mr. Eckersley may expect all his engineers to be clever, but that doesn't stop them being appallingly ignorant.

An hour later, Maisie was in the midst of a telegram flurry with John Maynard Keynes, whom they wanted for a series and whose schedule was making even a single broadcast impossible to set up. The economist was more popular than Charlie Chaplin. It was infuriating, both because she wanted to ask him about Germany and because she had to meet the man who had said: "Words ought to be a little wild, for they are the assault of thoughts on the unthinking."

"We should emblazon that around the office, shouldn't we?" Hilda said.

"He's so clever and seems charming. Why do you suppose he's not married?" Maisie asked, risking presumption for curiosity.

Fielden, overhearing, doubled over laughing. Hilda looked a little amused herself.

"Possibly he's married to his work. Anyway, here's luck. Alexander Fleming's agreed to a series of interviews. That will be fun, won't it?" Hilda said. "Bit different."

Interviews. Maisie's fingers froze on the typewriter keys. A nice little interview, with one of the prettier ladies.

She bolted from the office and ran at top speed all the way down to reception. Miss Mitterand was just shaking Beanie's hand.

"Miss Mitterand!" Maisie gasped. "Are you free for a drink later?"

There it was, in the next issue. Shiny and bold and bright. And a lesson in one of the pitfalls of ambition: Even getting something you wanted might not be satisfactory.

"Bert certainly likes to edit. It's half the original length, and I think only every third word might still be hers." Maisie sighed.

"Quite an achievement for a first effort," Hilda told her firmly. "But you obviously have a touch, Miss Musgrave. You ought to try again. And then again."

"And more after that," Maisie agreed, returning to her desk with a kinetically imperfect but emotionally exuberant pirouette.

TEN

"You ought to let me buy you a drink tonight. Say you can," Lola begged.

"I've got to work late," Maisie said between bites of toast. "We're so busy."

"But it's your birthday!"

"It's nothing to fuss about," Maisie muttered. If Georgina had her way, her daughter wouldn't even know her birthdate. As it was, May first always rendered Georgina defensive, embarrassed at having any child at all, but particularly Maisie, whose insistence on growing was beyond vexing. But once, in one of her occasional fits of communicativeness, she told Maisie her name derived from her birthdate, a choice that seemed fraught with romanticism and so must have come from her father.

Her father. In a blue cardboard box under her bed was the long-awaited letter from the General Register Office, a terse response to her query about Edwin Musgrave's birth and life, informing her that if she could provide a place, or at least an area, or an exact year of said birth, they might be able to assist. She couldn't, so they couldn't.

"You work too much," Lola scolded. "I never see you anymore,

and now I'm going on this European tour and won't see you at all
for who knows how long!"

Even though Maisie knew that Lola wouldn't give her another
thought from the moment she stepped on the boat at Folkestone, her
throat tightened. Lola was always so kind to her, and while it was
the benevolence of the worldly who adored the dark opposite, it was
still kindness, and genuinely meant.

"I'm sorry," Maisie said. "Let's do meet up after your show. A
drink would be swell. And we're toasting your soon-to-be-diva status in Europe, too!"

Lola struck a dramatic pose. "What do you think? Constance
Worth? A prettier Gracie Fields, maybe?"

"Your own unique self, wherever you are," Maisie insisted.

Lola smiled broadly. "Here. Happy birthday." She handed Maisie
what looked like a folded handkerchief and proved, on unwrapping,
to contain a white silk rose on a slide, for her hair.

"Oh, Lola! It's perfect. Thank you!" She set it in place before the
hall mirror, blinking hard and regretting the decision to apply her
new mascara. Lola reached over and adjusted the rose. It looked better. Maisie blinked at her reflection. Brighter eyes blinked back from
a rounder face. She hadn't known her hair and skin could shine. Even
her nose and chin seemed interesting, as opposed to just oversized.
She was never going to be the sort who was called "pretty," but that
didn't matter. Even she could admit that she now had a quality which
might be called "striking."

"I thought that would look well." Lola nodded approvingly. "See
you tonight!"

Hilda was at a breakfast with Lady Astor and "a few other political
women; I wanted to bring you, but they'd already booked the table to
bursting point." A year ago, the prospect of joining would have chilled
Maisie to the bone. Now she was disappointed not to be there.

"Morning, Miss Musgrave," Alfred trilled, wheeling in the correspondence as Maisie hung her hat and coat on the rack. "Good
Lord, is that all for you?" He stared at the gargantuan iced cake on

her desk, which was doing battle for space—and dimension—with the typewriter.

"Er, I think Miss Matheson might have left it for me," Maisie said. She barely managed to snatch the fork and napkin lying in the in-tray before Alfred tossed in the morning's first haul. It was a beautiful cake. That mascara was definitely a bad idea.

"If it's not awfully impertinent for me to say so, miss, you look rather well today," Alfred complimented her. "Hardly recognize you from when you started."

"Gosh. Thank you, Alfred," she replied, touched.

She was about to offer him some cake when he continued. "Never imagined you'd last, working in the DG's office and all. You're more suited here." He nodded and wheeled away, whistling the tune of a song Maisie had heard emanating from some of her local pubs—the one about a late-blooming girl and where she bloomed. Maisie dug into the cake (butter and vanilla cream sponge with lemon icing) as she worked through the correspondence.

The morning took a decidedly less pleasant turn when Fielden, feeling his power with Hilda away, and finding no page immediately at hand, ordered Maisie to take an interoffice memo to Miss Somerville in Schools. It was a place she tried to avoid, as it contained Cyril—but she had no choice. She strongly suspected Fielden had arranged this on purpose.

"Ah, thank you, Miss Musgrave," Miss Somerville said. "Bit beneath your position, doing the deliveries, isn't it? Awfully good of you, though," she amended, so as to be clear no offense was meant.

"It's nothing, Miss Somerville," Maisie said. She hadn't realized the woman knew her name. She ducked out, pleased to have evaded Cyril, and ran headlong into Charles Siepmann.

"Oh, you!" he said, adjusting his glasses to study her more intently. "Thither and yon! You're quite the industrious little thing, aren't you?"

She longed to observe that she wasn't so little, but Siepmann was quite senior in Schools, deeply admired by Reith, and described by the rest of Savoy Hill as an eel, "only more slippery."

He smiled. Damn, he could look awfully attractive. *Unpleasant people should look unpleasant.*

"Just doing my job, sir."

"Yes, and making an effort to look pretty, too, which is also your job. Bright flowers, that's what you girls are, and don't think we gents don't appreciate it."

Oh, lucky us.

"I'm only concerned with doing well for the Talks Department, sir," she told him, with as much asperity as she dared.

"Just Talks? Not the whole BBC?" He smiled again, but there was a hiss, a whetstone preparing for the knife.

"I—well, of course the whole BBC," she stammered, hoping he didn't see her gulp. His eyes were dancing. Was he teasing her or testing her loyalties? She remembered how much Reith liked him and was suddenly cold. "I'm the Talks secretary, though, so of course I want to do well there," she said, hoping to paper over any mess. "Doing well by one is doing well by all, isn't it?"

"Ah, that's nicely said, dear," he complimented her. A host of not-nice comments paraded through her brain as she stalked back to her typewriter. Only Hilda's pointed cough roused her from her assault upon the poor Underwood.

"Oh, excuse me, Miss Matheson. I didn't realize you'd be back."

"It was a very fine breakfast. And I see you enjoyed yours as well." She indicated the empty cake plate.

"It was delicious, thank you," Maisie said, wishing there was one last bite.

"You're most welcome. Many happy returns. Twenty-five is a pivotal time. Now, then, Miss Fenwick has just popped 'round to say they've been inundated and will have to take lunch much nearer the tea break, but she hopes I will allow you a longer break this afternoon, and I think that can be arranged."

"Thank you. I can take a short lunch."

"Well, to do that you'll have to keep track of the time," Hilda warned. Then she smiled. "This ought to help," she said, handing Maisie a cardboard box.

Perplexed, Maisie opened it to find a lilac-colored hard case. And inside that was a little enameled watch with a lilac face. It was already set to the right time. Maisie stared down at it, as though it were a face that could gaze back. She'd never received a proper birthday present in her life, and now she had gotten two . . .

"Oh! Miss Matheson!" The mascara was inching down her cheeks.

"I said twenty-five was a pivotal *time*, didn't I?" Hilda smiled. "And this will save you always having to check the clock. What did I tell you your first day? Efficiency. We run on efficiency. Now put it on and remember to wind it every night. It should run for years, I hope. Have you got that letter for Mr. Wells?"

Hilda was continuing to work her charms on H. G. Wells, who was blunt in his opinion that broadcasting was far sillier than anything he could ever write. Hilda's latest letter to him was a masterstroke, telling him that while of course she respected his position, he was robbing Britain of a special experience. She signed it in her firm hand, then asked for the morning's correspondence, simultaneously demanding Maisie take dictation on her observations from the breakfast meeting, because it was possible most of what had been said could be worked up into some very fine Talks. The chaotic normalness restored Maisie's face to some order.

It was, finally, a bright day, with the sky a pagan celebration blue and the flowers in the potted plants hanging from lamps along Savoy Street giving full vent to their bliss. Maisie, armed with a steno pad and a notebook full of Hilda's thoughts on broadcasting, headed to the Tup, warm thoughts of Mrs. Holmby's lamb chops putting a skip in her step, but the glory of the day and the majesty of her new watch turned her to the sandwich bar on the Strand. Laden with sandwiches, chocolate from Miss Cryer's, and, despite the promise of a long tea, two cakes, she strolled down to the Embankment.

She rolled a pencil through her fingers, staring at the Thames as it bubbled along. *I wonder how far it goes? I'd love to travel the whole length of it someday. And then out through the estuary and on and on.*

"I say, would you mind awfully if I shared the bench? Rotten impertinent of me, but this is the only one I've passed for the last half mile that's not overflowing with squawking children and snapping nannies. Gosh, doesn't 'Squawking Children and Snapping Nannies' sound like a music-hall ditty? I might be in the wrong business."

Maisie looked up at the tall young man hovering by the bench. His derby was set well back on his head, showing off waving brown hair, slicked back enough to be neat, but not so much as to be dandified. Chocolate-brown eyes, soft and puppyish, with a cheery snap around the edges. Crinkles under his eyes that went deep as he smiled. She felt as if someone had lightly brushed the back of her neck—a tickle she felt all the way to her toes.

"Well, it's a public bench, so I really can't lay claim to the whole of it."

"I can't know. You might have given money for it," he pointed out.

"Wouldn't that be a sight, miles of us all on our own benches? That takes entitlement a bit far."

"It could sound like free enterprise," he ventured.

"It doesn't sound like free anything," she told him with finality.

"Wise words," he said, sitting down and unwrapping a sandwich. Maisie sneaked one last glance at him and turned back to her own food.

"I must say," her uninvited companion piped up, "I'm a bit surprised to see a young girl out on her own like this."

She bristled. "You think I should have a chaperone?"

"Nothing so bourgeois as that," he said, chuckling. "I only meant that you modern girls usually go 'round in pairs, or a gag—er, group."

"You were about to say 'gaggle,' weren't you?" She was surprised by her own sharpness. It was so easy to talk to someone you weren't sure you wanted around, tickle or no. He was handsome, and perhaps clever, but she knew now that handsome young men were lethal.

He threw back his head and laughed, just like Hilda.

"Caught but corrected. And contrite."

"I like eating alone," she told him. She didn't want it to sound like a hint, but her hackles were rising. She refused to be seen as easy prey.

"Ah, but you're not alone. You've got a notebook. Do you write?"

She closed the book, protective of Hilda's privacy.

"A little."

"For business or pleasure?"

"Isn't most writing always both?"

He laughed again.

"You're a funny thing," he told her. "I'm a writer as well, journalism, some essays—well, they bleed together."

"Oh!" Interest flowered. "Do you write for one of the Fleet Street papers?"

"No. Far too bourgeois for me. I write for *Pinpoint*. Do you know it?"

"I don't, I'm afraid." Reams of periodicals coursed into Savoy Hill daily, buffeted either by staff who thought they might be of worth, or by Hilda's insistence that they all be familiar with more than just the principal papers. ("It's always useful to hear as many voices as possible. Even those somewhat lacking in coherence.")

"We're still new. Just starting to make some rumblings," he said, rubbing his hands together and grinning a little maniacally. Maisie always liked seeing men passionate about their work, but then, Guy Fawkes probably had been, too. "If you're keen, I'd be delighted to send you some copies. Wouldn't presume to ask your home address, but if you're one of the great new throng of lady laborers, I could post them to you there, if your employer would allow it."

"They would positively encourage it," Maisie said. "I work at the BBC," she told him, lacing her pride with a sliver of nonchalance.

"No! Do you, really?" He laughed again, longer than seemed warranted. "Ah, well, we all pay our respects to Mammon somehow. Secretary, are you?"

And a very good one. But she wondered what it would be like to be asked without the expectation of being right.

"But you do a bit of writing on the side—is that it?" He registered her nod and barreled on, pleased with his perspicacity. "Good show! Always try to do something more—that's my motto. Well, one of them. But a fun girl like you, seems you ought to be chatting with other clever girls in your free moments. You're all rather clever these days, aren't you?"

"Fun"? "Clever"? When had such language ever been applied to her?

"Maybe we always were clever, and you just never noticed." Was this really her?

"And here I always thought I was observant." He sighed, weighty with drama.

The watch, still cool on her wrist and heavy with newness, reminded her it was a short lunch. She wasn't overly sorry.

"Ah, of course." He nodded. "But do please tell me your name?"

"Maisie Musgrave," she said, shaking his extended hand.

"Simon Brock-Morland. Perhaps our paths will cross again?"

"I suppose people have written stranger scenarios." She smiled. She couldn't help it.

"That almost sounds like a challenge." He grinned back.

"It was very nice to meet you, Mr. Brock-Morland," she told him. "Good day."

The tingle lingered on her neck as she walked up Savoy Place. But she wrestled the feeling down, shoving it somewhere the fist inside could beat it till it broke. She wasn't going to fall for another handsome man, even if he thought she was funny, and clever. She wasn't going to run from anyone else again. Not ever.

Loyal to Maisie's request, Phyllida hadn't spread the word about her birthday. Not that anyone cared, but Maisie remembered her idea of where she would be by this age. All those carefully wrought plans, little boxes in the back of her mind, each labeled and filled with some segment of life. Love. Marriage. Home. All amounting to security.

Though she knew now that they didn't. She'd seen illnesses, injuries, work shortages strip households bare and send whole families into the streets, where even the other poor wanted to pretend they didn't exist. Both Phyllida and Hilda were advocates of a better system of helping "unfortunates." It sounded Utopian. Maisie found most people would rather *not* care than care, and not help if they could help it.

She blinked away the cobwebs and rejoined the tearoom, where Phyllida was presenting her with a walnut cream cake and a jug of chocolate to pour on top provided by Mrs. Hudson, who regarded Maisie's appetite as a glorious challenge.

Phyllida was rapturous over the watch. Her Yorkshire flowed like the chocolate.

"Yon Miss Matheson is the most gradley . . . nae, champion . . . *topping* woman in Britain, nowt finer. I knew she thought the world of you, and why not, but this is really super."

"Shh, don't let it get 'round," Maisie insisted. "I don't think she got Mr. Fielden anything for his birthday, and he's her deputy."

"Yes, but you can't buy a sense of humor in Selfridges."

"Or even Harrods."

Their giggles attracted the ire of the sound effects men, huddled in the corner.

"Do you mind?" Jones growled. "We are discussing how to create a tennis party."

Which only made them laugh harder.

"Hallo, oh, I say, that looks scrumptious." Beanie sat down with them in a great rustle of crepe de chine and a swish of her Sautoir necklace, whose tassel nearly took out Maisie's eye.

"It's special for Maisie," Phyllida put in quickly so as to allay any trespasses. She liked Beanie; they all did, generally because of, rather than in spite of, her rudeness, it being so wholly without malice or awareness. But Phyllida, an advocate of the classless society, was keenly aware of the breadth of Beanie's privilege and determined to shield that which was emphatically not hers from any reach.

"What for?" Beanie asked, but promptly forgot to wait for an answer in the wake of her desire to communicate. "Great *scandale* a-brewing—have you heard?"

They hadn't.

"Only just announced; quite a shock to the poor DG."

"Siepmann's a Russian spy?" Phyllida asked, ever hopeful.

"Wouldn't that be odd? No, the Great Shields is leaving to get married."

Maisie choked, sending crumbs sputtering.

"Good Lord, so now we know what it takes for you to lose some of your food," Phyllida said, thumping her on the back.

"Miss Shields?" Maisie asked, her head spinning much harder than the effect of four cakes in one day could ever manage. "But she's so . . . rigid."

"Oh, I don't know. She did have that torrid affair with the married man a few years back."

Now both Phyllida and Maisie were choking.

"If you're going to make that ghastly noise, you should at least do so where we can record it," Fowler shouted at them.

"Beanie, you can't be serious," Maisie said, almost imploring.

"Mama often says so, too, but I've proven her quite wrong, I think."

Miss Shields, straight-backed and straitlaced, slavish to Mr. Reith ("Sir John"). Inflexible tweeds, even more inflexible features. Engaged to be married.

"You wouldn't have thought a woman her age could manage it," Beanie went on, helping herself to Phyllida's cigarette lighter.

"I don't think she's much more than thirty-five," Phyllida said.

"Yes. Perhaps her fiancé's not very strong, or doesn't want children. But good on her. Not one of the 'Surplus Women' anymore!"

"You shouldn't use that phrase. It's ghastly," Maisie chided Beanie.

"Apparently the DG is devastated," Beanie continued, ignoring Maisie. "Silly man. Wants everyone to get married, but not if it means they'll stop serving him. Ah well. Cheerio!" She ground her cigarette in Phyllida's saucer and skipped off.

"She's got him absolutely pegged, yet *she's* the one who's the aristocrat," Phyllida said, shaking her head. "If anyone was ever going to return us to feudalism, it's the aspirant middle classes."

"I doubt the aristocrats would mind that very much, though," Maisie pointed out.

The Savoy Hill buzz quickly told more of the story. Miss Shields had asked to stay on after marriage and been denied. Maisie wondered how anyone could possibly know—none of the parties in question would have disseminated such information. But at the next meeting between Hilda and Reith, she saw for herself Miss Shields's elegant diamond ring and more-than-usual rigid face. As she looked closer, Maisie recognized what few others would: the light application of stage makeup, probably to hide red-rimmed eyes.

"Miss Matheson," Reith said, his tone attempting patience. "A great many of these books Lady Nicholson discusses are not at all appropriate. I've received a number of complaints, including those expressing the concern that some of the books advocate shocking ideas, perhaps even the overturning of all our most sacred traditions. As if these times aren't outlandish enough."

"Lady Nicholson would never be inappropriate," Hilda said, her chin jutted stubbornly and a decided snap in her tone. She had been to Long Barn, the estate of Vita and her husband, Harold Nicholson, for a dinner party, and her opinion of the whole family, but especially Vita, dwarfed the Eiffel Tower. "And if I may say, Mr. Reith, *we* have received reams of letters from librarians throughout the country saying that many of the books reviewed are high on request lists."

"Yes, but are people reading them or burning them?"

"Well, I don't think that would bode well for their lending privileges."

"Do please be serious, Miss Matheson. I've told you many times, we have got to tread with care. Minds are malleable, you know."

"Oh, yes, I know," she said.

"So you'll speak to Lady Nicholson?"

"I certainly shan't. She understands the parameters and has inimitable taste. Besides, if you'll recall, some of the honey we added to the pot when we asked her to take up the reviewing post was that she could choose to review whatever books she liked."

Reith inhaled on his cigarette so hard, it looked like he was eating it.

"I'd speak to Sir Harold, but I know the lady holds the whip hand over him. I do hope, by the way, that their union is not so unnatural as is rumored, or of course we will have to review her position here."

Hilda's stubborn chin was trembling and her jaw was turning white. Maisie leaned forward.

"If I may, sir, we've received quite a lot of complimentary letters from listeners, not just librarians, appreciating Lady Nicholson. I have a compendium in the Talks Department, if you'd like to see it?"

He had a way of blinking at her as though surprised she could speak in full sentences. He'd done it before, Maisie realized, but she'd always been too pleased to be acknowledged to notice his expression.

"Yes, well, I'm sure that's . . . very nice. But now really, Miss Matheson, I'd be obliged if you would at least *hint* that some discretion is advised? Even in these unrestrained times?" He said the word "unrestrained" with the sort of grimace someone might make if they'd just sucked down a whole lemon. One that was rotting. "The greatest loyalty must be to the BBC. We all need to put it first."

Maisie glanced at Miss Shields, who bit her lip as she wrote those shorthand marks.

Would she miss this? Maisie had always thought of marriage as going *toward* something. Now she thought about what you were leaving. The BBC was one of the few places in Britain where a woman could keep working after marriage, provided she was senior enough, and given approval. Maybe Miss Shields didn't qualify. Or perhaps Reith didn't want to feel like the woman serving him loved another man more.

The meeting over, the women dismissed, Maisie held out her hand to Miss Shields.

"Congratulations, Miss Shields. I hope you'll have great happiness."

Miss Shields actually smiled and took Maisie's hand.

"That's very kind of you, Miss Musgrave. Many thanks."

It was hard to remember that not quite two years ago, Maisie, pale and bony, first tiptoed into this office, a frightened hen on the way to the chopping block. Miss Shields hadn't thought much of her, but she'd given her tea. And the chance to speak the words that had brought her inside to stay.

Maisie wanted to thank her. But Miss Shields wasn't the sort of woman who welcomed thanks. And anyway, they both remembered that her wish to keep Maisie far away from the BBC had been thwarted.

I, at least, continue to put the BBC first.

She was hard-pressed to imagine anything more important.

Maisie and Hilda had not exaggerated about the amount of letters they received. Most were thanks, and congratulations, but there were also requests and even open suggestions for new Talks pouring in from every square inch of Britain. Not only that, but thousands of people, gallantly offering their time and expertise, were eager to come broadcast. The mail boys marveled at the sacks of correspondence that flowed in and out every hour. They were as pleased with their work as the rest of Savoy Hill, though they did grumble about Reith's rule regarding men's jackets. While shirtsleeves were allowed in the mailroom, jackets had to be worn when delivering correspondence. Reith's puritanical insistence on a dress code was one of those subjects that gave fodder for the satirical magazines that otherwise weren't always at their best skewering radio. "They should thank us for giving them such a challenge," Hilda observed, snickering over *Punch*.

The afternoon post, as if determined to further vex Reith, was full of letters praising various Talks, as well as invitations for Hilda to speak at this society or that charity or some other lunch.

Then Maisie came to a large square envelope—a parcel, really—and had the oddest sensation of her heart doing a loop-the-loop through her, like a carnival ride.

It had her name. on it.

Definitely her: *Miss M. Musgrave c/o BBC* etc., etc. Her hands shook as she opened it, risking death by a thousand paper cuts.

Four copies of *Pinpoint* magazine were inside. There was a note in a man's confident, elegant hand:

Dear Miss Musgrave, I can't tell you how I enjoyed our chat the other week. I wanted to send you some copies of our little magazine that very afternoon, but thought perhaps I would wait so as to include this latest issue. I should very much like to know what you think of it. If you're free Saturday afternoon, would you care to meet me for tea? Please don't let the prospect of my disappointment sway you, should you not be able (or willing; he cringes with mortification). Yours, very sincerely, Simon Brock-Morland.

Maisie's breath was short and ragged. It could be a trick, of course. A Cyril sort of trick. Simon Brock-Morland might think she was an advocate of free love. But tea, not a drink. An afternoon, not an evening. It all seemed quite civilized. Maybe.

"Ooh, what have we been sent?" Hilda's eager eye danced over the magazines.

"Have you heard of *Pinpoint*?"

"No, I haven't. It must be quite new if it's not one of our regular flow." Her eyes slid to Maisie. "I say, are you all right? You look a bit pale."

"No, I'm fine, thank you. May I read one of the copies as well?"

"Of course."

Maisie slid the note into the top copy and handed the rest to Hilda.

She would thank him politely but decline. One didn't meet men for tea after just an accidental and unwanted shared lunch. Even if he was a writer. Who called her fun and clever and made the back of her neck tingle. She would ask Phyllida if she wanted to go to the pictures; they could see the new Buster Keaton at the Odeon.

She still couldn't breathe.

ELEVEN

"Are there Russian spies amongst us and is this government doing enough to quash them?"

Audiences had been interested to see what sort of Talks they might expect now that "controversial" material was allowed, and thus far Hilda did not disappoint. This was the third of dozens of scheduled debates on slippery subjects of the day, and audiences were primed.

So were the broadcasters. Studio One seemed far too small and stuffy—though Maisie thought it didn't matter, as everyone was holding their breath.

The moderator, Mrs. Strachey (Rachel, but she went by Ray), introduced the speakers on each side, and the debate took shape.

"I have a quarrel with the very title of this debate," began the first speaker, "because the second question assumes the answer to the first is a resounding yes. And until such time as we have proof positive—by which I don't mean a sensationalist story in a publication favored by fluff-headed young girls titillated by the notion of white slavery—we cannot insist upon the government allocating precious time and resources to chasing down what doesn't exist."

"But the dissonant voices in Britain are growing!" he was countered.

"Trade unionists and Communists are advocating against our finest traditions."

"We have a long tradition of dissonance, which surely must be welcome in any free society. As effective as our system might seem to those who benefit from it the most, we must also allow that it has its imperfections, and we ought to be open to correcting them as such."

Maisie glanced at Hilda, watching the broadcasters, nodding along with each point. Reith liked to suggest that controversial material was simply to "educate and inform," but Hilda insisted it must go further. It must provoke thought.

The legions of the provoked made their feelings known in letter after letter. But by last count, there were two and a half million BBC licenses purchased, so Hilda felt emboldened to carry on provoking.

Maisie wondered if Hilda was what was termed "a radical." It seemed unlikely. Lady Astor was a Conservative, so why would she have employed a radical political secretary? Maisie and Phyllida often discussed it on Sunday walks.

"I've heard the rumor Miss Matheson's a Communist. Hardly matters if she can't vote, though, does it?"

"Miss Matheson *can* vote," Phyllida corrected her.

"But she's not married," Maisie said. "Doesn't a woman have to be married?"

"The stupid rule is you have to be over thirty. Then you have to either own property yourself or be married to a chap who does. Or be a graduate. It's mad," Phyllida scoffed. "The fight was for equal suffrage, not this cobbled-together rubbish. I don't want to wait. I want to make things happen now!"

"America doesn't bar women under thirty."

"Nae, because America was so late joining the war," Phyllida said, without judgment. "We lost loads more young men, so if women over twenty-one were allowed to vote here, we'd be the majority. And, you know, heaven forfend."

Maisie was looking forward to the debate on equal suffrage.

Billy gave the sign they were off the air, and everyone applauded.

The debaters were shiny pink with sweat, and Mrs. Strachey looked cheerfully harassed.

"Goodness!" she exclaimed. "That was stimulating! And here I always thought blood sports a lot of nonsense. I could moderate one of these every day of the week. Marvelous exercise."

Maisie wished the debates would answer the questions they asked, but she agreed with Mrs. Strachey. The constant asking was a thrill. She wanted to be even deeper in the midst of it. She'd certainly rather not keep asking herself about Simon.

"Why did I agree to this?" Maisie asked Phyllida, staring into the mirror in the favorite ladies' lavatory.

"Because he's handsome and witty and said you were clever, which means he's not stupid, so you'll go and have this tea, and then you're meeting me for chips and croquettes and the pictures after," Phyllida told her firmly.

Maisie had deliberately made no effort to look smarter, though the Garland Green dress had been given a careful brushing, and she wore Lola's white rose in her hair. Phyllida supervised a light dab of pink lipstick, laid a tissue on Maisie's lip and instructed her to blot, then barreled her off to the tram.

This is nothing. It's just tea. I have plans afterward. And he wasn't that handsome, not really, I think, or clever. He probably just—

"I don't know what the BBC's playing at, allowing that sort of talk." A man's complaint cut across her thoughts and captured her attention.

"Can't agree with you there. I thought it was rather useful. Good luck finding a paper that will ask those questions."

"Haven't we got more to worry about than Bolsheviks?"

"That's the point! Why worry about something that isn't going to happen?"

"I'm not sure that was the point at all."

On and on, as white-hot as the debate itself, though less eloquent and occasionally unbroadcastable. Maisie had to force herself off at her stop. It was one thing to read the correspondence. It was quite another to hear, live and in person, how much the BBC was engaging the public. Hilda was right; radio might not change anything. But she was also right in that it was forging a connection with people.

She was still smiling as she entered the poky teashop and Simon sprang up from his seat and smiled back. He wasn't as handsome as she remembered—he was quite a bit more so. That tickle on her neck ran all the way down her spine.

"Miss Musgrave! I can't tell you how pleased I am to see you again. Do sit down. What would you like to drink?"

"Well, it *is* a teashop," she said, feeling an obligation to state the obvious.

"They have coffee, too," he said, mock defensively. "And some sort of lemon fizz thing, probably for kiddies."

He ordered a pot of tea and a tray of sandwiches and scones.

"Shall we be wholly bourgeois and get cake as well? You like cake, if I remember."

"I wouldn't trust someone who didn't," she said, meaning it.

"I read that we're having a great revival of cake; it's our glorious new era. From Shakespeare to Donne to Hardy . . . to cake."

"The Bloomsbury crowd, the BBC, and cake? I'd say we're doing all right."

"Ah, I see that cunning hat tip to your employer!"

"They are changing the world, you know. They deserve a nod."

"Oh, certainly, certainly. And giving all you young ladies a chance at some interesting work," he said, winking.

"A few of us, anyway."

"So I must ask, Miss Musgrave, are you perhaps American?"

Is that why I'm here? Was that light touch of "other" really so alluring? Her accent, never definitive anyway, was much softer than it once had been. She didn't sound British, but she certainly didn't sound like she came from New York. Or Toronto. *I sound like someone who doesn't belong anywhere.* Which might have been what made her appealing—a cipher upon which to draw. The reverse image of Eliza Doolittle, but just as much clay.

"I'm Canadian, but I spent a lot of my childhood in New York."

"Oh, New York! Father took us in 1920. Ostensibly to look at some property he owns—or anyway has holdings in—but I think really it was to chastise the Yanks for taking their time helping us thump the Boche." He shook his head, chuckling. "Ah, you do have to wonder what it was all for. But never mind. I did my bit and it's sunny days now."

"Your father owns property in New York?" Maisie tried not to gulp. She could tell his accent was upper-class, but now she wondered just how high up it went.

"Owns a bit in Trinidad, too, but primarily it's the old seat here," Simon said with a shrug. "Matters nary a whit for a spare second son, so I'm just thrown an afterthought title and off I go to make my own way in the world."

Title? All of Maisie's deepest girlhood fantasies poked their heads from their box and sniffed hopefully. It seemed churlish to press the subject, though, so she forced herself to pretend disinterest and instead asked how he'd liked New York.

"Very much. I was twenty-one. I was decorated at Cambrai. I liked everything."

And just like that, she liked him.

"Thank you for sending the magazines," she said, remembering what he wanted to hear. "You're awfully talented."

Actually, she wasn't sure. *Pinpoint* was an odd magazine written in a jokey style but nothing like *Punch*. Simon's articles were either paeans to the best of Britain, or an attempt to consolidate the views of many newspapers, though usually pointing out that it was no wonder Britain was awash in myriad opinions. And the conclusions were that this was likely good, or else the government might really get to accomplish something.

"That's very kind of you, thanks," he said, ducking his head and grinning. "I wasn't sure what you'd think, you being at the BBC and all."

"What do you mean?" Maisie asked, surprised enough to set down her cake.

"Well, the spoken word versus the written, quite different, isn't it?"

"Yes!" Ha! Hilda had taught the public well.

"Quite, and when you really want people to absorb and understand something, well, it just has to be written."

He remained charming as he excoriated the whole concept of radio. But he courteously listened to Maisie's argument that the oral tradition was ancient and had the capacity to engage audiences in a wholly new—which was to say, old—way, and rouse their passions.

"True, true. It's why theater is still more vital than cinema," he said, shaking his head. "Though the theater's grown dreadfully bourgeois. We could do with a Master of the Revels like in the Elizabethan days, someone determining what's allowed to be staged and what's not. Save a lot of people a lot of money."

"I suppose there's an awful lot of tripe onstage," Maisie agreed, wishing his eyes weren't so liquid. "But someone saying what could or couldn't go forward . . . that doesn't seem right."

"I expect you think I'm a bit of a silly blowhard." (She did a little, though his voice was hypnotic.) "The fact is, I just want everything to be beautiful all the time. I want all theater to be profound, delightful, enchanting. I want to see nothing but magnificent art. Clothes, buildings, villages . . . I'm a forward-thinking man, I am, but what's more perfect in the whole world than an English village? Thatched roofs, a street of little shops, all the good people doing all their good work. And I can't think of a greater ecstasy than riding a stallion through an English wood, and up to the top of a mountain—or a tall hill, anyway—and looking down over the rolling expanse of all the glorious green. Just manor houses and quaint villages to disrupt the flow, but making it all prettier. That's my England, and the only place I want to live, always."

If she could speak, she would say that he'd proved her point. There was nothing like the spoken word for arousing an audience's passion.

"Will you meet me again, Miss Musgrave?"

"Maisie," she breathed, relieved to remember.

"Ah, yes, Maisie. A bit of May, a fresh spring. I suppose you haven't a telephone?"

"No, I'm afraid not." Mrs. Crewe would sooner install a swimming pool.

"Good. I prefer to write. Words to paper, it's my *élan vital*, you know."

She knew. She was the same way about words now. And she couldn't wait to read more of his.

"Oh good, you found your way. I knew you wouldn't let the side down."

Maisie blinked at Phyllida, not entirely sure how she'd found her way to the chip shop. She thought she might have flown.

"Was it that good or is there a Talk brewing in there?" Phyllida asked, tapping Maisie's temple.

"I . . . well . . . I enjoyed it."

"Aye, you're floating so high, you could make a few extra bob giving people balloon rides."

"He's rather swell. A swell swell," Maisie added.

"Which certainly trumps being swill," Phyllida rejoined. "Now tell me what you mean."

"I think he might be an aristocrat."

"Oh, good Lord."

"Possibly not a lord. He didn't say."

Maisie grinned shakily and dumped half a decanter of vinegar on her chips.

"You do look besotted," Phyllida said. "Before the fantasy gets too developed, just remember you're not senior enough to stay at the BBC if you get married."

"It was one date," Maisie protested. "And only tea." Though he did seem to be everything she'd ever dreamed of. *Except now I want something more.* She shoved a forkful of chips in her mouth, feeling guiltily ungrateful. Phyllida's father was content to think of her as dead until she got married and grew out her hair. Half the female working force in Britain had a similar story. The papers trumpeted their great modern times, but a lot of parents were still firm devotees of Victorianism, and nearly all the institutions and businesses embraced modernism only in so far as it enhanced their fortunes. The BBC was nearly a lone exception, and even its beneficence only stretched so far. *I wonder if my father would approve of me working.*

"Ah, that was rotten of me. I'm sorry," Phyllida said, misreading the meaning of Maisie's expression. "I'm glad you had a good time, as you should. 'All work and no play . . .' or whatever damn thing it was someone once said."

"Is it still work when you absolutely, totally, and completely love it?"

For once Phyllida didn't have a quick response. She broke into a wide smile and ordered them more chips. It was such luxury, being able to buy a meal and not feeling you had to skimp on something else. They were still poor, but there was a division in London—the same division that existed everywhere, Maisie supposed—between the poor who had regular work and those who weren't able to secure it. Those were the people the Poor Law forced into workhouses, another Victorian vestige, offering meager assistance and copious amounts of shaming.

"Why do you think poor people are made to feel ashamed for being poor?" Maisie burst out as she dumped half a bottle of HP Sauce over the fresh chips.

"Well, what? Would you have the rich feel guilty about their over-sized houses and collections of Greek sculptures and dead butterflies?" Phyllida asked, stabbing her knife into her chicken croquette.

"I'm serious." Maisie was suddenly livid. "London and New York are stinking rich. It's like the peasants and the lords still, and we should know better by now. Why isn't it the government that's ashamed 'cause so many people are poor?"

"Why, Maisie Musgrave," Phyllida shrieked, her laugh bouncing around the restaurant. "Aren't you just a wild, mad Bolshie!"

A dozen heads swiveled around to glare at Maisie. Phyllida sobered up at once.

"Only joking, not that it's anyone's business," she announced. An officious woman, her feather-festooned hat poised to take flight, glared at them.

"I will have you know I'm not above calling the police."

"It's not illegal to be a Bolshevist," Maisie told her. "Whatever some Tories might think."

"And I were only having a bit of fun with my chum here," Phyllida said, her voice steely. "I've nae read of any laws against having fun."

On hearing her accent, it was clear the woman was astounded Phyllida could read at all. The waitress hovered, hoping she would not be called upon to mediate or, worse, adjudicate.

Whether it was evident from the breadth of Phyllida's shoulders that she could thump a person soundly and return to her meal without missing a breath, or a general unwillingness to be one of those who caused a scene she could not control, the feathery woman merely harrumphed.

"You girls these days. So keen on your fun. Just you wait and see; you'll pay for that fun good and proper."

It was certainly a fine exit line—Georgina would have adored it—but she lost some ground as she was leaving because Maisie called after her:

"At least we'll pay with money we've earned ourselves!"

After which Maisie and Phyllida found it prudent to pay and leave as well. They each gave the waitress an extra penny, and congratulated themselves on being able to do so.

"I lost my eldest brother in Passchendaele," Phyllida said as they walked toward the cinema in the heavy blue twilight. "And not a day goes by I wish I didn't know how to spell that bloody name. But these are better times, whatever anyone says, and I like being able to work and if I don't want to marry, I won't, and I will not go back to a time when someone says otherwise."

A brother. Phyllida didn't tend to talk about her family, which Maisie well respected. She knew that nearly everyone they passed on the ten-minute walk had lost someone. Father, brother, son, uncle, nephew, cousin, friend. But these *were* better times. Weren't they? She was seized by an impulse to stop and ask everyone in Piccadilly Circus what they thought and write it all down. She linked her arm through Phyllida's to stop herself.

"I'm so sorry." Her mind wandered once again to the unknown Edwin Musgrave. Likely too old to have fought, she hoped. But he had family here; he must. Had she lost cousins, uncles, perhaps even half brothers? Lost before found. How would she ever know? "Why the heck did so many have to die to make these better times? It's a damn crying shame."

Phyllida squeezed her arm.

"Do you know, I can always tell when you're a little hotted up— you use American slang."

"Do I? Gads, but I'm years out-of-date."

"Or you're starting the trends here," Phyllida said, unfailingly loyal. "I shouldn't have joked on being a Bolshie, though. Not where stupid people could hear."

"Stupid is right. What's the matter with them, anyhow?"

"Pah. Nowt queer than folk, is what my people say. A bit pat, but does the job. Want to share a chocolate bar?"

Maisie did. But neither the chocolate nor Buster Keaton could stop her mind from asking questions.

The questions were still flowing as bountifully as the tea in The Cosy Rosy, where Maisie ignored the silly name and spent half her Sunday afternoons reading and working through two pots of tea and a mountain of Cosy's special digestives. The *Radio Times*, she found, was a great balm to the buzzing mind. She read it cover to cover every week, exulting in its perky nothingness and her own part in its existence. The same general advertisements ran in each issue. Bert likely found it both boring and convenient. There were also a few personal advertisements, and these Maisie couldn't resist reading. It felt like eavesdropping. She had technically outgrown the glossies, but she still pored over Lola's discards and found plenty of personals with which to sympathize. The personals in the *Radio Times* were less drenched in bathos but still intriguing. "If you love the evening Talks and want someone to sit and listen with, please write."

It felt like taking Hilda's notion of the radio as a form of creating connection to an absurd extreme.

Maisie glanced around the shop to be sure no one was looking, dunked a digestive into her tea, and transferred the whole thing into her mouth. She skimmed the last few pages of the *Radio Times* and turned to the *Independent*. Deep into an article about BBC listening groups (and another digestive), something clicked in her brain. She sat there, the digestive melting into her tongue, trying to figure out what she was trying to figure out. Something about listening, radio, meetings . . .

She flipped back through the *Radio Times* and stopped at the Siemens ad, extolling its most popular wireless. No, it wasn't the ad; the ad was the same they'd run for months (the stupid one the boys loved to quote around the typists: "She turns the knob and music wells out"). Maybe it was the text beside it:

"Listen in a like-minded crowd! If Siemens is your favorite wireless, opt to gather 'round with us. News of a *real* sort and refreshments, too!"

It looked like it could be part of the ad. There was an address in New Bond Street, probably a shop. Nothing to excite interest. Quite the opposite. Still, something was nudging her. She had two previous *Radio Times* in the battered holdall she'd bought in a secondhand shop. The magazines were wrinkled, crushed, and covered in crumbs. Hilda would be aghast. Maisie silently apologized as she opened the magazines to compare pages.

It had to be nothing, really. This must be the effect of all the constant certainty of Russian spies, or Hilda's interest in German propaganda, making her see things in the most innocuous of places.

Or her prejudice against Siemens, brought on less by the propaganda than by her dislike for Mr. Hoppel, Reith's friend at the company. But the longer she looked at the listings, the more something seemed odd. Nothing might, in fact, be something.

Hilda's laughing, encouraging voice sounded in her head: *Why don't you go find out and let me know?*

Maisie wrote Hilda's words again. "Siemens?" "Nestlé?"

Oh.

Siemens, at least, was German. Perhaps the largest German company to have a presence in Britain?

Maisie circled the address in the magazine. *What's life without a little adventure? And it does promise refreshments.*

TWELVE

Maisie was unreasonably disappointed to find the address in New Bond Street was, after all, a shop selling wireless sets. The shopkeeper, a Dickensian wisp of a man with pince-nez and a cravat, guided her to the favorite sets for "the young ladies."

I'm an idiot. It's just a listening party. Plenty of people still do that. Much cheaper than buying your own wireless. Her eyes caressed the wood and Bakelite radios, so pretty, so past her price range. Even if her room was wired for electricity.

"It is nearly closing time, miss," the shopkeeper said with a pointed cough.

"But I saw an advert, for a listening party?" She was here, after all. Might as well ask.

"I think you must be mistaken," he said.

"No, it's right here," she argued, digging in her bag for the *Radio Times*. As she did so, a young man strolled in.

"Have you got a Lion by any chance?"

"A very good choice, sir, one of our finest!" the shopkeeper answered. "Right this way, sir."

It was possible anyone else would shrug, or storm off in a huff. But no one else had suffered through any number of overwrought melodramas in which Georgina starred. Maisie immediately discerned an embarrassingly crude setup and the stagiest of poor line readings—and her body reacted with its usual automatic shudder. She tagged after the men.

"So you'll guide a gentleman to the Lion, but not a lady?"

"Begging your pardon, miss," the shopkeeper said, flustered. "I quite misunderstood you."

And she and the young man stepped into the back room together.

She was nearly knocked back by a man's booming voice. If it had been a listening party, they would have been intent on Vernon Bartlett's Talk about the League's plans for a constitution in Syria. But it wasn't. It was a meeting. Maisie cloaked herself in Invisible Girl and drifted into a corner.

". . . it is not just about our own good political fortune," the speaker said. He was quite handsome, with golden hair and a gentle smile. His accent was at once patrician and friendly. "We must and can do a great deal to advance the fortunes of our fine friends in Germany. They are most grateful for all our advice and assistance, and I am convinced they will repay us for it most handsomely. It will be an easy thing, convincing the British to admire Germany once again. But we must hurry. We must do more today, every day, to convince our local MPs of the urgency."

"Well, Lion, I find that donations to a pet cause go a long way towards currying favor with a politician," a woman in evening dress advised. Maisie was outraged on Lady Astor's behalf.

"But will they go far enough to close up all this openness we're seeing in society?" a blustery old man demanded. "Young people aren't being properly molded. It is appalling."

"Quite so," the handsome speaker—apparently the Lion—acquiesced with a shake of his golden head. "But all that will change once we have exerted our influence upon the BBC."

That fist in Maisie's chest nearly flew out of her mouth.

"That may yet take a great deal of doing," a man called from the other side of the room. "Things are well entrenched there. Although

I believe the election will mean a new board of governors and the opportunity to replace the director-general, should that be necessary, though I do hope not. The current man is, I think, amenable."

"I am most pleased to hear it," the Lion said. "We can have our own Five-Year Plan, you know, only ours will be accomplished more quickly. The BBC will be far easier to manage, once we have barred all women from working there."

What?! Maisie fought to retain the cloak of Invisible Girl. Who *were* these lunatics?

"And don't forget the newspapers," another man piped up in a gruff voice. "I am still arranging to purchase a number of newspapers, and searching for the right man to manage them."

"Yes, I daresay it is useful to have outlets for those who still read," the other man said, to much laughter. "But with sales of less expensive wirelesses growing apace, the BBC will allow us to make the Britain we want, and in good time."

Maisie spotted a table laden with sandwiches, coffee, and cakes, but had no appetite. Although she could only see his nose and avuncular smile, there was no question: The man with the plan for the BBC was Hoppel, of Siemens. Siemens, who also offered less expensive wireless sets. She slithered to the door. *Dollars to doughnuts he'd never recognize me, but what a damn waste of a doughnut if he did.*

Which wasn't going to stop her from calling again, after she'd raided Lola's trunk for a wig and some stage makeup. She wasn't Georgina's daughter for nothing.

Maisie was bursting with communicativeness the next day and was thwarted at every turn—it was simply too typical a day for a conversation in Talks.

"Mary Cartwright needs to be rescheduled again—so much for bankers having regular hours—and we've got to sort out Rebecca West, fine writer but my goodness, she doesn't understand broadcasting at all. Oh, and that mathematician at Oxford wouldn't change his script, insisting that women aren't capable of higher maths, so we're just going to replace him. That's censorship of me, isn't it? Very poor form, but a lesser crime than putting ladies off numbers. I am looking forward to telling him we're getting someone from Manchester instead; that should get him counting to ten a few times, and were you able to make any progress on getting us more storage space for files?"

Hilda sat on the floor, a cheery volcanic island in a sea of red-inked scripts and the week's schedule. Maisie sat at the edge of the papers, rearranging and taking notes as Hilda talked, as though she were dealing three-card Monte.

"I think we can manage Miss Cartwright for next Wednesday after Mr. Bartlett. We can push *Life in Roman Britain* to the following week. I'll draft the letter before lunch, and the only way we're getting more space is if we branch out onto the roof. We're growing so much, there's some real concern about the joists. Miss Matheson, if I may, I had a rather extraordinary experience last night that I think is not unrelated to the—"

"Miss Matheson, what the devil are you doing?"

Reith was standing in the door, glaring down at them. Just behind him was the despondent figure of Fielden, the messenger who had failed to warn them in time. Maisie wondered how much Reith had heard.

"Ah, Mr. Reith, welcome," Hilda said with the warmth of a hostess at a garden party. "Do join us. Would you like a biscuit? They're lemon-flavored, very nice."

"You are a senior member of this staff. You ought to be showing some decorum," Reith snarled. He looked ready to seize Hilda and jerk her to her feet. Despite their almost comical difference in size, Maisie could easily see Hilda pushing Reith back. In fact, she wouldn't be surprised to see Hilda thump him.

"Sitting on the floor helps me think, I've told you," Hilda reminded him airily. "It's hardly indecorous."

"What if an important guest were to walk in?"

"I've got extra cushions and plenty of biscuits," Hilda answered. Maisie hid her laugh in a fake sneeze.

"This is hardly a moment for levity, Miss Matheson. I'm very troubled . . . Will you take a proper seat, please?"

"Of course," Hilda said, ever gracious, and swept herself up and into her chair. Reith, however, chose to remain standing.

"Miss Matheson, I need you to replace Sir John Simon in the talk on Lord Birkenhead."

Hilda turned white. "But, Mr. Reith, we've invited him. He's accepted. It's all arranged."

"Yes." He helped himself to one of her cigarettes. "You'll have to disinvite him. He's not appropriate for broadcast—his personal life, you see."

"I'm afraid I very much do not see."

Neither did Maisie. Sir John was married to an activist of some sort, but that was as much as she knew of him. Reith rolled his eyes.

"Well, with the girl present, I can't say more. Just see to it at once. This isn't pleasant for me, you know. Do you realize I had MPs on the phone after that Bolshie debate, worried we might be creating panic? Panic, Miss Matheson!"

"Oh, what tosh," Hilda said, ignoring the disappearance of Reith's eyebrows. "The papers are constantly screeching any amount of dross about Russians, radicalism, revolution, probably even roller skates. *We* create a space for dialogue, and that calms things down rather than stirs them up. The more people understand—"

"You're not going to argue that radio forges *connection* again, are you?"

"I don't have to. I think it's been quite proven."

She was going too far. Maisie wanted to throw herself between them.

"Miss Matheson, I admire your hard work, but you must be more temperate. I see, for example, you are allowing Lady Nicholson to review that filthy Mead book?"

"Oh, it's not filthy at all, Mr. Reith. It offers an extraordinary insight into the Samoan culture! Remarkable people. Here . . ." She produced the book from her stack. "Do read at least some of it."

Reith shied from the book in more alarm than Maisie guessed he ever had from mustard gas.

"You'll disinvite Sir John, and I don't like the sound of this fellow talking about our oil interests in Persia. The Persians are lucky to have our business, you know."

"That's not really what—"

"You must be politic as well as political," he said. Feeling the impression of the exit line, he nodded to Hilda and Maisie and strode away.

Fielden stuck his head in. "Shall I reschedule the oil talk, then?"

"I suppose so," Hilda said. "I'll try to winkle more of what's troubling him. Do draw up some names to replace Sir John Simon, will you?"

Fielden almost smiled. Catastrophes and unpleasant tasks stimulated him.

Maisie flipped to a fresh sheet in her pad. "Do you want to draft the letter to Sir John now?"

"No," said Hilda. "I most emphatically do not. He must have crossed Reith. If everyone with a dodgy personal life were barred, there'd be no one left to broadcast." She lit a cigarette, leaned back in her chair, and glared up at the leaf-and-dart cornice. "Very silly, panicking about panic. Dangerous, too, really."

"Yes!" Maisie burst in. "It's funny you should say that, because—"

Rusty ran in, bearing aloft an urgent telegram for Hilda, just as the phone rang and Maisie jumped to answer it. One emergency turned into another, and somehow the entire week disappeared in a flume of radio waves.

Alfred handed her a card with the last round of correspondence. "Funny, people writing to you," he said, winking. Maisie ignored him and tore open the envelope. It was just one line, from Simon, asking if she was free to meet for a drink the next evening.

"Ooh, someone fancies himself a Bohemian," Phyllida said when she saw the part of Chelsea he was suggesting for their rendezvous.

"Maybe he is and the aristocrat suggestion was just a joke?" Maisie ventured.

They left their tea and ran down to the BBC's library—a grand appellation for what was basically a converted airing cupboard. Squeezed together at the single bookcase, they turned the pages of Debrett's straight to "B." And there it was. Simon's father, Charles Brock-Morland, was the Earl of Banbury. His older brother, Nigel, was the principal heir. Simon himself was an Honorable. A thrill of excitement ran through Maisie as she read this. *Damn, I thought I'd outgrown my Lady Astor fantasies.*

"'Honorable,' eh?" Phyllida drawled. "And do we suppose he *is*?"

"The evidence is in his favor thus far," Maisie said. She started to close the book, but instead flipped to "W." "Well! Look at that. Beanie's an Honorable, too. 'Hon. Miss Sabine Eugenia Warwick.' It certainly is a refined name, isn't it?"

Phyllida shut the book.

"Lot of maungy nonsense," she pronounced, and blew a raspberry at the cover for extra emphasis. Maisie whipped out her handkerchief to wipe the book clean of spittle before replacing it on the shelf. "Means sod all these days, and they know it," Phyllida added, folding her arms in satisfaction.

"Someone like Miss Matheson deserves to be in a book like this, doesn't she? There's *Who's Who,* but that doesn't seem illustrious enough," Maisie said, her finger still resting on the spine.

Phyllida drew her away. "Miss Matheson will earn her way into something much better, you'll see."

The Chelsea pub definitely attracted a Bohemian crowd. Maisie glanced around it in satisfaction. However much she might dislike Georgina, she always felt right surrounded by people who wrote and made art. Maybe Simon did, too?

"Maisie!" he cried, reaching for her hand. "Absolutely topping of you to join me. Quaint little snug this, isn't it?"

That seemed an abuse of synonyms, but he winked, and she noticed his eyes had flecks of gold in them. That tingle danced across her neck again, and she was glad to swallow her sudden heat in the gin-and-tonic he offered her.

"So! Have there been any great new adventures in Savoy Hill since we last met?" he wanted to know.

"Every hour is an adventure there," she said, not mentioning that there were some adventures the Talks Department could do without. She still hadn't had a moment to tell Hilda about the meeting. She hadn't even had time to think about Simon. Or not too much, anyway.

"Every time you mention your BBC, your eyes dance a little reel," he said.

She grinned, feeling herself blush.

"That's an awfully old-fashioned dance."

"I'm an awfully old-fashioned fellow."

Another wink belied the assertion, as did the achingly on-trend cuffed trousers, Fair Isle jumper, and two-tone brogues he wore. And of course there was his job, one of the few respectable lines for aristocrats. If he was old-fashioned, he'd have to work a bit harder to prove it. He kept smiling, and her hand slid to the banquette, clutching her holdall in an attempt to keep herself from tossing the gin down her throat in one go.

"Your Miss Matheson certainly sounds modern enough," he said, leaning back and lighting a cigarette. "Got rather a name for herself, hasn't she? 'Making the BBC,' and all that."

"Have you met her?"

"Not had the honor, tragically, but one does hear stories."

"I'm glad to report they are all true."

He laughed. Eyes twinkling, he reached out a hand as though to touch her hair. But Maisie, staring at his approaching fingers, didn't find out what he was about to do because her grasp on her bag was too tight and the cheap fastener snapped open, sending pencils, pad, several *Radio Times*, and a Cadbury Nut Bar tumbling to the grubby floor.

"I say, it's the great flood!" Simon laughed, helping her gather her things. Maisie lunged for the pad. Not so long ago, the Cadbury would have been her first priority for rescue.

"I hope they're paying you extra to ferry these around," Simon said, dangling a copy of the *Radio Times* between his thumb and forefinger.

"You don't have to treat it like radium," said Maisie, snatching it from him. "Actually, I write for it sometimes," she added, realizing as she said so that this was a slight exaggeration.

"Do you?" Simon regarded the magazine with increased interest. "And do these issues have something of yours inside?"

"Oh, no. No, I just—"

"No false modesty here, Maisie dear! I see writing of yours indeed."

Her notes, scribbled in the margin by the ad. Only not scribbled enough, because they were perfectly legible.

Maybe that's why Miss Matheson writes like she does?

"That's nothing, really, just—"

"I do believe you've tricked me, my dear! You're not a secretary. You're an investigative journalist! Or are you in MI5? No, I oughtn't ask. You might be able to have me killed."

"Don't you like living dangerously?"

He laughed. "I say, if you are an investigative journalist, do let a fellow in, man-to-man, will you? I've been longing to show up all our so-called papers, show them what a real media can be."

"What's wrong with the newspapers?" Maisie demanded. Simon threw back his head and laughed so hard, she worried he might burst a blood vessel.

"Oh my, Maisie," he gasped. "I would need such a lot more gin to answer that. But come, you must see most of them are no better than this silly rag your BBC puts out."

"The *Radio Times* is listings and supplements. You can't compare it to the actual *Times*."

He wasn't listening, but amusing himself by flipping through her other copies of the magazine until they were all open to the page with the Siemens ad, all of which she had circled. So much for her stint as a stealth artist.

"Are you shopping for a Siemens wireless set, or are these listening parties good fun?"

"More like bad theater," she told him, attempting to slide the magazines from his grip. "Silly meetings, really. Lots of babble about . . . about nothing."

"So you've been!" Simon cried. "Now you must take me. We can acquire rotting fruit to throw at the poor players."

"I think we'd need something more lethal," she said, though it was nonetheless tantalizing. Simon didn't seem to hear her; he was riveted on the ad in the new *Radio Times*.

"Maisie," he said slowly, studying the ad. "If I've cottoned on to this correctly, a bit of your bad theater is happening tonight. Quite near here—look. Moving locations around, how divinely medieval of them, a veritable traveling troupe!"

"Simon, really, I'd so much rather us just chat here, or perhaps over supper?"

He tossed back the last of his whiskey.

"Supper there will be, I promise, but it's always best after the show. This, my dear, is what we call 'kismet.' Let's go!"

"Well, the thing is, I—"

He was out the door, and she had to catch his arm to stop him.

"There was a man when I went before, a fellow I recognized, and I would rather he not see me if I can avoid it, is the thing."

"Curiouser and curiouser!" Simon cried. "All right, then. Let's have a squint, and if the blackguard is there and is too big for me to knock down, we'll make our great escape, shall we?"

Simon's smile was terrifically convincing. He ought to be in advertising. He could sell people on anything. Probably even arsenic.

"Well. All right. But we have to be careful," she pleaded. She cursed every circle she'd drawn around those absurd ads.

"Certainly. But there's such a thing as too much caution. Look at me. A second son, with no property to inherit, just a modest sum to live on. I could manage on the interest, but I wanted to do something useful. I want to always write what I think and perhaps make people cross by it. Make a real name for myself, speaking out. But I knew from the start I couldn't be afraid. Fear is for the weak-minded."

"Aren't you afraid of anything, Simon?"

"I try to leave fear behind and look to the future. Making Britain more glorious than ever and all that, what?"

"Didn't people think that before the war, though?"

"What do you mean?"

"Well, that Britain was so strong and glorious and everyone was certain there was nothing but a great future to keep on coming, because all those treaties meant war wasn't possible anymore. But then it happened anyway and now—"

"Yes, yes, you're quite right," he agreed with blunt but easy politeness. "But I prefer to think it's the sort of thing that makes us stronger going forward."

She hoped so. It was hard, though, not to feel a little trepidatious. Maisie didn't believe in ghosts, thought the obsession with spiritualism absurd, but could understand it, too. It was hard to walk through London and not feel the occasional shadow.

She looked at Simon. Tall, handsome, burnished gold and bronze, a man tanned from rough play, not work, sporty, beloved, educated, wealthy, and aristocratic. Born to *be* feared, not feel it. Not that most people feared aristocrats anymore. Except maybe Lady Astor. *A little fear in general can't be a bad thing, though, can it?*

"Maisie, if your head buzzes any louder, you'll be mistaken for a beehive," Simon chided.

"Yes. It does that," she apologized, shaking off the various thoughts.

"Doesn't it create interference at work?"

Maisie laughed until she saw his confusion.

"Sorry. I thought you meant . . . 'interference'? Because of the technical . . . ? Never mind. Anyway, it's good to think at the BBC. They like that sort of thing."

"Even from secretaries?" he teased.

"Would *you* want a secretary who couldn't think?"

"I daresay that would depend on her thoughts. But fair enough. My compliments to the BBC for welcoming thoughts, even from secretaries."

Then he bent down and kissed her on the lips. Lightly. Then not so lightly. Then she wasn't sure, because time stopped.

"Well, look at us," Simon breathed, his mouth still close to hers. Whiskey and cigarettes on his breath. She wanted to weave the scent into a cocoon coat. "We Britons don't behave like this, I'll have you know. Even in Chelsea."

Her laugh came out in a shuddering gasp, and he stroked her cheek.

"I think we may have arrived," he said, his tone a mix of regret and excitement.

They stood before the gaudy front window of a fortune-telling establishment.

"Inauspicious, to say the least," Simon said, chuckling. "Shall we venture in?"

Now that they were upon the meeting, Maisie was uneasy. She tugged her hat down as far as it would go. At the mention of "Lion," they were waved into the pink-and-purple shop's spacious back room without question.

She didn't see Mr. Hoppel, but it was otherwise much the same crowd. The golden-haired speaker—Maisie felt silly thinking of him as Lion—continued to detail their plans. His pleasant lilting tones, so perfect for broadcast, were somehow more disquieting than the expected roar.

"Of course, it's best that we prevent all women working, aside from servants. But we must better instruct them in the care of children."

Simon nudged Maisie. "Ah, you naughty workingwomen!"

Maisie knew he meant her to smile, but she couldn't.

"We can perhaps engage one woman for the BBC under the new regime, to broadcast solely to women, guiding them appropriately. An aristocrat, perhaps, so she commands authority and need only volunteer."

"Ah, they mean to put you out of work, methinks!" said Simon, chuckling. "This is capital."

"It's not funny," Maisie whispered.

"And we will certainly see that the press is more responsible as well. Some of what these so-called journalists are allowed to publish is virtually obscene."

Rather depends upon how you define the word, I think.

"I think the blighter means to insult me," Simon whispered, delighted.

Maisie saw a teapot-shaped man in a bowler hat gazing at them with an intent frown. Her heart chilled. People of a certain class knew their own, and a City man might recognize members of the aristocracy. And Simon had a face one remembered.

"We are going to save our country, and we will begin by insisting that the truth be told," the Lion assured everyone with a warm smile.

The truth. Their truth. So different from the truth as Hilda saw it. As Maisie saw it. As most, she hoped, saw it. But she didn't know.

Maisie's fingers twitched. She needed a pencil. She needed to write. It wasn't going to wait. And that man was still looking at them, with the look of one who wanted to introduce himself.

"I've got a merciless headache," she whispered, reflexively pleased by her first usage of the standard women's social maneuver. "I think I've got to get home."

Simon promptly proved what it meant to have been inculcated in gentlemanly gallantry since the swaddling stage. Within seconds they were on the street and he had hailed a cab, though she insisted she could manage with the tram.

"I'm grateful to you, Maisie, really. Another minute and they'd have stoned me to death." He laughed, then took her hand and kissed it, gazing into her eyes.

The treacherous fist in her chest clawed its way to her brain and nearly made her say, "I feel better now. Let's go anywhere, everywhere, now, forever."

But she was too dazed to form words, and he skillfully handed the driver some money and her into the cab and, with one lingering look, was gone.

The fist inside settled down and her fingers closed around her pencil. Words flowing across the blue lines in her boxy, conscientious script.

"Could the Fear of Communism Lead to Something Worse? Would the British People Willingly Sacrifice Hard-Won Freedoms for This False Fear? Thoughts from a Canadian."

She stared at that for a moment and amended:

"A Canadian-American."

She had no idea where she meant these words to end up. It didn't matter. She just kept writing, and writing, and was still writing when she got out of the cab, as she walked through the door, and by the dim light in the sitting room, not noticing that her fingers were growing cramped and she hadn't even taken off her hat.

THIRTEEN

Maisie was pacing outside Savoy Hill when Hilda sauntered up. "I've got to speak with you. Can we go inside the chapel a minute?"

"My goodness, Miss Musgrave, how very cloak-and-daggerish!" Hilda, always delighted with novelty, was glad to accommodate. They were as alone as Maisie hoped; the chapel's only other occupant was a red squirrel, genuflecting over an abandoned sandwich.

"Miss Matheson, I've been reading the *Radio Times* every week, cover to cover—"

"Oh, and here I thought you liked yourself," Hilda said, eyes dancing.

Maisie refused to smile.

"The thing is, I've been noticing these, well, adverts of sorts, for meetings. I've typed them all up so you can see." Hilda glanced at the notes and back at Maisie, encouraging her to go on. "And I went along, and it seems to be a branch of the Fascists. Or a splinter, perhaps. Anyway, the DG's friend Mr. Hoppel was there, and he works for Siemens, and you had once thought . . ."

Hilda exhaled heavily and leaned against the baptismal font.

"Well, well, well. You've been having quite an extracurricular time of things."

"What do you make of it?" Maisie asked.

"What do *you* make of it?" Hilda countered.

"Oh, don't do that, Miss Matheson, not this time, please!"

"I certainly shall! You've not taken up spying as a lark. You know there's likely something afoot. So? What are your instincts suggesting?"

"They were *your* instincts. They came from that German pamphlet you had."

"I'm well aware. Go on."

"All right. Well, last night, I was out with, well, a fellow—"

"The Honorable Mr. Brock-Morland?"

Maisie nearly toppled into a pew. "How on earth did you know?"

"He sent you that letter with the *Pinpoint* copies, and at least one other note besides. Remember, I was a secretary, too. Political, not clerical, but nonetheless, we see everything."

Maisie had a sudden flash on Miss Jenkins instructing them to be the eyes and ears of whatever business they were so fortunate as to gain employ with.

"Oh. Well, I . . . Well, they want to take over the BBC. Or at least influence, but it's the same, because they want to stop all women working here, all women working anywhere, and they want to take over newspapers too, so they 'tell the truth,' as they call it. But mostly the BBC."

"Ah! So they see what we're worth, do they? That's most gratifying. Almost compensates for the lack of original thinking."

"Miss Matheson, they're awfully serious, and most of the people there looked quite posh and important, the sort who can influence things. And if that man Hoppel is involved, and he's so high up in Siemens, and Siemens is one of the companies you thought those Nazi people were trying to get support from, and—"

"Miss Musgrave—"

"If MI5 is concerned, then—"

"Be quiet!" For once, Hilda looked enraged and, possibly, a little alarmed. "Some things you just don't say in some places." She stroked her onyx necklace. "We've got to go in. I'm three minutes late. Mr. Fielden has likely already rung Scotland Yard."

"But—"

Hilda held up a warning finger. "Later." Then she smiled her biggest Bonfire Night smile. "I promise."

It wasn't that Maisie didn't trust her, but "later" had a way of stretching into weeks in Savoy Hill. Despite Hilda's organization and Reith's dictatorship, things spiraled out of control almost hourly. Just that morning, the well-rehearsed Mrs. Lonsdale, discussing her champion border collies, meant to say, "I breed them," and instead said, "I bleed them." Hilda instructed Fielden to have the mailroom set up a temporary holding tent for the coming deluge of complaints. Billy forgot to give Mr. Wallis his cue to begin, leaving thirty-two seconds of dead air, and "Beaky" Brendon's "easy-to-train" singing parrots got loose of their cage in the corridor. Which might have been less of a problem if the string quartet hadn't opened the door to Studio One just as Rusty thundered down the corridor with a butterfly net procured from Sound Effects (people had long since given up asking why the effects men had certain objects). Eckersley could be heard baying for blood over the "destruction" of the studio ("Just a few feathers and droppings; you'd think it was a zeppelin air raid," Maisie said). Beaky Brendon himself had hysterics when Samson the cat got involved in the roundup, but since only a few tail feathers were sacrificed, no one else was particularly ruffled. The parrots were wrangled, Hilda slung some brandy down Beaky Brendon's throat, and he recovered after she offered to give the parrots some as well. Samson went back to scouring Savoy Hill for mice, and everyone else went back to being

206 · SARAH-JANE STRATFORD

several days behind in their work, a complaint so often stated, no one, including the complainants, paid any attention.

Much later that afternoon, while Hilda was attending a broadcast, the correspondence brought Maisie another note from Simon. *Dear Maisie, I do hope you're feeling better today. Many thanks for such a gloriously stimulating evening, and I shall no doubt beg of you your next free Saturday night. Yours, Simon.* Maisie pressed the note to her chest, then crammed it in her bag lest anyone spot it and returned to her immersion in cathode rays. The phone rang.

"Talks Department, Miss Musgrave," Maisie answered crisply.

"It's Lady Astor for Miss Matheson," said an equally authoritative secretary.

"I'm so sorry, but Miss Matheson is not available. May I take a message?"

"When will she return, please?"

"She's in the studio and can't be disturbed. May I have her ring Lady Astor back?"

There was a surprised yip, a shuffle, and Lady Astor's imperious voice came on the line.

"Miss Musgrave? Good. I couldn't abide speaking to that hang-dried misery-boot. The news can't wait, because I want to give Miss Matheson an exclusive, and as she trusts you, that means I can as well, doesn't it?"

It wasn't really a question. Maisie was glad Lady Astor couldn't see her smile.

"I always strive to be very worthy of trust, Lady Astor."

"Marvelous. Though in my experience, keepin' certain people a bit unsure isn't without use. Now, listen! They're going to announce it tomorrow, but they've finally just passed equal suffrage, and that's going to make for some very good Talks, I should think."

Maisie, writing the information on the Talks Department harvest-moon-orange memo (a clever choice of Hilda's—there was no missing a missive from Talks), knew she was meant to respond with enthusiasm. But Lady Astor knew they were still constrained as to the sort of news they could report, and when was there time for an exclusive?

"That's very good news, Lady Astor. Thank you so much for letting us know."

"Those are the words of a polite and professional secretary, my dear. Don't you realize what this means? All women over twenty-one can cast a vote next year, single or married, rich or poor. It's the law now, and it won't ever be changed again. It's rather a bit of something."

Phyllida would turn twenty-one next year. She would be able to vote. Everyone would. Then Maisie swayed and seized hold of the desk. A Canadian national, living in Britain, was allowed to vote. That meant her. And now she was going to get to spread the news.

"I've got to get Miss Matheson straightaway."

"That's better," Lady Astor trilled, her laugh ending in an unladylike snort.

Maisie slammed down the phone, snatched up her pad, and sprinted for the studio. Where of course the BROADCASTING IN PROGRESS sign kept her rooted to the corridor. She circled before the door, a bull trapped in a pen.

"My goodness, dear, you'll wear a hole in the floor!" It was Siepmann. With Cyril. She wanted to lower her head and charge. "You don't look like you're working. Doesn't Miss Matheson keep your nose well to the grindstone?"

She thrust her nose into the air to give him a better view. "She does, Mr. Siepmann, though it's hardly necessary. We in Talks are very dedicated to doing the best possible work. For the BBC," she added, remembering their last conversation. She was pleased to see Cyril look abashed at Siepmann's manner. Or maybe he was surprised at hers.

"I rejoice to hear it," Siepmann said. "I do sometimes wonder how you all manage, being so busy." He shook his head, as though the wonderment preyed on him. "I'm surprised Miss Matheson doesn't seek to expand the department, do more delegating while keeping the whip hand high. I'm sure if I ran it, I'd have to be a terrible tyrant."

I'm sure if you ran it, we'd all take up pitchforks and torches.

"Miss Matheson manages very well, thank you."

"Certainly according to the papers and listener numbers, yes," he agreed, as though such things were inconsequential. "Well, keep up your hard work, my dear," he said, and jerked his head to Cyril to chivvy him on.

If only I were one of those secret agents. I'd have a poison dart to shoot at him.

She shunted aside that pretty picture and focused on the real masterpiece: Lady Astor's scoop. There had to be a way to use it and not step outside their bounds. A special guest, perhaps, ruminating on the possibility that full suffrage would at last be the law of the land? And if that person was highly respectable, known, above reproach . . . maybe Lady Astor herself? No, not a sitting politician. Everyone knew they leaked stories all the time, but none would do so publicly. But it should be a woman. A suffragette! Emmeline Pankhurst had just died (such a lovely retrospective Talk on her life and work). Her daughter Christabel had moved to California. Perhaps the other daughter, Sylvia? No. An older suffragette would be better, someone who had fought long and hard and survived to see—of course, Millicent Fawcett. She was over eighty, not well, but very much alive and a dame, so decidedly proper.

Hilda came out of the studio and Maisie pounced on her.

"Miss Matheson, the most extraordinary thing! We've got to . . . It's so . . ."

A shadow loomed over her. She'd forgotten it was Vita Sackville-West who had been broadcasting.

"Holy smokes," Maisie whispered, gazing up into the great lady's steely eyes. "I . . . er . . ."

Vita laughed. "I do relish the sight of a woman passionate about her work. Do attend to Miss Musgrave, my dear Hilda. I can see myself out this once. Good day."

As soon as Vita was out of earshot, Hilda turned on Maisie in a rage.

"Since when are you unprofessional? Was my promise of 'later' somehow not clear? I'm a patient woman, but—"

"No, it's not that. I—" She barreled an astonished Hilda back into the studio, closing the door behind them. "Miss Matheson, Lady Astor rang, and—"

Billy was still in there, clutching a wilted bouquet of red and blue wires.

"Could you leave us be for a moment, please?" she asked him.

"But . . . I'm working," he protested. Maisie shot him her most ferocious glare, and out he went. She slammed the door behind him and leaned against its gloriously soundproof surface, grinning in the face of Hilda's fury.

"They've passed equal suffrage. Lady Astor said so. It's being announced tomorrow, but she's told us now on the chance we can do something with a broadcast tonight. Can we? I thought Dame Millicent Fawcett, maybe. She could speak to a rumor or some such, so it's not 'breaking news.' The papers can't complain at anything to do with Dame Millicent, surely? I mean, not the good ones."

Hilda's face morphed from purple with indignation to white with astonishment and was now pink with pleasure. She clasped Maisie's hand.

"Equal suffrage? Are you sure? What did she say?"

"She said it meant all women . . ." Maisie choked up. It had never mattered to her before, not politics, not anything. But women had died for this. Phyllida lived for it. It mattered a lot. Her words came out in a squeak. "All women over twenty-one can vote. No restrictions."

"Oh . . . Maisie." Hilda yanked a handkerchief from her pocket and pressed it to her face. Her head popped up quickly, eyes damp and glittering. She swan-dived onto the studio phone to ring Millicent Fawcett. Maisie stood behind her, bouncing on her toes. Even through her excitement, she couldn't help looking at the controls and thinking they'd be such fun to work. It couldn't be so hard if people like Billy did it. Women weren't allowed, but maybe . . .

"She said yes!" Hilda crowed. "I'll go fetch her myself. Oh, we'd best say something to the DG," Hilda remembered. "Can't risk an apoplectic fit."

Except that telling him meant giving him a chance to veto. Luck was with them; his secretary said he was gone for the day and no, he couldn't be reached.

"A jolly good night for him to be gallivanting," Hilda said, sighing with relief. They had, after all, attempted to follow protocol. Now they just needed to rearrange the evening schedule to accommodate the broadcast and write a script of sorts.

"Someday the BBC is going to have the right to do all its own news, hang the papers," Hilda grumbled with uncharacteristic vitriol. "Honestly, why can't the future be *now*? Even being a political secretary didn't require so much disassembly."

She clasped her hands behind her back and paced.

"Let's see: 'Rumbles from Parliament hint at the long fought-for right to equal franchise. If this is true, it will have some real bearing upon our next general election. Dame Millicent Fawcett, one of the great activists for women's universal suffrage, is here to reflect on the legacy of the struggle and what true universal suffrage might entail.' And then Dame Millicent can say: 'I hope this is the case, as we don't want to remain behind our American sisters, and it's important for Britain, generally a universal leader, to show it trusts all its women with this task.' Hm. This sacred task? No. This sacred duty? Bit hyperbolic? But we can't overstate the import." Her grin nearly split her face, and she hugged herself. "It will be a terribly interesting election."

<hr />

"Where's Our Lady gone?" Fielden asked Maisie, standing over her desk, arms folded, ignoring the furious gallop of her fingers as she typed the script.

"She's escorting Dame Millicent Fawcett here for a special broadcast," Maisie said, overflowing with the joy of superior information.

"Oh, Lord, not the Fawcett woman." Fielden moaned. "Perfect
name—turn her mouth on and it never stops running."

"She is an enormously important woman! One of the great suffragettes, and a dame, besides!" Maisie retorted, outraged.

"Damn the dames, I say."

"Mr. Fielden!"

"I'm a republican. Small 'r.' It means something different over
here, you know."

"Yes, I know," Maisie snapped. "I have actually lived in Britain
most of my adult life and I read all the newspapers." She slammed
the shift lever over, thundered through her final sentences, and
snatched out the papers.

"Well, look who's got a temper on her." He *tsk*ed, smirking.
"What are we coming to?"

"I'll leave you to determine," she told him, and flounced off to
the typing pool to scoop up Phyllida. The nearest spot for a private
talk was the second-favorite ladies' lavatory and, after checking under
the stalls for feet, Maisie broke the momentous news.

Phyllida gripped hold of the sink and stared at her.

"Nae. Is it really true? It must be. Lady Astor wouldn't spread a
rumor. Oh, my life!" She began to weep. "Can you believe it? We're
all of us going to have a voice at last."

"We really are," Maisie said, and she started crying too.

Both of them were still red-eyed when they emerged a few minutes later. Eckersley saw them and chuckled. "What would you poor
girls do without lavatories to bawl in?"

They were floating far too high to bother with a response.

Meeting Dame Millicent passed in a blur. She was frail, with
papery-white skin and trembling hands, but like Hilda, her eyes were
shining.

"I think I lived to see this out of sheer stubbornness," she declared
in a voice much stronger than her body.

She bore herself with extreme elegance and sat as upright as if she were still wearing corsets. Which perhaps she was. Mr. Burrows, the BBC's announcer, had to be brought into the secret so he could interview Dame Millicent—there was no time to find anyone else. And listeners would think the presence of a man added gravitas to the occasion.

Maisie stepped outside the door, set the BROADCASTING IN PROGRESS sign in place, and gave it a fond pat.

"I believe you just squealed," Fowler, the sound effects man, told her. A short performance was to close the evening's broadcast, and he wheeled up a trolley bearing a gramophone, an amplifier, a tea towel, and a head of cauliflower.

"I suppose I did," Maisie agreed. "Good thing I'm not in there." She jerked her thumb at the studio door. An unscripted background squeal was punishable by firing squad. "What's all this?" She waved a hand at the trolley.

"Items for sound effects, of course," Fowler answered, with that stunned expression the sound effects men always got when someone asked about their work, baffled as to how they were fated to work among such imbeciles.

"A gramophone, Mr. Fowler? That looks like cheating."

"Does it?" he asked sharply. "And do you see any records here?"

She didn't. Seeing her properly chastised, Fowler chose to educate rather than upbraid her.

"Here. Put your ear right against the amplifier, and have a listen." He wound the gramophone and set the needle on a tea towel, so it just brushed the fabric. He tapped lightly on the towel in rhythmic beats, creating a *thump-thump, thump-thump* that, she gradually realized, was the sound of a heartbeat. "Close your eyes," he advised. She did, the sound washing straight through her.

"Crikey, it's hardly anything to cry about," Fowler scolded. "You girls, you get weepy over the strangest things."

Maisie wiped her eyes and grinned, feeling no need to ask where the cauliflower came in. Even at its most mundane, the BBC was pure magic. That was worth a few tears.

"Tell me, Mr. Fowler, can you create a sound for being so happy, you just want to hug the entire world and never let go?"

He shrank from her in horror. "That's not for an upcoming Talk, is it?"

The newspapers outdid themselves with stories on what was formally titled the "Representation of the People (Equal Franchise) Act 1928," and were generous enough to congratulate the BBC on its prescience and fine discussion with the great Dame Millicent Fawcett. Reith's incandescence wilted under the weight of the congratulations that showered on him all morning, though Maisie wondered how many of those congratulations were more about his genius in hiring Hilda.

Reith towered in the middle of Hilda's office. He never seemed to fit there—Maisie thought cozy spaces made him uncomfortable.

"I appreciate that I was not available, Miss Matheson, and so you had to make a swift decision and you decided to err on the side of risk." His scowl contorted, indicating his general feeling about risk. "It does seem to have been successful. But in future, I hope you will show more discretion, or at least seek the advice and support of another senior. We can't have staff simply throwing on broadcasts without proper vetting. It will certainly lead to chaos."

Maisie could see that Hilda yearned to tell Reith that senior staff absolutely needed that discretion, and it was flexibility that would help the BBC grow. But she smiled placidly and nodded.

"Yes, of course, Mr. Reith. I do apologize."

"We have no idea what could have happened," he pointed out.

"No, indeed."

"Well, let's be more mindful on another occasion." He turned on his heel to leave, nodding at Maisie in a way that made her realize he was expecting her to accompany him. "We miss you up in the executive offices, Miss Musgrave," he said when they reached the corridor. "You were a pleasant girl to have around."

"Thank you, sir," she said, rather touched.

"What do you think of this voting business?" Ah, that was why he wanted to talk to her alone. He remembered the devotee of the Old World and wanted some youthful sympathy. "My wife has never seen the need for it—she's happy to let me make all such decisions. We were both quite troubled seeing any women vote, but single, and perhaps uneducated women at the polls, that seems a guarantor of trouble. I know it's all down to these times, but it does worry me."

"I suppose we'll just have to see?" Maisie said. She couldn't point out America's success with women's suffrage, since he considered Americans to be an ungrateful, degenerate rabble who should be corralled back into the empire.

"It doesn't worry you?" He was asking if she had become one of those. No longer under his watch, had she shunned her beloved traditions, been seduced by the big bad wolf of modernity?

"The British Empire is the greatest the world has ever seen," she assured him. "Having more of its people involved in its politics can only be to the good."

He favored her with his most smiling scowl.

"You are a diplomat, Miss Musgrave. And perhaps you are correct. I suppose we shall see. If the election goes poorly, I daresay they can revoke the law."

Revoke the law? Finally grant rights, then snatch them away again? That sounded like the stuff of satire. Or the Fascist meetings. It didn't sound like democracy. *Of course, there are always laws that someone doesn't like, but . . .*

"Miss Musgrave?"

Reith was scowling down at her, without a hint of a smile.

"Sir?"

"I said, 'good afternoon.'"

"Oh!" She had been dismissed. "Yes. Good afternoon, sir. Thank you."

"You really *are* a diplomat," Hilda teased when Maisie came back to the office.

"You heard all that?" The woman had the hearing of a bat.

"It comes in handy."

Maisie sat back down to the correspondence but couldn't concentrate. She wanted it to be the mythical "later." She wanted to write about men's fears of women voting, compare it to America. She wanted more stories they could tell, to go chasing stories herself. She wanted to interview women on the street. She wanted to tell Eckersley to work harder on developing a traveling microphone. She wanted to be able to print Dame Millicent's Talk in a magazine. She wanted to vote. Now.

"Miss Matheson!" Her shout nearly made the windows rattle.

"Gracious! Is there a fire?" Hilda looked more interested than alarmed.

"Can we . . . ? I remember we once . . . The general election is to be next year, isn't it?"

"That's the general idea," Hilda said.

"Perhaps we can do a series, something to teach—no, not teach, but, well, maybe teach—"

"You're wittering," Hilda said, but she was grinning.

"Yes. Something to help prepare women for voting, learn about the process, how to choose their party interests. I mean, masses of women will think they ought to vote as their father or husband does, won't they? But maybe that's not really what they want, but maybe they don't know . . . I'm still wittering."

"I wasn't criticizing. From a good witter, inspiration rises." Hilda leaped up and paced the office. "We can start something once a week. Do more nearer to the election. Invite women from all fields, positions, interests, and talk about politics and women's place in it. We'll be accused of being shills for Labour, obviously—"

"Or the Communists," Maisie put in.

"Oh, certainly." Hilda chuckled. "But we'll have Lady Astor first, and we'll keep it all very neutral and informative. Give it a nice, nonincendiary title. *Advice for Women Voters*. No, that's condescending. We'll sound like agony aunts. *Questions for Women Voters*. That might do."

"Can we? Ask questions, I mean."

"The traveling microphone?" Hilda asked, smiling. Maisie nearly fainted. Could Hilda read her mind now? Then she remembered the phrase was one she'd read from Hilda's notes on broadcasting.

"I hope we can try." Hilda glanced at the carriage clock. "I think we deserve a celebratory lunch. Get Rules on the phone, will you?"

Rules! That was one of the grandest restaurants in London. Maisie glanced down at herself. The Garland Green wasn't bad, but . . .

"You look perfectly smart. Ring them up and I'll book us a table."

Not as smart as Hilda, though. Maisie looked at her with envy as they approached the restaurant. It was an easy walk from the Strand to Southampton Street and then Maiden Lane. Hilda walked with that swift purpose, that little bounce in her step that was really quite attractive. What would it be like to wake up every day with such lovely skin, such bright eyes? She had just turned forty, but she was so young and beautiful. Vibrant. It was almost hypnotic.

As was Rules. They stepped in, and Maisie squeaked. The plush carpet, buttery lights, magnificent pictures and mirrors, heavy damask tablecloths. Her hands were shaking as she took the menu, burgundy leather and embossed in gold.

Maisie waited until the arrival of her Cornish fish soup to ask if it was "later."

"No. It's lunchtime." Hilda grinned. "But I do have some news. We're going to start a new magazine, printing transcripts of our better Talks. And other things. *The Listener*, it's being called. Bit prosaic, but at least everyone will know it's us."

"Crikey." Maisie whistled. "Do you think it'll accept articles from staff?"

"It might even run bylines," Hilda teased. Then she went on to divulge another piece of gossip—the BBC was deemed successful enough to warrant a purpose-built home, with ground to be broken in Portland Place in a few months.

Maisie was so stunned, even the arrival of partridge and bread sauce didn't immediately arrest her attention.

"We're leaving Savoy Hill?"

"Don't get sentimental about the old pile," Hilda warned, pointing a parsnip at her. "It's been a perfectly good starting spot, but the BBC is going to become something even more. If I have anything to do with it," she added with sudden blood in her voice. "We deserve it. We need a massive hulking beast of a building—elegant and beautiful, of course, but fantastically imposing, with 'BBC' emblazoned across the top. And we're going to get it. Not till 1932, though, dash it. I abhor waiting."

"I suppose it took longer to build St. Paul's?"

"Yes, yes. And the pyramids. And at least our builders will get a nice salary, but damn, I want that space. Imagine the studios! And the IEE will be pleased to have the whole of Savoy Hill to itself again. I bet they'll throw a monthlong party."

Even the thought of the Institute of Electrical Engineers indulging in Bright Young Thing–style frivolity couldn't make Maisie smile, not when it meant leaving Savoy Hill. It was home, probably the place Maisie thought more like home than anywhere she'd actually lived, she realized with some astonishment. Then she was more astonished to find she was expecting to still be there in four years. There wasn't anywhere she'd rather be.

"Now, Miss Musgrave, I must ask. Do you want to continue as my secretary?"

Maisie clutched the table to keep from smashing through the carpet and into the basement. Hilda's expression was merely curious, as if she'd only asked if she wanted more wine. She opened her mouth to insert something in the crater-sized gap Maisie created, but a sudden, "Ah, Miss Matheson!" made them both look up.

Lady Astor was standing by their table.

"Goodness, Lady Astor, hello!" Hilda cried, jumping up to shake her hand. "It was so good of you to give us that scoop. Do sit down."

"No, no. Shan't be stayin' but a moment. Knew you'd be here and wanted to offer my congratulations. Very nice work you did, though of course I knew you would."

"It was largely down to Miss Musgrave, really."

"Was it?" Lady Astor scrutinized Maisie as though she were a shiny trinket. "Marvelous. I suppose no good imaginin' Reith was admirable about it all?"

"I think the idea of any women voting is still a bit of a shock for him, to be honest."

"I've drunk sugar water made of sterner stuff than that man, though he's an impressive tyrant." She turned to Maisie. "I met his mother once, you know. Oh yes, he's got one. Brought her to lunch at the House of Commons, presumably to show off how grand and important he's become. Well, so he introduced me and, not being one to pass up an opportunity, I asked her if was it from her that he got his Mussolini-like qualities."

Hilda choked into her burgundy.

"What did she say?" Maisie breathed. It was extraordinary, what the upper classes could get away with.

"Oh, she seemed a bit put out," Lady Astor answered with shrug. "That sort always is. Not stern stuff, that's what I say. Not where it counts, anyway. Hence, tyranny. Though she probably thinks he's very fine. Well, shan't interrupt you any further. I'd recommend the Bakewell tart," she advised Maisie before sashaying off.

"How did she know how to find you?" Maisie asked after Hilda had ordered two Bakewell tarts and coffee.

"She had a tail put on me when I left her employ," Hilda said, finishing her wine. "I jest. This is where we always dined after a particularly memorable triumph."

They grinned at each other. Then Maisie remembered Hilda was upending her world.

"Try to look at it from an outsider's perspective," Hilda said, seeing what Maisie was thinking. "You're an excellent secretary, but with your first-rate mind, fearlessness, and knack for finding good stories, you could be just the sort of journalist the newspapers need more of. If you want to pursue it, I'd be happy to introduce you to some useful people. There aren't many women reporters, very few doing serious writing, but I'd lay money you'd be one to break through."

Even the arrival of the tarts didn't break through Maisie's whirring brain. A mind that was first-rate. Knack for finding stories. Fearlessness. She remembered reading about Nellie Bly, who had written some extraordinary stories. Was Hilda Matheson, Oxford-educated director of Talks at the BBC, extolled in all the papers for her own fine mind and taste and capacity, was she really saying this about Maisie? Mousy Maisie? Perhaps she could join a newspaper, or a magazine, and write every day. Nearly all of Simon's notes told her how tremendous it was to write articles, giving people information and with your name on it, too.

But she had something else to do.

"Miss Matheson, I . . . Thank you, truly. That is . . . Thank you. But I don't want to leave the BBC. I really don't. I love it there."

She hadn't known how much until now.

Hilda smiled and poured out their coffees. "Good. Because I'd like to promote you to Talks assistant."

Rules had become a roller coaster. Hilda went on, blithe and blasé. "It's still rather a lot of clerical work, as you know, of course, but it's the only way from which you can eventually be promoted to producer."

That roller coaster was taking a pretty hairy turn.

"Producer?" Maisie's voice was so high, only bats and Hilda could hear her.

"You certainly think like one. I'd be shocked if you couldn't work like one, and I loathe shocks. Do you want to be one?"

The only women working as producers were the very well-educated and even better-connected Beanie and Mary Somerville in Schools.

"But I'm not even educated," she felt the need to point out.

"By which you mean you didn't go to school. Not quite the same thing. How did you learn, anyway? I've always wondered."

"Libraries," Maisie said. "Well, I learned my letters first from a wardrobe mistress in a theater, very kind lady. Georgina—that's my mother—never sent me to school because we moved so much and she didn't really care anyway. So I went to libraries. Some librarians saw me as a project and suggested books and even explained things. One actually tried to help me learn sums and science. Others just left me in peace and I read everything. As much as I could, I mean. It wasn't the same as a real education, but I suppose it was something."

"I should jolly well say so. A testament to American libraries. But why didn't Georgina just lodge you in Toronto if she didn't want to raise you properly?"

"My grandparents didn't want to keep me full-time. I was more of an embarrassment than Georgina. I don't even know if my parents were married—I only know my father's name, Edwin Musgrave, that's it. In summers, they could 'educate' me but keep me partly under wraps. And I think they liked Georgina being stuck with me. Saw me as a fitting punishment for her."

"Gracious. Well, it proves what I've always thought: that it's not how you're born; it's what you make of yourself. Anyway, who gives a fig about your background? There's no point in a new industry if only the same old sort of people do the running of it. I'd promote you to producer now, but that would be blocked. Mind you, he might balk at this as well, though his courtship promise included my free rein over the department. So we can but try. Are you keen?"

"I am," Maisie said, her voice coming out in little pips—the BBC's pips at the top of the hour.

"Good. Who do you think might replace you as secretary?"

As though it were any question.

"Miss Fenwick is a very fine choice," Hilda said, before Maisie had opened her mouth. "We ought to be tootling back." She called for the bill. "It was rather a nice lunch, wasn't it?"

"I've never had better," Maisie said.

That evening, as Hilda was packing up to leave, she called out to Maisie, "I say, Miss Musgrave, have you got evening plans?"

"No, Miss Matheson. Is it another of Lady Astor's salons?"

"Actually, I was thinking it was 'later.'"

Maisie lurched from her desk, nearly taking the typewriter with her. Hilda *tsk*ed and tidied up the disrupted papers as Maisie threw on her hat and coat.

"You've got your hat on backwards," Hilda informed her. Then said nothing else, all the way up to the Strand, where she hailed them a taxi.

"Where are we going?" Maisie asked.

"I've got a friend I'd like you to meet."

Hilda ordered the driver down an alley, ignoring all of Maisie's questions as they entered a posh, silent building from the back entrance. Hilda murmured something to a man inside the door and pattered up the back stairs, Maisie close on her heels. Down a corridor covered in what looked like the Bayeux tapestry ("Victorians had a peculiar taste," was Hilda's whispered critique) and into a dark study, where a gaunt man with a toucan nose untangled his long legs and rose from a Renaissance Revival chair, grinning at Hilda.

"Topping to hear from you, old girl. Hardly recognize you without a notepad the size of the Ten Commandments in your hand."

"It's in my holdall," Hilda said, shaking hands with him. "May I present my secretary, soon-to-be Talks assistant, Miss Musgrave? Miss Musgrave, Mr. Ellis. Known to a few of us as 'God,' though of course quite ironically."

"I hope that's short for 'Godfrey,'" Maisie said.

Ellis raised an eyebrow and offered her a drink. She declined—the snifter looked as though it would engulf her head if she tried to sip from it.

"What about you, Matty?" Ellis said, turning to Hilda.

Matty?

"Always happy to take away some of the club's brandy," Hilda said. She turned to Maisie with a grin. "God likes doling out nicknames. But he's a clever sort, so we tolerate him. Also, he's a whiz at the sort of thing we're sniffing at, so I thought we might bring in his brains."

It was positively alien to think of Hilda needing anyone else's brains. Ellis lit a cheroot and grinned at Maisie.

"It's not actually my brains she's after, but kind of her to say."

Maisie looked back and forth between the two of them. "Is this . . . ? Are you . . . ? You are MI5, aren't you?" She sagged against the Regency table.

"Ah, girls and their fancies," Ellis said, winking at her.

"Yes, we're hopelessly frivolous," Hilda snapped. "Now, then, have a look at these, so as to offer your dubious yet valued opinion."

Maisie wanted to point out they hadn't answered her question, but Hilda was spreading their notes, German propaganda, and annotated articles across the table.

"I know you were putting it down to cleverness, Matty, but if the girl thinks you're a spy, it may be because that handwriting looks like desperately tricky code."

"What hilarity," Hilda said. "How are you not a music hall star?"

"I have a rotten agent. So, your little interest in the political lunatic fringe rises again, I see."

"Not so lunatic or fringe if they are attracting people with money. Miss Musgrave sneaked into an underground meeting . . ." Hilda turned to Maisie. "How were you able to get in, by the way? They weren't letting just anyone in, I should think?"

"No, there was a code word, 'lion,' which . . ." She paused, as Hilda and Ellis were laughing.

"Sorry, Miss Musgrave. It's only that these people are like little boys playing adventure games. Look at the advert again, just the first letters of every line."

Hilda ran her finger down the ad:

Listen in a like-minded crowd!
If Siemens is your favorite wireless,
opt to gather 'round with us.
News of a *real* sort and refreshments, too!

"And I daresay it's 'Lion' for the lion of England," Ellis finished, wiping his eyes. "But really, Matty, how can you think people who put on such a poor show are worth worrying about? I grant you, they would do better to take up good, solid hobbies like Onanism—"

"Ellis!"

"—but I fail to see anything illegal."

"They want to take over the BBC and stop women working there!" Maisie cried.

"Everyone wants to run the BBC. You're a great success. But I'll say to you what I said to Matty. I see foolishness and odiousness, but not illegality."

"The *Radio Times*," Maisie said suddenly. "Not just any magazine—they picked the *Radio Times* to alert people to meetings." She whirled to Hilda. "That quote. From that fellow Goebbels. Where he said that coup the Nazis staged in 1923 might have succeeded, if they could have taken over the radio." She turned back to Ellis. "That wasn't legal. And now they're trying to raise money, and from here, too. And if British Fascists are thinking along the same lines—"

"I said they were legal, not decent," Ellis muttered.

"Honestly, if captains of industry are giving up a free evening to attend Fascist meetings, they must see a business opportunity," Hilda said. "And that's rarely good for those who like freedom. They want to buy some papers too, it seems, to further exert influence."

"Ah, following closely in Mussolini's footsteps, eh?" Ellis asked with a theatrical wink. Hilda, to Maisie's surprise, actually blushed.

"My point," Hilda said, biting her lips, "is that it might be worth keeping at least a casual eye on them."

"That takes time and money," Ellis said. "Of which I have virtually none. But if the two of you wish to dig deeper and then share findings, there is always plenty of brandy."

"So you do think it's worthwhile!" Hilda cried.

"No. I'm just humoring you," Ellis said. "You always like to have your thousand and one projects. But I say, Miss Musgrave, do be careful. These fantasists rarely amount to much politically, but they can allow their ideas to run away with them, which can be a bit dangerous. Not really something a nice young girl ought to be getting muddled up in."

"That's very good advice," Maisie said gravely. "If I see any nice young girls, I'll be sure to pass it along."

FOURTEEN

London, September 1928

Dear Lola,

I'm so pleased the show is such a success and you're enjoying
Rome. I do miss you, though. You needn't worry about my moving
anytime soon. I'm earning more money as a Talks assistant, but
I'd rather build up some savings, and of course get some more
decent clothes and things. I do wish you were here to help me with
shopping (which wasn't true but it would delight Lola). Tell
me more about this visconte who meets you at the stage door every
night. I hope he's noble in every sense of the word! We all miss
you. Mrs. Crewe wants you to hurry home from such a disreputable
place as Italy, though she's glad you decided to keep your room
here. As am I, and thank you again for giving me free rein with
your things. I'm putting them to good use, and will tell all when
you get home.

Yours,
Maisie

Even if she had funds enough to move, there was absolutely no time for flat-hunting. In addition to her full days as a Talks assistant, she continued to type Hilda's notes on broadcasting as they accumulated, every few weeks. A fine book was taking shape. Her budget now allowed for her own copies of morning papers, and as she had mastered the art of balancing in the tram without holding a strap, she could read and mark interesting events or people that might generate a Talk. And now she was sniffing around at what this unauthorized branch of the Fascist party was up to, as it was trying to upset her apple cart. She never felt tired, only energized.

This week was particularly historic, as she was the first one to attack a submitted script with a red pencil. The Talk was *A Day in the Life of a London Postman*. She worked on it in the tram, in the evenings, even in the bath. *Make it conversational. Bring out the most interesting bits. Help him be his most natural self.* Then she presented it with high ceremony to Hilda.

"Excellent work, Miss Musgrave," Hilda said half an hour later, handing it back to her. Covered in blue writing. Hilda had made several dozen more revisions—all of them perfect.

"Sometimes I wonder why any of us even bother," Maisie murmured to Phyllida, who was reading the script over her shoulder.

"Hers is better," Phyllida said unhelpfully.

"I'm aware of that."

"And next time you'll do better, too," Phyllida said, bopping Maisie on the shoulder.

Maisie looked forward to getting her hands dirtier with *Questions for Women Voters*, which was an instant success. So much post came in asking follow-up questions, they had to run an extra five minutes at the end of each broadcast just to address a tenth of them.

"We need a daily program, frankly, and an hour long," Maisie told Simon, as they strolled through the National Gallery. He was keen to show her what he considered all the best art.

"If the ladies have so many questions, maybe they're not ready to vote," Simon said, laughing in the face of Maisie's lightning-bolt glare. "Joking! Rights for one should be rights for all, certainly. And it's far better than having women protesting on the streets, yowling like banshees and creating all kinds of mess. I remember seeing it as a lad, grim stuff." He pretended to shudder.

"If equal rights were just given from the beginning, then no one would have to fight for them on the street and create a mess," Maisie said.

"Ah, there's no arguing with the radical ladies."

"Not radical; reasonable, I think."

They laughed, and Maisie tried not to feel too pleased with herself. She couldn't entirely believe it, believe this was her, the former Mousy Maisie, exploring the National Gallery with a charming and handsome and honest-to-goodness aristocrat, who seemed to like her. She still felt a bit awkward around him. Even after an acquaintanceship of several months, she hadn't seen much of him. Indeed, their only contact over the last few weeks had been letters.

"Can you forgive me, dearest?" he asked. "I've been working at it like a family of beavers. The words, the words, eh? Well, you know, you do a bit of writing yourself. Awfully satisfying when it comes out right and is printed, isn't it?"

"It is," she agreed, thinking it was high time she tried to write something for print again.

"But I can't help wishing for a larger readership," he complained. "*Pinpoint* is doing such fine work, but so few know it." They stopped before *The Hay Wain*. "Ah, Constable. A great beauty, isn't it? He really knew how to capture the best of Britain, the country life, the ordinary worker. Now, you see, that's the sort of man I'd like my work to reach."

"Constable?"

"The worker, darling. Provided he can read. Ah, I suppose that is the advantage you have over me. With radio, it doesn't matter if the people are illiterate; you can still present them with useful facts and thus shape their minds."

"Well, we actually try to—"

"Wouldn't it be grand if the newspapers and BBC worked

together, after a fashion? Get the most important information to the people, make sure no one missed it?"

"But news does get everywhere," Maisie said. "Every town and village has a paper, and there's Reuters and—"

"Of course, of course. But it's not the same as a really brilliant editor, putting together all the best stories, not just facts but essays, opinions. Think of it, darling. A good, strong voice, clear of all the other dross that ends up in papers, that would provide some real meat for the man. Or woman," he added graciously.

"I don't know," Maisie said. "It sounds like it waters things down an awful lot."

"Not if the writing is masterful. Besides, isn't that rather what your BBC does? It is only a single entity, based in London and so not unreasonably viewed as London-centric, and travels unaltered all through the country."

"But that's what makes us so democratic," Maisie argued. "Anyone anywhere can hear a poem or a debate or a play and they don't have to be able to read or be in London and they can enjoy it equally."

"They don't have to be bothered with a lot of different views."

"But we *do* present different views! Miss Matheson says that's one of the most important—"

"Oh, Miss Matheson, Miss Matheson. Honestly, darling, she begins to sound like a deity. Come, let's pay obeisance to Vermeer."

He took her hand to pull her along. She was sure his argument was flawed and wanted to think about it, but when he touched her, the ability to think fell out of her ears. She just wanted to follow that touch wherever it went.

"If that's true, you'd best be careful," Phyllida warned. They were cranking out mimeographs, so they could steal a moment for a private conversation. "At least go to one of those clinics."

"Those . . . Oh!" Those sorts of clinics. She had come a long way from Cyril. She wasn't sure if she was in love, but she wasn't sure she cared. When she was with Simon, she just wanted . . .

"But what do you think when you're not with him?"

"Mostly about the BBC."

"Aye, so be careful. Don't want to get yourself in what they might call 'a situation.'"

"You have to be married to go to those clinics, though," said Maisie.

"So you borrow a ring and call yourself 'Mrs.' They're not going to check." Phyllida shrugged.

"How do you know?" Maisie demanded.

Phyllida gave Maisie a disdainful frown.

"I came up through the typing pool. Try to find something I don't know."

Maisie laughed, gathered the mimeographs, and headed for the corridor.

"As it happens, unlike some people we need not mention, Simon Brock-Morland is thus far as honorable as his title."

Beanie, hurrying past them, skittered to a halt.

"Simon Brock-Morland? Don't say *you* know him!"

"I do, actually." Maisie grinned.

"He's courting her," Phyllida added, smirking.

"Is he? Really? Fancy that—here I thought I was the one who specialized in unlikely scenarios. Anyway, must dash, rehearsal. Cheerio!"

Maisie had her own rehearsal to attend, so kept pace with Beanie.

"So you know him, too? You do, don't you? Do you like him?"

Beanie gave Maisie a sidelong glance, looped arms with her, and propelled her up the stairs, heads close together.

"I don't know him well, if that's what you're asking. I was just paraded before him a few times as a viable candidate, doing my show horse rounds."

"Sorry?"

"He's eligible. I'm available. Got to display all the wares. *Les parents*

230 · SARAH-JANE STRATFORD

may be tickled by my work, living the regular life, doing good, et cetera, et cetera, but I'm still who I am and there are expectations, don't you know? Can't let the side down. Duty will come for us all and can't shirk it forever. Got to produce more top foals and what."

Beanie was too well trained to let her real feelings show, even accidentally. But Maisie swore she heard a twinge of bitterness in that cut-glass accent.

"But you don't have to marry anyone you don't want to, surely? It's nearly 1929, for heaven's sake."

"You really aren't British." Beanie giggled, shaking her head. "Ah, well, in any event, the Honorable Mr. Brock-Morland didn't take my bait, even though the story says he could do with some extra dosh."

"Just because he's the second son doesn't mean he hasn't got money."

"Perfectly true. But I hear his father isn't the best manager of things. Of course, one can't ever be sure. And thank goodness for that, or what would we talk about?"

Maisie turned this information over and over. If Simon was concerned about money, but seemed to be interested in her and not someone like Beanie . . .

"He might like that you're clever, you know," Beanie said. "He's a funny one that way. Or he hopes to shock the family, of course. Shocking one's family is quite 'the fad' these days. This year's pea-shooting. Ah, here's for me, cheerio."

Beanie was halfway down the corridor when Maisie shouted after her.

"How do families like that lose money? It's not just taxes or peasant revolts. It can't be."

Beanie turned and stared at her. "It would take a lot more journeys up and down the stairs to answer that question."

"Can you, though? Answer it?"

"Are you looking for gossip about Simon? I can likely scrape some up for you. He was rather a pompous ass to me. You're not in love with him, are you? Not that it matters. On the other hand." She paused, studying Maisie. Her expression was so serious, she was unrecognizable. "If you really want to know more about reversals of fortune, there are any number of stories written on it, I should think. But if this is towards a Talk, you tell Miss Matheson I want to be the one to present it."

"You? Really?"

Beanie laughed, looking much more like herself.

"I told you. Shocking one's family is all the thing."

Georgina would certainly be shocked if she saw Maisie using stage makeup to good effect, and especially if she saw the disguised Maisie entering a secret meeting of Fascists.

Except she probably doesn't know what Fascists are.

This time, the Lion was dismissing any effect women voting might have, as he assumed most women were too featherbrained to even find their way to the polling booths. Maisie ignored him and inched her way to Hoppel, who was having a whispered conversation in the back corner. She was so intent on her quarry, she didn't notice his companion until she was upon them. The teapot-shaped man who had looked at Simon with such interest. His bowler hat was tipped back and a cane hung over his arm in a parody of Charlie Chaplin. Neither man noticed her.

"Your friend at the BBC really must try and control that impossible woman," the teapot-shaped man said in a gravelly voice. "She is making every attempt to see Labour win the election. I am convinced it's the fault of the BBC, and that ghastly *Manchester Guardian* drivel, that trade unions are allowed to thrive. Total disaster for business—we'll all be paupers if this carries on. Appalling state, might as well be living in Moscow."

"'Appalling' is the only word," Hoppel agreed. "I tell you, Grigson, plenty of men are willing to work for whatever they're offered, but then those damn unions give them notions. And these book clubs! That's the sort of thing that makes a workingman think he's better than he is. More of that dreadful woman's influence. The sooner we see the back of her, the better."

"Another who thinks she's better than she is," Grigson said with a disparaging sniff. "But here's good news. I have purchased a newspaper and think I have found the man to run it. Might have a bit of a time finding a few more sound fellows to write for it, but I think we'll manage."

"I know some writers," Maisie burst in. Good spies listened, yes, but better ones seized opportunities.

Both men turned to look at her, surprised. Grigson laughed in what he clearly intended to be a fatherly manner. It grated on Maisie like fingernails on a chalkboard.

"Do you now? And I suppose these 'writers' are in fact brothers or cousins in need of a good job?"

"Well, perhaps," she said, trying to speak in Lola's accent. "But truly, they are very talented and eager."

"Ah, that's very nice too," Grigson said. "I tell you what, dear. Take my card, and if you'd like to have these writers drop through their stuff to me, I'll have a look at it."

"That's very kind of you, sir. Thank you so much."

"Not at all, not at all. But, ah, I say, dear, have the boys just leave off envelopes addressed to me and not saying anything about what it's regarding, all right? You can manage that, can't you?"

"Certainly, sir. Thank you, sir."

She had a feeling they were the sort of idiots who liked to see a girl so elated by a nothing sort of promise, there was a skip in her step as she walked away. She skipped, they laughed, and she smirked. Then the old thought floated through her contempt, the question, wondering if she had in fact told the truth, and Edwin Musgrave had provided her with brothers and cousins.

On the tram, she shook off those thoughts and looked at the card. The fist inside sucked all the breath from her body. Arthur Grigson. A company director. At Nestlé.

She should have been flabbergasted. But she wasn't.

Neither was Hilda. "Although I would like to be, I must say." Maisie had met her at the door to Savoy Hill that morning and they walked up the stairs together. They murmured, though they could have bellowed and no one would have heard them over the din, even at that hour. "All this fuss, just to keep a wealthy company run by wealthy men earning a bit more money. And I wouldn't be surprised if they call themselves Christians, too. Silly idiots."

"They also want to keep women from working. Or voting."

"They wouldn't, if they thought women working and voting would earn themselves one extra half-farthing. Never mind. The more we educate our listeners, the harder their work will be."

"And the more fun for us," Maisie said.

It was a grueling day. Hilda asked both Maisie and Phyllida to accompany her in rehearsing Virginia Woolf, an uncomfortable hour during which the writer refused to meet any of their eyes. She gazed at the microphone as though she expected it to bite her and looked fully prepared to bite back.

"I enjoyed *Orlando* very much," Phyllida ventured, with her most winning smile. Virginia Woolf stared at her without blinking.

"Thank you," she said at last. "It was a great pleasure to write." This comment was delivered with what looked very much like a glare at Hilda.

"We're all very lucky, aren't we?" Hilda asked. "Getting to do work we enjoy? Wouldn't have been possible, even when you were born, Miss Fenwick."

"No, quite," Phyllida answered, but her voice was wavering under that ceaseless glare, and Hilda's usual cheer and disinterest in Miss Woolf's temper was making it worse. Maisie and Phyllida exchanged a look, but there was nothing to do except carry on until, at last, Miss Woolf rose to leave.

Maisie stepped forward to walk her out. Miss Woolf said nothing, but shunned the lift for the stairs, moving with such ominous solemnity as to unnerve anyone coming upstairs, so that they jumped aside to let her pass. Maisie didn't like the writer's behavior, but couldn't help be impressed.

"Are you working on something new, Miss Woolf?" Maisie asked, hoping she seemed polite. In fact, she wanted to punish Virginia Woolf by forcing her to talk.

"I am," was the succinct reply.

"Another novel, dare we hope?"

"Of sorts." They reached reception, and the writer gave Maisie the faintest of nods. "It is, in part, about the importance of having one's own space. And having that space respected." She raised an eyebrow at Maisie, then turned and sashayed out the door.

Well, what idiot's going to argue otherwise?

Maisie ran back upstairs, where Hilda had forgotten Virginia Woolf and wanted to address the problem of some letters they were getting in response to *Questions for Women Voters*, letters from married women whose husbands were angry about them registering to vote.

"What sort of marriage do you call that?" Phyllida demanded. "One that needs walking out of, is what I say."

"We can't be accused of promoting marital discord," Hilda said. "Or more scandalously, divorce. So, let's think about these women."

Maisie rolled her pencil up and down her pad. Just a few years ago, she wouldn't have wanted to vote, to do anything that required making her own decisions. The old ideas, home, safety, someone who loved her, a family at last. So here were women whose husbands still believed that their voices should be sufficient in speaking for the whole family. It had for centuries; why should it not now?

All right, so they were raised to be the head of the house, and they do still earn the money, most of them, so they want to feel in control. But why should a man want to control the person who's meant to be his partner? That can't really be pleasant for anyone, surely?

"I suppose it's something new to share, isn't it?" Hilda said, sounding unusually romantic. "That's what marriage is meant to be, sharing lives." Her eyes wandered; she took a thousand-mile journey in a millisecond. "Another member of the family voting isn't going to change real love."

"Speaking of love, Maisie, you've got a phone call," Phyllida said, her hand thankfully over the mouthpiece.

Maisie took the phone in surprise. Simon preferred to write rather than ring.

"Maisie!" he cried when she greeted him. "Glad the ever-so-important BBC can spare you a moment. Do you need to tell them it's work-related, lest you risk a whipping?"

"No, it's all right . . . Are you all right?" She thought he sounded odd, a bit sneerier of the BBC than usual, and almost frantic. Which wasn't Simon at all. Maybe it was just the strangeness of hearing his voice on the phone.

"Grand, grand. Listen, darling, can you dine with me tonight? Seven? The Spencer in Chelsea? Say you can!" He definitely sounded rushed and frazzled now, and her "yes" was as much to calm him down as because she wanted to see him. "Thank you, darling. Must dash, cheerio!"

Maisie hung up and stared at the phone.

"All right," Hilda said, returning Maisie to the office. "We'll convene a panel of married women to give a Talk addressing this worry about cross husbands. That will be nice and proper."

Maisie made the note, her mind running backward from marriage to love. *Is this love, between me and Simon? Could he love me? Do I love him? How does anyone ever know? I suppose if people were sure, it would put an awful lot of poets out of work.*

She glanced at the neat pile of Hilda's books. Several volumes of poetry, a novel—probably one of Vita's recommendations—and any number of pamphlets. Had Hilda been disappointed in love, once? Was that why she threw herself so wholly into work? Or worse, was the one she loved lying under poppies, somewhere in Belgium?

Maisie's mind spun far away from Simon now. Ten years had passed since the Armistice, but for so many left alive and alone, it was yesterday. Maisie loved the bold new world, this glory they were continually inventing, but it was hard not to walk through the streets and feel that undercurrent of rage and, of course, fear. Because if so much had changed already, what might happen next? Maisie wanted to tell people there was no point trying to control change. Far better to control fear, but . . .

Her fingers were itching again.

"Look at the busy little bee," Mr. Holmby at the Tup crowed as he brought Maisie more bread and butter with her lunch. "Writing a letter?"

"I'm working on a story," she said, beaming up at him.

"Ah, isn't that lovely, then?" He nodded in approval. She knew he was thinking of the sort of puff-pastry stories that ran in the glossy magazines. It would never occur to him, nor to her to tell him, that she was writing about the unreasonable fears of Communism, when in fact they should be more afraid of the effects of deep poverty on so much of the British population. Such information would disrupt the order of things.

And it would disrupt the bread and butter.

"It's going to be all hands on deck for the correspondence tomorrow, I should think," Phyllida exclaimed later that afternoon, rubbing her hands together. Fielden sighed heavily.

Maisie looked up from the script she was revising. "Hmm? What? Why?"

Fielden sighed again and Phyllida laughed.

"Maisie, I know you've not forgotten the evening's debate topic?"

She hadn't forgotten the topic, just that it was this evening. There were times when a single day at the BBC felt like it lasted a week, which was part of what she loved about it, but it did occasionally make life confusing. However, tonight's debate was *Should Married Women Work?*—a subject nearly all the women in Savoy Hill felt was already decided and were delighted to share with the world.

"Oh, goodness!" Maisie screeched, prompting another sigh from Fielden. "It's going to be a tremendous show, isn't it?"

They powered through their work that afternoon and Maisie skipped to the studio just before six thirty to ready it for the debate at seven. She was setting up the microphones when Reith strode in. Reith never entered the studios, and Maisie suspected this shift in habit did not presage anything good.

"Good evening, sir. You're here quite late. Is there something amiss?"

"Hmm? Oh, Miss Musgrave. No. I simply thought I had best supervise this debate. Best make sure all the right sort of things are said, mitigating against complaints and what."

She wondered how much he agreed with Hoppel's opinion that the BBC needed to be less progressive. She wondered how many other men held the same opinion.

"It's very good, having these debates," she said. "Very patriotic, really."

"Is it?" He looked as though she were using the word incorrectly.

"Oh, absolutely! They discuss the complexities of government and social policy, and of course question it, too, but maybe, perhaps, give ordinary people information for discussing with their representatives, which might mean changing policy, and you can only have that sort of thing in a civilized and democratic society like ours," she said, hardly pausing to breathe.

"Hm, well, it's a very interesting perspective you have, Miss Musgrave," he said, nodding. She felt like a dog who had just performed a trick, and that he was barely restraining himself from patting her on the head. "Quite extraordinary, that we can even ask the question, isn't it? These times, these times." He sighed and took out his cigarettes.

"No! I mean, er, they do ask that no one smoke in the studios, sir," she reminded him, feeling herself blush.

"Ah. Yes, of course," he muttered, tucking the case back in his jacket.

Maisie was relieved when Hilda and Phyllida came in, escorting the debaters and the moderator, Mrs. Strachey. All married women. Reith groaned softly, but then exerted himself to shake hands and welcome them—he wouldn't have it said he wasn't worthy of being called a gentleman.

"Awfully good of all you ladies to come in and give listeners fodder for chat over supper."

Supper. Simon. She had promised to meet him at seven. If she left now and took a cab, she would only be five minutes late. But then she would miss the debate.

Maybe it won't be that interesting. Maybe . . .

The woman arguing in favor of married women working was laughing at Reith. "My good man, unless she does absolutely all she wants every day and is subject to no one else's whim, I think you'll find the average married woman does work, just not for pay, which itself can hardly be counted as fair and ought to be changed at once."

She would ring the restaurant and leave him a message. She had heard of people doing such things. She whispered hastily to Phyllida, then nipped across the corridor to the engineers' second office and snatched up the phone.

"Number please?"

"Er . . . the Spencer, a restaurant. In Chelsea," Maisie specified.

"Do you know the number, miss?"

"No . . ." Maisie looked desperately across at Phyllida, who was holding the door open. It would have to close at any moment. The BROADCASTING IN PROGRESS sign would light up.

"One moment, please," the operator informed her, looking up the exchange. Phyllida held up five fingers. Then four. Then three. "I'm connecting you now, miss."

But the receiver was dangling well away from its rest and Maisie was back inside the studio with seconds to spare as the door closed, the switches flipped, and Billy gave the signal for the debate to begin.

If the Spencer had been a different sort of restaurant, it wouldn't have let in a sweaty, red-faced woman, coat and scarf akimbo, eyes wild. But Simon's penchant for "Bohemian" establishments meant that they were used to that sort of thing, so Maisie was admitted, at seven thirty-eight, and raked the room for Simon.

He was at the bar. He stood up and smiled, as he had been trained to do. But there was more ice in his manner than in the drink he offered her.

"I'm awfully sorry," she gabbled. "It was a terribly important debate—I'd clean forgotten when we spoke—and then the DG, Mr. Reith, I mean, came to observe, and I did try to ring the restaurant and leave a message, but I was called back and—"

"It's perfectly all right, darling," Simon insisted. "I do understand. I daresay I've had enough such nights myself and not been able to give you the attention you deserve, so it's no wonder you wouldn't be able to make the time for me."

"No, that's not—"

"Of course it isn't. Do forgive me. I'm in a beastly mood. Been rather a rotten week."

He tossed back half his whiskey and gave her a rueful smile. She wanted to stroke his face—a woman could behave such a way in a Bohemian spot—but she didn't dare. Touching him set something off in her. She knew that if he were to ask her up to his flat, she would go. She wanted him to ask. She hoped he wouldn't. She didn't know.

"I am sorry," she said. "It's only . . . the debates are so critical, and I'm needed."

She hoped he wouldn't guess she was lying. Even Hilda wasn't required to supervise the debates. They went because they couldn't stay away.

"And I'm sure it was exciting," he said. "But I can't help feeling you're more fond of your BBC than of me."

His voice was teasing, and he winked. She laughed, feeling like she was supposed to. But it was a thing that was lying there between them, a parcel neither of them wanted to pick up. She could easily have pointed out he was so keen on his work, and on the social duties he claimed to despise but engaged in anyway, that they had barely seen each other ten times in six months of acquaintance. But his work was important, and he was trying to build something. And there were notes sent back and forth, which made her feel he was present, even when he wasn't. And. And. And it was true. She was entranced by him, but the BBC had her heart.

He looked at her a long moment, then ordered another drink.

"I have to go away," he said at last, his voice flat and defeated.

"Oh. You mean for Christmas?"

"Longer than that, I think." He downed the glass again and turned to her. "Bit of a nuisance with the family, and they need someone to do a bit of managing here and there, so I am called. I cannot shirk."

Maisie forced her face to remain neutral. Beanie was right. His family was in trouble.

"Is there anything I can do?" she asked.

He took her hand. Again, that tingle. Running all through her body. He turned her palm over and buried his face in it. A long, slow gasp escaped her, which she hoped was masked by the din in the room. *Ask me home. Don't ask me home. Ask me.*

He looked up at her, his whole soul in his eyes. "Maisie. Tell me you care more for me than the BBC."

"I do," she breathed.

"Do you mean that?"

No. "Yes."

But she didn't understand why she had to rank them.

He pulled her toward him and kissed her a long time. She could feel his body melting into hers. Then she realized that in fact he was blind drunk, and it was all she could do to pour him into a cab, where he gave the directions and waved her off, not seeming to remember that this was a long goodbye.

It wasn't until she was mulling it all over on the way home that she realized he hadn't told her he cared more for her than his work.

He hadn't said he loved her.

She didn't tell Phyllida what had happened, and if Phyllida noticed that there were no letters from Simon over the next few days, she didn't mention it. Maisie had thought he would still write, but she kept seeing the look in his eyes when he surmised that she cared more about the BBC than him.

What she would like would be to talk to Hilda. In a neutral place, free from the demands of work, Hilda composed Maisie's idea of a favorite aunt, someone very much your champion who could also listen and counsel to great satisfaction. Maybe over tea and cakes.

There was just the matter of finding free time.

"Yes, yes, will give it a think, not a chance, good," Hilda said, running down a list of people Maisie had compiled as potential speakers. "And we're meeting with the governors in the New Year. I think they'll give us another bump in hours. We'll see how this series goes over." She was having lunch with E. M. Forster, who had agreed to do a broadcast, and his initial series of thoughts were so fine, Hilda decided it should be an open-ended series.

"I don't think the DG will be keen," Fielden said, bringing his own list of upcoming candidates for a series on scientific innovation throughout the 1920s.

"Mr. Forster is well considered; that's all he'll care about," Hilda grunted, stabbing at her curls with a comb. "I think this lipstick is too bright. What do you think?" she asked Maisie.

"Forster won't notice," Fielden put in.

"I think it's cheerful," Maisie said. "You need that on a rotten day like this." Fielden shrugged. He was used to everyone pretending like he hadn't spoken.

Hilda glanced at her watch. "Goodness, that was a long meeting. I'll have to take a cab. Miss Musgrave, you'll greet Miss Woolf when she comes in, won't you?" After that rehearsal, Maisie wasn't surprised Hilda was lukewarm toward Virginia Woolf, but the whole thing seemed odd. It wasn't like Hilda to shrug off writers. Especially as Miss Woolf was good friends with Vita.

But I had a hard time getting through To the Lighthouse, *too.*

It was Vera, the new head typist's birthday, and Phyllida was joining in the festivities. The rest of the staff was at lunch, so only Maisie and Fielden remained in the department. Maisie loved when it was quiet like this, and she could lose herself in thinking. The next debate in *Questions for Women Voters* was: "Should Boys and Girls Have the Same Education?" and Maisie was keen to interview the speaker for girls, the head of Cheltenham. "Oh, good Lord, I'll have to hide in the broom cupboard all morning," Beanie had wailed. *Why shouldn't boys and girls have the same education? The real question should be about the rich versus the poor—that would be something, all right. Someone would say the poor have to leave school at twelve because we need the laborers and then someone else will say that's awfully classist, and maybe we'll finally get Parliament to take up the issue of schools, and wouldn't that be something, too?*

Her legs kicked back and forth of their own accord as she wrote. Phyllida's status as the most outspoken avowed radical in Talks was being challenged.

"I don't suppose the copy of Woolf's newest magnum opus is to be found?" Fielden called from his desk.

"It is. I suppose you want me to fetch it for you?" Maisie asked. Fielden's icy stare only made her snicker as she went into Hilda's office.

The usual tower of books. Maisie ran her finger down the spines. Poetry, poetry, something called *The Well of Loneliness* (rather a poignant title), *All Quiet on the Western Front* (Reith was on the warpath over all the anti-war screeds getting so much credence these days), something in German Maisie couldn't read, and there it was, *Orlando*. She slipped it from the pile and straightened all the other books. *Ooh, hallo, a Bartlett script!* She picked it up and started to read, then noticed a BBC interoffice memo underneath it. Or rather, she noticed it was turned over. A venal sin, of which the all-capped DO NOT WRITE ON THIS SIDE commandment marching three times down the sheet was a fierce reminder. But under the top DO NOT WRITE ON THIS SIDE, Hilda had scribbled, "Shall!!"

Maisie, though exultant in Hilda's nose-tweaking, obediently turned the page over.

But it wasn't a memo; it was a letter. A personal letter. "Dearest Vita." Dearest. Vita.

Well, lots of good friends address each other that way. Very Jane Austen.
But she couldn't stop herself reading, as though it were any other
confusing bit of text that she wanted to understand. And there they all
were, sentences no one but the recipient should see, answering many
questions about Hilda but raising a dozen more. And then, at the bottom, in highly legible capital letters: "I LOVE YOU. I WANT YOU."

She stared down at those words, which went well past Jane Austen's milieu. There was no mistaking their meaning. There was no
mistaking any of it. Vita. And Hilda. Of course, the papers loved to
talk about the Bloomsbury group and their leisure activities, feeding
the disgust of some, the titillation of others. Maisie, despite her education in the theater, didn't pretend to understand it, but had always
shrugged it off as not her business.

Which this wasn't either. But Hilda and Vita. Hilda. So she did
love, after all. Loved, and wanted.

Maisie flipped the page back over—it was far more comforting
to see the familiar DO NOT WRITE ON THIS SIDE.

"Ah, Miss Musgrave, is Miss Matheson not in?"

Maisie yelped and spun around—Reith was looking down at her.
Her hands were behind her back, still on the memo.

"No, sir. She's lunching out."

Please don't let him see the "Shall!!" The "Shall!!" would be better
than what was on the other side, but he couldn't, he mustn't, he must
never think of Hilda as anything other than the brilliant if somewhat
radical director of Talks.

"Ah, of course," Reith said, scowling. "Where is Mr. Fielden?"

"Sir?" Fielden hovered at the door, radiating disapproval at Reith's
being in Hilda's office when she wasn't there. Maisie kept her hands
on the desk, her fingers reaching as far as they dared, searching for
the script to slide back over the letter without either man noticing,
but Reith wasn't turned away quite far enough. Likely he wouldn't
notice, but she wasn't prepared to take the chance.

"Fielden, good. Tell me, this Talk on banking, who is this 'Miss
Cartwright'?"

244 · SARAH-JANE STRATFORD

"A banker, sir. The first woman to hold such a position, it seems. We've had her in to broadcast before, sir."

"I see. And the other banker is one of the Rothschild men?"

"That is correct, sir."

"Ah. Might I ask that you arrange for a third banker? Someone a bit more traditional?"

"Certainly!" Maisie burst out, desperate to get rid of him, ignoring Fielden's glare. "We'll discuss it with Miss Matheson as soon as she returns."

"Perhaps you have someone in mind?" Fielden asked Reith. Maisie glared right back at him. This was not the time to be so protective of Hilda's taste.

"Well, I—" Reith began, but the phone rang. Maisie didn't dare leave her post guarding the desk. She pretended to cough violently, forcing Fielden to answer.

"Talks Department, Fielden . . . Oh yes, Miss Wo—sorry?" His voice twisted upward, turning suddenly, rarely, frightened. "But we can't . . . No, I . . . She isn't . . . Miss Woolf, please, if it's a matter of the fee, I'm sure we can . . ."

Virginia Woolf! And to judge by Fielden's wide-eyed mewling, there was a problem. Maisie's eyes unwillingly slid to the afternoon's schedule, where *A Survey of Women in Literature with Virginia Woolf* shouted at her in purple mimeographed ink. She jerked her glance away, only to see Reith eyeing it as well.

Fielden hung up. His skeleton seemed to have dropped out of his frame.

"Miss Woolf is, er, not able to broadcast as scheduled."

That letter under Maisie's hand grew hot. Now she understood Virginia Woolf's chilliness toward Hilda, and Hilda's indifference. Now she remembered that the character of Orlando was said to be based on Vita, with whom Virginia Woolf had been involved, according to gossip Maisie barely noticed. And now Vita was receiving letters from Hilda, who loved her, who wanted her.

"Women!" Reith boomed. "Completely unpredictable. And especially those Bloomsbury sorts. I suppose you have some sort of contingency plan?" Reith glared at them expectantly.

"Certainly, sir," Fielden said, and Maisie suddenly adored his ponderous voice, where sarcasm was so hard to discern. "We keep a score of potential broadcasters at the ready, just for such events as these."

"I'll leave you to it, then," Reith said, full of condescending beneficence, and wonderful undiscernment. "You'll convey to Miss Matheson my concern about the banking Talk?"

"She will treat it with the same consideration as all your concerns, sir," Maisie assured him. She shut the door and turned to Fielden. "What are we going to do? We've got to ring her!"

"It's the Dorchester. They don't put calls through to patrons. That sort of thing is 'very low behavior,'" he snapped, ripping off his glasses and rubbing his eyes.

Maisie folded her hands and paced, tracing Hilda's thinking route. "All right," she said. "Let's ring five of our usual people, and if we can't get anyone, I'll go to the Dorchester myself and tell her. She'll want to know."

"You just want to go to a posh restaurant," Fielden sneered, but fetched the bound book of names and addresses. "I suppose the Strachey woman is always keen," he said with a gusty sigh.

"No, it's literature. We should be able to get a writer," Maisie argued. "It's daytime. They'll be home working."

Fielden looked up at her through heavy eyelids. "If that's what you call it."

No one answered T. S. Eliot's phone. She tried P. G. Wodehouse and was told he was lunching out. She was wondering why all modern writers went by two initials when Fielden scored success. H. G. Wells, having been so thoroughly seduced by Hilda, was enchanted to be their white knight.

"In shining tweed, no doubt. Shiny and turning green," Maisie commented. "He can afford better."

"But then how would we know he was an intellectual?"

Hilda returned just before Mr. Wells was due to arrive. "Bad news, I'm afraid," Fielden greeted her, with a rare almost-smile. "Miss Woolf was unable to come do the Talk today. Fortunately, I was able to reach Mr. Wells, and he should be here imminently. I've made a few adjustments to the script—he should manage just fine."

Maisie waited patiently for him to acknowledge her contribution during the crisis. She wished Hilda didn't go first white and then red on hearing about Miss Woolf's cancelation. Inscrutable as Hilda was, it was obvious she had a very good idea exactly why Virginia Woolf didn't want to come anywhere near her.

Fielden presented Hilda with the amended script, and she skimmed it.

"Topping, Mr. Fielden. Excellent work. Emergencies will occur. We manage them as we can. And it keeps things interesting." She hung up her coat, fluffed her hair, and beckoned to Fielden. "Come along. Let's meet Mr. Wells and be obsequious in our thanks. You can manage obsequious, can't you?"

Fielden's answer was lost in the stairwell and the return of Phyllida.

"Crikey, you look mithered. What's happened?"

"Miss Woolf canceled, but Fielden found Mr. Wells to come in."

And Fielden had been the one to find him. All Maisie had done was help. Which was her job. They were all in it together. She didn't need credit for every small thing she did. Although a "thank you" might have been nice.

Then again, this is Fielden. If he were to utter those words, he'd probably have a seizure. And that's way beyond my nursing skills.

A nice enough vision, though, to help her get back to work.

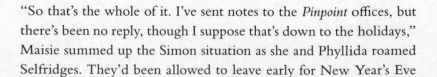

"So that's the whole of it. I've sent notes to the *Pinpoint* offices, but there's been no reply, though I suppose that's down to the holidays," Maisie summed up the Simon situation as she and Phyllida roamed Selfridges. They'd been allowed to leave early for New Year's Eve and combed the huge shop for possible bargains.

"He sounds a right maungy taistril!" was Phyllida's assessment, and Maisie didn't feel the need for translation. "I've nae heard such trammel. Does he expect you to fall all over him, declare undying devotion, when he can barely manage room for you in his diary?"

"I don't know," Maisie said. "But I miss him. I miss him awfully. I could easily have said the thing to please him and I didn't, not well enough. I did the exact same thing with the DG, who knows how many times. Why don't I ever learn?"

"I think you're quite well educated enough," Phyllida said dryly. "And is he here pursuing you, giving you reason to worship his pampered hide? He is not. He's off being errand boy for his family. You'd always come second, in a family like that. You're better off as you are. You'll see. Remember, we're going to vote this year! We're on the verge of many great things."

Maisie nodded automatically. She cast her eyes over the glove display and asked if she could try the plain chocolate-brown kidskin. They glided nicely over her hand and wrist, coming to rest halfway toward her elbow. She circled her wrists and wiggled her fingers as though she were typing. The gloves moved like new skin.

"They're beauty beyond, Maisie, but they're well nigh four pounds! You can get gloves nearly as good for half that."

Maisie clenched and unrolled her fingers a few more times.

"No. Georgina wasn't good for much, but she was right about one thing. It's best to pay the money for the top quality. These will keep me warm and look elegant for years."

And when they stepped back out into the dark, raw afternoon, the sharp droplets of rain and sleet promptly turned their faces red and wet, but Maisie's fingers didn't feel a thing.

FIFTEEN

January 1929

Maisie had a brief moment of melancholy, noting the beginning of the New Year and that, contrary to Lola's annual prediction, she still boarded at Mrs. Crewe's house. She had a dressing gown and slippers now, and a warm nightdress. And savings building up in an actual bank, of all things. But it wasn't quite enough. Lola herself had yet to return. She still maintained her room, as her family wouldn't hear of her storing belongings with them, not while she was on the stage,. She was now on a tour in Germany, that Italian *visconte* in arduous pursuit. Maisie had half a mind to ask Lola to put the man to use and find Simon. If nothing else, he might ask why being in Germany had robbed Simon of the ability to write letters to the woman of whom he claimed to be fond.

She'd wrapped this grim mood around her more tightly than her muffler when she returned to the office on January 2, but then Hilda swooped in announcing: "We're going to rehearse that fascinating woman who trumped the house in Monte Carlo, and I'll need you to reschedule the head of the Science Museum so we can have the Tunisian ambassador, very interesting man. I'd rather like to go to Tunisia. Wouldn't you? And we should talk more about oil interests.

I know the DG doesn't like it, but it's becoming such a critical issue. I really think . . ."

And Maisie forgot everything else.

The list of things Reith didn't like was growing by the hour. Fielden opened a departmental pool, taking bets on how many of their proposals Reith would fight them on through the year. Despite the regular meetings in his office, Reith had taken to storming into Talks at least once a week. Phyllida grumbled that he must like the exercise.

"Miss Matheson, it seems you have Mr. Forster booked for a series with no end in sight? Is that correct, or have you made an error in the planning?"

Hilda went marble white, less offended by the slight on E. M. Forster than the suggestion she had made an error.

"Mr. Forster is enthusiastic about the opportunity," she began.

"I daresay. It will mean quite a bit of regular money for him," Reith said, with a half glance to Fielden, seeking support for this wit. Fielden failed him abjectly.

"Sir, Mr. Forster is one of our preeminent modern novelists," Hilda explained. "Once again, we're the ones who are reaping the benefits, more than he. And I'm sure he's just as pleased to earn four guineas per broadcast as he was to earn thousands of pounds for *A Passage to India*, but I think he's quite comfortably fixed, regardless. He certainly hasn't tried to negotiate the fee."

"His books may be well liked, but he's not an upworthy man. Do you know he was a conscientious objector? And he's not married."

"Well, you know what writers are like. Hard enough to eat with, much less live with."

"I'm weary of it, Miss Matheson, positively weary. Must every man of letters you bring in here be a homo . . . that is, an inappropriate sort?"

"Mr. Reith, you asked me to cast a wide-ranging net and bring as many voices as possible to the BBC. I heartily apologize if their personal lives are not up to scratch, but they are only discussing their work. I'm glad to have a monk come in to broadcast, but none seems to be a bestselling author."

"Oh, will you stop being so infernally clever!"

"I would try, but it's inordinately difficult."

"Hallo, bit of trouble at t'mill?" Siepmann was leaning in the doorway.

Reith lit up on seeing him, but Hilda went even whiter with rage. To Maisie's horror, she was even trembling.

"Mr. Siepmann," Hilda greeted him in a colorless voice. "Many thanks, I'm sure, but this is a private matter concerning the Talks Department."

"Oh, certainly. Only I heard raised voices and thought perhaps I could be of service? One thing we are well versed in over at Schools is keeping peace. Still, right you are, Miss Matheson, and I'll be—"

"Please, Siepmann," Reith broke in. "Do give us your opinion. Do you think a man such as this E. M. Forster is the right sort to be given prominence by the BBC?"

"Ah! Forster. Very popular writer. A fine intellect, it would seem. Not my own taste, personally, but can't say his work hasn't captured the reading public."

"So it would seem," said Reith, talking over Hilda. "And we can't control what gets published. But should *we* be making a show of him?"

"Mr. Reith!" Hilda said. "We're meant to expose Britain to the whole of our contemporary society and let people draw their own conclusions based on complete information. If they come to dislike Mr. Forster, they are welcome to leave his books on the shelf."

"I think there's something in what our Miss Matheson says," Siepmann said, grinning. "That's what I like so much about Talks. You can take these delightful little risks. And I daresay a bit of controversy builds more of an audience, what?"

"I can't say I'll ever be keen on controversy," Reith said, though he was smiling. "But I suppose so long as we keep a steady hand on it, we should manage. And the *Times* has been very favorable to Mr. Forster, so he can't be all bad."

"What do *you* think of his work?" Hilda asked him, her voice a study in innocent interest. Reith wrinkled his nose.

"I haven't time to read all these modern novels; you know that," Reith scolded. "And especially not if they're written by that sort." He glared at Hilda's bookshelves, groaning under the weight of work by that sort. "These people are supposed to go to prison, not be given book contracts!"

"Yes, there is something very Byzantine about our justice system," Hilda agreed. Reith only sniffed and strode out the door, nodding to Siepmann.

"Ah, never a dull moment here in Talks, is it?" Siepmann said. "Glad I could help, Miss Matheson. We're all in it together—isn't that right?"

Hilda waited till they were both long gone before she sat down and sighed.

"Why does the DG get so aerated about . . . well, everything?" Maisie asked. "I suppose his intentions are decent enough, but—"

"Yes." Hilda lit a cigarette. "His spleen is in the right place."

Spleen seemed all the trend suddenly. Maisie could shrug at it in some places, like the *Telegraph*, but took it far more personally when yet another letter searching for Edwin Musgrave was answered with a sharp rebuke at her lack of information. She felt her own spleen rumbling when the Lion told the Fascists that the BBC didn't understand how people needed things to be simple, so they didn't have to think too hard. Maisie longed to ask how people who had no brains could possibly think too hard, but figured this was a question best left unasked, despite her interest in seeing their spleens explode.

"They're still not talking about anything illegal," Ellis said to Maisie and Hilda. They were convened in the study in a building neither Ellis nor Hilda deigned to identify. "Ask every third person on

Oxford Street and they'll tell you the BBC is a load of Bolshevist propaganda. Every next third person will insist it's a government mouthpiece."

The interviews Maisie still wished to conduct, using that traveling microphone.

Hilda looked over Maisie's notes, one hand idly twisting up her onyx necklace, the other holding a cigarette. She was smoking more these days.

"It's certainly gratifying to know we've done such good work," Hilda said. "Barely a blink ago the papers were swearing the BBC was a fad that wouldn't last. Now entire political factions want to bend us to their will. Nothing says you've arrived like a conspiracy. Except maybe a death threat."

"Most people are never that bored," Ellis muttered.

Maisie studied their pile of propaganda. More pamphlets, articles cut from German newspapers with notes in English, a two-volume book by Hitler claiming to be autobiography, but mostly just what Phyllida would call "political blether," and a lot of letters from Vernon Bartlett whose contents did not make it into his *Way of the World* Talks. There were also scribbled sections of letters from Vita, in Berlin. Maisie wanted to ask if she was acting as a spy as well, but was uneasy about venturing into any discussion that might touch on the word, "Shall!!"

"Vita tells me a great deal that doesn't find its way into the papers," Hilda said.

Maisie blushed at the name "Vita" being spoken out loud. She sneaked a glance at Ellis, but if he knew anything in particular about that name, his mostly bored expression didn't reveal it.

"She has noticed much in the way of a cosmopolitan atmosphere, and a great influence from Hollywood and even Asia in entertainments. But she's also observed more than once a club primarily attracting homosexuals being attacked by thugs."

"Hardly surprising," Ellis muttered.

"But then we have all this propaganda, from these Nazis—"

"A marginalized group of mostly laughable idiots, as I understand," Ellis interrupted.

"Yes, and Vita and Harold agree with you. But Harold, in his capacity as diplomat, notes that some political circles agree with the concern over interest in Bolshevism and, of course, everyone's favorite specters, trade unions and media. These circles would also like to see a more traditional Germany rise again. And increasingly there are those murmuring that given the opportunity, they'd lend support to whoever can help make it happen. And everyone thinks Germany is being stifled and robbed by the British and French, and is not to be borne."

"Yes, even your economist friend Keynes said that," Ellis pointed out. "And on the BBC no less. One would think the Fascists would appreciate him."

"Mr. Keynes is no Fascist!" Hilda snapped. "He was making a perfectly fair point, and his studies indicate that it will hardly improve our own economy to keep fleecing Germany."

"And continuing to kick someone when they're down is never a good idea," Maisie chimed in.

"Oh, I don't know," Ellis mused. "It does at least keep them down."

"Only until they get up again, at which point they want more revenge," Maisie said, remembering all her plans to destroy the Toronto gang kids. And Georgina, too.

I bet all those kids ended up dead anyway. Or in prison. Here's hoping.

"I've no doubt that Siemens, being German, wishes to see Germany rich and powerful again," Ellis conceded. "Patriotism costs nothing. But these are still businessmen, and they want to do business in England and wherever else they can. They won't be so patriotic as to interfere with business. And any number of corporations despise unions and want to see them excoriated in the newspapers. So if they wish to publish their own paper to do as much, they can, but they can't force anyone to read it."

"What if they buy up all the other papers?" Hilda asked.

"Oh nonsense, that would never be allowed," Ellis scoffed. "We've laws against that sort of thing, and it's just not the British way besides."

"It happened in Italy," Hilda reminded him.

"Not exactly a journalistic paragon prior to Mussolini, was it, though?"

"See here, my dear God," Hilda said, tapping the German papers. "This is very good propaganda, well considered and awfully compelling. Didn't Mussolini prove how useful that could be?"

"Certainly, but the idea that a few wealthy men would take such ludicrous steps all to maximize their profits is the stuff of high melodrama. Tell me, Miss Musgrave, do any of them twirl their mustaches?"

"Oh for heaven's sake, will you please help?" Hilda snapped.

"Seems to me what you need is a good investigative journalist, not me." He turned to Maisie, pointing at her with his cheroot. "Which are you more interested in becoming, Miss Musgrave? Journalist or spy?"

"Truth seeker," said Maisie.

Ellis fell about laughing and Hilda beamed like a proud favorite aunt.

"And truth teller," Maisie added. Just so everything was clear.

"I suppose in the best of worlds, journalists and spies do both those things," Hilda said. "That might make an awfully good Talk, now I think of it. But really, Ellis, will you help?"

"I'll see what I can do," he promised. "But I still think it's an enormous waste of your enormous brains."

"Ah well, it wouldn't be the first time," Hilda said.

Hilda and Maisie left soon after.

"I don't feel like going straight home. Fancy a stroll?" Hilda asked.

They got out of the cab near Piccadilly and walked through the crowds of people leaving the theaters and streaming toward restaurants and nightclubs. It was strange, being in the midst of so much finery and happy chatter and thinking of attempts to clamp down on most of it. Strange, too, having a deeply private conversation in such a place, but no one could hear them.

"Miss Matheson, how did you know about Siemens and Nestlé, specifically? Did you know Hoppel and Grigson were friends?"

"I have a number of friends in a number of places and they know I like information that might look esoteric. So they send me things. And then other people tell me other things, and I ask questions. But you're the one who's really done the, if I may, lion's share of the work here. I would never have had the time. I'm most grateful."

"But it's not just via friends, is it?" Maisie pursued. "You got some of that information through more official channels?"

"Ah. You're asking about a certain organization, of which very few people know the membership?" Hilda grinned and blew a smoke ring. "It's possible that a person whom you know has had something or other to do with said organization. As it happened, that person became known to T. E. Lawrence, just before the war—"

"Lawrence of Arabia?" Maisie gasped.

"He prefers to be called 'Ned,' actually," Hilda said, then grinned fondly. "Unless it's a formal occasion. Well, so, he was looking for a person who spoke Italian and German and was good with organization and whatnot to help set up an office for that said organization in Rome during the war, and so it went."

"And . . . are you still . . . ?"

Hilda shook her head. "I'm telling you what I'm telling you because you've more than earned my trust, but understand I've not really told you anything. I only want to show you I trust you, because you are playing quite a dangerous game, and I'm afraid I've led you into it. You should at least be assured you are playing for the right side. Now, then, I think the next step is to hook in one of my journalist friends, someone to do a bit of snooping, get some real dirt to stick. Someone who doesn't mind something a touch illegal, so long as the real crime is exposed."

"How illegal?"

"Oh, just going into some offices and looking at files," Hilda said, shrugging.

"That sounds like something a secretary could do. Isn't it?"

"Miss Musgrave, I know you're quite a young woman, but that sort of work is a bit out of your line."

"Maybe not. Miss Jenkins, the teacher at my secretarial school, said all offices are arranged more or less alike. Know the system, and you can find whatever you need, on your first day. Then you look competent and you don't have to ask too many irksome questions."

"It's far more complicated than that. There's a great deal you'd have to learn. We don't know how long it would take."

"Can we try?"

Hilda took another long drag on her cigarette. "All right." She smiled. "We can try."

Maisie supposed she ought to be leery, or frightened. Instead, she was exhilarated. She did, however, hate keeping it all from Phyllida. Hilda's warnings hung heavy on her, and Phyllida, though she was good at keeping secrets, would be even more enraged about the Fascists than Maisie and would have a harder time controlling it. There was some irony, Maisie thought, in withholding information for safety's sake, but until they knew more, it felt the wisest move.

There was no keeping it from Phyllida, though, when a letter arrived for Maisie postmarked from Germany. Maisie had the wild thought that someone had found her out and was warning her off. Excited, she ripped open the letter. And shrieked. It was from Simon.

> *My dearest Maisie,*
>
> *Can it really be three months since we spoke? I am sorrier than I can possibly say, especially as I was so boorish with you. And for no reason other than my concerns for family affairs and, I daresay, my own absurd ego. Only I do think of you, your cleverness and your devotion*

*to the BBC. I do know you are determined to help make it something
important, and this says more of you than I think you even know.
My darling, I hope someday you'll want to extend that same energy
to me. I confess I've thought a few times over these dreary weeks of
what you and I could do, were our energies combined. Conquer the
world, I should think! Truly, you are so much more than I know
you've imagined. But know that I have seen it and that I cherish it.
I hope to be home soon and beg your forgiveness properly for all my
stupidity and silence and begin to do the real work of winning your
most invaluable heart.*

That heart had become a jazz quartet in her rib cage.

"You'll be careful though, won't you?" Phyllida asked. "Don't
give away your heart without getting another in return."

"Well, I never." Maisie laughed. "Phyllida Fenwick is becoming
romantic."

"No," Phyllida said, shaking her head and refusing to smile. "Not
in the slightest."

"It's just one letter," Maisie said. "We'll see if he writes again."

She had noticed Hilda, in those rare spare minutes, using Talks
and BBC memos to scribble more and more letters, all to Vita. She
wanted to warn her, lest someone else see, too. But to warn her would
be to mention it, which she couldn't do.

The love that dare not speak its name indeed. Good grief.

But it wasn't just that. Maisie was starting to understand very well
that the heart just had to go where it wanted to go. She hoped Hilda
was happy. She didn't know anyone who deserved it more.

SIXTEEN

"Ladies! The election is the thirtieth of May. Are you registered to vote?"

"We most certainly are," Phyllida told their questioner, though with more politeness than the last one who accosted them on their stroll through Hyde Park, as this man's red boutonniere spoke him for Labour.

"Good on you! Embracing your hard-fought right, as you should. And only one party is determined to uphold the freedom and independence of all young women, be they single or married—"

"Labour, yes, though in fact the Liberals claim to be our champions as well. And the Conservatives, too, though I sense they wish to be seen as protectors."

"But you wish your interests protected, not your person, of which you can tend yourself, I think," the party man said.

"Oh! You are good!" Phyllida complimented him. "Give us a pamphlet, then, and we'll read it over with care."

Phyllida pawed through it as she and Maisie ambled on down the path.

"Really, Phyllida, that's got to be the fifteenth pamphlet you've taken."

"Yes, I'm hoping to paper a wall with them soon."

It was hard not to be excited. All the newspapers, noticeboards, and public walls were emblazoned with the upcoming election and aimed particularly at this enormous new crop of voters, courteous of their intelligence and thoughtfulness and pleased for their independence of mind and spirit—and determined to win them to a particular party and hold them there forever.

Maisie and Phyllida claimed a free bench by the lake, with a good view of boys staging a race between paper sailboats.

"I feel as though we ought to be doing something ourselves, not frivoling like this," Phyllida said, lighting a cigarette.

"Resting up, that's what we're doing," Maisie said, though she felt the same. The election fever was high, and even women who would never have called themselves political were buzzing about it. They could hear snips of conversations all around them, and discovered the sailboats were christened "Labour" and "Liberal."

"I can't wait till I'm running in an election," Phyllida said, stretching out her legs and crossing her ankles.

Maisie reached into her bag and pulled out another letter from Simon.

"Practice your political acumen by telling me what you think of this."

My dearest Maisie,

The beauty of this part of Germany is extraordinary. The food and wine are nothing to what one gets in France, but the people are far more fine than I imagined and I think they have learned their lessons well. I do miss all the beauty of home, of course, but business must be done and things must be put right before I can return. Be well and be good, and think of me.

"Still busy trying to renew the family fortune by exploiting the flattened German economy somehow or other, is he?"

"I hope not," Maisie said, biting her lip. "But somehow, the way he's always saying how keen he is on beauty—"

"Call yourself plain and I'll punt you into the lake."

"I wouldn't say that about me anymore. It's that, all right, he lives and works in London, and loves it, but he's always joking about his love of that other life: the great house, the manor, riding his horse every day. And I don't know that it's joking, really, and . . ."

"And you're wondering where you fit into that life?"

Maisie sighed. "Sometimes I imagine a . . . wild sort of world, I guess, me in a long dress and cloak, long hair, wandering through the countryside . . ."

"And after the five minutes are up, what do you think of?"

"A flat in Mecklenburgh Square, where I can read as late as I like and listen to the wireless and no one says boo about the electricity."

"And is Simon there, too?"

"I guess I can't help hoping so."

"Hmm. Well, no good getting mithered till he's back in Britain anyhow," Phyllida said with finality. "Come on, let's hire some mallets and join the croquet."

"I don't know how to play."

"I'll teach you. It's great fun. You just pretend the ball is the head of someone you despise and give it a solid whack."

"You're a champion at it, aren't you?"

"With the ribbons to prove it."

The spring of 1929 might have been beautiful or miserable, but no one in Savoy Hill could know for sure, because in those few weeks from the announcement to the election, the staff worked at a fever pitch. The broadcasting day was still short, but the preparations for each election-related broadcast took hours. And where there was time, Hilda swept Maisie off in the evenings to instruct her in the finer details of snooping through a stranger's office.

"The trouble is, Miss Musgrave, if you get caught, it's not going to speak particularly well for the BBC, is it?"

"It won't be official BBC business," Maisie argued. "It'll just be me."

"Yes. I suppose. All right, these are the sorts of papers you want to look for . . ."

She wasn't to start until after Election Day. Maisie was out the door in record time on May 30 to run to her polling station, and found a long queue already. Half those waiting to vote were women.

Maisie was bouncing on her toes, counting the heads in front of her, when a man's voice sounded in her ear: "Pardon me, miss. Might I ask you a few questions?"

"You mean me?" she asked the eager reporter, blinking at her from behind smeary glasses. He was so young, he still had spots.

"Yes, please. How did you decide whom you would vote for?" he asked, licking his pencil and holding it poised over his pad.

"Ah! The BBC series *Questions for Women Voters* was a great help," she told him, not lying. Then realized she was in trouble if he asked her name and printed it.

"You've got a bit of a peculiar accent," he told her.

"Thank you."

He frowned, but was too eager to get to his next question to dwell on her accent. "Tell me, did the appearance of the candidates sway you at all?"

"Appearance? I'm not sure what you mean."

He leaned toward her with a superior grin and winked.

"Maybe you're voting for a particular party hoping a good-looking representative will take the seat?"

"Do male voters make their decisions that way?" She was genuinely curious.

"We're just wondering what's driving so many women to the

polls. Do you think this is something you'll do again, or is it just a bit of a fad?"

He was very reedy-looking. It wouldn't be hard to overpower him, seize his pad, and write a proper story for him.

"Voting isn't a new hairstyle," she told him in a withering tone.

A stringy young woman behind her, pushing a baby in a pram and holding a yawning toddler at her hip, leaned around Maisie to glare at him. "It's just right we all get our say, is what it is. We work, too, in case you didn't know."

He gaped at her, possibly not realizing she had the capacity to be articulate.

Maisie was next, and stepped up to vote. She wondered how many hands had trembled already today, holding their pencils over the ballots, with all the little boxes. Did most women take to their new, belated right with aplomb, or did they take their time, marveling over the beauty of it all, the silent speech that would be heard?

Or did they think, like she did, that there was a long queue behind her and she had to get to work.

She wrote a thick X, drew over it twice, and dropped the paper in the ballot box.

That's how you spell a shout. With an X.

"Just you wait until we're allowed to report our own news," Hilda greeted Maisie. The day's programming was like a thrilling tease of what such reporting would be like, as it was all in reference to the election, and they were being granted a special report, an expansive twenty-five minutes long, that evening.

Reith strode into the office, unannounced and in such a bluster that they had to clamp their hands down over papers to keep things from flying into the fire grate. Hilda blew smoke out of the corner of her mouth and smiled up at him. Maisie noted the twist in his mouth as he watched her take another puff, but he said nothing.

"I realize it's a busy day for us, but as we're on the subject, I want you to coordinate with Siepmann to do a series suited to young people on politics."

Hilda started to interject, but he was far from done.

"I hear Labour is poised to win, with all these women voting," he moaned. "I read and hear the most appalling stories everywhere and now discover it is happening even under my own aegis. I understand that Mr. Eckersley is getting a divorce. He has been . . . involved . . . with another woman, a *married* woman, and she, too, is getting a divorce. It's not to be believed."

Maisie was inclined to disbelieve right along with him. Peter Eckersley? The grim and stuffy chief engineer? What must this poor woman have already been married to that she'd upend her life for an endless series of monologues on sub-mixers and oscillators and frequencies?

"Yes, I'm afraid I heard something to that effect," Hilda said, grinding out her cigarette.

"Is there anything that happens here you don't know about?" Reith asked.

"I hope so," Hilda said fervently. "Awfully dull otherwise."

"And why didn't you tell me?"

"I'm devoted to broadcasting, Mr. Reith, but draw the line at gossip."

"Well, I can't see allowing him to stay on. It sets a bad precedent." Reith sighed, shaking his head.

"He's a very fine chief engineer," Hilda said. "And it's not as if his personal—"

"He oversees men, young men, and they look up to him," Reith snapped. "I sometimes wonder what we fought a war for." He sighed again and stalked away.

"Well, that's certainly a fair question." Hilda sighed herself. "Poor old Peter."

The fate of Peter Eckersley, like the next installment of *The Perils of Pauline*, would have to wait another day. It was time for the final broadcast of *Questions for Women Voters*. Hilda had insisted that a coda on Election Day would be fitting.

"Want to come and help me oversee?" she invited Maisie. "After all, you helped birth it, didn't you? Fair enough you see it through to its end."

Maisie looked up at her and started to cry.

"You don't have to if you'd rather not," Hilda said.

"It's been such a superb program, exactly the sort of thing I want to do, and now it's over. And I've been so busy, I never properly appreciated it."

"This is why I warn the staff about egotism," Hilda said, passing Maisie a handkerchief. "But you don't really think that's your one and only idea that's going to make a series, do you?"

"I hope not, of course. But it was awfully good, and it mattered."

"And the next one will be better. Are you going to stop being a little goose now and come do your job?"

Maisie blew her nose loudly and gave Hilda an apologetic smile.

"That was my last little honk."

"What a relief."

The next morning, Hilda was almost buried in every newspaper in Britain, all blaring the headlines about Labour's win and the women who had helped make it happen.

"'The Flapper Election'? Really? Those silly lads, so prosaic," Hilda tutted.

Prosaic, but poetic, Maisie thought. And it was something, being touted as having counted for so much.

"The main thing is we brought results," Hilda said, echoing Maisie's thoughts. "The sun is even shining, and the world doesn't appear likely to end."

"Just beginning," Phyllida chimed in from her desk.

"Be upstanding," Fielden muttered, stumping into the office. "Apparently the DG is in a bit of a temper today."

"How can you tell?" Maisie asked.

Fielden gave her a baleful look. "The old Tory's displeased about the election results, it seems."

"*Quelle surprise,*" Hilda murmured.

"We should be grateful he doesn't demand to know whom we all voted for," Fielden said.

"Maybe he'll add that to the questions he asks potential new employees," Maisie suggested. "But just the men."

Even Fielden laughed, which made Maisie wonder if Hilda's observation that the world wasn't ending was perhaps a touch premature.

Later, when Hilda was going to lunch, she jerked her head at Maisie to follow her.

They were halfway up Savoy Street when Hilda pulled a lumpy parcel out of her holdall and handed it to Maisie.

"This will help you when you pay your little visit. Don't open it now."

Visit. To Siemens. A dozen snakes rose in Maisie's belly and began to do the cancan.

"So you think I'm ready?"

"As much as anyone can be. Go to Siemens first. Friday is a company meeting day."

"How do you know?"

Hilda grinned. "I don't know why I'm encouraging this. I daresay I've gone soft."

Later, Maisie sneaked the parcel into the lavatory and opened it. It was a pocket camera. She turned it over and over in delight.

Oh, Mr. Hoppel, Mr. Grigson. You might have a lot of money and influence. But I have the power to expose and embarrass you. Good luck buying your way out of that.

The offices of Siemens in London were in great behemoths that exemplified the worst taste of the Victorian era, though Maisie admitted she might be slightly biased against any building that housed Siemens.

The nearby restaurants had claimed most of the workers who weren't engaged in meetings, and the few who remained in the parts of the building where Maisie entered were only of the coffee-and-sandwich hierarchy, and thus too bitter to notice another mere secretary.

Maisie could hear Miss Jenkins's brittle voice lecturing her on office patterns. Circling the first floor. The second. The third. She found her target on the fourth. A corner office, because it would be, with Hoppel's name engraved in a rather florid style, very last century.

"Look for locked drawers first," Hilda had advised.

His secretary's lair featured files and drawers that opened with nary a creak. *But he wouldn't keep anything I'm looking for in here.*

Maisie felt thoroughly businesslike and even blithe as she entered Hoppel's office and tested the desk drawers until she found the one that was locked.

"An innocent nail file is one of the finest tools of the trade."

And per Hilda's instruction, Maisie's nail file bent the lock to her will with shameful ease.

The first few files were all the usual company documents. Reports, budgets, projections, the daily tedium that would have been her lot to type and file if she hadn't landed in the Elysium that was Savoy Hill.

Then her hand closed upon a fistful of pamphlets. Smiling the smile of grim triumph, she discovered copies of all the Nazi pamphlets Hilda had been accumulating, covered with annotations on plans for the media and how it would support the cause.

She took a picture, and for extra good measure whipped out her pad and covered it in shorthand. *All the best spies should go to secretarial school.* Then she found another report, this one indicating funds allocated for the promotion of the Nazi party, "should they prove to be the friend to industry they promise."

And then a file marked GIFTS.

She checked her watch. She'd been here seven minutes. "You want to never be longer than five minutes in any one spot, if you can help it," was one of Hilda's rules. But GIFTS!

The first gift was the shifting of a small portion of UK profits to the Nazis, with the understanding that Siemens would be given an exclusive government contract should they come to power. The second was a bit more oblique, merely indicating "valuable cause in education and edification."

The newspaper, most likely, or perhaps something about the BBC. Maisie grimaced and snapped a picture. She returned everything to its place and the drawer locked beautifully.

She was out the door; she was in the corridor; she was leaving. And there was Hoppel, walking straight at her.

Bloody hell.

She ducked her head, relieved her hat was already pulled low.

"You," he accosted her. "Who are you? What are you doing on this floor?"

"So sorry, sir. I'm a new girl, sir, and I got a bit lost." This time, she tried to force Phyllida's accent out of her mouth.

"I'll have to speak to Miss Hensley. Only executive secretaries are allowed up here. Were you running an errand for my girl?"

"No, sir. I lost track of what floor I was on, sir. Was supposed to pick up drafts, sir, and deliver them to . . . they who do our advertising," she improvised.

"Well, you won't find those up here. Go back down to Miss Hensley on two and get her to sort you out, and tell her to be more mindful in her instructions. I am not impressed."

"Very sorry, sir."

She hurried away, feeling great sympathy for the maligned Miss Hensley.

Maisie was rounding the second flight of stairs in Savoy Hill when she heard them. Men shouting. No one was allowed to shout in the corridors. They risked getting sacked. She sped up, nursing a foolish hope it was Siepmann.

As she bore down on the crowd that was trying to go about its business but couldn't tear itself away from the bloodletting, she saw Cyril and her hopes soared. He often trailed in Siepmann's wake.

"It's not your business, Reith!"

Oh. Eckersley. In a booming voice reverberating more than his beloved transmitters.

"I'd suggest you control yourself, but clearly that ship has sailed," Reith shouted back.

"And I'd suggest to you that he who's without sin cast the first stone, but you've never committed a sin in your life, have you? Maybe you should. It might loosen you up a bit."

"Gentlemen!" Hilda joined the fray, hands out in a gesture intended to be beseeching and instead looked reminiscent of Augustus Caesar. "Let's not create a ruckus, shall we? Mr. Reith, I understand your concern, of course, but you know Mr. Eckersley's the top in his field. We couldn't possibly ask for better. If the Engineering Department hasn't suffered, then surely—"

"Don't try to charm me, Miss Matheson!" Reith roared. "You may have bewitched every other snake in the garden, but you may consider me impervious."

Hilda recoiled, shrinking just enough to be noticeable before she tried again.

"Forgive me. I'm hardly trying to charm. I'm only thinking of what's best for the BBC. And Eckersley's part of that best."

Eckersley put a hand on Hilda's arm.

"No, Miss Matheson, not anymore. I'm not going to be treated like a naughty schoolboy, and certainly not because of my private life, which, may I add, is no one's business bar my own!"

"We have standards to maintain," Reith said, arms folded. "As I said before you lost your temper in such an appallingly schoolboy-like manner, if you are willing to heal your home wounds, I will be happy to forget I ever heard anything of it."

"No one cares except you," Eckersley told him. "You may be my superior here, but you're not a confessor. I tender my resignation, effective immediately. Replace me with an altar boy, or an aspidistra, or Samson—I'm sure one of them will perform to your standards."

Eckersley thundered off to his lair, and the others dispersed quickly, zigzagging on the theory that a moving target is harder to hit. Hilda remained steadfast, so Maisie hovered near her.

"I do understand that he and his wife were very unhappy," Hilda ventured, in her most winningly placating tone. "No one likes divorce, naturally, but the actions of the chief engineer in the BBC are hardly the stuff of interest to the general public."

"I am setting a tone here, Miss Matheson," Reith said. "I cannot abide anyone being unseemly towards their family. And I'd thank you not to interfere where you don't belong!"

He strode back to the executive suite, and Hilda, her face apocalyptic, marched back to Talks, not seeing Maisie.

"Well, one might see where he has a point," a faintly amused, silky voice snaked into her ear. Siepmann. "It is no great leap from 'unseemly' to 'unnatural,' after all, and that would have a dreadful effect."

She wished he didn't linger quite so lovingly on the word "unnatural." His smile made her appreciate the far more honest sludge of the Thames.

She kept her arms folded tight around her, staring after him as he left. *That's history, isn't it? How much damage a man can do, with so little?*

"I'm sorry," Cyril whispered. She hadn't realized he was there. They locked eyes briefly. He seemed to want to say something more, but she pulled away from his gaze and hurried back to Talks. There was a lot of work to do.

"Imbecile should have stuck it out or gone to the governors," was Phyllida's shrugged response to the dearth of Eckersley ten minutes later. "All right, so he's a louse to his wife, but what does that have to do with anything? If every man who behaved like a complete toad were forced out of his job, then . . . well, you know, it would open up a lot more jobs for women."

"Meaning what, you could be chief engineer?" Fielden said with a sneer.

"I'd put up a good fist learning. I'll tell you that."

Hilda crooked a finger at Maisie, beckoning her away from the brewing donnybrook.

"Margaret Bondfield's agreed to come broadcast," Hilda announced.

Hilda's charms worked where they counted. Margaret Bondfield was the subject of much scrutiny and some quiet scoffing, being the first woman who wasn't an aristocrat to be made a Cabinet member.

"Oh! How wonderful! May I work on the first draft of her script?"

Hilda grinned, blowing a smoke ring. "I remember a young woman terrified to take on such work, or even ask questions."

"I remember her, too," Maisie said. "I can't say as I miss her."

"She was a great deal more than she knew to credit herself for, though. Ah, and she still blushes, I see. Yes, Miss Musgrave, you may have a go at the script. That's the only way to carry on learning. Rather good, having a lady politician in so soon after the election. Feels like a continuation of *Questions for Women Voters*, don't you think?"

"It does. Maybe if we could keep bringing on women in politics in some way—"

"Just as I was thinking. But not haphazardly. Women are still so new to being part of the political process. Most of them haven't the foggiest idea how Parliament works. Mind you, I can say the same for some MPs. But what's good for the goose is good for the flock— what do you think of a weekly program that will educate women as to the goings-on in Westminster and we'll only have women MPs as broadcasters, and a woman as the presenter and moderator? Explain how the sausage gets made and talk about specific policy discussions. Good, eh?"

"The bee's knees," breathed Maisie.

"I admire all parts of the bee, myself. Anyway, jolly good. I was thinking we'd just call it *The Week in Westminster*, yes?"

"Yes."

"You are pliant today. And here's what else I'd like to propose. That you should be the producer. Yes?"

"No. What? Me?" Pliancy flew up the chimney.

"You'd be quite good at it. Lady Astor will be one of our regular speakers, obviously, and she already likes you. And you've come to rather enjoy politics, I think."

Maisie's fingers were itching. She wanted to write to every woman in Westminster at once.

"Do you think the DG will approve it?" she asked.

What she meant, though, was, *Will he approve me?* It felt like a long time since Reith had extended any sort of approval to Maisie. She missed it. Though in fact, it was a long time since she'd approved of him.

"He likes the women's programming," Hilda answered. "Especially when it's edifying and features upstanding women. And he's terrified of Lady Astor's wrath. And"—seeming to know Maisie's real question—"if I convince him that it's only a small sort of program, educating young women like yourself, then it's only reasonable that you should be at the helm and I'll keep a close eye as always, and that sort of thing."

That sort of thing. *The sort of thing of which minor revolutions are made.*

"Can you stay a bit late today, to discuss things further?" Hilda went on.

Maisie grinned. She knew perfectly well what that meant.

Hilda had prepared for the momentous chat and was equipped with bread and honey and tea.

"We might do a Talk on that fellow's new invention in Missouri," Hilda said, her knife singing through the loaf. "The machine that slices bread. Mind you, that's copping to the worst of people's laziness. There's an art to slicing bread, and each piece should have its own idiom. I'd like to say I hope the machine doesn't find its way into every bakery in Britain, but I daresay it will."

"People like being lazy," Maisie observed, sucking honey from her pinkie.

"Many find it preferable, yes. But you don't." Hilda waved a hand at the notes spread on the floor around them. With the door closed and barred with a chair, and the rain making it hard for them to hear each other, never mind be heard past the door, they were free to discuss Maisie's Siemens adventure.

"My goodness. They are ambitious," Hilda observed.

"It looks like they want to silence women and unions everywhere. And what's it for but money?"

"People are awfully funny. Always thinking lots of money makes them special, and thus superior, and so they ought to exercise that superiority."

"It's a wonder they don't try to revoke the Magna Carta."

"I'm sure there are those who wouldn't mind. But there you are. We simply carry on reminding people not to take anything for granted. You've done very well, Miss Musgrave. Are you prepared to carry on with this project?"

"They're not getting into the BBC without a fight."

"No. No, they're not."

As *The Week in Westminster* would focus on events of the week, notes on scripts were made every day. Maisie spent her morning tram ride scrawling ideas for themes and tidbits voters would want to know. She sailed into Hilda's office and was knocked into the umbrella stand as she was leaped on by a huge red spaniel.

"Steady on there, Torquhil," Hilda commanded, laughing.

Dogs made Maisie nervous. An admirer had once given Georgina an overbred puppy and Maisie had been deputized to feed it scraps from her plate. Whether because it was hungry or simply sensed the resentment, it sank its teeth into Maisie's fingers. The combination of screeching and growling prompted audience merriment, which made Maisie cry, which made everyone, especially Georgina, laugh harder. The dog soon disappeared, part of the ceaseless detritus flowing in and out of Georgina's life. The scars on Maisie's fingers were still visible.

"Isn't he beautiful?" Hilda purred, stroking Torquhil's red head. "He was a gift."

"Um, he's very nice," Maisie muttered, avoiding the dog's eye.

"Don't you worry," said Hilda. "Torquhil can't even do damage to a chewing bone." She scratched behind his ear and crooned, "If a man were trying to have my bag off me, he'd just sit there and look for a biscuit, wouldn't he? Wouldn't he?" She stood and studied him. "Or am I maligning your character? Many apologies, if so." She turned to Maisie and grinned. "Well? Aren't you going to tell me I'm off my nuts?"

"I was thinking of saying more like you're barking mad."

Hilda threw back her head and laughed.

"Well, there's no directive against bringing in dogs, and the DG did say he wanted us treating family well. Now that Torquhil's trained, no need to keep him at home all day, so here he is."

Her eyes were bright and challenging. Maisie wasn't sure who would be more displeased, Reith or Samson.

Phyllida came in with a green interoffice envelope. "Good morning. This just came. It's marked 'Urgent.' Oh, hallo!" She saw Torquhil and he, recognizing a friend, nudged her hand for a pat. "New Talks assistant?"

"Excuse me?" Maisie asked.

"Oh, good Lord, please no," Hilda moaned as she read the interoffice memo.

Maisie and Phyllida exchanged alarmed glances.

"Not another tour of inspection by the governors?" Maisie asked.

"Worse," Hilda replied in a hollow voice. "We're to have a Sports Day."

SEVENTEEN

It wasn't quite a Sports Day in fact, but rather a Savoy Hill–wide picnic, in the countryside, featuring games, amusements, dancing, and loads of food. All in all, a grand day out.

Maisie hopped off the bus Reith had hired for them, wearing borrowed brogues, a georgette ocher frock, and a straw hat, and carrying the good wishes of her whole boardinghouse. It was a startlingly warm day, and the park chosen for the event was a lush expanse of green lawn ringed by very fine oaks and shrubbery.

"Ah, the Hundred Acre Wood!" Phyllida cried. "Lord, the whole thing is rather tidy, isn't it? Bet it belongs to some landed gent, raking in a few extra shillings. They still have their names and houses, but the cash is running down. Excuse me whilst I weep."

Marquees stretched over tables groaning with food, and Maisie was second only to the messenger boys in making her first strike. She took her food and settled herself on a blanket, happily working her way through a cold collation and salmon aspic as she watched a rather brutal game of field hockey, with Hilda as one team captain and Beanie as the other. Maisie had long since reconciled herself to her lack of schooling, though she still felt a twinge at not being able to join this melee. Even Phyllida could play a little, applying brawn whenever there was a small lapse in her knowledge of the rules.

"Go, go, go!" Beanie shouted, a general leading a cavalry raid. "What do you call that?"

"Good form, troops, good form. Now move in, strike!" cried Hilda, equally militant.

"What a bother I can't join!" Mary Somerville said, coming to stand beside Maisie. She had married last year and was now six months pregnant. Not only did she still prefer to be called "Miss Somerville" at the BBC, but the rumor was she was intending on returning to work some months after the baby was born and had asked Reith for what she called "maternity leave."

"You could be goalkeeper for Miss Matheson's team," Maisie suggested. Though Beanie's team put up an impressive fight, the goalkeeper had not been much challenged.

"I think I'll go watch the cricket. It'll be more soothing," Miss Somerville decided after a particularly vicious attack.

Maisie watched her stride along the grounds, her gait only just becoming ungainly. *That's who I could be.* In Simon's last letter, he'd written, "I do admire you, my darling Miss Musgrave, working so hard as you do, devoted to your cause, and rising." He was a modern man at heart, and proud of her. He wouldn't mind her staying on, still being Miss Musgrave, still rising.

"Aren't they supposed to be the weaker sex?" Billy's voice sounded above her as Hilda performed a complex dribble, charging through half her opponents, sending them reeling, and launched an enormous thwack that tested the strength of both stick and ball and knocked poor Vera, keeping goal, to her knees.

"That's why generals avoid putting weapons in their hands," Cyril answered. Maisie glanced over at him and Billy, but they were too enthralled by the match to notice her. "So, whose knickers are you hoping to see here?"

"Oh, I'm not bothered. But I say, Underwood, look at that Matheson woman. Can't help admiring her. Is there anything she can't do?"

"Don't let the DG hear you say that. Speaking of, we'd best push on. We promised to join the cricket." Cyril's voice was heavy with martyrdom.

"Now, lads, we can't play anything so coarse as football," Billy said, in an eerie imitation of Reith's voice. They laughed as they trudged away.

Maisie took advantage of a time-out in the hockey to make her second assault on the food tables. While there, she thought she might as well examine the cakes, in the manner of a general's studying the movements of the enemy before he plans attack.

Siepmann was being served a Pimm's cup at the bar, and Maisie ducked behind a pyramid of peaches and plums, hoping he wouldn't see her. She was in no mood to hear his observations on her industry or littleness.

"Ah, there you are! Coming to watch the cricket, old man?"

Maisie was rather surprised Reith came to fetch his own drink. She would have thought he'd have someone tending to him. But possibly he wished to be seen as one of the staff. The lads, specifically, to judge by his straw boater and linen jacket. He looked alien in light colors, a bear without its skin.

"Lord, yes," Siepmann replied. "I just needed a drink after watching the girls go at it. I know sport is meant to be healthy for them, but it's quite unfeminine."

"I know, I know, but I would have been lambasted if I hadn't allowed them some sort of game. I'd certainly rather they play hockey than take up some of that ghastly dancing people persist in these days. I won't have any BBC girls behaving like that, not on my watch."

"You know Miss Warwick goes to those parties," Siepmann said.

"But she was properly brought up, so we trust she knows how to behave."

"Did you see Miss Matheson leading the fray?"

"I rejoice to say, I did not."

"Our Miss Somerville would have given some back, I'd think, but for her condition. Awfully decent of you to keep her on. And the fact is, she's really very good at the job. So much so that if what we're talking about comes to pass—"

"Yes, yes, precisely. I can't pretend to understand her marriage at all. That Mr. Brown of hers must be a strange fish if he has no quarrel with her retaining her father's name. But she's married, she's going to be a mother, and she's a very regular sort of woman, quite moral and decent. She won't try to impose advanced fare if she agrees to replace you."

A replacement for Siepmann! Maisie wanted to run, skip, turn cartwheels. If he was leaving the BBC, that would be worth one hell of a party.

"A very good choice, I think," Siepmann remarked with only a hint of oleaginousness. "If it must be a woman, she has certainly proven herself."

"As have you, Siepmann, as have you."

"I'm only thinking of what's good for the BBC."

"That's what makes you such a fine man. And arguably, Miss Matheson does think much the same way, but whatever the governors say, she just seems more and more like a woman who oughtn't have quite so much influence. Those damn unreasonable demands."

"But she's extremely popular."

"Yes. She's done well, certainly. Ah, let's not spoil the day with the same old chat, shall we? Come, let's see how the lads are getting on."

Fortified, they walked over to the cricket pitch, and Maisie stood there, eyes locked with the bored bartender, who professionally hadn't heard a single word. She mindlessly crammed cake into her mouth, the heavy plate in her other hand quite forgotten.

Hilda would say it was her foray into investigative journalism— or espionage—that was making her see conspiracies in what was just churlish grousing. But there was no way, no way she was wrong.

278 · SARAH-JANE STRATFORD

Those sleek heads had stuck together to plan the clipping of Hilda's wings, for no reason other than that they didn't want to keep looking up as she flew by.

Even if Hilda had heard the whole exchange, she would likely only shrug. Unsurprised that there were those who sought to take some wind from her sails, she would carry on charting her waters. Phyllida would point out, with infuriating reasonableness, that Siepmann couldn't be promoted to Talks until Hilda left and she wasn't going to and Reith could never justify sacking her. The governors would sooner dismiss him.

But Phyllida didn't know about Vita. And Siepmann might. And if Reith ever found out . . .

I need to talk to someone who has some muscle. The sort of cynic who wouldn't be surprised . . . Where's Fielden?

It was important to look as meandering and dreamy as possible, just one of the girls, enjoying the novelty and the buffet. She wandered with increasing impatience, almost despair—was he even here? He had to be. This holiday jaunt was mandatory.

Her plate was nearly empty by the time she found him, perched under an umbrella, watching the sound effects crew play a highly querulous game of croquet.

"Good afternoon, Mr. Fielden! May I join you?"

"I know the DG considers this a social gathering, Miss Musgrave, but we don't need to humor him beyond a nod. Do please feel free to finish off the buffet instead."

Since there was nothing to be gained by breaking the plate over his head, she sat down as if she'd been invited, or at least not discouraged. It would be so preferable to talk to Beanie! Both as an aristocrat and an adept of an elite school, she must know everything about shifting allegiances and how petty quests for greater personal power must operate. But Beanie was very deliberate in her avoidance of trouble at the BBC, and very loving of gossip. Fielden might not like Maisie, but he didn't like anyone, except Hilda. So there it was.

He looked at her a long moment, as if trying to ascertain that she really was sitting there and not moving.

"I suppose the geese are watching from the shrubbery, and if you trouble me long enough, you win some sort of prize?"

"Er. No. What?"

"Direct and clear-spoken as ever."

"Mr. Fielden." She cast a nervous glance around her to be sure they couldn't be heard. Then again, there was little chance of being heard over the shouts of the sound effects men. It seemed inadvisable to let them handle wooden mallets. "What would happen, do you think, if someone in Savoy Hill was thinking of disrupting the Talks Department?"

His eyebrows shot up. She wouldn't have guessed his features could be so animated.

"Seen a bad play, have you?" he asked, though it was clearly just to maintain form.

"A multitude," she agreed. "But that's beside the point. I overheard a discussion I wasn't meant to hear—"

"That's what 'overhearing' generally is, Miss Musgrave."

"—and it made me think there is an effort to elevate . . . a certain person . . . in a way that would, er, affect our department."

"Ah. Siepmann," Fielden stated.

"What have you heard?" Maisie demanded.

"Only what you're failing to tell me in worthwhile detail. But the DG's fading enthusiasm for Our Lady is legion enough that it may as well have been broadcast, and who else could he connive with within the ranks to try to splinter us? He's not going to pull from outside, not these days. Strictly an earn-your-way-up man, save where himself is concerned."

"We've got to do something."

"We can't do something against nothing. We couldn't even if it were something."

The whole of the BBC opined that A. A. Milne had modeled Eeyore on Fielden.

"We've got to warn Miss Matheson," Maisie insisted. "There must be a way to do it without upsetting her."

"There is. We say nothing, but rather double our efforts in producing brilliant Talks. We support the genius of Our Lady and of course be sure that there is no chance of the Dear Generalissimo missing a single positive response, either from listeners or the press. Whatever he thinks of Our Lady, his greatest love is for the BBC itself."

"Can't help feeling sorry for his wife," Maisie said.

"For so many reasons. My point is, he's not going to interfere with the growth of his child, even if one of its godmothers irks him. He's far too pleased with his nose to cut it off."

"But the thing of it is, Mr. Fielden, we do a top job already, and if he's thinking—"

"You don't really know what the Dire Gargoyle is thinking, and he could simply be letting Siepmann know he has faith in him." Fielden hid a faint smile in his drink. "Thinks he's good enough to do a woman's job."

"What's that supposed to mean?" Maisie snapped.

Fielden looked surprised. "Do they not have jokes in your homeland? Or is the entire dominion of Canada joke enough in itself?"

His head was saved by a shout from Fowler and an errant croquet ball crashing into the table between them. Fielden pulled his drink to safety but jerked too hard and half of it landed on his summer tweed.

Maisie seized the ball and pitched it back to Fowler so hard he yelped.

She sat back down and handed Fielden her napkin. "You needn't always be so nasty," she said.

"No," he agreed. "But I generally prefer it to the alternative." He suddenly drew close and conspiratorial—she could see all the droplets of gin fizz in his mustache. "No one in Savoy Hill is better at what they do than Our Lady. Some are just as good, maybe, but no one is better. The DG knows it. And he knows the logic of it. Where does a brilliant person go but up? And where else is 'up' for Our Lady?"

Oh. The fantasy. Hilda as DG. And if Fielden left, perhaps Maisie could . . .

"That's lovely but ridiculous," Maisie snapped. "The governors like us modern, but they know perfectly well that the BBC wouldn't be seen as serious if it were headed by a woman. Besides, I don't think Miss Matheson would want the job." But even as she said it, she thought of all the meetings between Hilda and Reith and how Hilda had a stronger sense of audience and technology and content and Reith knew it and hated every bit of it.

Fielden gazed mournfully into his empty glass.

"Whatever else the Deathly Ghoul is, he wants the BBC to be admired. Siepmann hasn't the imagination to do better in Talks than Our Lady. So they can grumble all they like, but speaking as a master of grumbling, I can assure them it doesn't tend to come to anything."

It was strange, Fielden being more optimistic than her. Perhaps it was the effect of the sun.

At least he knows to be on the lookout. And I'm not going to let anything happen to Miss Matheson—that's for damned sure.

Another croquet ball flew toward her and she caught it and stalked away, tossing the ball up and down, to a harmonized chorus of disapproval.

As the afternoon melted into evening, the staff was encouraged toward the marquee stretched over a temporary dance floor. Despite a host of grumbling, the small band held firm to their instructions and played no dances from later than 1921.

"I suppose we should be grateful it's not minuets," Phyllida said.

Maisie, nibbling grapes, was determining where she could drag Phyllida to tell her what had happened when a voice sounded beside them.

"Enjoying the day, Miss Musgrave?"

Cyril. She glanced at him, and took her time finishing chewing and swallowing before she answered.

"Very much, thanks. You?"

"Copacetic."

"Now who sounds like they're from New York?"

He laughed, the sun glinting off his hair and all those freckles standing out on his cheeks, and she couldn't help it—she smiled back.

"Maybe you've been a good influence on me," he suggested.

"That's debatable," she said.

"Is it? Can you have it be a Talk, perhaps?"

"Now, now, Mr. Underwood. Some of our subjects are arcane, I'll grant you, but never inane. You hear the difference?"

"Clever. I don't suppose you've ever read Latin, Miss Musgrave?"

"I've never even read Pig Latin."

"Do you know what 'pax' means?"

"Well, yes, I am a moderate disciple of Mr. Bartlett's, you know. He's fond of any word that means 'peace.'"

"Well, then. Pax?"

She studied him. Two years had passed since their fraudulent date. Not only did she continue to keep her head up, but she had risen through her department and was on the brink of becoming a producer. His equal. And she had an absent but still fond young man. She stuck out her hand.

"Pax."

"Thank you. I don't suppose you'd like to dance?"

Maisie gulped and glanced around the venue. Phyllida was being guided in a very expert fox-trot by Billy. Hilda was across the marquee, having a deep tête-à-tête with Mary Somerville.

"You don't have to," Cyril said hastily, tossing his head to hide his embarrassment at her silence. "I was only—"

"No, it's all right," she broke in. They'd made peace, after all. "But I'm a spectacularly lousy dancer."

"I bet that's not true," he said, taking her hand.

Twenty seconds later, she asked if she could call in that bet.

"We didn't set the terms," he said, laughing. "Actually, Miss Musgrave, you move rather nicely. You just need a few lessons. And you really need to relax."

"I never relax. It's the New York in me."

He laughed again and adjusted his arm more firmly around her waist. Her feet got a vague sense of how they were supposed to move, and she found herself doing something that approximated dancing.

"There, you see?" he asked.

Unfortunately, she did. Over his shoulder, she saw that Siepmann had connived Hilda into a dance. Something about seeing Hilda letting herself be touched by him made Maisie's skin crawl. She wanted to run over and pull him away. No, she wanted to rip his arms from his torso.

She stumbled, and she and Cyril knocked right into Phyllida and Billy.

"Maisie, are you all right?"

She wasn't sure which of them asked. She shook her head.

"Sorry. I . . . I think I need something to drink, actually."

It was Cyril who took her over to the bar.

"It's still quite hot. You do look very flushed. A lemonade should refresh you."

"Thank you," she said, not hearing him.

It was all too much. The late-summer heat lying so heavily all around them like a gas cloud. She preferred the cooler weather, trusted it more. This blaze was too blinding, encouraging them all to let loose. And she had meant what she said. Relaxing was treacherous.

"Feeling better?" Cyril asked after she downed the lemonade in one gulp. He looked genuinely solicitous.

"I think so. Thank you."

But there was Siepmann, talking to Reith again, and he had inveigled Hilda into the conversation. His hand was clutching her elbow possessively.

"You know, Miss Musgrave, you . . . ah . . . you're really very—"

"I'm sorry," she said suddenly, a wave of dizziness overwhelming her. She was not going to faint or scream, not where anyone could see. "I've got to . . . I'll be back in a minute. Thanks."

She wandered through the dusk, trying to think, yearning for silence and solitude. She found herself back at the croquet set, now abandoned—the sound effects men were just as Dionysian as she was when it came to the buffet.

She seized a mallet and began thwacking wooden balls, hitting each of them so they soared into the air and bounced away, lost until tomorrow's sunrise in the neatly mown grass.

EIGHTEEN

As soon as Hilda saw Maisie, she turned into the chapel outside Savoy Hill.

"Or should we perhaps be strolling down the Embankment, feeding the ducks?"

Maisie didn't smile. She told Hilda everything she had overheard between Reith and Siepmann, words tumbling out all over but more or less comprehensible.

Hilda hoisted herself onto the altar. She crossed her ankles and stroked her onyx necklace.

"Funny, really, that there are so many greater things for people's energy and this is how they spend it. Ah well, what can you do?"

"Miss Matheson, I think it's quite serious. We've got to be on guard."

"We can't be on guard and do good work, and the work must not suffer. As I see it, Siepmann would like to be the next DG, and I daresay he'll succeed. I would be most surprised if Reith isn't grooming him thusly. No doubt there are whispers of a new position for Good Sir John, something quite high somewhere or other. The mind reels. In any event, he's likely trying to persuade the governors to give him a deputy, thus creating a clear line of succession."

"But—"

"I know. The DG has long since lost love for me. But he can't sack me without cause. That would create the sort of publicity that would end up with his own head on the grass. Besides, much though some of our content makes the governors nervous, I think they would argue for me rather than against."

Maisie didn't want to admit what she knew—didn't even want to hint at the name "Vita"—but she thought that Hilda was afflicted with a rare case of shortsightedness. The DG had perfect cause, if he ever came to know of it. The question would only be who would prevail in public—Hilda, because she was so widely extolled for her brilliance, or Reith, because whatever went on among the Bloomsbury Bohemia, someone had to take a stand somewhere.

"I think you've got plenty else to worry you, Miss Musgrave," Hilda said, with a fond smile. "No point taking on something that isn't anything. We'll just carry on doing excellent work, and no one can fault us, can they?" She gave her necklace a final pat and hopped down from the altar.

"Miss Matheson?" Maisie asked as they headed for the BBC. "Your necklace, was it a gift?"

"It was, as a matter of fact. From me to me." She grinned and held the door open for Maisie. "It was the first thing I bought when I could afford myself a small luxury."

A luxury. Once all the needed things were in place, and a new home settled, a woman who earned her own money could give herself a small something, just because.

Mine will be a jade brooch, I think.

Such thoughts didn't banish all the cobwebs, but they didn't hurt.

Though Hilda had warned her to stop attending meetings now that she was snooping on a higher plane, Maisie couldn't resist. It was fun, seeing the Fascists so aerated now that Labour was in power. The fact that no one had advocated the closing of churches, the stripping of titles, or nobility sent to salt mines didn't mitigate their apoplexy one iota.

"That infernal BBC is poisoning the minds of the British youth!" Lion insisted.

Maisie checked her watch. Four minutes before a mention of the BBC; he seemed a bit off his game tonight.

"I hear of boys thinking that a coal miner should be treated with the same respect as a landowner! And my own younger sister hopes to go to university and study medicine! She doesn't even wish to get married! These are the spoils of the so-called progressive mind."

I love being spoiled.

"We must defend our small island against those who would attempt to call it home, while having no right to it. We are the true Britons! I was born in Windlesham. Where were you born?" He pointed to a man near the front.

"Shepherd's Bush!"

"And you?" A woman with a spray of peacock feathers flowing over her ear.

"Holland Park!"

Shouts everywhere, even before the question was asked. "Stow-on-the-Wold," "Berkshire," "Leigh-on-Trent," "Selby!"

Maisie, at the back, heard more ferocity than pride in each voice. The whole room had become a sing-along and the song was a macabre tour of Britain.

"You!" A young man grabbed her by the shoulders and glared straight into her face. "You're awfully quiet. Where were you born, Big Nose?"

"Jew Nose, more like," his friend sniggered.

She looked down her nose at them very hard. *Be Beanie.*

"Savoy Place!" she said, in an accent she didn't know she could emulate.

"Oh. Well, that's all right, then," he said, releasing her.

"I'm so pleased," she told him, wishing the acid in her voice were enough to burn him as she pushed past and outside.

Hilda was, as usual, right. Maisie called a moratorium on the meetings.

The DG's hedging on my promotion, Maisie wrote Simon. *But at least he hasn't said no. Nothing's changed since that chat I overheard with Siepmann, so I'm hoping it was just a lot of sound and fury.*

She bit the tip of her pencil, then wrote:

It's been the most beautiful September. The skies are such a brilliant blue, and all the Georgian buildings look like paintings in the afternoon light. You ought to see it. Will you be home soon?

Then she crossed that out. She didn't want to sound needy. Hilda and Vita, if Maisie's calculations were correct, must have enjoyed only a few weeks together before Vita went to Berlin with Harold. Maybe they, too, felt their love grow stronger in the absence. Maisie was sure it was Vita who had given the gift that was Torquhil. It was probably just as well Simon didn't give gifts.

He'll allow the promotion, I'm sure, Simon wrote back. *Who's more right for it than you? And this is just the sort of program we should have more of, good, solid information about the intricacies of government, so that we dispel ignorance. Ignorance is quite passé, very nineteenth century. We want a capable public, strong minds, strong bodies. That's how we retain our glory, and aren't you just the right sort of person to be one of the leaders thereof?*

Sometimes he was the one who sounded like a Communist.

The Week in Westminster had, at least, been approved. "Another political program, really?" was Reith's initial squall. "Lady Astor will be a regular contributor, and Megan Lloyd George. All the best women," Hilda promised in her most soothing tones. "And it will be at eleven in the morning, when workingwomen are drinking their tea." This example of the stalwartness of British women charmed him enough that he forgot the crumpets would be served with politics.

"But he doesn't want to pass around promotions," Phyllida said, with a sigh both supportive and selfish, because Maisie and Hilda were angling to have her made Talks assistant when Maisie stepped up.

"That would be three women in vital positions in the most important department in the BBC," Reith fretted. "I think we had at least be sure this new women's fare is a success before we risk anything so radical."

"I'm not sure how making me a producer is 'radical,'" Maisie said to Phyllida, who reported all the details of every meeting with a thoroughness that made Maisie think she should apply to MI5 herself.

"To be fair, this is a man who still thinks women riding bicycles is radical."

Reith's hedging notwithstanding, Maisie was involving herself more and more deeply in the preparations for the program. Broadcasters were already giving them scripts, discussing assorted minutiae about days spent in Parliament. Maisie huddled over a cup of tea and a script by Megan Lloyd George, the sole female MP for the Liberal party. A fascinating story, but one that read like a dry news report.

No, no, you've got to talk to us, Miss Lloyd George. Talk to us like we're good friends and just as clever as yourself. Every word counts, and then it will be your delivery. But if I just shift this and change that, and let's make the story of a first day in Westminster after an election more personal. That will make everyone just love you, and then I think . . .

Two hours later, she presented it to Hilda, who read it straight through.

"Very good work, Miss Musgrave. I can't add anything. You've done it most satisfactorily."

"I know," said Maisie. Then she blushed. "I mean, thank you."

Hilda grinned. "You meant what you said the first time."

Maisie grinned back. "I know."

Planning to break into Nestlé was more difficult than Siemens. Maisie made several reconnaissance visits and confirmed Hilda's observation that, British arm or not, being beholden to their Swiss overlords subsumed the company with a penchant for high order and exactness, which didn't allow for deviations and unauthorized visitors. But she had to get in. She wanted the evidence of Grigson's lack of ethics, at least, and if he was found to be engaged in anything worse, so much the better.

After the morning tea break, Maisie knocked on Hilda's door for their meeting. Hilda was sitting bolt upright in her chair, hand pressed to her heart, staring at a mountain of telegrams.

"Miss Matheson?"

Hilda didn't look up.

"The American stock market crashed yesterday."

"But that's happened before," Maisie said, remembering her vague attempts to understand the wilderness that was nineteenth-century American banking.

"It appears to be rather bad," Hilda said, struggling to light a cigarette. Her hands were shaking. Maisie moved to help her just as Phyllida came in with a brandy.

"The whole business of stocks never made much sense to me anyway," Phyllida said. "Unless they're talking about cattle."

Maisie read a few of the telegrams. Whatever a "run on the banks" was, it didn't sound good.

"So people will get their money, and—"

"There is no money," Hilda interrupted, her voice hollow. She threw back the brandy in one gulp. Phyllida hovered uncertainly, the bottle cradled in her arms.

"You, er, didn't have money in American stocks, did you?" she asked.

Hilda glanced at her and shook her head. Then she fixed her eyes on Maisie.

"America was doing a great deal to prop up the Weimar Republic."

Germany was still struggling. And if there was to be no more American money, and Mr. Keynes and other economists urging the end to reparations weren't heeded, Germany might become desperate. And here was the example of Italy, who had neatly turned its desperation into a thriving dictatorship. And here were these German patriots, building their agenda, helped by corporate money and ideologues.

"What's Germany got to do with anything?" Phyllida asked.

"God, I hope nothing," Hilda said, staring into space. "I really, really hope nothing." She slipped the bottle from Phyllida's grasp and poured herself another drink.

The story of the disappearing American money—a magician's greatest feat—was the only tale told in all the papers. In some there was gloating, because the bounty of American cash had been a source of some irritation in a Britain struggling with its own sluggish economy. In others, there was worry, but only because the crisis was being handled so poorly. There was no whisper of Germany.

"We can't be the only ones who know, can we?" Maisie asked.

"No. We might be the only ones who care," Hilda said.

Which wasn't particularly encouraging.

"Bit of a poor show our homeland's puttin' up, wouldn't you say?" Lady Astor greeted Maisie when she came to broadcast the inaugural *Week in Westminster.* "Terrible mess. I can't imagine what the boys were thinkin', but I daresay they weren't, and that's how messes get made. Shouldn't be surprised if it's mostly women who do the cleanin' up, or would, if they're allowed in."

Hilda came in to lend further gravitas to the occasion. Billy was finishing the setting up, and the presenter, Miss Hamilton, prepared the introduction. Maisie's old friend, the fist inside her chest, was the size of a boulder and doing serious damage.

"I find every new program gives me butterflies on its maiden voyage," Hilda whispered. "You as well?"

"Swap butterflies for pterodactyls," Maisie said through short breaths.

"You've done marvelous work, and I've told the DG so."

292 · SARAH-JANE STRATFORD

Billy signaled, and Maisie and Hilda gripped hands.

"Good morning, and welcome to our new program, *The Week in Westminster*," Miss Hamilton greeted the listeners. "Every week we will hear from different female members of Parliament, who will explain the workings of Parliament and the business before the House of the previous week. Our inaugural presenter is Lady Astor, MP for Plymouth, of the Conservative Party. Good morning, Lady Astor."

"Thank you. I'm terrifically honored to be here and to assist in educating all the young ladies who have just enjoyed their first vote as to the workings of our system. I've talked to far too many ladies who think politics sounds too confusin' to manage, or just a dreadful bore. I assure you, nothing is further from the truth. A lady does require a powerful voice, though, and some very serious backbone. Now, then . . ."

Fifteen minutes later, Maisie exhaled.

"Marvelous!" Lady Astor said, though it was hard to be sure if she was congratulating them or herself. "And not a moment too soon. Some of the letters I've gotten lately . . . Gracious, there are a multitude of muttonheads out there. Honestly thinking that America's example shows too much democracy leads to scrapes. 'The firm few, not the muddled many, are what's needed for a strong nation.' That's what one imbecile wrote. Do hope this helps sort people out."

Which seemed a lot of pressure for fifteen minutes a week. But Maisie was keen to try.

By that afternoon, they had early notices from papers and a number of congratulatory telegrams.

"There, you see? I knew it would be a success," Phyllida said, giving the telegrams an approving pat.

"Surely the more people care about our political system, the more they'll fight to maintain it, right?" Maisie sought confirmation.

"What idiot would look around the world and think anything's better than what we have here?" Maisie just looked at her. "Oh, all right. Plenty, but they're not going to do anything except make fools of themselves shouting in a pub."

Maisie smiled. But for once she thought Phyllida might be overly optimistic.

By the time she left that evening, her brain felt so full, her hat was tight. It wasn't a train of thought; it was King's Cross Station. The damp cold was a relief. It tugged at some of the threads in her mind and unspooled them so they floated behind her as she headed up to the Strand.

"Pardon me, miss." A hand tapped her on the arm.

She screamed.

It was Simon.

"Easy, easy. We'll be arrested if we keep on like this," he said, finally managing to pry her away. But he kissed her again, too.

"Were you waiting for me out here? You could have come inside, you know."

"But that wouldn't have been as romantic."

His lips were moving, he was talking, but Maisie couldn't take any of it in. All this time, and now here he was. He seemed too big, too much, as if he'd been consigned to memory and was now made solid—it was like a series of fun house mirrors, with everything too big and small and distorted. She had the most horrible sense of wanting to break out and be in normal space again.

"I'm overwhelming you, aren't I? I'm so sorry, darling. It's just I . . . I don't know what to . . ."

"Neither do I," she breathed.

"I can't tell you how I missed that voice." He picked her up and kissed her. "Have dinner with me," he whispered into her neck. "At my flat. Come home with me."

She wanted to. She wanted to be with him. Feast off him. Feel everything she'd only ever dreamed about and wondered and hoped. But the suddenness of it, the popping up of him, a jackrabbit in spring . . . Her head was too distorted. Somewhere in the din, she heard Phyllida's firm advice, reminding her to keep her head, at least, if she couldn't keep her heart.

"No," she whispered. "Not at your flat. Somewhere in Soho or Chelsea."

"I'm longing to be alone with you, darling," he murmured, stroking the exact spot on the back of her neck where he always made her tingle. She leaned into him, feeling that melting sensation. *Just go. Just let go. Just let yourself have this.*

"No," she said, and saw his brows jump at her firmness. "No, it's too soon, after all this time. No. We're going for a meal and then I'm going home."

He looked startled, then smiled and was more gallant than ever, whisking them into a cab and soon after a bistro. And they talked, and ate, and laughed, and she wondered if she saw something in his eyes, some sort of unease, but decided that was the peril of journalistic pursuits. She was always looking for something more in things, creating a danger of seeing things that weren't there.

I must work on that. Can't be devoted to the truth if I'm living in even half a fantasy.

For all that some people decried the Marie Stopes clinics as hives of immorality, only married women were officially allowed to partake of their wares. Maisie felt more of a fraud wearing one of Lola's more understated rings as a wedding band than in a wig and heavy makeup. She tried not to fidget with the ring as the reception nurse was asking her a few rudimentary questions and taking her through to a little examination room.

What she really wanted was a pencil. So many questions, a long story to write, asking about the numbers of women who came in, their ages, their backgrounds. Were they excited? Desperate?

"Good afternoon, Mrs. Simon," the rosy-cheeked young midwife greeted her. "I understand you want a diaphragm?"

She had a brisk, cheerfully magisterial sort of voice, and Maisie wanted to ask her to come broadcast. She listened to the midwife's brisk explanation of the device and instructions, hearing the voice rather than the words and thinking how useful this would be for their female listeners. Then she heard what Reith's response would be to such a proposed Talk.

"Yes, it really is that easy," the midwife said, mistaking Maisie's smile for a response. "Now, just relax and take a few deep breaths. It won't hurt, but it's not terribly comfortable, I'm afraid."

It wasn't. The midwife was professionally gentle, though the word "manhandling" came to mind.

"It's easy to get nervous giggles, but do try to just relax and breathe steady. It'll be much quicker," the midwife ordered. "There! You are now wearing a Dutch cap."

"Can you fit me with wooden shoes, too?"

The midwife chuckled.

"How many of the women ask that?" Maisie wanted to know.

"Only a few," the midwife assured her. "Any questions?"

A thousand. But none that the midwife meant.

"No. I think I'm all right."

"Well, any discomfort or concern of any sort, you come straight back to us. Don't feel awkward."

Considering where the midwife had just had her hands, Maisie thought it was past time to mention feeling awkward. But she only said, "Thank you."

"You're welcome, Mrs. Simon. Good afternoon."

"Well-done," Phyllida congratulated Maisie after the whispered confession in the tearoom. "Though after all this time, I'd keep him waiting a month at least."

"I don't want to."

"No. I suppose you don't. Well, here's hoping you're a producer soon and that saves you from the Marriage Bar."

"And you'll be Talks assistant."

"I will, won't I?"

Their delight was tempered by the reality of Reith. His deep chill toward Hilda escalated the more popular Talks became.

"You'd think instead he'd hire four strapping lads to carry her on their shoulders wherever she went," Phyllida said.

"Or keep us drowning in sandwiches and cakes all day long," Maisie countered.

"Or meet us every morning to bow thricely and wish us maximum productivity."

"Do you girls really have to giggle so much?" Fowler said, looking up from his Chelsea bun. "It's highly distracting."

"Just trying to inspire you with sound, Mr. Fowler," Maisie assured him.

And so here she was, sitting down to a supper she could barely eat in Simon's "awfully bourgeois flat" in Primrose Hill. "But it's part of the family pile and a lovely view of Regent's Park," he said, both introducing and dismissing the place.

They were served with an excess of deference by "my man, Trent. He's all right. Aren't you?" He looked dyspeptic, actually.

The room was almost overbearing in its insistence on masculinity, with heavy, dark furniture and drapes. A walnut bookcase was stuffed with leather-bound books, and Maisie counted two rolltop desks, one closed, the other with a typewriter peeking out between piles of papers and vases full of bouquets of pencils.

"I don't believe in gifts, Maisie," Simon announced, smiling. "But I daresay I'm an incorrigible hypocrite." And he slid a small black box across the table to her.

One fist in her chest became a dozen.

This can't be real.

She opened it. A ring. An emerald ring. Emerald for May. For Maisie.

RADIO GIRLS · 297

"Possibly it's not really a gift, since I'm asking something rather large in return," he said, reaching over and slipping the ring on her finger. "My father doesn't approve, I'm afraid, but I explained you were devoted to England, an admirer of king and country, and whatnot. And that I was determined to marry you because I couldn't imagine trying to talk with anyone else of an evening."

This was one in the eye for Georgina. Maisie wondered where Edwin Musgrave was, and wished he were someone she could go to and share this with.

"You'll marry me, Maisie?"

"Is that a question or an order?" She laughed, and he did, too.

"Oho, the orders come after marriage, my dear! You will swear an oath to obey, don't forget. Joking! I rather like the idea of a working wife, and in fact I'd be keen to put those magnificent brains to work for me. Think of it, darling. Think of me owning a string of newspapers and magazines and having you to help me! And you'd write. Of course you would. Your name would be all over the pages, connected with your ideas, far more than as a Talks producer, or even if you ever became director. You'd like that, wouldn't you? 'Maisie Brock-Morland,' doesn't that sound superb?"

He turned her hand around and kissed her palm, looking up into her eyes.

"Yes," she whispered, though in fact she was answering a very different question. One he didn't need to ask. He simply scooped her up and carried her into his bedroom.

She wasn't sure what her body was supposed to do. His body, however, was less alien than it might have been. She had bathed so many bodies in Brighton. And long before, before all the breaking, all the white beds, she'd walked alone through the Met in New York, unsettled and thrilled by the nakedness of men in the classical wing. No one ever sculpted a hero cut down. Hercules always succeeded in his labors. There was no shot, no gas, no bayonet, nothing to land him crushed and limp in a white bed, a body becoming infant-spongy under blue pajamas. But Simon's body was solid, rangy, unblemished, unbroken, and it knew exactly how to warm and melt her own flesh. Somewhere, sometime, he'd had a different training from hers.

Imagine asking the sound effects men to re-create this.

"Why are you laughing?" He grinned at her, teeth flashing in the semidarkness. "I'm not comical, am I?"

"No. You're wonderful."

He was. It was. She was. This was the great wild wood, a primeval forest, and she was a creature unbound.

She blinked awake with a suddenness and completeness that startled her. It was still dark. She was sure that was moonlight peeking in through the drapes. It bathed them in a silvery sheen, keeping alive the woodland fantasy. Imagine making love outside, a midsummer night's dream indeed, a bed of grass, a roof of trees.

Goodness, I lose my virginity and turn into a libertine.

She looked down at herself. She'd never slept naked before. Her body was still strange to her, no longer scrawny and pasty and scaly with the sheen of unhealthiness barely masked by youth. She had satiny flesh now, pink and plump, and actual curves. Unfashionable, perhaps, but really very nice. Simon seemed to like them, certainly.

A sudden bellow, like from a water buffalo, made her jump, and now she knew what had woken her. Simon snored. He was sunk in sleep, curled on his side, one foot resting on a knee, right hand folded under his face, the knuckles digging into his cheek, left arm underneath it, stretching out, the hand dangling helplessly over the bed.

Maisie squinted at her watch, the only thing she was wearing besides the ring. Four in the morning? There was no point in going home. She would just go to Savoy Hill from here.

She eased herself out of the bed, though the way Simon was snoring, she could probably tap-dance on his head and he wouldn't budge. Her clothes were in a heap. She scooped them up and made her way to the bathroom.

As she used her fingers as a comb, the ring caught her hair. She patiently unwound it, thinking of all the things she would have to learn now as she adjusted to this new life, this life of wearing an engagement ring. She could see the park outside, bathed in fading moonlight. Wouldn't that be something, to have this as one's view every day? A wolf stepped into the light and she gasped. A wolf, in Regent's Park? She was dreaming. She was in the wild wood.

A man joined the wolf and fixed a lead to its collar, and she realized it was an Alsatian and they were out for a predawn stroll.

The hour of the wolf, they call it somewhere. I remember that. Dreams and reality colliding, all very dangerous and tempting.

Her fingers were itching. She hurried back to the sitting room and dove upon Simon's open desk. She snatched up a pencil but couldn't find any paper and had to search the drawers. In the messiest, she found some plain, if slightly crumpled, sheets. She sat on the squashy brown leather sofa and scribbled notes for a Talk: the things you see in the night, so different from the daylight, the tricks our eyes play upon us. Was this how fairy tales had been developed? She quickly covered one side and flipped the page over. Her heart stopped. It was a letter.

It's only a discarded draft, nothing to worry about, she told herself. But it was addressed from London, and the date was practically scratching at her eye. "15 August 1929." When Simon was still meant to be in Germany.

"Dear Grigson . . ."

The fist inside blew up, forcing her breath into icy gasps.

No. No, no, no.

Words jumped out at her, screeching and biting like pixies. "Delighted to make the arrangement." "Grateful for your investment and your faith in me." "Will not disappoint you."

Sun was breaking in around the drapes. Maisie forced herself not to think, to just go to her bag, where the camera was still nestled among a mound of chocolate and the latest *Listener*.

Don't shake, Maisie ordered her fingers as she smoothed the letter, set it under the desk lamp, and took a photo, hoping it would be clear and legible.

Five thirty now. Her mind and body worked on auto, searching the desk with the clinical precision of a surgeon. Then she looked over at the closed desk.

The desk was locked. In his own home. Out came the trusty nail file.

More letters. Letters, letters, letters. She snapped seven more pictures, finishing the reel, and then confined herself to shorthand, not thinking about what she was writing, not thinking about all the talk of cacao, of exclusive contracts with Nestlé, of a great family restored, of plans for an illustrious future as head of a media empire, so natural, with a man of Simon's breeding and connections and caliber. Simon couldn't possibly know what he was doing, or whom he was doing it with. He was desperate to help his family. That was honorable, and he was an Honorable. He wasn't going to be proof against the offer of real help, and especially if it gave him something more, something he always wanted. But he wasn't going to be a puppet on a string, doing as his benefactors demanded. He just needed to understand whom he was dealing with, what it all might mean, and then he and Maisie could have a bonfire with these papers.

She slipped the camera and pad back in her bag, locked the desk, and glanced back at the messy open desk. She could just see the corner of brown leather—a diary, it must be. She shifted aside some papers.

"May we help you?"

Maisie lurched forward into the desk, banging her knee so hard she thought it might be fractured. It was the dyspeptic Trent, looking as though he'd like to beat her to death and refraining only because he didn't want blood staining the parquet floor.

"I was just looking for some international letter paper," she explained. "I wanted to write to my mother and tell her about my engagement."

"And did Mr. Simon say you could have the use of his desk?"

"I was going to use the sofa, actually. He's still asleep. But I'm a lark type of girl. Very keen on catching worms."

He looked her up and down, probably wondering what the attraction was. Eyes locked on hers, he pulled out a drawer and withdrew several sheets of thin blue paper.

"Ah, there you are," Simon murmured. Maisie turned to see him, clad only in pajama bottoms resting at his hips, running his hand through already tousled hair. That body. Smooth, sculpted, strong. She had touched every inch of that lightly burnished flesh. She could go to him now and touch him again. She wanted to. Better to do that, better to touch him, to kiss him, to lose herself in him, take him back inside her, than to believe all her eyes had told her. He had been drawn into something he didn't understand. Who among us didn't make mistakes, after all?

"I thought you'd used and abandoned me," he said, pulling her into his chest and kissing her neck. "Let's go back to bed. I'm never up before nine. Trent must think the end is nigh."

"I've got to be at work long before nine," she reminded him. "Very busy day ahead, I'm afraid." *Just got busier, too.*

"Mm, busy little bee. And I suppose you want to go home and change. Do you want breakfast first? Trent makes a rather lovely mess of bacon and eggs."

"No, that's all right," she said, instantly regretting it. Her turning down food was a dead giveaway. "Miss Matheson said she was going to stand us muffins and jam this morning, and, well . . . for once, I'm not feeling hungry for food." She ran her hand down his back, thrilling to his shiver. She could do this. She had the right to touch him now, to . . .

What the hell am I doing? He's not . . .

"I hope you weren't riffling too much in my desk, there," he said suddenly, and she wondered if there was an edge in his voice.

"No. Just hoped to find some blue letter paper. But the mess was a bit of an allaying force."

He laughed.

"Yes, I imagine your secretary brain looks at that dog's dinner and wants to fill it with any amount of bourgeois in-trays and labels and files."

302 · SARAH-JANE STRATFORD

"Nothing bourgeois about organization," she snapped. "And I'm not a secretary anymore. I'm a Talks assistant."

"Of course, of course, I know. And soon you'll be a producer and then the director and have the power to come in whenever you like and dictate the whole course of action."

She barely heard him. She had to get to the BBC. She had to talk to Hilda.

"If you're not going to be a good girl and come back to bed with me, then it's cruel to stay," he chided her. "Shall I give you cab fare?"

"No," she said. She wanted to walk, clear her head. "No, that's all right."

"I promised the lads a drink tonight, but will we have dinner tomorrow?"

"I'd love that," she said, hardly registering either of their words.

"And what else do you love?" His eyes were teasing, and so warm. So honest.

"You," she told him, kissing him again. "I love you."

But I have no idea who you are.

NINETEEN

Maisie walked slowly down Eversholt Street. All around her was the pulse of early-morning life. Dustmen, milkmen, postmen. And boys, newsboys, delivery boys, shoeshine boys. But not Tommies. Not anymore. No more war. They had fought, and won, and now the former enemy was subdued and come to heel and peace reigned.

And I'm the Queen of Sheba.

Maybe it all meant nothing. It might. She looked around her. It was later now. The street was full of the working and middle classes, all heading to different jobs, none as important as her own. Because she had power, didn't she? She was part of something that was doing something. She was . . . She was on the verge of running late.

She was hot and flustered when she reached her desk, and slammed her coat and hat on the rack. She stared at her neat piles of paper. There was a great deal to do. Letters from assorted experts in fields, hoping to be considered for broadcasts. Scripts to revise. Letters to draft.

Phyllida hissed in her ear, "You look hellish. Are you feeling all right?"

Maisie just nodded.

"Rubbish. Can I get you some tea? Or bicarbonate of soda?"

Maisie burst out laughing. If only, if only she were nursing a hangover! What a marvelously fashionable, mundane ailment that would be.

"Oh, *there* you are, Miss Fenwick," Fielden said. "I made the mistake of looking for you at your own desk."

"What luck Miss Musgrave's desk is less than twenty feet away. Otherwise I'd feel dreadful about your having to trek so far."

"I don't know how the pair of you aren't making a fortune in the music halls," Fielden said, including Maisie as part of the great comic duo. "Can you type these, please? And we've got to reschedule Mr. Jennings from Lloyd's."

"We need more broadcasting time." Phyllida sighed, looking at the schedule.

"We need more everything time," Fielden agreed, glad to have company in his complaints. "More time, more space, more staff."

"Maybe when the new building is ready," Maisie said automatically. The already designated "Broadcasting House" was well under construction and on schedule for 1932, but seemed like Arcadia, something not to be reached.

Almost as if she were listening, they heard Hilda cry from her office, "But we haven't space as it is!"

They looked at each other, alarmed. When did Hilda ever raise her voice?

They crept to the edge of her door, as near as they dared. Reith was there, arms folded, rocking back and forth on his heels.

"No, you misunderstand me," he said, his voice calm and sing-songy. "It's just a bit of departmental rearranging. A better use of all our best resources."

"You cannot be serious." Hilda was standing, white-faced, her eyes wide and glassy.

"You've said you need more staff, that you are all at full pressure. Everyone knows you in Talks work later than everyone else. It's too much for just one person. And I am not taking away your title, far from it. I do think you're getting a bit hysterical. Really, you should be grateful."

"Grateful? You are telling me I am incapable of running this department."

"Now, you see? That's the hysteria talking. My dear Miss Matheson, I am including you as one of those best resources I mentioned, and I doubt there is any man in Britain who doesn't know of your brilliance in running this department. This little change—"

"Little!"

"—will allow you to focus on the Talks you like best. Everyone can be more carefully designated, without so much mishmash. Focused minds, focused work. And you and Mr. Siepmann are doing such similar work anyway. It makes sense to consolidate your mental acumen, no? Miss Somerville will head up the Schools Broadcast herself—she's delighted to do so—and you and Mr. Siepmann can divide the spoils here and thus bring more to Talks overall."

"Mr. Reith," Hilda said, licking her lips, "I do appreciate what you are attempting to do, truly, but whilst I do need more staff here, my hope was for some more fine producers and one or two additional administrative staff. That's all. I think if you talk to my staff as stands, they will assure you that I am a very good director. If you add another director, however much you may pretend he is doing different work, it will only add confusion. You are a man of great experience. You know that's true. Would you have had a second captain serving with you in the trenches?"

"To help me manage a thousand troops? Absolutely. Now, my dear Miss Matheson, I know this all seems a bit of a shock, but try to take it as the compliment it is. You have done a great deal in building up this department, and now it is simply too much for one person to handle all on her own."

Maisie was on her way in to tell him just how wrong he was, but she couldn't move. Fielden's arm was encircled around her waist, holding her with surprising strength. To push back would create some very undesirable contact; to pull forward risked toppling into the office. He was infuriating, Fielden, but damned clever.

306 · SARAH-JANE STRATFORD

"You and Siepmann and I can meet in my office and we'll talk it through," Reith said, grinding out his cigarette in Hilda's ashtray. "I guarantee by the time you've talked to him, heard his persuasive arguments, you'll be overjoyed."

"So this was his idea?"

"Hmm? Oh, no. It's long been my concern and he's always asking how he can be more useful. When I said I thought Talks needed some reworking, it became obvious that he was the man for the job."

"I see."

"Good! Well, see you in my office later, then. Cheerio!"

Fielden's fingers dug into Maisie's side, urging her away. They all shrank back as Reith strode off, whistling. Maisie was about to go into Hilda's office when the phone rang. Phyllida, controlling the tremble in her voice, announced to Hilda that it was a personal call and they didn't give a name.

Which must mean Vita. Hilda closed her door.

Maisie pushed at Fielden in a blind rage.

"Didn't I tell you?" she snapped. "Didn't I warn you? Now everything is going to be ruined."

"What could we have done differently, Miss Musgrave? You're so clever; you tell me. What else could we have done?"

His eyes were full of their usual sarcastic fury, but there was a hint of pink around the edges of his eyelids. And the only answer was "nothing." Because the only option would have been tamping down Hilda, and that was never going to happen.

Hilda avoided them all until after the promised meeting with Reith and Siepmann. When she returned, she called Maisie into her office and shut the door.

"Here. I've brought you a bun," she said, setting it on a trestle table.

"You didn't have to—"

"I know you all heard enough. Apparently there will soon be a memo. The department is to be split. I am director of General Talks and Siepmann director of Adult Education. And it is hoped the politics might be 'toned down.'"

She methodically stabbed her blotter with a pen. She looked drawn, even ill.

"Miss Matheson, we can manage this," Maisie said in a sudden swell of confidence. "The DG will hate bad publicity. We just need to make it obvious that anything Siepmann is handling is going poorly and have it be known in a few quarters that the new regime is confusing and making for bad Talks and he'll set it all right."

Hilda looked at her with misty eyes. "You sound like me, you silly goose."

"Good."

"Miss Musgrave, I'm afraid it only gets worse. The DG has determined that you do not have the necessary qualifications to be the producer on *The Week in Westminster*."

There was no reason to be surprised. Maisie frowned at the bun. She gouged off the top.

"I made the point as plainly as I could. But the DG—"

"I know."

It was foolish of them to think this was going to go any other way. A woman's program, by women, for women, should not have spurred his interest. But he had warned Maisie against ambition once. This must be her punishment for not heeding him.

"I'm still a Talks assistant?"

"You are."

Maisie stabbed her finger farther into the bun, making it bleed cream.

"Who gets the position?"

"Cyril Underwood."

Hilda spoke without expression. She wasn't the slaughterer, just the messenger.

"He wanted to be a producer on an important program," Maisie stated, ripping off a chunk of bun and shoving it in her mouth to stop her chin shaking. "He had better consider this a compliment."

"If Reith wanted the program to fail, or didn't think it had worth, he would have let you have the position."

"Yes. I suppose so."

There was nothing to do but look at each other.

"He's a schoolboy," Maisie said at last, without bitterness.

"Some of them never recover from it," Hilda agreed.

The phone was ringing. Business had to go on.

Maisie stood and brushed the crumbs from her skirt. "It is a terrific program," she said.

"One of our finest," Hilda agreed.

So there was that.

And something else.

"Miss Matheson, may I send one of the lads out to have some film exposed?"

Hilda raised an eyebrow. For the first time that day, she smiled. "You have more information."

"I do. The sort that had made me think the day couldn't possibly get worse."

"That's the BBC for you. Always surprising."

They smiled, though neither of them felt like it.

Everyone did their best to smile when Siepmann descended on them, Cyril in tow, "just to say hullo." He was quick to assure everyone that nothing was really going to change, even though there were going to be immense changes.

"Ah, Miss Musgrave, industrious as ever, aren't you, dear?" Siepmann bent his head around to examine her work.

I wonder how hard it would be to accidentally topple him out the window.

"Yes, I understood you were rather hoping to be producer on the little *Westminster* program, but you understand that Underwood here needs that sort of experience more than you, don't you? Of course you do. Very clever little thing. I've always said so."

"And I've always appreciated it, Mr. Siepmann."

"Ah, isn't that nice? Well, must be tootling on, but of course we'll soon be seeing a great deal more of each other."

Cyril lingered, biting his lips.

"Did you need something?" Maisie asked. "Because we're really very busy, you know. Apparently, that's the whole reason for this little massive upheaval."

"I'm sorry," Cyril said.

"No, you're not. Don't bother lying. It's really never suited you."

"Maisie . . ." Her sharp glare backed him down. "Miss Musgrave. I didn't ask for the *Week in Westminster* assignment. I want you to know that."

"All right, so I know."

"I really am sorry. I know you'd have done a fine job."

"If you believed that, Mr. Underwood, you'd thank your bene-factors and ask that I be given the assignment instead. It's not a plum for you anyway, being a woman's program and all, and in the morn-ing. It's not as though you were being assigned to Mr. Bartlett's broadcasts. It would have been a great chance for me, but for you it's just another notch as you clamber your way on up. Well, congratu-lations, and good luck to you."

She turned around and typed as loudly as she could, even long after she knew he was gone.

Somehow, the terrible day came to an end. Not a single person in Talks felt like staying late. Hilda and Maisie left together and hailed a cab. The driver gave them an apologetic grimace.

"Sorry, misses, but the backseat's got a poorly spring on one side—bally kid wouldn't stop jumping on it. One of you will have to ride jump, I'm afraid."

"I don't mind," Maisie said, hopping in to prevent Hilda from taking the awkward seat facing backward. Hilda attempted to give the driver the address in between his tirade on lax child-rearing and all the ills it forebode.

"You could go to the governors, you know," Maisie said once they were finally en route. "They want a tight ship, not a sloppy one.

What amounts to two directors of Talks won't go down well at all. The salaries, if nothing else."

"I certainly shall not go to the governors. I'm not going to be seen to be crying like a little girl because Papa doesn't like me."

"But that's not—"

Hilda held up her hand. "He must have already persuaded them. If I were even to try, it would be evidence of my churlishness."

"But they like you! Or anyway, they like the good press you get. It's good for the BBC and then they look good, too, and—"

"Yes, everyone's very quick to assure me I'm indispensable and invaluable and all the things that have led me to this sterling moment."

It was unsettling to see Hilda be bitter. Maisie jerked her eyes away, staring instead at the ever-disappearing street behind them.

"Miss Matheson?"

"Hmm?"

"I think there might be someone following us."

She'd thought she noticed a car idling at the bottom of Savoy Street when they were waiting for a cab, but there was always some activity or other around there. And she had maybe registered it starting up when they drove off, but that wasn't odd in and of itself. But over Hilda's shoulder, out the tiny rear window, she saw the same headlights following them.

"What makes you sure?" Hilda asked.

"It's been following us since we left Savoy Hill. I know it. One of the lamps is dimmer than the other."

"Very good!"

Hilda was suddenly almost cheerful. She turned and knelt on the seat to study their pursuer.

It continued to wend its way after them. Hilda turned back and tapped on the driver's shoulder. "I say, cabbie, change of plan. Can you take us to 31 Sumner Street instead?"

"Wha'? But that's miles the other direction!"

"Terribly inconvenient, I know. Will another two shillings compensate?"

He whipped around and roared off with a new spring in his acceleration, if not the cushion.

And they lost their tail.

"Not even trying to turn 'round? That's a poor show," Hilda tutted.

"What's on Sumner Street?" Maisie asked.

"My flat," Hilda answered simply.

Sumner Street was one of the many London streets sporting rows of elegant white Georgian houses with pillars, on which the house numbers were painted in black. Each house was indistinguishable from the other, unless its residents had done something with the patch of concrete that stood in for a front garden. They didn't need a garden, really, having ready access to the square around the corner. And the houses themselves boasted their own beauty.

Hilda chivvied Maisie inside number thirty-one just as Torquhil hurtled down the stairs and flung himself on Hilda, barking and wagging his tail in danger to the Staffordshire likenesses of himself on the coat rack shelf.

"There's my favorite lad. Had a good day?" Hilda crooned. "Not all by your lonesome, are you? Hallo, anyone in?"

"You don't live alone?" Maisie asked, following Hilda downstairs into the kitchen. She could certainly afford to.

"Landlords aren't especially keen on renting to lone women," Hilda said, loading a tray with bread, cheese, and fruit. "Though I could have had my father or brother stand for me, but it's not a bad thing, having other people about. We can look out for one another, and it means I've been able to buy a car. Gorgeous beast. I'll show you sometime. Yes, you're a gorgeous beast, too," she assured Torquhil, and opened a tin of meat for him. After several jetés and a circle around Hilda, he settled to his food.

"I'm feeling some affinity to him," Maisie remarked. Hilda laughed, set the tray in a dumbwaiter, and rolled it upstairs. They followed their supper to Hilda's domain, a large sitting room with a bedroom beyond. Hilda stoked the fire and tossed cushions on the floor.

The room was as bright and warm and cheerful as Maisie could have imagined. But she remembered why they were there and what she had discovered in Simon's flat that morning, a thousand years ago. Hilda handed her a glass of sherry just as she started to cry.

"Your photos were developed with great haste and I've had a look at them, so I have somewhat more of a sense of what's bringing on the great floods. I'm so very sorry." She pressed a handkerchief into Maisie's hand. "You have notes, too?"

Maisie passed her pad to Hilda, and shoved a chunk of Wensleydale in her mouth.

"Isn't it possible," she asked through the cheese, "that Simon doesn't know what he's doing, or who he's involved with? He wants to run a newspaper. He's said so a dozen times. And now here's his chance. Maybe he doesn't know the rest."

"I hope so. And I'm sure you would have noticed if he has Fascist inclinations."

"He can't have. He was so horrified at that meeting I brought him to." Maisie hesitated, remembering. "Actually, he thought it was hilarious. And they were talking about wanting to control the press." She paused. "And Grigson was there, looking at him. But then we left before they could talk. Or . . . I wonder. I suppose he could have gone back in after I left?"

Hilda lit a cigarette and slid a cake tin off a shelf. Victoria sponge. Maisie laid a slice of Wensleydale on the cake. They went together nicely.

"It's possible," said Hilda. "It's also possible Grigson recognized him. I knew who he was myself, remember? He's been plastered over the society pages at various and sundry times. A big man in business would know of someone like that, especially when the aristocrat in question is trying his hand at journalism."

"But he . . . he can't . . . ." Maisie slugged down some sherry. "He's made a lot of remarks about newspapers—calls them 'bourgeois,' actually—and definitely wants to show them how to do the job, but of course he believes in a varied and free press. He must, surely."

Hilda refilled Maisie's glass. "There's a sort of man who thinks he ought to have power. As of the divine right of kings. Hideously ata-vistic, of course, but impervious to evolution. And it's a media baron who can wield real power. Think of William Randolph Hearst."

"Must I?"

"It looks to me as though Grigson—and likely Hoppel too—courted him more with power than money. He runs the one paper they start with. Then they buy more, and he remains the voice behind them all. And then it's easy to disseminate whatever information you like. 'Nothing to fear from Fascism. The real fear is, et cetera, et cetera.' Once that's the majority opinion in all the respectable papers, anyone disagreeing looks foolish. You don't have to silence them by aggression. Much more civilized."

Torquhil nosed his way in and assayed the cheese plate. Hilda snapped her fingers and he withdrew to lay his head in her lap.

"How can he like someone like me if that's the sort of power he really wants to wield?"

Hilda took a long drag of her cigarette.

"He may have some severe shortcomings, but he'd have to be a hopeless idiot not to like you. And if he were a hopeless idiot, you would have no interest in him. So there we are."

Maisie took the ring from her bag and turned it this way and that, catching the light from the fire. Torquhil watched with desultory interest. She looked again at the photos she'd taken of Simon's papers.

"So this is where we stand. Grigson has arranged for a contract between Nestlé and the Brock-Morland cacao holdings, which might get the family out of debt, and asked Simon to run his newspaper. I wonder if Simon even went to Germany at all."

"That's easy enough to find out, not that it matters. But he likely did. His family does have business there. Possibly less than they used to."

"So it is bad for them."

"It does seem so."

Maisie ate another piece of cake. "I have to go to Nestlé," she said.

"I don't think that's wise, now that we—"

"No. I know what I have to do. I know what I have to prove. You won't try to stop me, will you?"

"I hope you know me better than that by now."

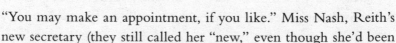

It was almost surreal, being back at the BBC the next day and trying to pretend things were ordinary. Especially when Siepmann strutted in again to, as he said, "assess the space."

"We're going to be a bit snug, aren't we? And still dreadfully busy, I'm sure." He turned to Phyllida and put a consoling hand on her shoulder. Her eyes flitted toward it, but he bravely kept it there. "I'll be bringing my girl over as well. You don't need to worry about being the lone secretary here."

"I can hardly contain myself for relief," Phyllida said. She made a sharp turn back to the typewriter, forcing off his hand.

"Now, now, girls," he said with a tinkling laugh. "Do let's all be more cheerful and obliging. I would hate to have to recommend any of you be removed. And after all, this little reorganization is all to the good. We can't have people thinking Talks is a woman's sole domain, or the men won't listen in."

"We have a good number of men in the audience," Maisie said.

"Most certainly, but that doesn't stop us needing to be mindful. Best not to rock boats."

"Of course, Mr. Siepmann," she said. But she wondered if it was too late to keep the boat from changing course.

She'd once known how to talk to Reith. Maybe she still could.

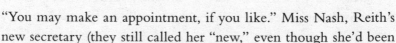

"You may make an appointment, if you like." Miss Nash, Reith's new secretary (they still called her "new," even though she'd been there nearly two years), looked at Maisie with dislike.

"Isn't he having his tea now, though?"

"Yes, and he's having it alone."

"Would you mind terribly asking him if he'd like company?"

Miss Nash raised her eyebrows over her wire-framed glasses. But she asked and the question was answered. Maisie went in.

"Ah, Miss Musgrave." Reith waved her in with his warmest scowl. "Yes, do join me. Most delightful. Still not smoking? Glad to hear it. Quite a bit of water under the bridge since you first joined us, hey?"

"Quite a bit, yes, sir. Coming to the BBC was the best thing that ever happened to me."

"And very good for us, too," he assured her, with a generous nod. "It does seem as if you've done well."

"I think so, sir. Thank you. It was very good of you, sir, to let me work solely in the Talks Department. Wanting to do good work there was the best way I could thank you." She hesitated, wondering if that was enough to warm him. "I do think Talks has done well. People seem to be pleased."

"Yes, that's my understanding overall," he agreed. She wondered how many of the Talks he ever listened to. Or liked.

"Sir, I know you're keen on expedience, and I'm wondering, perhaps, if it's not too late to rethink the plans regarding Mr. Siepmann? That is, he's excellent, of course, and done such fine work, but if Talks are doing well as they are, and Schools, too, maybe that's a boat that shouldn't be rocked?"

"Ah. Yes, I understand." Reith nodded. He leaned back, folding his hands behind his head. "The trouble with success, Miss Musgrave, is it creates its own problems. Miss Matheson has said she needs more staff, the best available. Now she has it and someone to help her with the duller parts of managing as well."

"But Mr. Fielden does very well as her deputy, helping with managing, and all the rest of us work very hard to keep things running so smoothly," Maisie said.

"Of course you do, and it's very much to your credit. But I suspect Miss Matheson's great ambition is causing all of you to wear yourselves out in her service. Under this new scheme, all your energies will be better allocated, and Miss Matheson will be better able to hone her considerable talents and produce fare that is more suitable to the times in which we're now living. You see, Miss Musgrave, the world economy is now in a frightful state. People need comfort, and we must provide that."

"But don't they need good, well-rounded information, too?"

Deep disappointment crinkled Reith's face.

"I would advise you against assuming too many of Miss Matheson's qualities, my dear. You must understand I have to please people. The governors, you know, they're always trying to keep us up to the mark. They worry, Miss Musgrave, and they charge me to keep them assured, and that's a very heavy charge."

His eyes were wistful, and she could see he meant every word. She wondered, though, what might happen if he allowed the BBC's popularity to assure the governors instead.

"Besides which, Mr. Siepmann will bring a great deal to the department and allow Miss Matheson and you girls on her team to focus on the sort of Talks you like best. I know this sort of change is difficult to understand, dear, but trust me. You always said you did, you know."

She looked into his piercing dark eyes. He was testing her, testing the memory of her gratitude.

"Of course I trust you, sir."

And she did. There was something to be said for knowing exactly who he was and how he operated. What the rest of them needed to better master was how to work within that operation to achieve their ends. But it was an unending game, wherein they kept drawing near and he moved the goalposts.

"I rejoice to hear it, Miss Musgrave. Thank you."

And thus was Maisie defeated.

"So that's that, then." Phyllida sighed, frowning around at the crowded Tup. "I suppose it was to be expected."

"It shouldn't have been, though."

"All parties come to an end."

"This is work."

"It certainly will be. But we're still here, and still fighting, aren't we?"

"Damn right."

"Onwards and upwards." Phyllida tossed back her gin with the brio of a sailor.

"We're still the modern women, aren't we?" Maisie sought reassurance.

"We are. A force to be reckoned with. We'll just have to make Siepmann sorry he ever wanted to be part of Talks."

"Yes. And we'll have to see what we can do about making Miss Matheson the next DG. After that I'm going to stand in the next election."

"And I'm going to leapfrog Mr. Fielden and be director of Talks. With a regular column in the *Listener*, with my name on it."

Several patrons frowned at the angry laughter of the two young women, who paid them no attention.

Maisie visited the Drama Department, on the pretense of asking about actors for broadcasting poems. It wasn't hard to get Beanie alone. She perked up, smelling excitement.

"You told me ages ago that Simon's family was in trouble. Have you heard anything further?"

Beanie nodded. "His father put a great deal of money into American investments. And as you know, there's been a bit of a bother over there."

"So the earl's lost money?"

"It's possibly quite desperate." Beanie giggled. "And it's said their cacao holdings in Trinidad are wobbly as well, but that might just be adding fat to the fire."

"Which would make them frantic for any sort of good contract to keep the cacao flowing."

"Begging for it, I'd think." Beanie lit a cigarette and poked a (rather sharp) fingernail into Maisie's shoulder. "Maisie, I've been involved in theater one way or another since I could toddle. I know the makings of a plot when I hear one."

"Yes. I'm writing a play."

"Most certainly you are. Do you know, it's dreadfully funny, but I warrant I could help you a great deal if you were to actually trust me with the full story."

Maisie looked into Beanie's challenging green eyes. Not the full story, no. Especially when Phyllida knew nothing. But Beanie understood things about the waters Maisie was about to chart that even Hilda didn't.

What would Hilda do? What would an investigative journalist do? Some sources had to be trusted, surely?

"It's a bit . . . tricky," Maisie began, faltering. "I don't really know what . . . All right, to be honest, Beanie, it's an enormous secret, and I don't know if I can trust you to keep it quiet."

Beanie's eyes twinkled further. "Learning how to keep the right sort of secrets is the only way to survive a posh girls' boarding school, Maisie."

Maisie leaned closer to Beanie.

"Listen carefully . . ."

TWENTY

Nestlé's London office was a hulking maw of a Gothic atrocity. Maisie studied her reflection in her pocket mirror, pleased to see her efforts with the stage makeup continued to mask her well. She smoothed her coat and swept inside.

"May I help you?" the receptionist, an overpolished Home Counties young man, too young for his ostentatious pince-nez, intoned in a ponderous accent.

"Good afternoon," Maisie said in a crisp tone, articulating well enough to not be putting on a fake accent, exactly, but not be readily identifiable as her usual wherever-she-was-from self. "I have an appointment with Mr. Grigson's secretary. It's to discuss advertising."

An authoritative voice, nondescript appearance, and meeting with a secretary rather than the man himself garnered no interest. She was waved in and given directions without ever making eye contact.

Authority faded and Invisible Girl took over, as Maisie measured purposeful steps toward her quarry. The man at reception fulfilled her expectation in thinking nothing of a secretary's schedule, and forgetting, if he even knew that Grigson's secretary left early on the afternoons of the long monthly board meeting.

Maisie's careful research did not fail her. At 5:31, she was inside his office.

She went straight to work, forcing herself not to think about what it meant. About Simon. A man who had given her a ring. Who maybe loved her.

The nail file again. This lock was trickier. Or she was shaking. She fussed at it, sweat beading her neck. It was loosening. It was loosening—the nail file broke, the tip stuck inside.

No! Oh, no, no.

But the drawer was open.

Letters. Documents. Reams of them. Something in German, with notes in English. A contract? Notes, letters. A letter to someone about Simon, indicating that a man like him, so well connected and man-nered and educated, was just the right sort for building a trusted new media. Eventually, Nestlé was sure to be sponsoring content on the radio, and that would help secure more contracts as well as custom-ers. Maisie took her eight pictures, though she hardly knew what she was looking at and hoped her hands weren't shaking too much.

Six minutes. She had to go. His diary was open on his desk, appoint-ments in baroque handwriting. Her secretary's training made her glance at it automatically, confirming his meeting. But it wasn't open to today. It was open to next week. Drinks. With Simon. And the words: "Final contract." Maisie had to force her hand to make the marks, writing down the time and place. She hadn't ever crashed a party in her life. It might be time to start.

She made it all the way to the office door—and bumped into Grigson hurrying in.

"Who are you? What the devil were you doing in my office?"

"Nothing, sir. It was a mistake," she said, her head firmly down, heart pounding. He must have forgotten something, not that it mat-tered. She just hoped he'd forgotten her face. She attempted to slither around him.

"I'll say it was a mistake, all right. Don't you dare try to get away from me!" He grabbed her arm. A few passersby stopped and stared.

"Let go!" Maisie snarled, attempting to twist free.

"I won't until you tell me who you are." He pulled her close with surprising strength and jerked her head back. "I know you, don't I? I've seen your face before."

"No!" she yelled and jerked away from him and ran down the corridor.

"Stop her! Stop her!"

She could hear feet. She passed faces of people too startled to grab her. Even if they had tried, they would not have held her. No one in this building knew how to run like the girl who had grown up as Mousy Maisie.

She was down the stairs. She was past reception. She was in the street. She ran, and ran, and ran, and didn't look back. Didn't think of anything, except reaching Hilda. She made a cursory stop in a café to wash her face and generally make herself presentable and headed on to Lady Astor's salon, where Hilda, obliged to attend, had arranged for them to meet.

Maisie came in and saw that half of London was in attendance as well. The butler admitted Maisie with a resigned expression. Probably he'd hoped she was the fire brigade.

"Ah, Miss Musgrave!" Lady Astor glided through the throng to clutch Maisie's hand. "I am so desperately cross about the goings-on at the BBC. Miss Matheson is takin' it on the chin and you're holdin' up your end well, but to not even be made producer on our *Week in Westminster* when you've as good as *been* it, it's beyond appallin'. I've half a mind to tell the governors to step in, but Miss M says best not to and I expect she's right. Only she's always too nice by far, and that's a fact. What do you reckon, hm?"

Maisie wasn't sure if she was to weigh in on Hilda's niceness or whether Lady Astor should use her influence. The thought of how good Hilda was and her taking it on the chin made Maisie's throat tighten.

Someone called to Lady Astor.

"Must tend these people. Don't know where our Miss M's gotten to. Around somewhere, I expect. You go on and find her. We'll talk later."

From the reception room that only Lady Astor, Virginian at her core, called a parlor, to the study, to the dining room, no Hilda. Maisie heard laughter from the library, but met only a single man leaving it as she entered.

"Hullo." He nodded, friendly, because if she was here she must be important.

"Hullo." She greeted him, for much the same reason.

Maisie lingered in the empty room—it was, after all, a library. A small, stuffy library, but still full of books. She was just perusing the shelves when she heard laughter again and noticed a narrow door in the corner. She pushed through into the billiard room.

Hilda was in there. With Vita. And they were . . .

"Oh!"

Hilda giggled into Vita's hair.

"Ha! Caught you with your hand in the biscuit tin," Hilda teased. Vita took her time withdrawing her hand from inside Hilda's chemise and sighed as Hilda fastened her dress. "I suppose if mice will play where the kittens are. Evening, Miss Musgrave. You see Miss Sackville-West has returned to England."

"Er, yes. Good evening," Maisie muttered to the floor, which was inconsiderately refusing to swallow her. She had a long practice of mortification, thanks to Georgina, but this was on quite a different plane. She had never seen two women kiss before, and though it was no different from seeing anyone else kiss, well, a person never wanted to walk in on other people kissing. Especially one's boss. Maisie tried to leave the room, but her feet had forgotten how to move.

The women were irritatingly unembarrassed and made no attempt to shift away from each other once Hilda was dressed. Vita stood over her and Hilda stayed sitting on the billiard table, legs swinging idly. "Don't look so horrified, Miss Musgrave. I rather assumed you knew," she said.

Did Hilda assume Maisie was so much like her now that she knew everything?

"How did you get on?" Hilda wanted to know.

Maisie glanced at Vita but realized Hilda wouldn't ask if it wasn't all right for Vita to know.

"I, er, well, I found an awful lot, and took snaps and notes. But there was a lot more. And . . . he caught me."

"He WHAT?"

"I got away—well, I suppose that's obvious, but he saw my face. Though I did have makeup on, but nonetheless . . . Well, it doesn't matter, I hope. We've got to develop these photographs. And he's to have drinks with Simon next week, something about a contract. I was thinking I ought to attend?"

"Goodness," Hilda marveled. "It was a productive journey."

"Unfortunately," Maisie agreed with a sigh.

"You really have a fine girl here, Stoker," Vita pronounced, caressing Hilda's neck.

Stoker???

"You have no idea," Hilda agreed.

Maisie agreed to have lunch with Simon to try to allay suspicions. She had explained that the season of Christmas and New Year's was a particularly busy time at the BBC and so it was harder to get away.

"Even at night, darling?"

Part of her still tingled and melted when he looked at her. That face, that body. The smile, the laugh, the brilliance. She badly wanted to sleep with him again. Again and again. But she couldn't. She wouldn't. She still hoped he had no idea what Grigson really wanted, and that the whole deal was just about the cacao, not the newspaper, but until she was sure, she couldn't be alone with him anymore.

"My family's having a massive gathering, the classic bourgeois Dickensian Christmas. I was hoping to introduce you properly," Simon went on, spinning the fantasy of her welcome, her entrance into the great house and the ancient name.

A house that, if Beanie's information was correct, they were currently clinging to by their fingernails. Maisie might have more money in her own bank account—her own account, in her own name; it still felt like a miracle—than the Brock-Morlands had left in their fortune.

But maybe he believed it. Maybe he believed he loved her.

I hope so. Because that would be nice. Because otherwise no man ever has.

"Care for a pudding?" he asked.

"Yes, please."

You can't think how I want to believe it's all at the behest of your father, saving the family name and fortune. And you're just being his errand boy— or are you an errant boy? But I've got to stop you. I hope you don't see what you're doing. I'll show you.

"Say you'll come to the house. The BBC can spare you a little while, can't they? It's only the most bourgeois frothy programming over the holidays, surely?"

On the other hand, I would rather eat live entrails than hear the word "bourgeois" again . . .

"We've got such a lot of planning to do," she said, shaking her head.

"Ah. Planning. I say, do tell your Miss Matheson that her goal for 1930 should be a bit more fair-mindedness in broadcasting, what?"

"What?"

"Well, one only need look at the listings to see there's a great deal in favor of Labour and such-like. I hear that Bolshie economist Keynes has been on a great many times."

"And he's brilliant. But we have people who disagree with him, too."

"And there, you see? That's the trouble with your BBC, throwing around all those opinions, confusing people."

"No, that's not it at all. People are understanding more all the time. It's the best thing there is, Simon, and growing and changing and getting better, and I'm a part of it, and—"

He seized and kissed her. And for the length of that kiss, she was his girl again, cleaved to him and would fly with him over the whole of the world.

"I always said I loved your passion, Maisie. You're quite the rare specimen—you know that?"

"Do you mean that?"

"Of course I do, darling."

"Thank you," she said. Meaning it. But she still didn't go home with him.

Maisie had also meant it when she said how busy they were and how much planning was under way. There were new series being prepared with all-encompassing titles like *Points of View* and *People and Things*. A veneer of polite banality that masked the heady politics beneath. Hilda vented her rage, both with Reith and the world economy, by exploring more controversy than ever and seemed to be daring anyone to stop her.

Siepmann, heady with victory and busy arranging his new offices to suit his exalted position, didn't seem to notice the programming. He did notice Torquhil, though.

"And here I thought he was an innovative broadcaster." Siepmann patted the tolerant dog, who glanced at him suspiciously before returning to his pride of place by Hilda's fire.

"He is very nice," Cyril said, watching Torquhil trot away. "I like having a dog about the office. Makes things friendlier."

"So glad you think so," Phyllida drawled, barely beating Fielden and Maisie to the same line.

It was all their triumph, though, to see Cyril bow his head and return to the arrangement of his desk.

The newspapers were curiously quiet about the change to Talks, perhaps because it had been presented to them so as to look like the triumph of Hilda's good work that Reith insisted on saying it was, even within the BBC. It was only Maisie's determination to keep Hilda from reproach that stopped her leaking the truth to the press.

"Er, Miss Musgrave?" Cyril again, twisting his hands together. "I hate to trouble you for the *Week in Westminster* files, but—"

"Yes, of course," Maisie said, in a tone she decided sounded breezy. "They're all here in this drawer." She indicated said drawer. "Do you wish to move them closer to you?"

"Oh, no. No, you can still store them. You're still Talks assistant on the program."

"How smashing for me, thank you."

"Smashing for me, actually, or I'd be quite at sea. Er, I don't suppose you'd like to go over programming for the next year—perhaps over lunch . . . ?"

"Dreadfully busy today. Can't manage, I'm afraid." She couldn't put off a meeting forever, but she certainly wasn't giving him her free time.

"What are you working on now?" he asked, with polite curiosity. She couldn't resist giving him a sly smile.

"I'm booking a Miss Rachel Klay of the Fabian Society for *Points of View.* Subject: Do the Fascists Want to Control Our Information? Last-minute replacement. We're airing it next week."

"That, er, sounds rather incendiary," he said, his tone both quavering and admiring.

"Oh, I don't know. It's only an opinion piece. Nothing for anyone to worry about," Maisie said with a shrug. But she didn't stop smiling.

"If you wanted to break into files, why didn't you ask me for picklocks?" Ellis demanded when Hilda and Maisie showed him the takings from Maisie's espionage.

"Because if she were to be searched, a nail file is an expected thing for a woman to possess. Picklocks tend to raise eyebrows," Hilda pointed out.

"They could be a prop, or used for radio sound effects, and they don't leave evidence," Ellis rejoined. "Really, Miss Musgrave, you could be done for burglary now."

"Gosh, thanks," Maisie said.

"Oh, never mind that!" Hilda snapped. "Look at this mess. Look at what people are saying, about unions, women, media, Jews, homosexuals, books, music. They would probably stop science if they didn't think it was a moneymaker. The talk is only growing, Ellis—look at it."

"Whispered, Matty. Whispered on fringes, the way people always have. No one's ever liked Jews, homosexuals, or women who make noise—you can't get aerated about all history."

"I bloody well can," she retorted. "And I'm going to see them exposed."

"The trouble with you sort in media," said Ellis, lighting his cheroot, "is you think there's great power in printing things. It never really changes anything, you know."

"It does, though. Knowledge is power. Why else do you think they want to control media? Apparently this man Goebbels is quite the acolyte of American advertising. His writing is brilliant in its simplicity. If only he were using it to sell washing powder."

"It's just a load of tosh, shouting in the wind."

"No, it's really good propaganda. If they can keep capitalizing on it, they won't stay marginalized for long. Look, just look at this contract. These Nazis have promised that if they come to power, they'll give Nestlé a government contract. Nestlé can supply all the chocolate for the whole German army."

"Well, that will make the soldiers rebel for sure, and that will be the end of it."

"Stop it!" Maisie screamed. Then she clapped her hands over her mouth. "Oh, I'm sorry. I didn't mean . . . Actually I did, but not quite so—"

Hilda put a hand on her shoulder and turned to Ellis.

"Miss Musgrave speaks for us both."

"I do apologize," Ellis said, for once meaning it. "There is so much happening just now, it's hard to spare energy for suppositions about the future. And you must admit, it all looks like angry little boys playing at silly adventure games."

"Everyone thought it was an adventure in 1914, too," Hilda said.

Ellis sighed heavily and slugged down half his brandy. "You haven't many options when you want to stop something before it starts. You need better proof than photographs, for one thing. Anyone can swear they are faked."

"They'll do that anyway," Maisie said. "But I can get the contract they're planning to give Simon. I don't know if it's illegal, but it's got to be unethical."

Ellis looked at her with deep admiration. "Good. And this is everything you have thus far? You had better leave it with me now. I can be sure it's properly managed and analyzed. If anything proves to be beyond the usual ethical flexibility of business, I can arrange for further steps to be taken."

"All we need, I think, is to embarrass them," Hilda said, running a finger along the papers. "If it's obvious they're wishing to upend the BBC, it's possible people might choose not to purchase anything made by Siemens or Nestlé. As much as a business might hate a union, bad publicity that affects their bottom line is a different circle of hell altogether."

"Yes," Maisie agreed. "And I've been wanting to tell them to go to hell for such a while now."

Maisie and Phyllida took their lunch to the chapel—a good enough place for a confession. Maisie felt guilty, breaking her promise to Hilda, but she felt worse keeping such secrets from the only real friend she'd ever had. And Phyllida, to her credit, was far more appalled by what was going on than the fact that she was so late in hearing it.

"D'ye know," Phyllida said, lighting a cigarette, "they're not wrong. We should bring back some sort of feudalism or what have you. Something where treason's punished by being burned at the stake. Or is it drawing and quartering? I always forget."

"It's not treason, exactly, I think."

"Near as, damn it. Useless mongrels."

"He asked me to marry him, Phyllida. He gave me a ring, said he loves me. And I'm stupid enough to still want it to mean something." Maisie drew up her knees under her chin.

"Eh, it probably does. But, Maisie, go on. If even half of this is true, you can't have any softness for him now. You can't. You know that."

"I do."

"And your life isn't without love. You know that, too."

"I do."

"Good. So that's sorted." Phyllida ground her cigarette in the baptismal font. "I never liked him anyway."

"You never met him."

"I didn't have to."

For once, it was hard to concentrate on her BBC work. Maisie's mind kept wandering to Simon. Was it really possible he would take steps to compromise Britain's press, its whole democracy, just for money? Money, and to feel his power as an aristocrat? Whatever Phyllida said, it just didn't seem right. It couldn't be. The times had changed too much. He had to accept that, surely? The questions ping-ponged about in her brain as she brought a script to Hilda to examine.

"Miss Musgrave, what is this?"

"A script, for the competitive bridge players you hated so much."

"No, this. Are you awake?"

It was the sharpness of the tone rather than the words that snapped Maisie back to attention. She couldn't think how, but one of the photographs was in Hilda's hand, rather than Ellis's safekeeping. The photograph of Grigson's letter indicating the intent to remove women from the BBC, along with all the most popular programming.

"Ellis was going to analyze this. No paper can print it without verification. And we haven't much time."

"I can't think what happened," Maisie said, staring at the photograph as though it was an unexploded grenade.

"Post it to Ellis now, tonight." Hilda said. "Here, I'll write up an envelope for you."

"Maybe you should take it to him in person?" Maisie was suddenly panicked.

"I think at this juncture it's safer going through the post. If you get it by the seven o'clock and send it express, it might even reach him tonight."

"I'm so sorry, Miss Matheson. I can't think how I—"

"It happens, Miss Musgrave. But it's the sort of thing you can't ever let happen again." She sealed the envelope and slipped it back between the pages of the script.

"Go."

She knew. As soon as the BBC's wooden door shut behind her, she knew that the man on the corner was looking for her. There must be hundreds of people in every building on Savoy Street, but she knew. He was looking for her.

She glanced up the street. She didn't have far to walk. And it was a perfectly innocent thing she was about to do. Anyone could mail a letter.

She'd been seen. She couldn't be Invisible Girl even if she wanted to be.

She walked, strutted, actually. *Go on, try something. I dare you.*

But the fist inside her was heaving and hawing like a ship's bellows. This had all become suddenly, achingly real.

"Hallo. You're leaving almost early, aren't you?"

Cyril and Billy joined her on the path, heading for the American Bar. It was very strange to be happy to see them.

"Why don't you come along?" Cyril urged. "Have a bit of a chin wag about the old pile?"

"That would be super," she said, grinning with relief. "Only I've got to get to the post office first, a letter to go express. You know how Talks business is. Care to walk with me over there first?"

The men were just agreeing when they were joined by someone else, coming the other way.

"Is that my girl, strolling down the street with two other chappies?"

Simon. And she wasn't wearing the ring.

She pretended to be even more flustered and fidgety than she was so that the men took over the task of introductions. The ring was in her bag, in the mirror pocket. She slipped her hand in and worked the ring on, blessing the British traditions of proper introductions and polite nothings that gave her time. Her hand clasped around the envelope in her bag.

"I rang your office and the Yorkie girl told me you'd be leaving about now. I thought I'd come and surprise you," Simon said.

"I'm so happy to see you," she cried, throwing her arms around Simon. She caught Cyril's eye over Simon's shoulder and glanced at the envelope in her hand. Too surprised to do anything else, Cyril took it. She nodded in a way that she hoped told him to run and post the letter without thinking about the address and to not let Simon or Billy see. But there wasn't too much one could convey in a nod. Cyril tucked the envelope inside his jacket, staring at Maisie.

"My goodness, such ardor!" Simon cried. "And, darling, you're rather excessively glowing. Some powder, I think." He took her bag and opened it. "Only a lipstick! *Tsk.* Let's get you to Selfridges. You need a few girlish treats."

She took his arm, not knowing what else to do. She knew Cyril and Billy were staring at her, and hoped Cyril would hurry to the post office.

TWENTY-ONE

"I was able to get that letter posted for you," Cyril assured her the next morning, outside Studio Three. "I know it's not my business, but I did want to ascertain you're not in any trouble. That all looked a bit rum, to be honest."

"No, I'm all right. Thank you. Very good of you to post that letter for me. I just, er, didn't want Mr. Brock-Morland to know about it," she finished lamely.

"I rather got that idea," Cyril said dryly, nodding. "He seems an all-right sort of chap?"

"Unfortunately, I think 'seems' is the word of choice these days."

"Do you, er, need any help?" he asked.

His eyes were serious, but she was sure she caught the whiff of a boys' adventure tale.

"That's very good of you, Mr. Underwood, and I'll keep that offer in mind, should I get in a scrape."

She nodded and he nodded back.

"Coming, Underwood?" Billy called from the studio. "We're ready for broadcast."

"Yes, coming," he said, still looking at her. He went inside and the light flashed red. Broadcast in progress; enter and perish.

Maisie was just turning the corner back to the Talks Department when Hilda strode out, a file in hand, Torquhil at her feet. She nodded to Maisie and jerked her head. Maisie fell into step and they walked, silently, all the way to the Sound Effects Department.

Hilda threw open the door, and all the men jumped up to shout at the interloper, but went quiet and respectful on seeing who it was, joining in a rather harmonious, "How do you do, Miss Matheson?"

"Good day, chaps. I've got a speaker coming in to Talk about winter sport, and some sound effects might be nice. Can you have a think on it?"

"Certainly, Miss Matheson." Fowler nodded, eyes gleaming. "Does your dog bark?"

"Only when provoked. Or when he's playing."

"May we try recording him?"

"Certainly."

Someone produced a large rope and tested Torquhil on his tug-of-war skills, while someone else paid attention to all the cheerful growls. Within minutes, the sound men being what they were, the usual noise had the improvement of Torquhil's leaps and barks and all the men and dog scrabbling about in a game without rules.

"The letter got posted, but someone was definitely following me last night," Maisie told her. "And Simon came to meet me, which can't have been coincidence." She still felt queasy. Maisie had upgraded the headache to the age-old excuse of "women's complaints," which rendered her free from any chance of supper or his flat. Simon had been repelled.

"Yes, I got wind of something along those lines, never mind how. I've arranged with Vita and Harold. We're going to go there tonight and practice for your appearance at the drinks tomorrow. You'll have to be ready for all possibilities."

Fowler leaped right beside them, catching a ball. Torquhil leaped at it with an enormous bark, and they both crashed to the ground. And still Maisie and Hilda didn't move.

"These people wouldn't be following us if they weren't worried, would they?" Maisie asked.

"That's a fair assessment."

"Which means you're right, and they really are playing a big game. A nasty one, too."

"It's not always pleasant, being right," Hilda said, as Torquhil circled her, with what looked like a gramophone arm in his mouth.

"I'm learning that."

Despite the circumstances, it was quite pleasant to be in the Belgravia home of Vita Sackville-West and her husband, Harold Nicholson, on Ebury Street. They seemed hugely fond of each other, and Harold plainly adored Hilda.

"Miss Matheson says you're a very good egg, Miss Musgrave, but I hope this level of Bohemian immorality doesn't put you out." Harold Nicholson handed Maisie a drink.

"Not at all. My mother is an actress."

The other three burst out laughing, and Maisie felt she was part of the circle.

They had a superb meal, with Vita and Harold complimenting Maisie on her gastronomic capacity and discerning taste, but all the while the real reason for their visit hovered over the proceedings, twinkling in the chandelier.

"I have a few men on watch, just in case any of your friends think they can pay a visit here tonight," Harold told Maisie, as she helped herself to roast chicken. "Part of the advantage of being in the diplomatic service, what? And my man Vaughn is an old hand with this sort of thing. Have some celery sauce. It's a rather cunning little taste. I don't think we'll be troubled. I think they are hoping to take you by surprise. They may not know you know they know, that sort of thing."

"Do you know how to fight at all, Miss Musgrave?" Vita asked with polite curiosity.

"I can run," Maisie answered, making the company laugh again.

"Stoker—er, Hilda—tells me you're engaged to Simon Brock-Morland. I've met his family a few times. How well do you know him?"

"I think not well enough. And too well, obviously."

"I'm going to be blunt and tell you I don't think much of him. It's not my business, of course, but I like you and know Hilda does as well, and since your own mother sounds perfectly useless, someone needs to advise you on these things."

"Miss Musgrave has a very sharp mind," Hilda put in.

"I am well aware of it." Vita grinned. "But we all know how the heart can interfere with the mind. Have you slept with him?"

Maisie fumbled her fork, sending leeks jetéing across the table.

"Now, Vita, really!" Harold shook his head at her.

"I have," Maisie answered, locking eyes with Vita.

"And he was your first. Yes, we know how it can be. But you're a levelheaded young woman, aren't you? Not the type to go all moony and thinking it must have very great meaning and what?"

"I suppose it doesn't mean anything at all," Maisie said, rhythmically stabbing a potato.

"Well, maybe it did and maybe it didn't. Can't ever know with the fellows—sorry, Harold dear."

"No, no, quite true," Harold agreed.

"And you're not an old-fashioned sort, thinking you're now ruined or anything ridiculous like that?"

"Vita!" Hilda admonished her.

"No," Maisie whispered. "I don't think that."

"Good. Because I'm going to be very impertinent, Miss Musgrave—"

"There's a belated warning," Hilda muttered.

"And tell you that you can do a great deal better."

It was said with prim matter-of-factness, and whether it was the honesty of it, or Maisie's own confused feelings, or the enormity of whatever she was about to face, she found her eyes welling with tears.

"Miss Matheson says you do great justice to puddings," Harold said, and almost as if it had been conjured, an enormous dish of sticky toffee pudding was placed in front of her.

And it did help.

It was like playacting, working out all the possible scenarios, and what Maisie might say, and how she was going to get the contract and get away safely. Hilda would have her car at the ready, and Vaughn was being deputized to assist, but the main work was Maisie's alone.

Harold leaned back, lighting a cigar.

"And then what happens? Bring the stuff to me? Or your man, Ellis? Bit of an anticlimax, that. I suppose you're putting together enough to print it all in the papers and make them look fools?"

"Nothing like seeing something in black-and-white," Hilda said.

"But people should hear it first," Maisie said.

"Sorry?" Hilda asked.

"Yes! Yes, that's it. Miss Matheson, it's equal suffrage all over again! They're meeting at six, and surely by the time I get whatever it is, we can get back to the BBC by seven, and that's prime listening time. We'll just read it out, the whole of it. Sort out some sort of script—that can't be hard. And it doesn't matter if they say it's all a load of codswallop, because announcing it during peak listening time will mean maybe four million people or more get it all at once. Good luck countering that, right?"

Hilda just stared at her, cigarette dripping ash onto the carpet.

"And the DG will have left by then, too," Maisie remembered happily. "So we're clear of him."

"Mr. Burrows would never announce it," Hilda said slowly, shaking her head. "He'd be too likely to be sacked. I suppose I could do it, but—"

"You need a man," Vita said. "Authority and what. Harold, perhaps you can do it?"

"Not me, darling. They'll say I'm part of some homosexual plot. Look here, Hilda. I can have some chappies from the diplomatic service ring Reith afterwards and say you're spot-on and doing a great service," Harold said. "And your Ellis may well do the same. It won't necessarily prevent sackings, but it won't hurt. So then it hardly matters who presents it."

"Of course it does. Don't be silly," Vita scolded. "There's Lady Astor, if we can't find a man," she went on. "But it oughtn't be a politician, I think. Still, it's got to be someone with a very crisp, authoritarian voice. The sort that just commands respect and attention."

"May I use the telephone?" Maisie asked, though she was already halfway there.

The men were meeting at the Ritz, which must chafe at Simon's affection—or perhaps it was just affectation—for Bohemia.

Maisie was alone in the lavatory. She combed her hair and applied mascara and a lipstick lent by Vita. She slid her hat—new, a rosy pink with a mulberry trim—over her hair and gave herself a battle-ready smile.

As Vaughn was attending them, he waited at Hilda's car and Hilda herself chose a position near the front door of the Ritz so as to be nearer at hand if a distraction was needed. "Or something of that sort."

"I'm still not entirely sure what I'm going to do or how," Maisie confessed.

"Yes, that's the general way of espionage," Hilda said. "Journalism, too. Life, certainly."

So Maisie threw back her shoulders and went upstairs.

The Ritz might have been the most beautiful hotel in the world—though probably not—but Maisie saw nothing of it. She walked with steady purpose to the bar and scanned the leather and wood and consequence until her eyes rested on them. Hoppel had joined the party, creating a genteel circle of hostility. He wasn't German, any more than Grigson was Swiss. Why were they ultimately so happy to twist and bend Britain to make their companies more money? But perhaps they saw their own personal swelling bank balances as a sort of patriotism, and the rest was fluid.

Two other men, leaning against the bar and smoking, looked at her, impertinent grins and unmasked sneers. A woman in a place of men, she wasn't allowed to expect anything else. She fixed her eyes forward and crept toward her quarry.

"No, it's we who are grateful to you," Grigson was assuring Simon, his gravelly voice simultaneously toady and condescending. "I believe this will be a most fruitful alliance."

"Ooh, my goodness, is this another marriage you're making?" Maisie asked, approaching Simon and laying a hand over his, the ring he'd given her glinting in the somber lighting.

Either Simon was an actor to flatten Barrymore, or he was genuinely delighted to see her.

"Most clever dearest! How on earth did you know to find me here? I'm just closing a contract that will do more for me—for us— than even I could have imagined."

His companions evinced no delight at all—quite the opposite. Simon came in for his share of glares once he started to speak.

"Oh no, gentlemen, let's not get any silly ideas. This is Maisie Musgrave, my fiancée and a very bright girl. She will be a most able assistant in this venture if I can tempt her away from the BBC."

"What a lot of papers!" Maisie exclaimed, attempting to bely Simon's assertion of her cleverness. "What's in all of them?"

"Complicated bit of business, beloved. Nothing that need worry you too much."

"BBC?" Hoppel interrupted, gaping at Maisie. "Brock-Morland, I appreciate your industry, but you didn't have to compromise yourself."

"What do you mean?" Simon asked. "Maisie's all right. I liked her even before I knew she was so beholden to a beast." He turned to Maisie and winked. "And once we're married, you'll be beholden to another, you know."

"Simon," Maisie said, looking into his eyes, trying to read him. "You haven't signed these yet, have you?"

"Of course I have. We have plans, far bigger than anything in any storybook you've ever read. We'll get married and I'll tell you all about them."

"You." Grigson was staring at Maisie. "You are one for papers, aren't you?" He breathed slowly, lips twisting in a sour smile.

Simon turned to Grigson in surprise.

Maisie had hoped to use more elegance, but she saw the recognition in those oily eyes and there was no more waiting. A long contract, a letter. She slapped her hands over both, snatched them to her, and ran.

The men yelped and shouted, busily untangling themselves from the table. Maisie zigged and zagged through the bar and into the lobby.

A hand latched around her wrist, jerking her almost to the floor. It was one of the men who had sneered at her as she came in.

"Well, well. I think you'll be giving those papers back now, won't you?"

"No!" She twisted away from him and this time made it out the door and almost to Hilda. The man's companion was there, sneer on full display, and a nudge of his jacket displayed a pistol as well.

Maisie curled the papers more tightly in her fist. There were so many people around. He couldn't possibly think he could do her real harm in so public a place?

"Put the papers in your bag, then, and let's go for a little stroll," the other man whispered behind her. "Make it look all very natural."

She did as he suggested, hoping Hilda could see all of it. This was something they hadn't rehearsed. The men didn't even touch her, just flanked her almost politely and walked with her around the corner, into an alley.

"Maisie, what on earth are you doing? My friends seem to think you're in league against me." Simon had caught up to them.

"Your 'friends' are out to amass fortunes to surpass the king and don't care what they hurt along the way," Maisie told him.

"No, you don't understand," he said. "They're giving me the opportunity I've always wanted, to really help the ordinary man and restore Britain to its greatest glory. Strengthen the empire—people think it's waning, but we'll prove otherwise."

"You are a Fascist," she breathed in sudden recognition.

"I prefer not to use labels, Maisie. You must know that," he said.

One of the sneering men yelped and fell to the cobbled ground—hit by a rock.

"Run!" Hilda shouted.

And Mousy Maisie burst through the gang of street thugs and into the light.

Not that they were giving up easily. Hoppel, it seemed, was not such a gentleman that he couldn't give chase. He went after Hilda, while the other sneerer, the one who had so politely indicated his pistol, pursued Maisie. She could hear it, even as she vaulted over a pair of Yorkshire terriers, a cheetah in double-strap heels, and tore along the pavement. The click, ready to hurt her and anyone else, all to get these papers back. But she was well ahead of him.

Hilda could run hard herself. She was barely ahead, but ahead nonetheless.

Hoppel reached out. He grabbed her by the neck—and a shower of onyx stones shot into the air and fell in black rain on the concrete.

Vaughn saw them and had the presence of mind to hop in and start the engine. Maisie dove into the backseat and Hilda vaulted over the door, yelling at Vaughn to move over. He did, and Hilda slammed her foot on the accelerator.

Her eyes were flaming. She shot them through the traffic as though they were thin as an arrow and fifty times as fast.

"Does this car run on rocket fuel or something?" Maisie screamed.

"It's a very good car," Hilda yelled back, swerving around a corner.

They bulleted down a narrow road. Faint blurs of shocked faces and surprised, frightened cries bounced once and disappeared.

Another tight swerve and they were bearing down on a traffic stop.

"Miss Matheson!" Maisie squeaked.

But Hilda had it well in hand. She pulled up the brake with gentle ease, as though they'd simply been going on a Sunday drive.

Maisie panted. Sweat was pooling in her shoes and dripping from under her hat. Hilda was as cool as if she were ice-skating. But she was also a coiled mass of eager tension, a mongoose ready to spring on a snake. Maisie knew that as soon as they were clear of this intersection, the mad dash would begin again.

"Where did you learn to drive like this?"

"Italy."

The way was cleared and they jumped past two cars. Angry honks chorused after them as they rounded hard, plummeting down to the Embankment with a fury that had Maisie wondering if they were going to end up in the Thames. She wouldn't be surprised if Hilda would simply propel the car along the water, primarily through force of will.

Maisie cast a quick glance behind them.

"I don't think we're being followed. I think we lost them ages ago."

"We did," Hilda agreed, a half smile playing on her lips. "But we're behind schedule."

Maisie dug in her bag, flipping over the notebook, and wrote, attempting to keep her hand steady as Hilda wove in and out of cars.

Maisie leaped from the car as Hilda pulled up before Savoy Hill and pelted through reception, knocking through a waiting choral group like ninepins.

"I say!" one of them exclaimed in delight. "It really is the jungle they say it is in here."

The cheetah soared up the stairs, two at a time, Hilda just a few steps behind her.

Beanie was waiting for them, eyes wide and mad as if she, too, had torn halfway across London bearing a story fit to shock the nation. Phyllida was there, too, prepared to guard the door.

"Is the script legible?"

"We'll write it as we go," Hilda promised.

"You'll what?"

Cyril came out of the studio, escorting his broadcaster. He stared at the deputation in astonishment.

Maisie seized him. "Is Siepmann still here?"

"Yes, but—"

"Get him into a meeting. Give him any old story. We only need ten minutes."

His mouth opened. Then something seemed to click and she saw a spark in his eyes, something that reminded her of the day she came for her interview, a lifetime ago. He nodded and ran off.

"Go!" Phyllida yelled.

Billy watched with great interest as Beanie settled herself to the microphone.

"This isn't exactly a planned broadcast, is it?" he asked, grinning.

"No," Maisie told him. "And yes. Give it your best, Billy."

He grinned and gave her a big thumbs-up.

Hilda was scribbling the whole time. She set the first of the pages before Beanie.

Beanie leaned forward and began to speak.

And this, Maisie thought, was the purpose of the aristocracy. Beanie's voice could pitch deep, and those plummy tones, round and sharp, warm yet brisk, were effortlessly commanding. Beanie was young, but she sounded like a woman who had sat upon the throne for twenty years. She was awakening something atavistic in the nation's core, even among the staunchest republicans. To not listen to her might mean decapitation. But it wasn't fear. Not really. It was reverence.

"The BBC has discovered action and business that we felt the public ought to know and understand."

Hilda selected passages from Grigson's letter to Simon and wrote copy for Beanie, while Maisie tried not to be sick.

"The British Fascist Party, though of course small and of every right to its existence, seems willing to turn to dirty tricks in an attempt to make known its distaste for unions and Communism and even, it seems, the free press, while also attracting adherents. But in particular, we have found that men representing two great corporations, Siemens and Nestlé, have colluded in an attempt to go further. We have proof they secretly purchased the *Daily Express* and plan to buy several more newspapers, all in an attempt to print only that which they think is worth the public knowing. We ask, is this the way of a democracy? Is this the British way?"

Beanie was not outwardly editorializing, of course, but the disgust in her voice was unmistakable.

"But print is not enough for them. The British Fascists also intend to overtake the BBC. Not only would they remove all women from its ranks. They would suppress any programming that does not adhere to their narrow view. Beyond the BBC, they intend to cut wages, to roll back rights, and education. All this, so as to consolidate fortune and power, for corporations and a few select individuals. Their progress is such, they have forged an alliance with the Brock-Morland family to bring credibility to their mission."

Beanie's eyes flicked once toward Maisie, but she went on reading.

"We know the media baron is not such a new thing. We know of Mr. Hearst in America. But newspapers sponsored by corporations and corporations supporting political movements that seek to upend cherished liberties, all for the sake of greater profits? This is, we think, something of which the public should be aware and be wary. The BBC is, we hope, able to speak to the whole of society and present every point of view, however unpalatable, all so the public can further understand the world around them and think critically, so that each

344 · SARAH-JANE STRATFORD

listener can be a well-informed citizen and thus the best possible Briton. The BBC is itself objective, but it will always be a strong proponent of the greatest freedom of the press and is sure the public is strongly in agreement thereof. Thus we feel it our duty to reveal this very well-planned attempt to undermine that freedom. You may be sure that these documents will be printed in full in all the newspapers— yes, the *independent* newspapers—for citizens to read thoroughly and determine their own opinion. That is, after all, what a democracy allows. Thank you, and we now return to our scheduled programming."

Billy cut the mike and Beanie leaned back and grinned.

"Well. That was a jolly good show, I'd say."

TWENTY-TWO

"You two are looking a bit all in. Stay a moment and collect yourselves." Billy was shockingly courteous. Maisie didn't need to be asked twice. Her head dropped straight onto the desk. Hilda patted her back.

Someone had passed on the word that the broadcast had been heard by Reith at his club, and he returned, breathing fire, only to be met by Beanie, who insisted that the whole affair was primarily her doing. "I'm well aware of what a number of my so-called compatriots have been involved with, and I don't like it," she said, and tendered her resignation. Which, as she said, was the perfect Act Three finale.

Maisie was gutted. "But you love your job, and you're so good at it!"

"It was about to happen anyway," Beanie said with a shrug. "The chickens have come home to roost and roost I must. I'm getting married, tra-la!" She wiggled her long fingers, showing off a new diamond.

"Oh," said Maisie. "Congratulations. But . . . but look at Miss Somerville. You're a producer. You can carry on working so long as you want, even if you have a baby."

"Goodness, you are modern. But no, not for my sort. The fun

has been had. The real work begins, as Mama says. Duty calls. I cannot shirk!"

"The BBC will be the lesser without you here. And so will we."

For a moment, again, there was a twitch in Beanie's eye. But she was too well trained to show regret, and she laughed her musical laugh and seized Maisie's hand.

"We'll have the most marvelous weekend house parties, and I'll invite any number of interesting people. You will have to attend! Everyone will love to hear your stories. And of course we can have luncheons and things when I'm in London. So we'll still see absolutely loads of each other and be great friends."

"We will. That all sounds copacetic."

When she was alone, Maisie wiped her eyes. She wouldn't be surprised if she never saw Beanie again. But it would be nice to be wrong.

There was a certain amount of amusement, kept silent, at Reith's contorted efforts to hide his blind rage, because not only did the newspapers treat the story as an epic Christmas gift, but each one was also quick to credit the obvious brilliance of the BBC. Everywhere Reith turned, he was thwarted in his desire to punish. Two days later, the *Listener* ran a long article "by Maisie Musgrave" as a companion piece to the story, with extra details and so much wit, papers said: "It's almost as if the author were part of the action." An editorial in the *Telegraph* congratulating Reith on his selection of excellent staff forced him to retract his outstretched claw.

"I'm glad. The place wouldn't have been the same without you," Cyril told Maisie. "And you can really write, too. I mean, you're really very good. You should keep it up, but you'll stay here, too, won't you?"

"I hope so. I've got a lot of stories to tell, you know."

He nodded. The conversation seemed finished, and Maisie grabbed a notebook to go attend a rehearsal.

"Miss Musgrave!"

"Hm?"

"I just wanted to say, also, you don't need any powder."

"Er, what?"

Cyril turned bright red. "That Brock-Morland . . . when I delivered that letter for you. He said you needed powder. But you don't. You look really . . . swell . . . without it. Just as you are."

Maisie felt herself returning Cyril's blush. They stared at each other, trying to find something to say. The phone rang, breaking the spell.

The story went on for days. Hoppel and Grigson resigned, and their respective corporations insisted they were mere rogue operators, and safeguards were in place to prevent such occurrences again. But that didn't stop the newspapers from writing more and more. They didn't even complain when it was announced there would be no further restrictions on the BBC's news reporting. They had proven they could do fine independent journalism, so no reason not to let them keep on doing it. Especially if it helped the papers, too.

"But we haven't really changed anything!" Maisie complained to Hilda one lunchtime, as they walked Torquhil on the Embankment. "Why can't they all be prosecuted?"

"Fear of entrapment, apparently. Good countersuit."

"Who cares?"

"The rule of law. But we've spoken the truth and gotten results, and the rallies are right 'round the BBC. The British Fascists have lost half their numbers, the unions are emboldened, and there's a sense that being worried about Russian spies is perhaps a waste of energy. And Nestlé is doing poor business. I like Rountree's chocolate myself. That Nestlé stuff is like sugary chalk."

Maisie kicked a pebble. "And Simon's gone."

His family's estate was ruined and they'd all fled. The papers were full of rumors as to where they might have gone, but no one knew for sure. Maisie hoped she would never find out. She had posted the ring back to him, and it was returned to sender.

"It's like ill-gotten goods," she fretted.

"Ach, you more than earned it," Phyllida said. "Think of it as a nest egg. I bet Miss Matheson can advise on investments."

Maisie put the ring in a safe-deposit box at the bank. Provenance notwithstanding, it was nice to feel cushioned. Georgina wrote an almost plaintive letter, detailing the difficulties of finding a new sponsor and a new job as the Depression set in and asked if Maisie might think of "coming home."

"I am home," Maisie wrote back. But she enclosed twenty pounds.

She couldn't seem to stop thinking about Simon, about those strange final moments, trying to make sense of it and succeeding only in disturbing her sleep.

"He probably meant it, you know, that bit about making Britain great again." Hilda said as they strolled the Embankment. "Fantasists usually do."

He might really have loved her. She was both the things he wanted—clever, with the capacity to be pliable, though that last was changing apace. And as to the suddenness of his return and proposal, she need only bear in mind that a wife couldn't testify against a husband.

"Not that I think he expected to be caught, but might as well hedge the bet. The whole family seems to have gone a bit mad after the crash. I'm inclined to agree with Vita. You can do better."

"I don't want to get married until I'm sure I can keep working."

Hilda's answer was lost with the arrival of Nigel, the new messenger boy, who'd come running to find them and chivvy them back to Savoy Hill, where there were twenty new crises to contend with.

Maisie allowed herself to believe that peace would reign in the BBC, despite the presence of Siepmann. He was so determined to make his own work superior, he primarily left Hilda's team to its own devices. Besides which, there was so much excitement about the rapidly rising new Broadcasting House and the steady expansion of operations that there was far less time for petty squabbles. But Reith won a strange battle. Someone, somewhere, agreed that content should be controlled in these more difficult times. More conservative, more measured, more quiet. More music, more light entertainment, much less to challenge tired listeners. It meant almost daily battles for Hilda, who was starting to look pale and drawn.

And there was nothing the rest of them could do about it.

Harold Nicholson—of all people—was set to come in to broadcast about James Joyce's *Ulysses*. Hilda and Vita had gone their separate ways, but they all remained good friends.

"Who the devil does that woman think she is?" Reith spluttered to Siepmann as they were climbing the stairs to the executive suite just as Maisie, having delivered a set of proposals for upcoming debates, was going down them. She shot back up the stairs and attempted to melt into the wall.

"I've said no Joyce, no *Ulysses*. All disgusting stuff. Bonfire's too good for it, and that poofter Nicholson! Nicholson! By God, she lives to provoke, and I won't bear it another minute."

"I think if you just delete a few lines in the script, it should be all right," Siepmann said in his oily, soothing tones. "I've marked the most offending passages."

"They are all offending," Reith insisted, but Maisie could hear the scratching of a pencil even from up the stairs, which they were still climbing. She cast her eyes around desperately, edging herself along the wall.

Reith and Siepmann came up the stairs just as Maisie closed the nearest door behind her—the door to the men's lavatory, which was thankfully unoccupied.

"Shall I go and give her the revised script?" Siepmann asked, hopeful.

"No. I'll ring her and tell her to come and get it herself," Reith growled. "Get me Matheson, will you?" he shouted to his secretary.

Maisie listened hard. She could only get the gist, but it was enough. Hilda must be shouting back just as vigorously as Reith. And Siepmann, that worm, was enjoying all of it.

She peeked out the door. The corridor was empty. They were all in the office. Hilda had taught her well; her footfall was silent as she ran down the stairs and all the way back to Talks.

Hilda hadn't gotten far, only halfway down the corridor. She saw Maisie but didn't break stride.

"Miss Matheson, please. It's just his insane vendetta. It'll burn out eventually, and all the criticism about how Talks aren't as good as they were will force his hand. And it's Siepmann, you know, that spider on his shoulder. We just need—"

"Miss Musgrave, they've won at nearly every turn. I want to work, not battle. And I will not work in a place that advocates censorship."

"No, of course, but you can't face him like this."

"I bloody well shall."

Maisie tried again to stop her, but they only ended up going into Reith's office together.

"What do you mean by this?" Reith demanded. "That Harold Nicholson is a poof, and his lady just as unnatural, and that repulsive Joyce novel is banned! How dare you allow such a thing to be discussed?"

"Who are we to be banning books?" Hilda shouted. "My God, you moralists are such a pack of hypocrites. You decry Communism, screeching that it forces all its peoples into the narrowest of strictures, and then impose much the same in a presumed democracy! Why can't any man, woman, or child try to read *Ulysses* if they wish to? And if they like it, grand, and if they don't, fair enough, and if they find it disturbing to their morals, they can soothe themselves with some appropriate balm, and if they find it a stimulant to mind and heart, then they will carry that with them all their days and be always seeking out new books to treasure, and isn't this the whole point of the society we supposedly fight for and value?"

"I will not be spoken to like this!" Reith was bright red. "Why can't you comprehend that there are a great many people who must be guarded, who depend upon their betters to guide them to the sort of culture that will be pleasing and comforting but not taxing—most people cannot manage with being challenged—"

"So then they leave those books aside!"

"No, because they might be damaged with even just a little reading! These are delicate people, and the world is really far more dangerous than a girl like you can understand—"

"I beg your pardon?"

"—and we have a solemn duty. You will go to your poofy little
friend, and you will tell him that whatever he does in his own life,
his bandying about with his aristocratic 'wife' and all their estates
and travel and importance, and then all that time he really spends
with men, doing just as he wants, with no judgment upon him, and
no consequence, just living like a hedonist, all that pleasure . . ."

Reith was as scowling as ever, but as his words folded over and over
one another, Maisie stared at the contours of his face, his eyes, enraged,
but full of . . . Was it pain? Was it envy? Was it both? Her glance slid
briefly to Hilda, and it was clear she saw it as well. There was almost a
flash of pity in Hilda's eyes. Bits and pieces of Reith's actions and words
over the last five years tumbled through Maisie's brain. His obsession
with men's morality. His unreasonable rage when someone was having
sex outside marriage. And the way he smiled and fawned over Siepmann.
He had a wife. He had children. He had been given honors and had
worked his way into immense importance. But there was something else
he really wanted, and perhaps he hated himself for it, or hated everyone
else who got to have it. And it colored absolutely everything else he did.

It made Maisie speak to him with more sympathy than she otherwise might have.

"Mr. Reith, of course we understand your concerns, but Harold
Nicholson is awfully well considered and respected, and think of how
many times you've had a similar worry and it's all come to nothing,
really?"

He ignored her.

"Miss Matheson, you will instruct Nicholson to remove the
offending passages from his script if he wishes to broadcast. What's
more, you will now vet every last one of your speakers and their
scripts with me and submit to all my direction."

"I will do no such thing. Not one last bit of it."

"Perhaps we can compromise?" Maisie suggested.

"Miss Musgrave!" Reith shouted. "I have been more than toler-ant with you from the beginning. You are no one and nothing, and you've risen quite high. I insist you retype the script to my specifi-cations. But if you back Miss Matheson in this folly of hers, I will have your employment terminated."

The words were on Maisie's lips. She was quite ready to tell him she wasn't going to submit to threats or blackmail or censorship. But she caught Hilda's eye. Hilda did not move a muscle, but her expres-sion told Maisie she could do more with staying on.

"I'll adjust the script," Maisie whispered.

"Thank you, Miss Musgrave. Perhaps you might be elevated to producer rank after all."

"Mr. Reith," Hilda said, her voice very plain and casual. "You have made yourself very clear, and there is nothing else for me to do other than to submit my resignation."

"No!" Maisie cried, unable to stop herself. But neither of them seemed to notice her.

"Miss Matheson, that is being a bit extreme." Though he looked pleased. "I am hardly asking you to leave, and I do think the BBC will be somewhat diminished without you."

"For a while, perhaps. But what is sure is that this entire venture is lesser for submitting to such diktats. I've never heard of open cen-sorship of literature leading to anything good, and I will not be seen to tolerate it. I shall deliver my formal letter of resignation in the course of the afternoon."

And that was that.

The carriage clock was packed last, nestled lovingly into straw. Up until that moment, Maisie had thought for sure there would be one more reprieve.

"Cheerio, all. Onwards and upwards!" Hilda cried, sauntering out of the office.

As soon as she was gone, Siepmann turned to Maisie.

"I'll have you know I expect total loyalty. This department is due for a shaking up, and I don't know that we need quite so many girls running around."

"I do understand." Maisie nodded gravely. "I might be better off writing a massive exposé on the inner workings of the BBC and how staff is reorganized."

Siepmann fixed her in a hot glare, and she smiled back, placid and almost bored.

"You're not only angling to stay, but you want to be a producer, don't you? Do you think I'd let you on anything other than *The Week in Westminster*?"

"'Let'? No, but I think I'll earn my way onto more shows."

"And I suppose you want that Yorkie girl as your Talks assistant."

"Miss Fenwick? I would, but Lady Astor has just engaged her as her new political secretary and protégée, despite their being of wildly different parties. Don't worry. I'll make sure she sees that Lady Astor still has plenty of time to come and broadcast for us. You know how popular she is. The Talks Department will start getting good press again, I'm sure."

"Your first failure, little lady, and you're out," Siepmann hissed.

"Good job I've got no intention of failing," she assured him.

In fact, she'd just scored a success. *He called me a lady, not a girl. Before he knows it, he's going to stop calling me "little."*

Lady Astor fought hard to have Hilda appointed to the BBC board of governors, but Hilda declared herself sick of broadcasting. At least for a while.

"You know, Lady Astor's coaching me to stand for office," Phyllida confided as Lady Astor was giving her broadcast. Her new role as Lady Astor's political secretary had bought her a tweed suit and attaché case, but she was still her pretty and pugnacious self. "Bit tricky, as I've been living down here, I want to represent the North properly, you see."

"You always have," Maisie said, but her voice was shaking. She would have rather Phyllida had stayed at the BBC a little longer.

"None of that now, you dozy cow," Phyllida warned, though her voice wasn't as steady as it could be. "We'll still have lunch three times a week at least, and larks at the weekend. Onwards and upwards, remember?"

"Onwards and upwards."

"And anyway, not all change is bad, is it?"

"No. No, it's not."

EPILOGUE

1932

Hilda leaned back in the chair and smiled around the pretty pub back garden.

"I can't believe I thought life would be more restful after the BBC, but here I am, traveling all over Africa with Lord Hailey, and oh, did I mention? A publisher is interested in the little book on broadcasting, so it's back to that as well. I'm doing revisions now."

"I suppose you don't need a typist?" Maisie asked. Hilda laughed, shaking her head.

"A producer at the BBC, a columnist for the *Listener*, and how many magazines have you written for now?"

"Five."

"Yes, I can just see you making time to type my notes for me."

"Also I've probably forgotten how to read your handwriting."

Hilda laughed again.

It was really too early in the year to be sitting outside, but it was a bright day and the pub garden was very pleasant and they had it all to themselves. It had been several months since she'd met with Hilda, and Maisie was pleased to see her looking so happy. Besides doing work on the African Survey with Lord Hailey, and some work in independent radio—so much for being sick of broadcasting—and the book, she was also involved with Dorothy Wellesley, the Duchess of Wellington.

"Seems it's you who has the taste for the aristocracy more than I ever did," Maisie teased her.

"Yes, I'm quite the social climber," Hilda agreed, raising her eyebrow.

She asked, so Maisie told her about Broadcasting House, where they were about to move, and how Siepmann was still upset because the Talks director's office had been designed to Hilda's specifications, down to the furniture, and no one would give him the money to change it.

They were still laughing when a distant church bell rang.

"Goodness, I'm afraid I have to get on," Hilda said. They each looked at their watches—Hilda smiled to see Maisie still had the lilac one she'd given her.

"I have almost an hour before I'm meeting Cyril," Maisie said.

"Ah. He grew up nicely, didn't he?"

"Well, we'll see," Maisie said, but she was smiling. This was only their third proper date. She didn't count the one from 1927. She had told him not to get any ideas about her, and she had come a long way from being the marrying kind. He said he'd take her company however he could get it.

Hilda paid the bill, waving away Maisie's money.

"Stay and have another drink. I know you. I know you don't relax enough." She squeezed Maisie's shoulder, dropped a green folder on the table, and was gone.

Maisie stared at the folder. She knew Hilda was still involved with MI5. Was it a lead, maybe? Maisie was constantly chasing stories these days. It was always nice to have one handed to her.

She opened the folder and read.

"Musgrave, Edwin. Born 1881, Selby, Yorkshire. Died 1915, Belgium."

He had immigrated to Canada in 1900, worked as a painter in the theater. Which must have been how they met. "Married Georgina Allen, 1902. Issue: Maisie Edwina, born 1903."

Edwina? Georgina had always told Maisie to be grateful enough just to have one name. Edwina. For her father.

"Divorced: 1904. Returned to England: 1904."

A year. Or less. He had been there that long. Known her. But maybe not. It only opened up more questions.

Worked as a joiner. And joined the army, even though he was thirty-three and could have done his bit from a safer locale. And died before she'd joined the VAD and was stationed to the hospital in Brighton. Died in Belgium, so she wouldn't have seen him anyway.

There was a photo. Rare, in those days, for a man to have his photo made. Had it been for Georgina?

He was young, with stick-straight hair and Maisie's prominent nose. His eyes were solemn, chin pointy. His expression was appropriately placid, but there might be something behind his eyes that suggested he was interested in hurrying off to do something else.

Hunger.

Maisie wiped her eyes and went on reading. There wasn't much left. He had a brother, Maxwell, invalided home in 1916, living in York. A clerk for the county. Two children, Peter and Hannah. Each married. Two grandchildren, Gerald and Samuel.

She closed the folder so as not to let tears drip on it and rested her head in her hands.

She had a family. An uncle Max. Cousins. And she was from Yorkshire, just like Phyllida.

She could write to them. They might know nothing about her, but she could write. Maybe go to York. It would be good to travel more anyway. There was a lot to see. Phyllida might take a holiday with her. And maybe she would come away with a family.

She wiped her face again and tucked the folder into her holdall— stuffing it in with the newspapers, notebooks, pencils, two novels, and a primer on beginner's German.

Hilda hated being thanked.

I'll send her tickets to a concert. Something very lively and modern. She'll love that.

Maisie sauntered off into the evening, swinging her holdall beside her.

AUTHOR'S NOTE

It perhaps goes without saying that I wanted to write this book because of Hilda Matheson. She was such an extraordinary woman, and seemed to embody the adage of truth being stranger than fiction. If I have made her a bit too perfect, well, that was hard to help. According to many who knew her—admittedly writing after her untimely death—her flaws were an excess of passion and a determination to see through what she felt to be right, despite strenuous opposition. Even though this led to her downfall at the BBC, she never wavered—and it didn't hurt her throughout her (too few) remaining years.

Because the real history was so fascinating, I wanted to use as much of it as possible. However, it was imperative that the story itself come first, this not being a literary biography, and so I strove to weave fact and fiction together as seamlessly as possible.

While there are some sources that begin Hilda's tenure at the BBC commencing in 1927, I decided to have her start in 1926 (per some other sources) because I liked the energy of her coming in to change the BBC soon after the national General Strike.

I knew I wanted to fold in Hilda's real-life membership in MI5. The facts that she had been recruited to MI5 by T. E. Lawrence (aka Lawrence of Arabia); helped set up the MI5 office in Rome in 1918; and was there when they hired a young Italian journalist with a gift for propaganda to help keep Italy in the war—a certain Benito

Mussolini—were just too delicious to leave out. While she wasn't really involved with the organization after World War I, she apparently kept a hand, or at least an ear, in. As my story developed, with the fictional Maisie a budding journalist, it felt right that Hilda, so engaged with current events and always thinking toward the future, would take heed of quality propaganda and that she and Maisie would ultimately work together as they discovered the intents of the Nazis were intertwined with the agenda of the British Fascists and aimed at taking over the BBC. This last is pure fiction, extrapolating from Goebbels' real comment that a takeover of German radio in 1923 would have forwarded the Nazi cause immeasurably. The British Fascists may not have specifically mentioned the BBC, but it felt reasonable that they would have seized the inspiration and seen the opportunity to consolidate their message and power through this powerful new medium.

The fear of foreign spies was indeed paramount during this era. The 1920s in Britain were deeply complex times, as the nation had been financially and emotionally devastated by World War I, and many of the returning soldiers found that they could not secure employment. Economic uncertainty remained high, and there was a lot of anxiety surrounding societal changes. The lines were drawn between tradition and progressivism, as exemplified so neatly by Hilda and Reith, despite their being contemporaries and both children of Scottish Presbyterian ministers.

The spies people feared in the 1920s were Russian, and the panic was about Bolshevism. Though trade unions and the Labour Party were not communist—and in fact, the Communist Party of Great Britain at its peak enjoyed a membership of about sixty thousand—it was common practice to associate the push for unionization with communism. This of course was a useful straw man for fascists.

As I read about concerns of spying, both genuine and trumped up, I became convinced that this concern, combined with the rise of the BBC and some people's fears of it, was a thread I must weave into the narrative. It seemed natural that Hilda, thanks to her involvement in Italy, would have spotted the brilliance of the early Nazi propaganda and wondered if it was something worth worrying about, especially as Fascism garnered interest in Britain. I was inspired by a few real-life MI5 operations during World War II, particularly the Jack King sting, and chose to use threads of this story for my rising journalist and producer, Maisie, and her mentor, Hilda.

I particularly wanted to highlight the early complicity of corporations. The 1927 propaganda pamphlet *Road to Resurgence* was felt to make some headway in attracting corporate money to the Nazi Party at a time when they were considered marginal at best. It did lay out that the Nazis, despite calling themselves socialists and using proworker rhetoric in speeches, were in fact antiunion and would do much to assist corporations become richer. I chose Siemens and Nestlé as companies whose business relationship with the Nazis is well-known, although they did not establish ties until later than the timeline I present. I wanted to use more than one company to indicate that it was the involvement of many people with money and influence who helped fascism take hold, and did so primarily in the hopes of garnering yet more money and influence.

The BBC was very progressive in the 1920s and urged to be less so following the economic downturn. Reith was very ready to comply with this. However, the BBC, despite Reith's Puritanism, was one of the few entities where women could hold positions higher than clerical staff and men and women received equal pay. While it did institute a marriage bar, this was only nominally put into practice. Mary Somerville, the Director of Schools, was both married and a mother during her tenure at the BBC, and indeed took maternity leave. I deliberately kept the directorship of Schools Broadcasting nebulous, as Mary Somerville was its first director but was not given the title until 1931. She was, however, one of the first women to work as a producer at the BBC, and she was in Schools all that time.

One of my biggest changes regards Charles Siepmann, whose initial position was actually in Adult Education Programming. As the nature of the programming seemed so close to both Schools and Talks, I felt it read more clearly to have him in Schools and thus streamline the narrative. This was especially the case as the whole idea of "shaping the minds of the youth" runs lightly through the book and Siepmann's willingness, as I portray it, to toe the more conservative line made it feel right that he would be specifically in Schools, one of Reith's most prized departments in my rendition. I was also very imaginative with Siepmann's characterization, using his conservatism and his preference for hiring men (as noted in an internal memo) over women to inform his behavior and speech.

While the relationship between Reith and Hilda began to decline not long after Hilda's tenure at the BBC began, Hilda herself thought that Lionel Fielden, himself gay, "accidentally" outed her to Reith, which thus marked her for dismissal before the Harold Nicholson incident. The journalistic coup is wholly fictional, but Hilda's determination to resign rather than submit to censorship is real.

My only composite character is Ellis, whom I based loosely on Maxwell Knight, the head of MI5 and, apparently, one of the models for M in the James Bond series. I chose to make him a composite because Knight was said to have Fascist sympathies.

Maisie is a wholly fictional character, as is her initial job straddling the two offices. I wanted to place someone at the center of these volatile characters, with Reith, the traditionalist, and Hilda, the progressive. In one of Hilda's letters, she refers to her need for a capable young woman to whom she could readily delegate. She did secure a fine secretary and assistant, but I preferred to keep my character free of any of their qualities so as to allow her to follow her own inclinations and instincts.

I was fairly inventive in my rendering of the studios, as most of the controls were not so close to the microphones, but I wanted to keep the engineers more in the mix.

Nearly all of the Talks programs mentioned are real titles. This is especially true for *The Week in Westminster*, developed by Hilda in 1929 and broadcast to this day on Radio 4, though it is now more of a summation of political events of the week.

If there are things I have forgotten to mention, or details I have left out or mistaken, these are all faults of the author for which apologies should be considered duly made.

A brief biography:

HILDA MATHESON, OBE
(1888–1940)

Hilda Matheson attended what was then called the Society of Oxford Home Students, now called St Anne's College. She was not technically a graduate, as women were not allowed to obtain degrees until 1920. She worked for MI5 during the war and afterward became political secretary to Lady Astor. After her wildly popular tenure at the BBC, and in the wake of her much-discussed resignation, Lady Astor attempted to have her made a BBC governor. Hilda declined, instead becoming a radio critic and columnist, and then writing the first comprehensive book on broadcasting, *Broadcasting* (1933), alluded to in this novel. This remained the only textbook in use on radio broadcasting until the late 1960s (some say early 1970s). She later worked with Lord Hailey on producing the African Survey, published in 1938, taking on most of the work when Hailey became ill. This garnered her OBE in 1939. She became involved with Dorothy Wellesley, the duchess of Wellington, beginning in 1932, and it was by all accounts a long, stable, happy relationship. Hilda returned to MI5 at the commencement of World War II, working as director of the joint broadcasting committee. Among other work, she prepared instructions in wartime broadcasting including propaganda. Despite her unexpected death during surgery in 1940 (she died of Graves' disease), these instructions were so thorough, they were used throughout the remainder of the war.

You can find more biographies of real people mentioned in this book at www.sarahjanestratford.com.

ACKNOWLEDGMENTS

Researching and writing this book was a joyous yet arduous experience, and I cannot fully enough express my gratitude for the many people who gave me such tremendous help in a variety of ways as I crawled to the finish line.

As Maisie says, librarians are an endless source of assistance. Three libraries in particular were invaluable to me: the Mortimer Rare Book Room at Smith College, and especially Barbara Blumenthal. The Bienecke Collection at Yale, whose invaluable staff was also so kind as to mail back the hat I accidentally left in the locker. UCLA library—where a certain lovely mother (mine!) is happily one of the librarians—was especially terrific in allowing me a long loan of Hilda's book, *Broadcasting*, which was a wonderful talisman to keep at hand while I worked.

I spent a lovely two weeks researching in Britain, where I was hosted by one of my oldest and dearest friends, the writer Allie Spencer, and her wonderful husband, Christopher Daniell, and their two fantastic sons, Matt and Jamie.

Enormous thanks are due the BBC Written Archives Centre in Caversham and Archives Researcher Jeff Walden. The wealth of material was such that I could have happily wallowed in it for weeks.

The generosity of Kate Murphy, author of *Behind the Wireless: An Early History of Women at the BBC*, is simply unparalleled. Not only did she invite me into her lovely London home, where we spent a wonderful day discussing Hilda and the BBC, but she also allowed me to access what was nothing less than an absolute gold mine of information, photographs, recordings, and ephemera. For anyone who wants to learn more about Hilda and other real pioneering women at the BBC, Kate's book is a treasure.

I was immeasurably lucky to be in London soon after the opening of the Science Museum's exhibit Information Age, which featured the original 2LO transmitter, described in this book, among other radio treasures. John Liffen, the Curator of Communications and Electricity Supply, very kindly gave of his time to guide me through the exhibit and tell me more about the 2LO and 1920s broadcasting.

Luck continued in that Hilda's house on Sumner Street is about a five-minute walk from the Science Museum, so I was able to pay it a visit and take pictures. I hope it will soon bear a blue plaque marking Hilda's residence there.

Jon Cable, the assistant archivist at the Institution of Engineering and Technology, was so kind as to give me a tour of Savoy Hill House, show me photos, and answer a number of questions.

Back in the US, I am beyond grateful for the sanctuary that is Paragraph Writers Space and all my many friends there. Special shout-outs to readers, champions, and purveyors of hugs and cookies: Allison Amend, Kate Bernstein, George Black, Athos Cakiades, Lisa Dierbeck, Elyssa East, Sophie Jaff, Anne-Sophie Jouhanneau, Rebecca Louie, Ilana Masad, Amy Meng, Caroline Rothstein, Sia Sotirakis, Laura Strausfeld, and Cynthia Weiner! And so many others—we are a very special community.

Special thanks always to my agent, Margaret O'Connor of Innisfree Literary, who is not only a tireless champion but also a good friend.

I was lucky to work with two terrific editors on this book. First, Ellen Edwards, who saw the potential and took a chance, and then Kate Seaver, whose perspective and passion helped strengthen and deepen the story.

Many, many friends were endless sources of love and support. One superspecial shout-out to Melinda Klayman, my oldest friend and "sister," who is always a critical champion. I got to spend time with her, her terrific husband, Michael Zbyszynski, and their amazing little daughter, Anya, in both the early and the final days of piecing the story together. Though this book doesn't have a specific dedication, it's girls like Anya I have in mind—girls I hope will grow up unafraid to use their voices.

Further hugs to Sarah Canner, Jen Deaderick, Nathan Dunbar, Rob Intile, Amanda Kirk (another major hero during the final crunch), Karol Nielsen, Alisa Roost, Joe Wallace, Jerry Weinstein, and so many, many more. I am very lucky.

Hilda and Maisie have been very good friends to me as well. I am sorry to bid them goodbye, but if I may quote the inimitable Carol Burnett, "I'm so glad we've had this time together."

RADIO
GIRLS

SARAH-JANE
STRATFORD

QUESTIONS FOR
DISCUSSION

1. Despite the restrictions many women faced in work in the 1920s and '30s in Britain, the BBC was very open in its hiring practices and most of the time did not discriminate in terms of pay. Do you think this decision affected the staff at Savoy Hill and the nature of the programming the BBC offered? Note Hilda's point that presenting informational programs like *The Week in Westminster* at 11:15 in the morning meant it would come on just as "women were having their tea."

2. A great deal of politics surrounds the characters and life at the BBC. Hilda pushes for more political programming and quietly busies herself gathering Fascist—specifically Nazi—propaganda in the hopes of raising awareness about the growth of European Fascism. Hilda's contact at the intelligence agency MI5 is dismissive of her concerns, noting that the Nazis are a fringe group. What parallels can be seen in politics today? What might Hilda and Maisie have done differently to try to raise awareness about Fascism, and how might they have had greater influence?

3. British society changed radically after the First World War, with more women seeking work and living in semiautonomy. Maisie and Phyllida recognize that women of their class and educational background would never have gotten professional work in an earlier era. As the class system slowly erodes, we see the factions represented by Hilda and Reith, with Reith upholding tradition and Hilda the voice of the progressive movement. What do you think it was in each of their personalities that prompted their stances?

4. Hilda sees radio as an opportunity to educate the public and is especially keen on having more books and poetry discussed on the radio, as well as presenting sociopolitical debates. Does media still serve an educational purpose today? How might media broaden understanding throughout society?

5. Women like Hilda Matheson and Mary Somerville, who were at the Director level, were allowed to marry, and Mary was an even rarer case of a working mother. Women with children were rarely allowed in the workplace in Britain in the 1920s and '30s. How much have things changed for workingwomen today? What about working mothers?

6. Despite the fame of the Bloomsbury Group, and the general acknowledgment that many of the people working in arts and letters were gay, Hilda is quiet about her sexuality in general and closeted at work. Do you think she would have been as quiet about her personal life if Reith weren't so particular about his staff's "morals"? In the final explosion between Hilda and Reith, Maisie is given reason to think that *he* in fact might be a closeted gay man (an opinion shared by a number of historians).

Do you think his being closeted affected his attitudes toward those around him?

7. Maisie is initially mistrustful of both Hilda and Phyllida—Hilda because she is, as Maisie sees it, a woman in a man's job; Phyllida because she appears to look down on Maisie. Both these women become her closest friends and allies. How do you think they help her become a stronger, more confident person? Discuss how Maisie's personality—the wit she's kept under wraps most of her life—blossoms as a result of her friendships.

8. Many people in 1920s Britain are worried about the effect of technology and media. Mrs. Crewe, Maisie's landlady, is fearful of the idea of disembodied voices in the house. Are there any parallels to how technology is viewed in society today? How was the radio in its early days similar to the Internet today? How are the privacy concerns similar and different?

9. British women gained the right to vote in 1918, but 1929 marked the first election where all women over twenty-one could vote, irrespective of marital status or property. Two radio programs, *Questions for Women Voters* and later *The Week in Westminster*, were specifically designed to help women make informed political decisions. Do you think these programs had an effect upon the political process? Are there similar programs today in any form of media that you think legitimately assists citizens in becoming more active in politics and government?

10. When we first meet Maisie, she claims to be determined to use her job to improve her life and eventually attain the family she's always dreamed of. Despite her crush on Cyril, she's very

quick to fall in love with her job and devote all her passion to it. Do you think she really wanted to get married at all, or was she just telling herself that because it was what women were expected to want?

11. Several quotes from Hilda's book *Broadcasting* appear in the novel. Here is another one: "Broadcasting and other forms of electrical communications have sprung up to meet the urgent requirements of a world which must perish unless it can devise an organization capable of expressing its human and economic unity. The need for rapid interchange of news and views, for familiarizing each country with the ideas and habits of all other countries, and above all the need for an education which may fit men and women, literate and illiterate, for the complicated world of tomorrow—all these needs should find in broadcasting an instrument marvellously fitted to serve them." What do you think of this thought regarding the nature of broadcasting? Does it have any relevance to today? If so, in what way?

Sarah-Jane Stratford is an author and essayist who has written for the *Guardian*, *Boston Globe*, *Los Angeles Review of Books*, *Marie Claire*, Slate, Salon, and Guernica, among others. She is a member of WAM! (Women, Action, and the Media) and lives in London.

CONNECT ONLINE

sarahjanestratford.com
Facebook: @SarahJaneStratfordAuthor
Twitter: @stratfordsj
Instagram: @sarahjanestratford